"SO THAT'S WHY YOU ASKED ME TO DINNER!"

Emily stood up indignantly. "Just to pump me for information." For some reason that disappointed her, even though she'd known it from the beginning. But she felt more like the fictional Emily Lane every day, and Emily Lane would love to be courted by a man like Josh MacKenzie.

"Emily, I'm sorry. Please forgive me."

"There's nothing to forgive, Josh. I understand; you were just doing your job." She sighed for effect. "I should have known a handsome man like you wouldn't really want to take a plain woman like me to—"

His kiss cut off her words.

She'd been kissed many times before, but never—ever—like this. The contrast of his soft lips on hers and the scrape of his beard along her jaw created a throbbing sensation deep inside. His body was all angles and heat, while hers was curves and ice. They fitted together like two halves of an unknown whole—a whole she wanted to know very badly.

Other **AVON ROMANCES**

THE MACKENZIES
JOSH

ANA LEIGH

AVON BOOKS
An Imprint of HarperCollins*Publishers*

This is a work of fiction. Names, characters, places, and incidents are products of the author's imagination or are used fictitiously and are not to be construed as real. Any resemblance to actual events, locales, organizations, or persons, living or dead, is entirely coincidental.

AVON BOOKS
An Imprint of HarperCollins*Publishers*
10 East 53rd Street
New York, New York 10022-5299

Copyright © 2000 by Ana Leigh
Inside cover author photo by Fantasies Photography Studio
Library of Congress Catalog Card Number: 99-96452
ISBN: 0-380-81102-2
www.avonromance.com

First Avon Books paperback printing: May 2000

Avon Trademark Reg. U.S. Pat. Off. and in Other Countries, Marca Registrada, Hecho en U.S.A.
HarperCollins ® is a trademark of HarperCollins Publishers Inc.

Printed in the U.S.A.

WCD   10   9   8   7   6   5   4   3   2   1

I dedicate this book to Lori Handeland,
a dear friend whose help and encouragement
got me through a very stressful time
in my life.

Thanks, Lori,
for always being there.

Prologue

 ❧❧❧

May, 1890
Long Island, New York

Emily Lawrence cocked her blond head at a defiant angle, thrust her chin in the air, and with her green eyes blazing, angrily met her father's glare across the table.

"I don't care what you say; I'm not going to get married. The example you and mother set for me will deter me from *ever* getting married."

Her poor mother had been devoted to a husband who never gave her a thought other than to criticize her dress or hairstyle. Her self-absorbed father had always put his needs and job ahead of others—especially his wife and daughter. Despite this, her mother had loved him devotedly. Yet on the day she died, he'd delayed returning home and arrived too late to even say a final good-bye. Emily vowed she would never accept that kind of behavior from any man.

Hiram Lawrence slapped down the morning newspaper and gritted his teeth. "I will not tolerate any more of your selfish and headstrong attitude, Emily."

1

"Selfish! How am I being selfish, Father? Because I won't bow to your demands?"

"My demands or any others. Your obstinate reputation precedes you, Emily: only my position in society and your inheritance offers you any appeal to a man. You are rapidly approaching spinsterhood, and you know how badly I want a male heir to carry on my business. You've denied me a grandchild too long."

"I am only twenty-three, Father. I refuse to wed any of these indolent, insipid fops whose aspirations are limited to winning a regatta or polo match. When and if I find a man I can respect, with qualities worthy enough to raise a child, I'll marry. Then—and only then—will you get the grandchild you want."

Emily flinched as he slammed his fist on the table, displacing the silverware. "I've been patient long enough, Emily. Either you choose a husband from among those half-dozen suitors you have, or I'll do it for you."

"Do as you wish. That doesn't mean I'll marry him."

"We'll see about that! You do as I say, or I'll—"

Up shot her chin again. "You'll what, Father?" She tossed aside her napkin.

"I'll disinherit you—cut you off without a penny. You criticize your suitors' aspirations, but is your life any better?"

"No, it isn't—and I'm not proud of that. I'm as bored with my life as I am with them. But if you expect me to marry a man I can neither love nor respect, you can keep your money, Father. Mother left me a small inheritance, and I'll find a way to support myself."

Hiram snorted. "And how will that be, my dear," he

said sarcastically, "teaching lawn tennis or conducting garden shows?" He stood up. "You've heard my ultimatum."

Emily looked up at him defiantly. "And you've heard my response."

After he strode from the room, she stood up and walked to the window. She watched her father get into his carriage and drive away. Witnessing her mother's misery through the years had hardened her heart against this selfish man, but despite her resentment, deep down she loved her father and yearned for a happier relationship. Still, she refused to let him control her life.

As much as she'd loved her mother, Emily had none of her mother's submissive qualities. She had an independent nature and the one characteristic her father had passed on to her—stubbornness. And although she sometimes compromised for the sake of tranquility, his insistence that she marry was the one demand she refused to concede, no matter what the consequence.

Sighing, she walked back to the table, sat down, and picked up her coffee and the newspaper. After perusing it casually, she was about to put the paper aside when she stopped and looked closer at one of the advertisements. The Fred Harvey Company was seeking young women of good moral character and neat appearance with at least an eighth grade education to work in their restaurants along the route of the Atchison, Topeka, and Santa Fe Railroad. If interested, one was to apply to the employment office in Chicago.

Emily was no cook, but she did know about proper table settings and fine dining.

Lawn tennis, indeed, Father!

Grabbing the newspaper, she bolted to her feet.

Chapter 1

August, 1890
Chicago, Illinois

A fat man slammed into the dark-haired young woman, knocking her into Josh Mackenzie with a force that rocked him on his heels. He grabbed her and managed to keep both of them on their feet.

"Look where you're goin', lady," the man mumbled past the fat cigar clenched in his mouth. He hurried off without checking on the woman's welfare.

Josh bent down and picked up her fallen purse. "Are you all right, ma'am?" he asked, handing it to her.

Adjusting the spectacles that had been knocked askew, she looked at him as if he were an axe murderer. "Yes, I'm fine."

She rushed away without so much as a hi or goodbye—one of Maude Malone's favorite expressions for rude people—and Josh grumbled, "You're welcome, lady." She disappeared through a door marked LADIES.

His sapphire gaze swept Dearborn railroad station. As much as he loved his job, he'd had just about enough of these rude and impatient city people shoving their way through crowds in their hurry to get to Lord knows where. Too bad they didn't take life slow and easy, like the folks back home. A few lessons in courtesy might help, too.

Funny, how that old expression of Maude's had leaped immediately to mind. She'd been like a grandmother to him. He'd been in the East for four years now but still clung to the familiar lingo of his Texas upbringing.

All right, MacKenzie, so you're homesick!

He was that, all right. He missed the family and the Triple M. But trying to follow in the footsteps of his father—the finest man he'd ever known—as well as of his famous uncles, had been a frustrating, losing battle. The three years he'd spent in the Texas Rangers had merely established him as Luke MacKenzie's son, or Flint and Cleve MacKenzie's nephew. Their exploits in Texas were legendary— and their boots had been impossible for any young man to fill.

Yeah, he was homesick all right, and when he was through with this assignment, he'd take some time off and go back to Texas for a visit.

And that shouldn't be too long. His instinct told him that he was closing in on Emily Lawrence; it was a sixth sense to him. While he was growing up on the ranch, his dad had often told him that he had his Uncle Flint's knack for trailing. The instinct had proven invaluable, and had saved his skin many times, both when he was a Texas Ranger and now that he was a Pinkerton agent.

Back home, time and time again he'd been told

by others that one day he'd *probably* make as good
a lawman as his father had been; *might* have the sure
eye and steady hand with a Colt of his Uncle Cleve;
or could follow a trail *almost* as well as his Uncle
Flint. Though the remarks were meant as praise, they
were the very words that had driven him out of
Texas. Coming east had been a painful decision—
but it hadn't been a mistake. He loved his job. These
past four years as a Pinkerton agent had been ad-
venturesome and exciting; but more importantly, he
now felt good about himself. He had established his
own identity, and at twenty-eight was considered to
be one of the top Pinkerton agents in the country.

Josh pulled the small photograph of Emily
Lawrence out of his pocket and studied it. The face
in the picture stared insolently back at him: wide,
generous lips curved in a faint smile that hinted of
mockery; a delicate round chin set at a defiant angle;
and high cheekbones that flowed into almond-shaped
eyes glowing with defiance. Oh, this Emily
Lawrence was a real jewel all right—her face tele-
graphed trouble.

Another poor little rich girl, he thought with ran-
cor. Beautiful. Wealthy. Spoiled. So what made a
woman with all of those advantages run away from
home? These vain, pampered women were always
looking for a thrill before they settled down and married one of their own kind. He'd learned that lesson
the hard way.

What the hell, Josh thought, forcing aside the
brooding memory of Diane Huntington that had
slipped into his thoughts. His job wasn't to analyze
the missing person; his job was to find Emily
Lawrence and bring her back.

He'd traced the runaway to a rooming house in

Chicago, where the landlady remembered a blond boarder who'd called herself Emily Lewis and resembled the picture. She'd rented a room for a week, and left about a month ago with talk of going to Kansas City.

Slipping the picture back into his pocket, Josh continued to scan the depot for the face in the photograph.

"You're out there right now, lady. I can feel it."

Breathless, Rose Dubois entered the ladies' room, rushed over, and sat down on the settee next to Emily.

"There's a cop out there and he could be looking for you."

"Oh, no!" Emily groaned. "Are you sure he's a policeman?"

"Honey, I could be blind and still know a lawman when I see one."

Emily always found Rose's penchant for contradictory statements as endearing as it was amusing. With a patient grin, she said, "Rose, if you were blind, how could you see him?"

In the short time they'd shared a room during their training as Harvey Girls, the two women had become close friends. They'd confided their backgrounds to each other, and a bond of loyalty had formed between them.

They had fled from their homes for opposite reasons: Emily to escape from the indolence of wealth, Rose the squalor of poverty. Raised in a New Orleans slum, the nineteen-year-old, street-smart Rose Dubois had gotten Emily through a few lies she had to invent about her past; Emily, in turn, had coached

Rose in the social skills necessary to become a Harvey Girl.

"Let me help you," Rose offered, when Emily began to adjust the black wig Rose had advised her to wear as a disguise until they reached New Mexico. The masquerade had gotten her this far without being recognized, and once she got to her assignment in the West, she could toss it away for good and stop looking over her shoulder.

"I hate this thing," Emily complained, as Rose added several more hairpins to hold the wig firmly in place. "It's hot and heavy and feels like I'm wearing a fur hat. When we reach Las Vegas, the first thing I'm going to do is burn this darn wig."

"Why wait till then, Em? Take it off now and just go out and give yourself up. I'm sure that good-looking detective out there will appreciate it."

Emily pinned the bonnet back on her head. "What makes you think he's looking for me? He could be after a criminal."

"I watched him for a while. He's looking carefully at every blonde he spots."

"Don't most men?"

"Not when I'm around, honey." Rose rolled her eyes and readjusted the feathery boa on her shoulders. The two women broke into laughter.

In truth, her friend hadn't exaggerated. Emily had observed that men's gazes always followed Rose when she passed by. Besides having incredible blue eyes fringed with long, dark lashes, the tall, vivacious redhead had the curves to match Lillian Russell's—even when she wore the unbustled, proper, and very demure Harvey Girl uniform.

Emily replaced the pair of wire-rimmed spectacles, then blinked several times to try and focus her hazy vision. Everything she looked at through the thick lenses, tinted to make her green eyes indistinguishable, appeared blurry. "How do I look?"

"Perfect, like a young old lady. And hunch your shoulders a little to look even older. Although the spectacles and the black wig worn in a severe bun at the nape of her neck succeeded in making her look plain, Emily doubted the disguise made her appear elderly. "Maybe you could kind of shuffle along, too," Rose suggested.

"Do you prefer a juba or just a plain two-step?"

Engrossed in the mission of deception, Rose ignored Emily's tease. "And listen, if he stops us, we don't say anything—I'll do all the talking."

Before Emily could point out this latest contradiction to her, Rose linked her arm through Emily's and helped steer her out the door.

Leaning against the wall near the gate, Josh noticed the two women come out of the ladies' room and board the departing train. The incongruous pair were hard to miss: the redhead was a knockout and slowed her steps to accompany the shuffling gait of the other woman at her side. He recognized her as the woman who had almost been knocked off her feet earlier.

He now regretted his hasty assessment of her rudeness. She'd just had the wind knocked out of her and probably been scared to boot. Poor little thing, half blind as she was.

He jerked to attention. What the hell! He didn't remember her shuffling away from him then. Come to think of it, she'd taken off like a rabbit. *Yeah, Uncle Flint, I hear you. "If something smells of dead fish in the middle of a desert, it ain't fish!"*

He ran to the train and boarded it just as it pulled out.

"Oh, no!" Rose groaned. "That cop just got on the train."

"Which one is he?" Emily asked.

"He's that tall, good-looking guy in the aisle at the end of the car."

Raising the glasses off her nose, Emily peered down the aisle. "He looks like the man I collided with in the station."

"Drat! Here he comes. I bet he's on to us. Close your eyes and pretend you're sleeping."

"Rose, if he's been watching, he'll know we just got on the train."

If he did suspect her, Emily knew he wouldn't fall for such a ruse, so she turned her head aside and stared out the window.

"Excuse me, is this seat taken?" The man had a deep voice with a pleasant huskiness that conjured up a vision of candlelight and wine. She'd been too agitated to notice that earlier. Curiosity caused her to shift her gaze enough to see that he had pointed to the seat facing theirs.

"No, it isn't," Rose said politely. "If you don't mind riding backwards."

"That doesn't bother me."

"It surely does me, sir," Rose said flirtatiously.

"May I introduce myself? My name is Josh MacKenzie."

"And I'm Rose Dubois."

"My pleasure, Miss Dubois."

After a pause, it was clear he was waiting for an introduction to Emily, so she turned her head slightly, nodded, and then returned to staring out of the window.

"Do forgive me. This is my friend Em . . . ma."

"How do you do, Miss . . ."

"Lane. Dear Emma is feeling slightly under the weather. The motion of the train. You understand?"

"Yes, of course. I hope the unfortunate accident at the station hasn't added to your discomfort, Miss Lane."

This time Emily couldn't avoid responding. "No, not at all, Mr. MacKenzie." She closed her eyes in the hope of discouraging him from including her in any further part of the conversation.

"So where are you young ladies bound for?"

"New Mexico," Rose replied quickly.

"I see. Do you have relatives there?"

"No. I soon will, hopefully," Rose said lightly. "I intend to wed."

"Really?"

Rose was really getting into the lie; her voice lifted an octave. "My future husband will own a large ranch."

"So New Mexico will soon be your home. Who is this fortunate fellow?"

Rose giggled. "Actually, I haven't met him yet, but I'm confident I will. Until then, Emma and I are going to be Harvey Girls."

MacKenzie chuckled. "I admire your confidence, ma'am, and feel regret for all the poor men who undoubtedly will fall in love with you in the process."

Rose tittered. "Why, thank you, sir. That is most gracious of you."

"Do I detect a slight southern accent, Miss Dubois?"

"My goodness, Mr. MacKenzie, you are observant! You'd make a fine detective, sir."

"Matter of fact, I am one. I'm with the Pinkerton Agency."

Emily winced when Rose poked her with an elbow. "How exciting. Did you hear that, Em? Mr. MacKenzie is with the Pinkerton Agency. Do tell us, are you in pursuit of some nefarious blackguard, Mr. MacKenzie?"

"No. Actually I'm looking for a young woman."

Rose giggled. "Lordy, lordy, sir! I can't believe a handsome fellow like you would ever have a problem finding a young woman."

He pulled a picture out of his pocket. "By chance, have you seen this young lady? Her name is Emily Lawrence."

Rose studied the picture then shook her head. "I've never seen her before. Look, Em, isn't she lovely?"

Emily glanced at the picture, but the thick glasses prevented her from even recognizing her own features. "What horrible crime has this woman committed, Mr. MacKenzie?"

"Nothing too serious. Her father wants her returned home."

The fact that this man would take money to force a woman against her will to return to a place from whence she'd fled incensed Emily. "I would think if this Lawrence woman wanted to return home, she would do so. She looks old enough to make that decision for herself."

"Perhaps you're right, Miss Lane," he said, slipping the picture back into his pocket. "Thank you for your help, ladies. I think I'll look for the conductor." He tipped his hat. "Good night."

Rose stood up. "Mr. MacKenzie, I wonder if you'd remain with my friend for a few minutes. I hate to leave her alone when she isn't feeling well."

"I'd be glad to," he said.

Rose put a hand on Emily's shoulder, her fingers biting into the flesh. "I'll be right back, dear," she said, in a tone that carried more warning than casual concern. "Close your eyes and try to sleep while I'm gone." She hurried away.

Emily couldn't believe it. What was Rose thinking of? The man had been on the verge of leaving, and she'd stopped him. In the hope of avoiding any further conversation with the detective, she did close her eyes.

To her consternation he said, "I noticed your accent is different from Miss Dubois's, Miss Lane."

"I lived in the East for several years."

He nodded. "That would explain the difference."

"Are you an expert on speech patterns, Mr. MacKenzie?"

"No expert, but it can often be helpful to recognize them in my line of business."

"You mean the business of tracking down innocent women who flee from unhappy homes."

"After stealing a large sum of money from that home."

What was he talking about? The money she took had been willed to her by her mother.

"Actually, Miss Lane, I normally wouldn't take this kind of case. I was given the assignment because I haven't fully recovered from a near brush with my Maker on my last assignment. I usually pursue the more violent suspects—murderers, bank and train robbers, and similar unsavory types."

"So you were wounded. How?"

"I was shot in the line of duty."

"How courageous, Mr. MacKenzie. 'Into the valley of death,' et cetera, et cetera."

"Wrong again, Miss Lane. No jaws of death, no cannon to the right or left of me, and not even a single one in front of me. He shot me in the back. I assume the painful jolt you suffered at the station accounts for your rudeness, Miss Lane."

"I'm sure it does. My apologies, Mr. MacKenzie."

Embarrassed, she closed her eyes and was relieved when Rose rejoined them.

As soon as he departed, Emily opened her eyes. "Why in the world did you encourage that man to remain?"

Rose smiled confidently. "To get to the conductor before he did. I convinced the dear man—whose name is Charlie, by the way—and Amos, the porter, that if they helped us, we'd let them eat free at our diner."

"Rose, it's not *our* diner! That'll cost me a dollar and fifty cents every time the two of them make a stop. I only make seventeen dollars and fifty cents a month. In a month's time those free meals you promised them could cost me more than half of what I earn."

"That's still better than going back, isn't it? When MacKenzie shows them your picture, they promised to tell him that they recognize Emily Lawrence and she took a train bound for St. Louis a couple of days ago."

"Didn't they ask you why you wanted them to lie about it?"

"Of course. I told them Emily is a dear friend of ours and she ran away from a father who abused her."

Emily relaxed. Rose's plan did sound like a good idea, and if it worked, it certainly would get rid of that nosy Pinkerton man. Smiling, she leaned her head back and closed her eyes.

This time she slept.

The next morning Emily and Rose got off the train to eat breakfast. With a dramatic flourish, a white-jacketed busboy struck a gong and directed the passengers to the Harvey restaurant.

"I'm so hungry I could eat a five-pound steak," Emily declared as they entered the restaurant.

They were immediately greeted by fifteen smiling Harvey waitresses. "Good morning," one said, seating them at a round table covered with a white linen tablecloth and set with fine china and crystal.

"Just think, Emily, that'll soon be us," Rose whispered.

"Good morning, ladies. May I join you?"

Recognizing that husky Texas twang, Emily didn't bother to glance up.

"Yes, please do, Mr. MacKenzie," Rose exclaimed. "I hope you had a pleasant night." She flashed her eyes coquettishly. "I just bet a big, tall man like you must have trouble fitting into one of those Pullman berths."

"I can sleep anywhere, Miss Dubois." He turned his head to Emily. "I hope you passed a pleasant night, Miss Lane."

Forced to look at him, Emily nodded. "As pleasant as can be expected when one doesn't feel well and is confined to a berth, Mr. MacKenzie."

"Now, I always say it depends on who's in that berth with you." Rose giggled.

If Rose continued flirting with the man, Emily was certain she actually *would* turn sick.

Seeing Emily's glare, Rose quickly added. "You poor dear." She picked up the compote of fresh fruit the waitress had just set down in front of Emily. "Honey, take this away. My friend is feeling indisposed, so bring her just a cup of tea and a piece of dry toast."

Emily started to protest. "But I—"

"Trust me, Emma," Rose declared, cutting off Emily's words. "I'm not dumb smart when it comes to settling upset stomachs."

"What a shame, Miss Lane. This railroad line offers the finest dining in the country."

"I'm aware of that, Mr. MacKenzie," Emily said, with another scathing glare at Rose, who'd just popped a slice of banana into her mouth.

The meal continued, and Emily nibbled on the slice of toast as Rose and the Pinkerton devoured chicken livers and eggs *en croustade* covered with soubise sauce garnished with dill.

Unable to watch them consume the delectable fare any longer, Emily excused herself to return to the train.

MacKenzie rose with her. "I'll say good-bye, Miss Lane, since I'm not continuing on. It's been a pleasure meeting you, ma'am. I hope the remainder of your trip will be more comfortable for you."

"Thank you. I'm sorry to hear you're leaving, Mr. MacKenzie," she said, hoping her relief wasn't too evident. "I assume you've cornered your quarry."

He arched a brow at her sarcasm, then flashed a devastating grin that forced a return smile even from her. "Not quite, Miss Lane. But I did get a good lead on her, and I'm heading to St. Louis."

"I wish you luck in your endeavor, sir." *And may it all be bad.* Hmm. *Bad luck,* she thought—a contradiction if there ever was one. She was getting as bad as Rose.

Her grumbling stomach matched Emily's mood as she boarded the train and sat down to await Rose's return. She had plenty to say to her lying-through-her-teeth, gluttonous, self-indulgent *ex*-friend.

In a short time Rose and MacKenzie came out of the restaurant, exchanged a few words, and then he tipped his hat and walked away.

"I do hope you had enough to eat," Emily said, when Rose sat down beside her.

"And dear Mr. MacKenzie paid for our breakfasts, too. You see, he's a very nice bad man."

"That may have appeased your hunger but not mine."

"Well, you're the one who brought up the subject that you still weren't feeing well."

"I was trying to discourage conversation with him. However, I noticed you had no such intention."

"My goodness, do you always get this vicious when you're hungry?" Rose asked, good-naturedly. "Maybe I should have brought you a piece of raw meat instead of this, honey." She reached into her pocket and pulled out an orange. "I managed to pilfer this from one of the fruit displays."

"Tea and dry toast!" Emily muttered, her anger cooling. "And you claim to be my friend." She hastily peeled the orange.

"I'm sorry about that, but they *were* the first things that popped into my mind. They do help an upset stomach."

"But I didn't really *have* an upset stomach, you silly." She bit into a slice of the sweet, succulent orange. "Oh, this is delicious! God surely knew what he was doing when he created oranges."

"Forgiven?" Rose asked contritely.

"Of course. But next time you can be the sick one, and I'll do the eating."

"I don't think there'll be a next time, honey. As handsome and charming as he was, I think we've seen the last of Mr. Josh MacKenzie."

Chapter 2

A wire had informed the Harvey House at Las Vegas, New Mexico, to expect twenty-five passengers for breakfast, and the girls hustled to finish setting enough tables before the train's arrival.

When Rose laid down a napkin, Emily gave her an affectionate frown. "Rose, have you forgotten what I taught you already?"

"Oh, yeah." Rose began to recite, "On the left put the fork and napkin bright, and the spoon and the knife go on the right." She quickly rearranged the linen napkins and heavy Sheffield silverware. "And not a minute too soon. Here comes Fallen Britches now."

"Shh, Rose. One of these days he's going to overhear you."

"What is the delay here, ladies?" Fallon Bridges asked as he came up to the table. "The train will arrive in five minutes, and you two still have one more table to set," the restaurant manager pointed out.

"We'll be ready, Mr. Bridges," Emily said politely.

"I hope so. I expect you two to be on your toes."

19

"Fortunately, we took ballet, so we're up to the challenge," Rose said sweetly.

Bridges looked down his long nose at her. "I do not find your attempt at humor amusing, Miss Dubois." Using the distance between the tip of his thumb and the first knuckle as a gauge, Bridges began to measure the distance of each piece of the silverware from the edge of the table.

"Tsk, tsk," he said, shaking his head in disapproval, "these are not placed properly, Miss Dubois." He replaced them to his satisfaction.

"Must be my fingernail's longer than yours, Mr. Bridges."

"Then cut it off, Miss Dubois."

"Do you think Fallen Britches meant the nail or my finger?" Rose whispered, when the officious little man moved on to the next table to continue his inspection.

"Come on, Rose, we've got another table to finish. I'll put the silverware on; you get the cups and saucers."

Emily smiled as Rose hurried off. Although Bridges was a pompous martinet, she loved her job. The smartest thing she'd ever done—besides running away from home to begin with—was join the Harvey Girls. In the two weeks since she and Rose had arrived in New Mexico, she'd discovered a whole new world. Everything here was a lesson in contrasts to the life she'd known.

The town had not moved into the nineties but still retained the primitiveness of an early western town. Much of the landscape was barren and flat, broken up occasionally by spectacular rock spires rising out of a prairie sea—a far cry from the lush, green manicured lawns of Long Island and the blue of the ocean lapping at its shores.

The men rode horses for transportation, not for polo matches or fox hunts. Most of the women wore gowns of gingham or homespun cotton, as opposed to the jacquard silks and satin brocades she'd been accustomed to.

She loved the simplicity of everything around her. But the thing she loved the most about her new life was waiting on people instead of being waited upon. For the first time in her twenty-three years, Emily felt useful. And the diversity in the personalities she encountered three times a day was like discovering a buried cache of treasure she'd been seeking for a lifetime.

The mournful wail of the whistle on the inbound train brought the heads of both girls up with a jerk. Emily glanced over the dining room and gave a satisfied nod. They were ready. She smoothed her white apron, which went over a white uniform at breakfast and lunch but a black uniform for the more formal dinner hour.

To be honest, white was not Emily's color. One could not have pale skin and light hair, then wear white, and look anything other than awful. Although most of what she'd learned in finishing school had been nonsense, they'd been correct about not wearing white with blond hair. Black was even worse with her coloring. But Emily had not come to Las Vegas to attract men, as most of the girls had. She'd come to escape them.

When one of the busboys sounded a gong to signal the passengers had arrived, Rose stepped up beside Emily. "Shall we?"

Emily nodded and glanced at Rose, who, as usual,

looked stunning. Her flamboyant beauty and snapping eyes were accented by the staid dress. Rose joked that the Harvey Girl uniform, plain though it might be, had been designed with her and her dreams of a rich husband in mind.

Arm in arm, Rose and Emily stepped out to the front porch and joined the other Harvey Girls waiting to politely greet the new arrivals. Anyone eating at a Harvey House was made to feel welcomed from the moment they stepped off the train.

"Oh, oh," Rose muttered, "I thought the wire said twenty-five for breakfast."

"It did."

"I may not be educated like you, Emily, but I know twenty-five when I see it; and that," she said, pointing a finger at the ravenous horde descending upon them, "is not twenty-five."

"I'd be thinkin' 'tis more like thirty-five." The lilting brogue of Katie Cleary came from behind the two girls.

"I think you're right, Katie," Emily agreed.

"I'm thinkin' we've got our work cut out for us."

"And you love it; you know that," Rose teased.

"Darlin', I've already spent half me lifetime workin' much harder than this."

Katie Cleary was a favorite of Emily's as well as all the girls. She had come west after her entire family had died in a measles epidemic in Boston. Despite that tragedy Katie was a cheery sort and one of the best workers at the Las Vegas Harvey establishment.

The stream of hungry passengers—mostly men—went in the door. Some tipped their hats to the ladies on the porch, while others just shouldered by in their headlong rush for the best food this side of Topeka.

"Fallen Britches isn't going to like this," Rose murmured as the girls followed the passengers inside. "Someone read the wire wrong or counted wrong on the train."

The two girls hurried to set up additional tables. "There isn't going to be enough food prepared for ten more people." Rose glanced at the guests standing about waiting to sit down. "The portions will be smaller and the service not as good."

"That's nothing to smile about, Rose."

"No, it's not. But it would be a great time for Mr. Harvey to show up here. Just the other day, news trickled down the rail that during one of Mr. Harvey's surprise inspections, he discovered that the manager of the Harvey House at Lamy was serving smaller portions and buying shoddier products. Even though the man had saved the restaurant five hundred dollars, Mr. Harvey fired him on the spot. What do you think he'd do if he found out Fallen Britches had served the customers smaller portions? Poor ol' Fallen Britches would be kicked out of the dining room."

"You know, Rose, Mr. Bridges might be the lesser evil."

"I doubt anyone could be worse than that stuffy, thin-nosed creeper."

"You never know."

Rose sighed. "I guess you're right. We'd best save his bacon this time around." Then with a toss of her head, she grinned. "Besides, I can't let these poor people go without the food they've been looking forward to or the promise of our sparkling company, which I'm sure they've heard so much about."

Emily couldn't help but laugh. Rose might get annoyed with people, but she always got over it and just kept on going. She knew she could probably take a lesson from that, but she doubted she'd ever forgive what her father had done to her and her mother. She'd just make herself a new life in this corner of the West that she'd grown to love more and more with each passing day.

The kitchen bustled with activity as the cook hurriedly sliced extra fresh fruit, fried more bacon, and cooked additional omelets. Emily and the other Harvey Girls ran to serve the meal.

She was helping a little girl butter a slice of toast when Bridges came out to serve the main course, as was the custom for all Harvey Restaurant managers. He blanched when he saw the girls hustling to keep up with the demand. Emily gritted her teeth to keep from cringing when he announced in his high, squeaky voice, "Ladies and gentlemen, there was a bit of a misunderstanding today, but please be assured you will all be fed and back on the train in time."

"Sonny, I remember the last time I was on a train in '72," an elderly man said to Bridges when he served him.

Bridges paused and listened politely, although his gaze flicked back and forth across the dining room, trying to make sure his assurance of quality and quantity in the time allotment of thirty minutes would be met. Though Fallon Bridges could be a prig at times, Emily had to concede he knew his job. Fred Harvey only hired the best—and fired the worst.

"The food back then was poison," the old man continued, "if you even got to eat it. Most times you paid ahead for your meal, ate a few bites, and the dang-blamed train pulled out. I remember running out of the door of the diner with a piece of pie in my hand."

"That won't happen here, sir. Mr. Fred Harvey has studied the European art of presentation and makes certain his restaurants practice that art."

The old man, caught up in his story, ignored Bridges. Although Emily knew she should keep working, she couldn't help but listen.

"Then them polecats would take the meals we'd paid for but didn't have time to eat and serve them to the next rube who arrived."

The listening guests froze with their forks halfway to their mouths and glanced down at their plates in horror. But the fare served at Harvey restaurants could not be mistaken for second-hand food. It tasted too good and looked even better.

Still, Bridges paled at the unspoken implication. "Sir, you'll see that you will have plenty of time to finish your breakfast. And not that we would ever do something so disgraceful as you described, but there is rarely enough food left after a meal in the dining room of a Harvey House to resell a single plate." He sniffed and moved on to serve the next table. As he passed Emily, he hissed, "Get to work, Miss Lane, or they won't have enough time to eat before the train whistle calls them back."

She nodded and did as she was told. Although Bridges did know his job, he didn't know how to ask nicely for others to do theirs. That attitude was why Rose was so riled by the man. Emily, however, was used to living with a man just like him.

Amazingly, despite the overflow, they did have all the people fed and out the door in time to keep the train on schedule.

Every Harvey Girl worked seven days a week and

served three meals a day. For this they were paid in room and board plus almost eighteen dollars a month in spending money and a rail pass on the Santa Fe once a year. For most, this was more than they'd ever dreamed of having.

At night, after the last train departed, the girls would go to their rooms. There they shared their hopes and their dreams and bonded in friendships that would last for their lives.

Such was the case with Rose and Emily. They were kindred souls—sisters of the heart, if not the body.

"Did you see Fallen Britches's face when he realized we had more guests than food?" Rose laughed out loud as she lay back on her bed in her underclothes.

Emily had a robe on over hers. Though they'd been roommates for weeks and shared their most intimate hopes and dreams, she still couldn't lounge about in her unmentionables—at least not yet. Rose, however, didn't seem to have a shy bone in her body.

"Did you hear him yelling at the poor busboy who brought the message?" Emily asked. "The fool asked a nearly illiterate child to read him the wire then got mad at the poor boy for making a mistake."

She hung her wet uniform up to dry. While white might look virginal and pristine to the guests, by the end of a long day serving food, it was filthy. Though their black dress fared better, the white apron did not.

Thank goodness Rose knew a few tricks on how to get antelope-steak stains out of white material, for the Harvey Girls were responsible for keeping their uniforms clean and bright. Emily, who had never washed anything other than her own person, would have been hard pressed to do so. And appearing before Fallon Bridges and their guests in a stained uniform would not only get her fired, but would prove her different from all the other girls.

So Emily had taught Rose how to set a table, and Rose had taught Emily a whole lot more.

"Yeah, I heard him yell at the poor kid." Rose gave a disgusted snort. "He's lucky he didn't fire the kid, or I'd have done something worse."

Emily froze, then turned slowly to face her best friend. "What exactly do you mean by 'worse,' Rose?"

Rose stared at the cracked paint on the ceiling of their room as if she hadn't heard the question.

"Rose?" Emily repeated.

A roar from below made her jump nearly out of her skin, and she ran to the window. All the other girls were hanging out the windows of their rooms, too, watching in amazement as Fallon Bridges sneezed loudly and uncontrollably, then held his nose as if to stop the next onslaught. But he was unable to. "A . . . choo! A . . . choo! Achoo, achoo, achoo!"

The man twisted and turned, dancing about the courtyard as if possessed by a sneezing demon. At last, in seeming desperation, he ran to the horse trough and dunked his head beneath the water. She couldn't believe a man like Bridges, who believed cleanliness was next to godliness, had put his face into watered-down horse saliva! She choked back a laugh, afraid that if she started, she would not be able to stop. All she needed was to be caught laughing at her boss.

A quick glance at the other girls revealed that they

were as dumbfounded as she. After a few moments, Bridges raised his head. His hair was plastered to his skull, and rivulets of water ran down his face like tears. But when he took an experimental sniff and did not sneeze, he let out a sigh of relief and stood up.

"Be ye all right down thar, Mr. Bridges?" Katie called.

He stiffened and glanced up, scowling, at the windows of staring Harvey Girls. "Get back in your rooms, ladies. Must I remind you every single night your curfew is at ten?"

He sniffed in disdain, then gave another violent sneeze. Rose laughed, the sound carrying through the open window and floating down to Bridges. He looked up at Emily with narrowed eyes.

"Something funny, Miss Lane?"

"No, sir."

"I didn't think so. Good night, ladies." He walked back toward his rooming house with the stiff, practiced gait of a British butler, the effect spoiled by his attire. She never would have believed scarlet underdrawers lay hidden beneath the suit and tie of their proper manager.

"All right, confess—what did you do to him, Rose?"

"Nothing permanent."

"What," she repeated in a stern voice, "did you do to him, Rose?"

"I put red pepper in his snuff."

Emily blinked. "You what?"

"You heard me—and he deserved it. He'll think twice before screaming at a child the next time."

"Why would he think twice, unless you tell him

what you did and why? Then you'll just be fired, and I doubt he'll learn a thing."

"Oh, he'll remember. Deep down where it counts, he knows he's being punished. You'll see."

"Rose, sometimes you're a complete mystery to me."

"Mysterious and beautiful; that's Rose Dubois. How long do you think it will be before the richest man in the territory shows up and proposes marriage?"

"Any day now, I'm sure," Emily replied as she lay down on her bed. "But you know money can't buy happiness."

"That's what people with money always say."

Emily turned onto her side and Rose turned onto hers. The two girls smiled at each other. They'd been sharing their dreams for weeks now—or rather, Rose had been sharing hers. Emily didn't have a true dream, only an ambition: to stay out of her father's clutches and lead her own life. So far she'd done pretty well. And because Rose had the fervor of a true dreamer, she had helped Emily every step of the way. So Emily wanted to help Rose attain her heart's desire, even if she thought that marrying a man for his money was mercenary. Who was she to judge?

"Didn't you ever want to find true love, Rose?"

Rose scoffed bitterly, then rolled her eyes. "Ha! You can love a rich man as well as a poor man, I always say."

"I've met a lot of rich men, Rose, and believe me, I couldn't love any one of them."

"Bet you I could. Men are men. What's the difference?"

"What about Mr. Bridges? Could you love him?"

"He's not a man."

"I beg to differ. I just saw him in his underwear. He's a man."

"You what?" Rose asked, sitting up.

"You missed the show, Rose. Your little trick sent him outside in his underclothes for all the world to enjoy."

Rose winced and lay back. "Please, I'm about to go to sleep. I don't need any nightmares."

They laughed together, then Rose reached over and turned off the lamp. Darkness filtered over the room. Silence, blessed and deep, descended.

"Emily, who is the richest man in the territory, anyway?" Rose asked.

"I have no idea."

"I'll find him."

"I have no doubt you will. And he'll be a very lucky man."

"That's for sure."

Silver moonlight spread across their beds, and peace filled Emily's heart. She was happy here. So very, very happy.

For the first time since they'd gotten off the train, she thought about the detective her father had sent. She prayed she'd never see him again. From the look in his eyes, he would take her back. If Rose could put red pepper in Bridges's snuff just to give him a lesson on meanness, how far was she herself willing to go to keep her dream alive?

Emily had learned a lot from Rose, but the most important thing was that dreams mattered, and you had to reach out and grab them before they danced away.

She wasn't going back to Long Island. No matter what she had to do.

Chapter 3

⌒⌒◯◯⌒

Josh didn't like being tricked. He'd never known how much he hated deception until now, because he'd never been tricked before.

Lied to by thieves and ruffians, yes. That was to be expected in the business he was in. Heck, he'd been at this so long he never believed anyone anymore. Maybe that's why he was so annoyed that he'd believed the conductor on the train. He'd asked questions of everyone he could find, shown the picture to anyone who would look, and traipsed all over St. Louis. Emily Lawrence was not there. Probably never had been. Obviously, the redheaded beauty and her spectacled friend had gotten to that conductor before he had. A wire to the Harvey office in Chicago had confirmed his suspicion: they had an Emily Lane working for them but no Emma Lane.

He shook his head in disgust as he boarded the train for Las Vegas, New Mexico. He was losing his touch. That upset him more than he cared to think about. If he lost his instinct for detecting, he might as well go on home.

For losing his edge would come next. He'd seen it happen. And once an agent lost his edge, death waited just around the corner. You could not make mistakes in his business and live to joke about them. Not that he had any desire to joke about this.

So he was back on a westbound train, and he knew exactly where to start looking for his suspect: with Rose Dubois and her shifty friend, Emma.

Gritting his teeth in disgust, he cursed himself. How could he have been so stupid? There were just too many women with nearly the same name: Emily Lawrence, Emily Lewis, and this Emma/Emily Lane. Coincidence? Not a chance. In his business he'd learned that "coincidence" usually meant "clue."

Another few days on this blasted train, and he'd know the truth. Then he'd drag Miss Rich Long Island back home, head to Texas for a while, and hope a visit with his family would soothe his aching loneliness.

And then what?

Watching the miles roll past the train window, Josh wished he could find a dream as strong and beautiful as the one that had guided his father. His dad's dream had been and still was Mom, the ranch, the family. It was a good dream. A dream Josh understood.

But where, in the life he'd made for himself, would he find someone as brave and true and as beautiful on the inside as she was on the outside? A woman just like the mother he'd worshipped from the first time he saw her. In his business he only met women he could never bring home to Mom. Which only made him lonelier and sadder and more homesick than ever before.

But before he could get home, he had to find Emily Lawrence. The woman stood between him and his family—and no one did that and got away with it.

"I won't wear that dang-blamed jacket. I don't care what you say, little man. I paid my money for a meal at this here restaurant. No one said nothin' about dressin' for dinner."

Emily continued to serve her customers with a smile as she listened to the argument between Fallon Bridges and a mammoth cowboy at the front door. Jackets were required in the dining room at dinner, and if the guest did not have one, jackets were provided.

Unfortunately, this man had taken umbrage at that. Looking at the size of the fellow, Emily could understand his reluctance to squeeze into the black coat in Bridges's hands. The cowboy had to be six and a half feet tall and weigh over two hundred pounds. If the cows wouldn't argue with him, why was Bridges bothering?

"Rules are rules, sir. If I let you inside without the required dinner garment, then the next fellow who doesn't wish to wear a coat would be within his rights to refuse, as well."

"So what?"

Bridges paled as the huge man leaned over him threateningly. "S-so then we'd have anarchy, sir. Out here in the uncharted west, Mr. Harvey has recruited us to bring some of the amenities of the east. Good food, fine dining, proper ladies, and jackets at dinner. We can't let things backslide to the way they were."

"What's wrong with the way things are? I like it out here. Ain't interested in any of those dang-blasted eastern customs, and I *don't* need no snooty, white-shirted, thin-nosed, black-jacketed fellas like you tellin' me what to do!"

Emily tried not to laugh. Bridges looked like he'd swallowed one of the lemon slices they put in the iced tea. Really, trying to get a cowboy to wear a dinner jacket was silly, but Bridges didn't understand anything but rules.

"I do like a man who knows his mind," Rose said, eyeing the cowboy with obvious appreciation.

He was kind of attractive if you liked big, strong, angry men. Emily didn't. She'd learned that when the Pinkerton agent found her. He was big and strong and a little angry—at her. Still, he was handsome as sin and twice as tempting.

Now where had that thought come from? She'd been listening to Rose too long.

"But cowboys definitely do not have money," Rose continued.

"Too bad. Seems like all we've got out here are cowboys," Emily replied.

Rose handed her some extra napkins. When Emily reached out to take them, though, Rose wouldn't let go of them. Frowning, Emily glanced at her friend's face and found Rose staring avidly at the kitchen door.

"This should be interesting," she murmured.

Emily followed the direction of Rose's gaze. Katie Cleary approached the mountainous man, who looked even more mountainous next to skinny Bridges and tiny Katie.

Katie took the jacket from the manager's hand. "Ach, and t'be sure now, ye'd look silly as a sausage in a casing, stuffed into this wee garment. A big, strong man like the likes of ye. But come with me. I'm thinkin' I saw a bigger jacket in the coat room.

No one wears it 'cause no one's big enough. 'Tis hidden behind the others, it is."

"I don't want to wear a damned jacket!" the man roared.

The room went silent, and Bridges scuttled away, like a rat deserting the ship.

Katie stepped closer, put her tiny, care-worn hands on her black-clad hips, and shouted right back at him. "Ye'll *not* be talkin' t'me that way, sir. If ye want t'eat, ye'll be puttin' on a jacket, and we'll be havin' no more of yer nonsense. Ye hear me? I'm thinkin' ye'll look right handsome in this coat. Now, come along."

She walked past him toward the coat room. Everyone held their breath as the huge man's face turned red. Would he grab Katie and shake her? What would they do if he did?

The giant hung his head, turned about, and docilely followed Katie from the room. A sigh swept the dining area.

"Another tragedy averted." Emily turned to Rose, and finally succeeded in wresting the napkins from her friend's hands.

"With another right on its heels." Rose took one of the napkins back and tossed it over Emily's hair.

"What are you doing?"

"Look." Rose nodded at the front of the room.

Emily looked and nearly fainted.

Josh MacKenzie filled the doorway.

He'd lost over a week chasing to St. Louis and back, so Josh was not in a very charitable mood when he walked into the Las Vegas Harvey House.

Seeing Rose Dubois scuttling between the tables and disappearing into the kitchen, dragging behind her another waitress who wore a napkin atop her head, made him even less charitable and more suspicious.

Having a thin-nosed little man step in his way when he tried to go after the woman made him downright cranky.

"Where do you think you are going, sir? The dining room is full. You have no meal reserved." He sniffed, sneezed, then looked at Josh's wrinkled and travel-stained shirt with a grimace. "And no dinner jacket."

Josh was just reaching for his Pinkerton badge when a giant in a formal dinner coat walked out of the coat room, followed by a fairy sprite in black and white. Josh blinked at the incongruity of the couple, then shook his head at his fanciful turn of mind. He was too tired, too hot, too hungry, and getting too darn old for this. He just wanted to get his hands on that woman and take her home.

"Are they givin' you grief, too?" the giant asked.

"Excuse me?"

"About not havin' a jacket just to eat some beef?"

Josh glanced at the manager, who had suddenly shrunk back against the wall. "I suppose you could say that," he allowed.

Before he guessed what the man intended to do, the cowboy lifted the manager off his feet. "I can hold him if you want to eat quick."

Josh grinned in amusement. He understood what Harvey was about, but men like this tall cowboy would never be tamed. And he couldn't say that was bad, either, because men like this had won the West. Without them, they'd all still be cowering on the other side of the Mississippi.

"Ye'll be puttin' him down, and mindin' yer own business, Francis."

"Francis?" Josh couldn't help but repeat the name.

The red-faced giant growled like a grizzly, and Josh wished he'd kept his mouth shut.

"Stop that, now!" Katie declared, stamping a tiny foot. The giant did, in midgrowl. "Sit down and eat before the train whistle be blowin', or ye'll be leavin' with nary a bite in yer belly."

Amazingly the big man did as the fairy said, dropping the manager to the floor, where he slid on down the wall and stayed there.

Francis winked as he passed Josh on the way to a seat at one of the tables. "How can you not love a woman who knows her own mind?"

"And tells you yours?"

The man's smile looked drugged by love. "Yeah. Ain't she the dangdest woman in the world and as cute as a bug's ear?"

"In your world," Josh agreed. "Grab her while you can." Skirting Francis, he headed for the kitchen, hoping his quarry had not disappeared out a back door.

The sound of a resounding slap stopped him in his tracks. He turned to see the fairy facing the giant once more.

"Dinna be grabbin' me, ye big bear. I'm nay yers for the takin'!"

Francis thudded to his knees, causing the dishes to rattle on the tables. "Marry me, Katie."

"What are ye sayin', Francis?" She smacked her palm against his forehead, as if to jar loose any sense he had.

He took both her hands in his and kissed the

work-roughened knuckles. "I've fallen in love with you, Katie Cleary."

Her face softened, and she withdrew one hand to run it over the top of his tousled hair. "Dinna look at me like that, Francis. Ye'r breakin' me heart. Ha'e ye not heard of courtin' a miss before takin' the vows? What kind of wife would I be if I'd be weddin' the first stranger who comes in and asks me?"

"Mine, Katie love."

Josh felt his throat tighten. What had begun humorously had turned into something very sweet. He swallowed and forced himself to turn away from the tender scene. He had work of his own to do.

Bursting into the kitchen, he ran right into Rose Dubois and her black-haired friend. Josh narrowed his gaze on the friend.

One of the Harvey House napkins was tied over her hair like a kerchief. A few wisps escaped near her brow—wisps that were black as shoe polish. He frowned. Her glasses were different from the thick glasses she'd worn on the train, and his frown deepened.

The Chinese cook chattered away angrily, but Josh ignored him.

"Well, Miss Dubois and Miss *Lane*." Josh bowed, staring at the face that looked familiar, yet not. "So we meet again."

Emily Lane nodded but did not offer her hand. He very much wanted to touch her hand to see if it was soft as a spoiled little rich girl's hand would be or hard and calloused from the work expected of a Harvey Girl. But she put her hands behind her back.

Rose grabbed his hand, trying to draw him away from her fascinating friend.

"Why, Detective, how lovely to see you. And you

remembered that we worked in Las Vegas. Come, I'll get you a seat at one of my tables."

Not a man to be led as easily as the cowboy in the dining room—or told what to do and when, either—he stood his ground, frowning at the napkin on Emily's head.

"Interesting scarf."

She shot a glance at her friend, who quickly said, "Ah, yes, isn't it? We didn't know what to do when we found them."

"Them?"

Rose leaned against his arm, put a finger to her lips, and whispered conspiratorially, "The lice."

Emily choked, and he glanced her way, only to find her pink-faced and glaring at Rose.

"Now, no cause to get angry, Emily. Such things happen out here. Nothing for you to be embarrassed about. And the detective understands, don't you?"

"Uh, sure."

"So did you come to Las Vegas just to see little old us?"

Rose batted her eyelashes at Josh. He'd never actually seen a woman do that. It was quite effective when done by a woman like Rose. He forgot the question, but only for a moment.

"No." That sounded rude, but he'd been dragged to hell and gone, and he'd had just about enough. "I came to ask if you'd seen the woman I'm looking for—Emily Lawrence."

"Now didn't I already answer that question, Detective? Do you think I'm hiding something?"

"Are you?"

"No. I never hide anything. Disguise, perhaps— that's a woman's prerogative."

He narrowed his eyes. "And what are you disguising, miss?" The question was intended for Emily, but when he glanced her way, she was disappearing through the door to the dining room. He took a step to follow, but Rose now blocked his way. "Me? At the moment, not a single thing."

"It's interesting how your new friend has nearly the same name as the woman I'm looking for."

"Yes, isn't it? Funny how the world is so small, yet really so big. Fascinating, life's little coincidences."

"I don't believe in coincidence."

"What *do* you believe, Detective? That the woman I met a few weeks ago, who works dawn to dusk at my side without complaint, is the woman you've been searching for? The woman whose picture you showed me, who is blond, when my friend's hair is as dark as ebony? A woman who, from what you told me, wouldn't be able to work an hour a day, let alone twelve? And if she stole the money you claimed she stole, why would this woman you search for wait around here for you to find her? Why would she become a servant rather than *have* servants, as she's had all her pampered, pretty life?"

She had a point. Several of them, in fact. He shrugged. "You make it sound foolish."

"Isn't it?"

Looking into her eyes, he nearly agreed. But he still had a feeling he was right, and he'd learned to trust his instinct.

So he tipped his hat, said good-bye to the self-admittedly deceptive Rose Dubois, then went back into the dining room. He was not leaving Las Vegas until he discovered the whole truth about the multitude of women named Emily, Emma, or just plain

Em. And the way to do that was to get closer to her. Much, much closer.

Emily continued to work, although she jumped every time someone spoke to her or a door shut or opened. What was Rose saying to MacKenzie? And how had he found them in Las Vegas? Was the man part bloodhound?

When she'd returned to the dining room, Fallon Bridges had frowned at her blackened bangs and makeshift scarf and the glasses they'd "borrowed" from Yen Cheng, the cook. At least they weren't as thick as the pair tucked away in her room, which, if Bloodhound MacKenzie stayed around, she'd have to wear again. Just the thought made her stomach lurch.

Thankfully Bridges had been too busy carving the roast to bother her about her appearance. His encounter with the giant cowboy had thrown off their schedule once again, and in order to get the guests back on their train in time, no dawdling would be allowed. Emily had no doubt he'd demand a full accounting later—especially when he discovered his shoe blacking missing.

Thank the Lord for Rose and her quick mind and quicker tongue. Emily was so scared MacKenzie was going to drag her off then and there that she couldn't think, much less speak. She'd have to practice both if she planned to stay free.

MacKenzie came out of the kitchen with Rose right on his heels. His glance immediately went to Emily, and she fought not to lower her gaze. She couldn't continue to act guilty or he'd guess the truth, if he hadn't already. She glanced at Rose, who smiled. So far, so good.

MacKenzie strode through the dining room, headed right toward her. Her breath got stuck in her throat. That dark hair . . . those blue eyes . . . He really was quite breathtaking. How could a man be that handsome yet such a cad?

He barreled down on her, but she stood her ground. When he stopped in front of her, she craned her neck to meet his eyes.

"Ma'am." He tipped his hat that he'd neglected to remove.

Emily nodded, hoping he meant good-bye. No such luck. He began shifting his feet as if nervous, and she frowned. What on earth would he have to be nervous about?

"I'm going to be in town for a spell. I'd be honored if you'd let me call on you."

Her mouth fell open. He had to be joking!

"Ma'am?"

Her teeth clicked together as she snapped her mouth shut, then opened it again to speak, but Rose quickly blurted, "Of course. She'd be delighted."

Josh grinned, and the expression changed his face. When he grinned like a boy, he was something much, much more than handsome—he was dangerous.

And Emily was in big, big trouble.

Chapter 4

Emily made it through the rest of the dinner hour without spilling anything; it helped that MacKenzie left and did not return. As soon as their guests got back on the train, Yen Cheng came out of the kitchen, jabbering, and snatched his glasses from her face. Thanking him profusely, she didn't see Fallon Bridges approach.

"And what, may I ask, is going on here, Miss Lane?"

Before she could answer, Rose saved her from having to. "Nothing is going on but cleanup, Mr. Bridges."

"I saw you two run off in the middle of your shift. Then you"—he jabbed a bony finger at Emily, and she jumped back before it poked her in the nose—"come out of the kitchen wearing the cook's glasses and a napkin on your head. Yen Cheng is swearing a blue streak, or at least I think he is. I'm not an idiot. You two are up to something."

Emily opened her mouth, but what on earth could she say to explain her behavior yet keep Bridges from giving her away, now that MacKenzie planned to hang around? At least he didn't know her real name.

"Why are you so suspicious, Mr. Bridges?" Rose asked innocently. "Emily wanted to stop wearing her glasses. You must know how women are, being around so many of us all the time." She gave Bridges a dazzling smile that would have floored most men. Unfortunately, Bridges had seen it too many times and had become immune. He merely scowled harder. Rose was undaunted. "Anyway, dear Emily found she couldn't see well enough to do her job to the high standards of perfection you require, Mr. Bridges, so she borrowed Yen Cheng's. Tomorrow she'll wear hers again."

Folding his arms across his chest, Bridges tapped his foot. "And her hair?"

She shrugged. "Feminine vanity, Mr. Bridges. She looks much better with black hair, doesn't she? Dark hair will look exquisite with her ivory coloring and green eyes. In fact, I think we'll finish the rest tonight. Right, Emily?"

Emily just nodded, not trusting herself to speak. Bridges didn't believe them, but what could he do? They hadn't done anything wrong beyond leaving the floor for a few moments. Unacceptable, but not cause for dismissal. Especially when the Las Vegas Harvey House needed all its waitresses to keep up with the continually increasing crowds that poured into New Mexico.

Bridges contemplated them for a long moment. "I know you two girls are up to something, though I can't figure out what. Just make sure you stick to the rules and do your job." He sniffed and turned on his heel.

Emily and Rose let out a collective sigh of relief.

"We'll have to figure out some way to dye your hair tonight," Rose said.

Nodding, Emily moaned, "And I'm going to have to wear those glasses again. I'll probably be stumbling into everyone while I'm working."

"Just pull them down on your nose and look over the top. You'll get used to it."

Emily groaned.

"Would you rather go home to Daddy?"

"Of course not!"

"Then do it."

"It doesn't matter what I want or what I do, Rose. MacKenzie knows something. All he has to do is show that picture of me to someone here."

"MacKenzie won't be showing your picture around here."

"And how do you intend to stop him? Flirt with the man twenty-four hours a day until he forgets why he came here?"

"As appealing as that sounds, honey, it won't be necessary."

"You seemed to enjoy rubbing yourself up against him while you talked." Her voice sounded shrill and annoyed. It had to be because of her anxiety over the situatiion—nothing else.

Rose smiled. "While I did enjoy my temporary closeness to that tall, handsome Texan, there is always a reason for everything I do." She pulled her hand from the pocket of her gown. Tucked in her palm was the picture of Emily.

Emily's mouth gaped open, then changed to a smile of pleasure. "How did you do that?"

"I'm a woman of many talents. Some for the better, and some for the worse."

"You picked his pocket!"

"Shh." Rose put a finger to her lips. "Do you want everyone to know?"

"What happens when he discovers the picture is missing?"

"He'll think he lost it somewhere between here and St. Louis."

"You don't think he'll remember you and your friendly behavior?"

With a wry smile, Rose said, "Oh, I'm sure he'll remember me, and look back fondly on my friendly behavior. But MacKenzie's a gentleman. He'll never think that a woman like me would stoop so low."

Rose had a point. She so often did. Emily grinned. "I do love you, Rose."

"Of course you do, honey. Everyone does. Now let's do something about that hair of yours."

Luckily for them, Katie Cleary was a wonder with potions of every sort. They took her fully into their confidence—but only her. Although the girls at the Las Vegas Harvey House were for the most part friendly, the fewer who knew the truth, the less chance for someone to spill the beans by accident or design.

"Me grannie was of the *dione sidhe*," Katie whispered as she mixed her concoction later that night in their room.

Emily and Rose sat on their beds in their nightclothes and watched, amazed, as Katie's small but quick and clever fingers worked their magic.

"What's the don . . . she?" Emily asked, stumbling over the words.

Katie rolled her eyes. "Ye Americans ha'e no idea of the magic in the Old World. The *dione sidhe* are fairy folk, darlin', the ones who do magic."

"Witches?" Rose asked, looking intrigued.

"Ach, no." Katie narrowed her gaze upon Rose. "What d'ye know of witches?"

"Where I come from there are all sorts of people who do black magic at midnight. Voodoo and devil worshippers and the like." Her reflexive shiver enhanced her point.

Katie nodded, her attention focused on her potion once more. The mix had stopped bubbling and looked like harmless black water.

But Emily wasn't sure how harmless it was. "Have you used this before?"

"A hundred times. As I said, me grannie was of fairy blood and knew all the secrets of the earth. She used herbs and leaves and berries to heal. This canna hurt ye, darlin', and it'll last for weeks no matter how many times ye wash it."

"Weeks!" Emily exclaimed, alarmed. "I only want it until the detective goes away."

"Aye. And I've mixed ye a potion to dye your hair back to its lovely shade. None will be the wiser for it." Katie put her hand on her hips. "Come here, now, and dinna be a babe."

"Yes, Emily, don't be a baby." Mischief gleamed in Rose's eyes.

"Why don't you test it first?" Emily suggested.

Rose patted her hair. "What, and blemish this head of red hair? You don't fool around with perfection, honey."

It was clear to Emily that she wasn't going to change anyone's mind. Desperation left her no choice, and she had to try anything to throw Bloodhound MacKenzie off her trail. Sooner or later he'd have to give up and go away. Hopefully sooner, once he got a look at her with completely black hair and the thick spectacles.

"All right, ladies." She stood up. "Let's get this over with."

"That's the spirit, Emily darlin'!" Katie exclaimed, advancing on her.

Several moments later, Emily sat in a straight-backed chair near the window with a foul-smelling black goo smeared on her hair as the other two girls chattered.

"Katie, you certainly avoided a problem today with that giant of a cowboy. Everyone else, especially Fallen Britches, was scared to death of him."

Katie waved her hand airily. "Ach, I had me eight brothers in the Old Country. Huge, gruff men they were. And great big soft hearts beat in every one of their breasts. I've found the bigger the man, the more gentle he'll be."

"You're lucky Francis was gentle," Emily observed, wrinkling her nose. She could taste the scent of her hair.

"Lucky? Pshaw! Men like that are just waitin' fer someone t'tell them what t'do and how."

"And now he loves you," Rose teased.

Katie had no quick comeback for that, and Emily glanced at her. The girl had turned beet-red. "Katie, don't tell me you think you love him, too."

"I'm thinkin' it cud be. We spoke kindly together in the coat room. He's a fine man, he is. Gentle and kind, like me sainted father."

"Katie Cleary, you've fallen in love!" Rose exclaimed. "If he's rich, you have my blessing. Marry him."

"How can she love him?" Emily protested, trying to offer a semblance of reasoning to the conversation. "She just laid eyes on him today."

" 'Tis known to happen that way," Katie said softly.

Emily was astounded. "You can't mean you really do love him."

"I'm thinkin' I do, Emily."

"Then why did you chase him away and tell him you wouldn't marry him?" Rose asked.

" 'Cause I'll not let Francis be thinkin' I've no say in the matter. He'll jest ha'e to be waitin' till I can make me a weddin' gown."

"And what if Francis can't wait—won't wait?" Rose pressed.

Katie's sea-green eyes darkened with sadness. And in the no-nonsense tone she used on the cowboy earlier, she said, "I know 'tis a strong will I ha'e, and I'd be lyin' if I said otherwise. And I'm thinkin' Francis is much the same. So I'll leave it in God's hands, for what's t'be, will be." She winked. "But I'll nay be closin' me eyes or ears to a sign from Him."

The way she said it made Emily wish she could be as nonchalant about the men who were trying to rule her life as Katie Cleary was.

Josh was fortunate enough to rent a room that gave him a good view of the Harvey restaurant. The town of Las Vegas was growing rapidly due to the good fortune of being on the line of the Santa Fe. In the eighties Las Vegas had been considered the wildest town in which Harvey chose to raise the roof of a Harvey House, but the advancement of the railroad—and Fred Harvey—had not only brought law and order to the town, but an influx of settlers.

Exhausted from traveling to hell and gone in his

search for the elusive Emily Lawrence, he went directly to bed.

Unfortunately his dreams were haunted, as they had been for quite a while now, by the image of Emily Lawrence. What he'd heard of her he didn't like. But looking at her picture for weeks on end had an effect on him—there was something about that face he liked a lot.

And his dreams were embarrassing. She was a lady—albeit a thief—yet his dreams about her were anything but gentlemanly.

The sound of a train whistle woke him just past dawn, and he opened his eyes to the blaring, glaring sunlight that came through the thin curtains of his single window. The aroused state of his body did little for his foul mood.

He would have liked nothing better than to march over to that Harvey House, grab the Emily that *was* there, and drag her back to Long Island. But he could do very little as long as she only resembled Emily Lawrence in facial structure and insisted she was Emily Lane.

So his choices were few: catch the girl in a lie, get her to admit she was Emily Lawrence, or find someone who knew the truth. He didn't think much of any of those options, but the last one was the best shot of all three. He'd start by showing the picture to that prick manager.

Unfortunately, after he finished dressing he discovered the picture was gone. A frantic search of his bags and the room revealed it was, indeed, missing.

Had he lost it himself or been relieved of it with a little help? He could wire for another, but it would take at least a week before a new picture arrived.

He'd have to continue the investigation without it for a while.

He cursed all the way to the Harvey House. Though he knew it wouldn't do any good, cursing was better than smashing something or someone. Upon entering the restaurant right behind the guests arriving from the incoming train, he saw the skinny manager flitting about in the background and headed straight for him. Now was probably not a good time for questions, but his patience was gone.

A sharp gasp of surprise caused him to turn toward the sound just in time to catch Emily shoving her glasses up her nose. He frowned. She wore the thicker glasses again, and he could barely see her eyes. Apparently the lice problem—if there actually had been one—had been resolved, because she no longer wore the kerchief over her coal-black hair.

Pen and pencil in hand, she scurried away to take orders, and he resolved to talk to her later. But first things first.

"Excuse me," he began when he caught up to the manager.

"Yes, sir. Is there a problem?" The man showed no sign of remembering him from the previous day.

"Not yet. I'm looking for a woman named Emily Lawrence. Do you know her?"

"No." The manager tried to scoot past him, but Josh was too big for that to happen unless he wanted it to. Shifting, he blocked him. An annoyed hiss slipped past the man's thin lips.

"Sir," he huffed, "I have work to do!"

Josh flipped out his Pinkerton badge. "Me, too. Your name?"

"Fallon Bridges. I'm the manager," he said haughtily. He eyed the badge with a narrow glance, almost as if he didn't believe it was real, then shifted his gaze to the Colt Josh wore—which was very real. It was enough to encourage the skinny little man to give him his full attention.

"Mr. Bridges, I'm looking for a young woman who's run away from home: Emily Lawrence."

"I don't know her. The only Emily I know is the Lane woman who works here."

"And you know for certain that Lane is her name?"

"That's the name that came to me from the Harvey office, and we do not question Mr. Harvey, Detective MacKenzie. Actually, Miss Lane is a very good worker. It's her friend, Miss Dubois, who's the problem." Bridges's nose twitched when he mentioned Rose's name, and Josh tried to restrain a grin.

"Do you happen to know where Miss Lane is from?"

"East somewhere."

"Everyone out here is from 'East somewhere' unless they're Apache."

"True enough. But I don't—"

A sudden high-pitched shout—rivaling one of his Uncle Flint's finest—halted all talk in the dining room. Josh had heard that cry often enough while growing up in Texas not to recognize a Rebel yell when he heard one, and he turned to discover the source. Everyone was staring at the front door. Hoofbeats clattered up the porch, and Francis, the giant cowboy, rode through the open double doorway on horseback.

Bridges swore profusely and impressively, but from the sheet-white shade of the man's face Josh figured that was as far as the manager planned to go.

"I've come for my Katie," Francis announced. "Where are you hidin' her?"

His gaze swept the room, lighting upon then glancing off every white-uniformed girl. He gave another earsplitting holler, which had some of the guests putting their hands over their ears, and kicked his horse into motion.

Pandemonium reigned as people scrambled around tables to get away from the horse. Food splattered the walls, plates shattered on the floor. Josh had to admit the horse was well trained. The animal didn't flinch or skitter or buck, but just kept trotting down the aisle between the tables.

"Katie, love!" Francis bellowed.

The Irish girl came out of the kitchen, her face flushed red—from heat or anger or embarrassment, Josh wasn't sure. But he was sure of what he saw in her eyes. He saw that look whenever his mother looked at his father.

Pure love—and it stopped him cold. He eased his hand from his Colt and sat back to enjoy the show.

The tiny spitfire put her hands on her hips and tilted her head back to glare at the cowboy who had dared to ride a horse into the best dining room west of Kansas.

"And jest what in blazes d'ye think yer doin', Francis Burgoyne, ridin' in here on that beastie?"

"I've come to take you away, Katie love. We'll wed and live in sunshine the rest of our days."

"Dinna I tell ye last night—when ye stood beneath me window mewlin' like a cat at the moon— that I'll nay be weddin' ye until the courtin's done proper and ye gie me time to sew me weddin' gown?"

"I can't wait. I've got a homestead over yonder that I've got to get back to."

She opened her mouth, whether to say yes, no, or go to blazes, Josh couldn't be sure. But Francis, bless the man, knew what to do. He leaned over with the agility of a Comanche on horseback, put a long, strong arm around the little lady, yanked her over his saddle, and rode out the door.

Everyone in the room just stood gaping for a minute, then there was a mass scramble of humanity to the windows and out the front door. Josh reached the nearest window in time to see Francis kiss his Katie-love. And Katie kiss him back. And kiss him back, indeed.

Then they rode off.

Stepping back, he caught a glimpse of Emily at the next window. He sucked in his breath at the expression on her face; it was beautiful to behold. His mother always said that true love made everyone beautiful, but he'd never thought it had the power to make even an observer beautiful. He'd been wrong.

Bridges groaned at his side. "Oh, no, there goes another one."

"This happen a lot, does it?"

"Not quite like this; a horse in the house is a first. But these girls run off and get married at the drop of a hat."

In the woman-scarce west, ripe with men needing wives, Fred Harvey's high standards made his waitresses in great demand. Harvey Houses were the largest employers of women in the West, and although Harvey initially required a six-month contract by which the girl agreed not to marry, many of them married the day their contract expired—or merely disappeared into the wilderness, never to be heard from again. It was hard to prosecute a woman for breach of contract if she couldn't be found.

"That's the third one since I've been here," Bridges complained, "and I only arrived last month. I can't keep this place staffed to save my soul. Aren't you going to do something to stop that vulgar behemoth? Do your duty, Detective."

"What would you suggest?"

"Go after them. Chase them down. Drag her back. Shoot him!"

"I don't think so."

"You still have a duty to perform. You're the law, aren't you?"

"No, I'm the hired help. And right now I have a job."

"But . . . but . . . he kidnapped her. Right in front of your nose."

"She didn't look kidnapped to me. She looked—"

"Ravished?" Bridges sneered.

Josh raised an eyebrow. "Not yet," he allowed. "But as soon as they find a preacher, I'm sure good old Francis will take care of it."

He turned away from Bridges, intent on talking to Emily. She stood close enough to touch, staring at him with a strange look on her face: dreamy, misty, and with a little bit of the magic he'd seen on Katie's face right after Francis grabbed her.

Shaking his head to dispel the image, he figured he must be losing his mind, the result of the long hours and frustration—both sexual and professional—of this job. He took a step toward Emily to question her further, but the train whistle blew loud and long. People crowded in between them, closing the gap. He tried not to lose sight of her, but she disappeared in the horde of people flowing toward the door. By the time he saw her again, she was occupied in the massive and somewhat frantic cleanup taking place after the introduction of a horse to the dining room.

Bridges rushed around, flapping his arms and shouting, "Hurry, hurry, hurry. We'll soon have a lunch crowd coming down the rails, girls."

As time wore on and the dining room still looked like a cyclone had come through, his shouts turned to shrieks and his flapping to frantic waving. In order to keep himself from collapsing with laughter, Josh pitched in beside Emily to lend a hand.

"If he doesn't calm, down he'll have some kind of attack."

Emily looked at him warily. "Or perhaps take flight from all that flapping."

Laughing, he exclaimed, "You made a joke, Emily. Does that mean you have a sense of humor?" He bent to pick up another broken plate, which he dumped into the refuse bucket with the rest.

"At times. But only if I'm with someone who seems inclined to laugh."

"Do I?"

She paused and peered at him. Those thick glasses magnified her eyes so she looked like she was squinting. But if she had to squint behind the glasses, then why have them? That made him wonder even more.

"I think you might have laughed once upon a time, Detective. But not recently and not well."

"Care to change that?" he asked, grasping her hand. She started at his touch and made as if to pull away, but he tightened his hold. Beneath his fingers her skin was cool, and he had a sudden urge to warm her chilled hand with his own.

All around them people bustled, but suddenly the world was just the two of them. She smelled like lemon soap and lavender perfume. The scent enticed him. Strangely enough, so did she. She was plain and shy, as well as being intellectual. He'd never been attracted to that type of female, but he found her intriguing.

He ventured closer, and she stepped back, as skittish as an unbroken mare and just as dangerous. He reminded himself firmly that he was courting her to get the truth, to discover her secrets. And she definitely had some. The woman was a liar of the highest order, and he aimed to discover where the lies ended and the real Emily whoever began.

"Well?" he pressed as she continued to stare at him as though dumbfounded.

She frowned in confusion. "W-well what?"

"Would you care to make me laugh?"

Grimacing, she tugged to free her hand once more. "I doubt that's possible. I find very little that's funny out here in the wild west."

"Really?" He considered her face for a moment. She was lying, but why? "Didn't you think that this"—he indicated the broken room with a nod—"was funny?"

"Of course not!"

"What did you think?"

"I thought it was romantic, adventurous. What dreams are made of."

He chuckled. "See? You can make me laugh."

Her frown deepened, and she yanked again on her hand. This time he released it. "I wasn't trying to be funny, Detective. I've had a lifetime of men thinking I'm amusing just because I have a brain and I choose to use it."

"I'm not like that, I assure you, Miss Lane. Now, about our engagement tonight."

"What?" The word came out a screech before she realized he was referring to dinner. Scowling, Bridges approached them. "Now you've done it," she murmured.

"I can handle him."

Emily merely arched a brow, crossed her arms, and waited as Bridges descended upon them.

Looking apoplectic, Bridges stopped in front of him. "You aren't planning on running off with my waitress, are you, Detective MacKenzie?"

"No, sir. She just refused my offer to ride off into the sunset with me."

"Very amusing. I'm warning you, if you're planning to pirate her away, she has a six-month contract to fulfill, and I'll know where to find you, Pinkerton man."

Josh's response was as steely as the look in his eye. "And I know exactly where to find you, Bridges."

Bridges's mouth worked, but no sound came out. He looked like a fish on a line, hanging above the water. Emily choked, then coughed, so Josh let the man off the hook.

"I'm only asking Miss Lane out to dinner. I promise not to ride off into the wilderness with one of your girls."

Bridges snapped his mouth shut and nodded sharply, then turned away, muttering as he walked toward the kitchen, "She'd be the fourth girl this month. If Mr. Harvey shows up any time soon . . ."

What Bridges thought might happen was lost as he disappeared through the kitchen door. A stream of furious Chinese spilled out the opening before the door swung shut again.

Josh glanced at Emily and saw she had left his side. He took two long strides and caught her arm.

"I've got to work," she declared, trying to pull away.

"I'll be happy to let you go as long as you consent to have dinner with me tonight."

"I'm busy."

"Tomorrow night, then."

"I work through the dinner hour, remember?"

"You have to eat. I'll be here at seven tomorrow night."

Releasing her, he walked away.

Chapter 5

"Wasn't it the most romantic thing you've ever seen in your life?" Rose gave a dramatic sigh and rolled onto her stomach to look at Emily. "The way he rode right into the room, all big and strong . . . Then when she hollered at him, he just yanked her up on his horse and rode away. I wonder where they went?"

The heated night breeze blew into their window, doing little to cool their room. As they did every night, the girls lounged upon their beds in their undergarments. Whether from the extreme heat or increased comfort in her new existence, Emily had even left her robe on the peg and come to bed wearing only her shift.

"I doubt we'll ever know. Do you think she'll be happy?"

"As a pig in a wallow."

"Nice image, Rose. Do you think we should have stopped him?"

"Do you think we *could* have stopped him?" Rose countered, arching a curved brow.

Emily sighed, remembering the determination in the cowboy's eyes—and the adoration in Katie's. If she'd seen a speck of fear in the Irish girl's eyes, Emily would have grabbed onto that cowboy's boot and never let go. But what she'd seen when she looked at Katie had made Emily's heart ache with envy. Would there ever be that kind of love for her—or within her?

"You're right," she admitted. "We probably couldn't have stopped him. But Katie did say she wanted to be courted and needed time to sew a wedding gown."

"She also said she loved that crazy cowboy."

Emily still struggled with doubt. "Do you think she really could love him after meeting him only once?"

"He has a ranch, or so he said."

"What does that have to do with anything?" Emily asked, scowling.

"If he owned a big enough ranch, honey, I could even love his horse."

"Rose, you don't mean that!"

"Don't I?"

"You talk big, but I know your heart is just as big. And one day you'll fill it with love for one special man."

Rose snorted. "One special *rich* man."

"If you're so set on marrying for money and forgetting love, then why were you all misty-eyed when that cowboy dragged Katie off forever?"

"I never said I didn't believe in true love or that I didn't think it's the sweetest thing on God's green earth; I only said I plan to marry a rich, rich man."

"Sometimes, Rose," Emily said, half asleep already, "I wonder if you hear what you're saying."

"I hear all right. No down-on-his-luck cowboy is ever going to get me to an altar. If a rich cowboy wants to drag me off, I'm sure not going to struggle too hard. Just like I'm sure if that long, tall Texas detective carried you off, you wouldn't spit and scratch for too long."

"Not so," Emily murmured and slid into dreamland.

The thunder of hoofbeats woke her. She opened her eyes, confused and disoriented. She was still in bed, but it was morning, and Rose was gone. Why hadn't anyone wakened her? Bridges would have her head if she missed serving breakfast. They were short enough waitresses with Katie gone.

The hoofbeats kept coming, louder and louder, filling her head with a drumbeat that pulsed at the base of her skull. She had only a moment to wonder why she heard hoofbeats coming up the stairs to her room, and she sat up just as a horse and rider burst through the door.

They filled the doorway. She was so amazed to see them that she forgot she was virtually unclothed until the rider's sapphire eyes skated over her and made her shiver, then heat up. His gaze didn't return to her face, as a gentleman's would be expected to do; instead, it seemed frozen below her neck.

She glanced down, saw that her breasts nearly spilled from her shift, then gasped and pulled her unbound hair in front to cover her naked flesh. "Sir, you are no gentleman, invading a lady's bedchamber when she has yet to get out of her bed!"

"I never said I was a gentleman. I'm a cowboy, and I've come to carry you off to my ranch."

"Against my will?"

"What other way is there to carry someone off?"

His voice was full of Texas, and she wondered if that's where he planned to take her.

"Do you search for a wife like Francis Burgoyne?"

"No, ma'am! I'm seeking a lying, cheating, stealing blond woman. Would that be you?"

"Certainly not! Can't you see I have dark hair?"

"That's not how I heard it."

"Well, you heard wrong. You've probably been talking to that awful detective."

"MacKenzie?"

"How many awful detectives do you know?"

"Now, ma'am, I wouldn't say he's awful. Truth be told, I've heard he's quite the bloodhound."

"If you're comparing him to a dog, you're absolutely correct."

"That little gal he's a-lookin' for had better watch her back."

"And why do you say that?"

"I saw that there picture MacKenzie is showing around; she's one fancy lady."

The way he said that made her heart beat faster. "Oh, do you really think so?" Perhaps this cowboy wasn't so misguided after all, she thought with a pleased smile.

"Sure do. I wanted to look at that picture again. But seems MacKenzie misplaced it." He gave her a long, searching look that made her wonder if he could somehow know why the picture was missing.

Clearing her throat, she said, "Well, that's too bad. But once again, why are you looking for the poor woman?"

"If I couldn't look at her picture, I figured I'd look at her. But you'll do. Let's go."

"I don't understand. If you don't want a wife, why would you take me to your ranch?"

He grinned like a devil, and her toes curled in anticipation of things she did not understand. She put her hand to her nearly bare chest and felt the rapid thud of her heart beating harder and faster than ever before. "Do you intend to ravish me, sir?"

"Ravish you? Heck, no, I plan to have you cook my meals."

Emily blinked, uncertain of what she'd heard. "You've come to steal me away to be your cook?"

"I figure you could throw in a little housekeeping, too. Why else would I want you?"

"Be-be-because you've been pining with love for me. Because you can't live without me. Because your life will be worthless if I'm not in it."

He guffawed, and his horse snorted along with him. "You sure can make me laugh. If I can't have that lying, cheating, stealing blond woman, I guess I'll settle for *you*. A woman with a sense of humor is worth her weight in gold, even though you do talk too damned much."

Emily stood and stamped her foot, then grimaced because she was barefoot. "I have no intention of being *any* man's cook and housekeeper. So you can just take yourself and your stinking horse out of my boudoir, because I'm not going anywhere with you."

"Lady, it's one thing to call me names, but you've got no call insulting Buck like that. Out here, his horse is a man's best friend."

"Then advise ol' Buck to wipe that snicker off his face, or I'll call him a lot more than stinking."

"Reckon we've heard enough of that kind of talk, right Buck?" He leaned down and swept her into his arms.

"Put me down! I said I wasn't going anywhere with you." She struggled and kicked, but he just held her and laughed.

And laughed and laughed and laughed.

Emily awoke with a start to find herself drenched with sweat and tangled in her bedclothes. Rose was laughing in her sleep. At least *her* dreams were pleasant.

After disentangling herself, Emily smoothed out the sheets, then lay down and listened to the twittering of the morning birds. As the dawn spilled light across their room, Emily continued to stare at the ceiling. She thought of the cowboy who'd taken Katie away to a lifetime of love—and MacKenzie, who wanted to take her back to a lifetime of boredom.

Tonight she was having dinner with a man who could ruin everything she'd worked to attain. One wrong word and she'd find herself back on Long Island, married to an idiot, living the life of her mother, and dying inch by pitiful inch.

She didn't believe for a moment MacKenzie was interested in Emily Lane. A man like him would never look twice at a shy, myopic, plain girl, as she pretended to be. Now, if she could be herself, Emily had no doubt she could have MacKenzie groveling at her feet.

"That's it!" She sat up so fast she nearly fell out of bed.

"What?" Rose mumbled. "What time is it?"

"Time to get up."

"Go away," Rose groaned.

Rose was never at her best first thing in the morning, so Emily ignored her, and soon her friend was chuckling in her sleep again.

Unaccustomed anticipation for tonight made Emily tingle. If Bloodhound MacKenzie became smitten with her, he'd never take her back to Long Island. He might just steal her away himself.

Relaxation was overrated, Josh thought; merely another word for boredom. And he was bored.

Las Vegas, New Mexico, might have a train stop and a Harvey House and a hotel, but if you didn't live and work there, you might as well get back on the train. There wasn't much in the way of entertainment—unless you drank, gambled, or whored. He only indulged in any of them out of necessity: when he was thirsty, broke, or horny. Right now, he was the last—thanks to his dreams about Emily— but since he was going to "court Miss Emily," he couldn't risk being seen frequenting the local brothel.

He'd done all the detective work he could do. Many of the folks in Las Vegas had eaten at the Harvey House a time or two, but they didn't even know which of the Harvey Girls was Emily. And the girls did not mingle with the town. They didn't have time; they were there to work.

And no one at the restaurant knew anything about Emily Lane, much less Emily Lawrence. He'd spoken with the manager and her roommate, Rose; he'd even tried to talk to the Chinese cook, who chased him out of the kitchen with a meat cleaver that made Bowie's knife look like a toothpick. He had no intention of invading the crazy Chinaman's kitchen again.

He'd also spoken to a few of the girls, but every time he mentioned Emily, they just pointed at her and hurried on. He'd have to wait until tonight and question the woman herself.

Josh lounged about watching Emily during the lunch hour, and he had to admit she was very good at her job. She smiled and served and talked and cleaned. He found it hard to imagine this woman, who was on her feet over twelve hours a day, could be the spoiled little rich girl he searched for.

But if she wasn't, Josh was up the Rio Grande without a canoe—because if Emily Lane was *not* Emily Lawrence, then Emily Lawrence was not going to be found. She'd disappeared in Chicago, and he'd followed the wrong trail west. By now the right trail would be stone cold. But he wasn't ready to admit that yet.

He went back to the hotel after the noon meal, bathed and put on fresh clothes in preparation for returning to the Harvey House at dinner to await Emily.

Strangely enough, he was looking forward to this meeting, he reflected as he left the hotel. Emily was a welcome change from the beautiful, outgoing, and extraordinarily wealthy Diane Huntington, who had cured him of that kind of woman forever.

Although his mother and aunts were beautiful, he'd also heard all the stories about the trouble that had come along with them. Perhaps a plain woman was a better choice for a wife. You didn't have to fight off the ravening hordes or worry about her being stolen away or running off.

Upon entering the restaurant, Josh's gaze immediately sought Emily. When he found her, his smile turned into a frown. She served a table full of rough-looking men, and instead of eating their food and ignoring their plain, bespectacled waitress, they all leaned forward, gazing at Emily with equally besotted expressions.

"What the hell?" Josh muttered.

As she moved about the table, she stumbled occasionally and bumped into chairs. But it didn't seem to bother the men or interfere with her speaking softly, smiling, and laughing her quiet laugh, which trilled along his spine like summer rain.

Just then she tripped and fell against a huge, bearded hulk. The man drew a deep breath, inhaled the fragrance of her perfume, and his face went slack with wonder. Josh balled his hands into fists, prepared to step in and save her from being pawed by the big bear, but the man only thanked her kindly and never touched her at all.

She might be plain, with that stark hair and those tinted, thick glasses, but her figure was willowy and her smile was genuine. In the West it didn't matter anyway: a lady was a lady. Someone would steal Emily Lane away quick as a wink if he wasn't careful.

Why should I care? It wasn't as if he loved her. He thought she was a lying, cheating, thieving rich girl.

But . . . what if she wasn't?

He found that he liked that idea far too much.

MacKenzie had been hanging around watching her all day. By the time evening arrived, Emily was a nervous wreck. She glanced over to where he was lounging by the window, scowling at her table of guests. They were sweet, lonely men who'd been nothing but kind; yet he'd been glaring at them as if they were convicts from the time he came in the door.

"Look at him," she whispered to Rose. "How can the man have such a sour disposition all the time? It's probably the reason he chose that occupation."

Rose tried to console her. "Let him look, honey. The more he looks, the more he'll see that you aren't who he thinks you are."

Emily lowered her head and whispered, "But I *am* who he thinks I am, Rose!"

"No, you aren't, honey. If you believe you're Emily Lane, then Emily Lane is who you'll be. And if you believe—then so will he."

Emily glanced at MacKenzie again. "I doubt that. What will I do if he asks me right out if I'm her?"

"That's the spirit! She's her, not you. Remember that. Laugh. Flirt. Bat your eyelashes. He won't know what hit him."

"He'll know. He doesn't look dumb."

"They never do. But they're men; they can't help themselves. Look at him now—he's steaming that those men at your table are half in love with you."

Emily gaped. "They are?"

"Of course they are. If you so much as hinted you'd like a husband, you'd have five burly guys throw themselves at your ankles, begging."

Emily took a cautious glance at her table from beneath lowered eyelashes, only to find her guests staring at her raptly while they ate their pie. She looked back at Rose, who was grinning from ear to ear as if she was having the time of her life.

"See?"

"If they think they love me, looking like this, they'd be besotted by you. Since you're the one looking for a husband, why don't you give them a wink and have them drool all over your ankles?"

"No mountain men for me. No prospectors, no

farmers. Rich ranchers—that's all I'm interested in."

Emily took a step toward her table just as MacKenzie raised his sapphire gaze. His eyes met hers, and in their depths she saw something that made her reach out and grab Rose's elbow.

"What's the matter, honey?"

"What if MacKenzie wants more than supper?"

Rose glanced at him. "Hmm, I see your point. Well, if he wants a kiss, I suggest you give him one."

"Rose!"

"It's just a kiss. And I bet that man knows how. Have you ever been kissed?"

"Of course." How could Rose think otherwise?

Laughing, Rose teased, "I bet you've never been kissed by a man like that one. Believe me, honey, you won't forget the experience."

"But what if I don't want him to kiss me?" she hissed.

"I doubt he'll force it. He seems a gentlemen. But there is one thing you should know about men, and it's a very handy secret."

"There's a secret? And you haven't told me?"

"Well, not exactly a secret, but seeing as how your mama's gone and your pa's the way he is, I doubt he informed you of this little trick."

"Trick?"

Rose hesitated. "Well, not exactly a trick—"

"Rose," Emily warned, her exasperation mounting.

"All right, all right. If a man gets too familiar, all you need do is use your knee."

"My knee?" Emily frowned. She couldn't for the life of her figure what she'd use her knee for. All sorts of images came to mind, none of them very helpful and most too complicated to manage without assistance.

Grabbing Emily's arm, Rose pulled her behind a potted palm and placed her hands on Emily's shoulders and looked her in the eye. "Like this, Em." She made an upward motion with her knee. "In that private area they're all so proud of. Do you see what I mean?"

"And what good will that do?"

"It'll stop them in their tracks, honey. Do it right, and they'll be lying at your feet, gasping like a fish in the summer sun."

"You've done this before?"

Rose shrugged and didn't answer, but that was all the confirmation Emily needed.

"One other thing, honey. Once you do it, run like hell. Don't wait around to see if they're okay."

"Why? That doesn't seem very nice."

"If you need to use the knee, they weren't very nice to begin with. And when they get their breath back, they're going to be even less nice. You want to run—and don't look back. I'm serious about that. Men get very nasty after you've used the knee."

"All right."

Emily peeked out from behind the palm. MacKenzie was looking in their direction. Offering a weak smile, she raised a hand and wiggled several fingers at him. Grinning, he waved back. She couldn't imagine having to use her knee on him. Her face heated at the thought of touching him where Rose had indicated, even if it was with her knee.

Suddenly her dress felt too heavy and the evening too hot. The air too thick . . .

The train whistle blew. She jerked up her head—she was running out of time.

The travelers filed out the door and into the quickly approaching nightfall, until only Josh MacKenzie filled her vision: handsome, tall, dangerous—and definitely too much detective for a woman to handle. Emily swallowed the lump in her throat.

"Time for supper!" Rose called lightly.

Emily doubted she'd be able to eat a bite.

Chapter 6

～⌒⌒⌒～

S he had guessed right about not being able to eat, but wrong about the reason. She'd become spoiled, eating at a Fred Harvey establishment. Anything else paled in comparison. Since the meal at the Las Vegas Hotel and Livery could only loosely be referred to as food, she sipped her iced tea and studied her companion while he dug into his meal.

At least she tried to study him—she could barely see at all, since she couldn't slide the glasses down her nose and look over the top, which was what she always did when he wasn't around.

The man could eat, that was for certain. How he could eat that tough steak, fried to practically charcoal, was a puzzlement.

He glanced up in the middle of cutting his steak and caught her watching him. "Something wrong?"

"No, I'm simply not hungry." She cast her gaze downward and managed a maidenly blush. "But I'm enjoying the company."

"Thank you, but I know this fare can't compare to the Harvey House."

"Not much can."

"True, but 'waste not, want not,' as Maude always

73

lectured." He grinned sheepishly, looking adorably boyish. "Guess I've been on the trail so long I don't notice the food. Just eat it and move on. This"—he pointed his knife at the steak, which, if it was as tough as hers, could pass for boot leather cooked three days under a desert sun—"is the best steak I've had since Chicago."

Emily choked on her tea. "I'm so glad your steak is good," she said sweetly.

"I didn't say it was good. I said it was the best since Chicago. Out here, you're just lucky to eat at all and not die from it."

"No wonder Mr. Harvey is doing so well. I'm surprised we don't have riots to get a place at a table."

He flashed a winning smile. "Could still happen. You never know."

Josh cut another piece of meat and popped it into his mouth. His skin was bronzed from the sun and rough with an evening shadow of beard, yet those blue eyes and long, black lashes softened the effect. He spoke sharp words with his drawling Texas twang, and he wore a Colt on his hip, yet she'd never seen him touch it. His occupation was dangerous, yet his face always gentled when he spoke of his home. MacKenzie was a man of such contrasts she couldn't help but be confused—and intrigued—by him.

"And so, Miss Lane"—he put a twist on her last name that made her frown—"you never speak about your home. What brought you to New Mexico?"

Interrogation in the guise of courting talk. Well, two could play at that game—and she'd always been very good at games.

In keeping with her plan to entice him, she leaned forward and smiled.

"The Atchison, Topeka, and Santa Fe Railroad."

He smiled back in a friendly sort of way. "How long have you known Miss Dubois?"

"Rose and I met during our Harvey Girl training." It was best to stick to the truth whenever she could.

"Really? You two seem so close, one would think you've been friends forever."

She clasped her hands to her breast. "Do you really think so? I feel that way, too. As if we're kindred spirits. Sisters of the heart. Daughters of the soul," she declaimed dramatically.

For a moment he stared at her, stunned, holding his fork frozen in midair.

"Miss Lang, Sarah Bernhardt could not have conveyed it more eloquently." He popped the bite of meat into his mouth. "Now, where did you say you were from?"

So much for appealing to his finer senses—the bloodhound only had a nose for pursuit.

Darn! She should have changed from her black Harvey uniform into something with color, style, and a low-cut bodice. She might have been able to distract him with a show of flesh—even bloodhounds got distracted by a crossover scent.

On the other hand, if she'd worn one of her better gowns, MacKenzie would be more suspicious than intrigued. How would a girl like Emily Lane, who needed the money from her job, afford a silk or satin gown?

"Miss Lane, where *are* you from?"

"The East." She gave an annoyed sigh. Oops— she wanted to captivate him. Unfortunately, she was much better at annoyance.

"Out here, Miss Lane, everyone is from the East."

Patting his hand, she giggled. "Oh, you silly! You're not from the East, and I doubt the Indians are, either. And please, do call me Emily."

She tried batting her eyelashes, but he didn't even blink. He probably couldn't tell what she was doing behind the blasted glasses. She had to get rid of them.

Glancing around, she saw that their table was secluded in a dark corner. Pulling off her glasses, she intentionally knocked over the hurricane lamp on the table. "Oh, how clumsy of me!" Feigning the need for haste, she quickly extinguished the candle. "We don't want any fire, now, do we?" She batted her lashes so vigorously, she could have whipped a spark into a prairie fire.

"Something in your eye, Miss Lang?"

"There was," she snapped.

When he made a move to relight the candle, she reached out and closed her hand over his. "Please don't." Attempting the most seductive gaze she could muster, Emily murmured, "The light bothers my eyes, Mr. MacKenzie."

Nodding, he leaned back, pushing away the remains of the meal. "Whereabouts back east, Emily? And please call me Josh."

Despite his smile, which could charm the skin off a snake, Emily decided he was more like a terrier than a bloodhound—or whatever type gnawed a bone to death.

She tried to think of someplace he might never have been. All she needed was to mention a town and have him say, "Ah, Cleveland, I know it well!" And start babbling on about the wonders of the city, when she'd never seen Cleveland in her life. She wasn't going to fall into *that* trap.

"I'm from Ohio."

"Cleveland?" He perked up.

Aha, MacKenzie, I'm ahead of you this time. "No."

"I've always wanted to see it, but I've never been there."

Damn! A missed opportunity.

"Columbus?" he asked.

"No."

"Never been there, either," he said, leaning back in his chair.

"Have you been to Ohio at all?" Her voice came out sounding exasperated, and his lips twitched. Damn it, he was playing with her, too—and was much better at it than she was.

"No, ma'am, can't say that I have."

"Lovely place. I expect to return someday."

"Hmm. What do you like about it?"

Since she'd never been there, she hesitated. "It's just home—and home is always lovely."

"Yeah, it always feels good to go home." The skepticism was gone from his voice, and his face had softened again.

"Who's Maude, Josh?"

"Oh, Maude was like a grandmother to me and my cousins. She died two years ago." He smiled in loving memory. "She was one of those tough old Texans with a backbone of steel and grit. She ran the local diner in Calico—that's the town our ranch is near—until she moved to the Triple M when I was around eight or so."

"The Triple M?"

"My home."

"But Maude wasn't actually related to you?"

He glanced up at her, and once again she saw a tender glimmer in his eyes. "Only in our hearts."

"You seem to miss your home quite a bit, Josh."

"Yes, I do. Lately, more than ever."

"Then why don't you go back?" That certainly would solve her immediate problem—which was him.

His eyes narrowed, and hard suspicion replaced his dreamy memories. She'd spoken too quickly and too bluntly. "You sound eager to see me leave, Emily."

"Whyever would you think that? You just seem so homesick, I thought you'd be happier at home."

"My job isn't at home—and I do my job. That's very important to me."

It was her turn to frown. He sounded just like her father whenever her mother had begged him to leave home later in the morning, to come home early—or come home at all. Her father's voice echoed in her ears. *My dear, please cease your interminable whining; my job isn't at home.* Emily shuddered.

"Are you cold?" Josh asked, leaning forward, concerned.

"No, just a goose on my grave." *Or my mother's— but you wouldn't understand, MacKenzie.*

"You're welcome to my coat if you'd like."

The thought of putting on his garment—warm from his body's heat, the scent of him enticingly near her face—made gooseflesh prickle along her arms. She was attracted to this man, and in that attraction lay a danger more threatening than the man himself.

"I'm fine," she said. "But thank you, Josh." She

meant it sincerely. Despite his mission, he was truly a gentleman.

"I have to admit, Emily, I do miss home. And I plan to get there for a visit just as soon as I finish this assignment."

Since the assignment was her, part of her hoped he didn't finish, despite the danger. Emily's stomach danced in an intriguing sort of way.

He smiled and looked so sweetly sad, like a puppy who'd been left behind when the family went for a walk. She wanted to pick him up and cuddle him on her lap, until he spoiled it by becoming a terrier once more.

"Seems like I've been doing all the jawing here, young lady. What about your parents, Emily? Do you miss them, too?"

"Parents are part of home, aren't they?"

His lips tightened.

Her answering questions with questions had to drive him crazy—but it was so much fun.

"Have you ever heard of an Emily Lawrence?"

"Isn't that the girl you're looking for? The blond woman in the picture you showed Rose and me on the train?"

"Yes."

"Why would I know her?"

He shrugged. "Just wondering."

"You know, I never did find out why you showed up here. I thought you were chasing that poor woman."

"Why do you call her a poor woman? Could be she's a terrible person—a thief and a liar."

"And it could be she isn't. I have to feel sorry for any woman who tries to leave home and gets dragged back. If she wants to disappear, she must have a very good reason."

He grunted. "Yeah, a whole purseful. You seem to know her quite well."

"I know women like her. They're all over the West."

"Like you?"

"Me?" Her hand fluttered to her chest. "I'm just a working girl trying to take care of myself until I meet a man to marry." If he believed that, she'd be able to convince him of anything.

"You don't appear to be the marrying type."

Apparently she wasn't getting any further with the glasses off than she had with them on. "Because I'm plain?"

"No. I've been watching you, Emily. You don't give any man a second glance—no matter what he looks like. Furthermore, I don't think you're plain."

She couldn't tell if he was sincere or not. "If you believe that, then you must be more blind than I am."

"I can see perfectly. I look past the surface to the woman beneath."

The words sounded more like a threat than loverlike, but Emily couldn't let on how nervous he made her, or all would be lost. So she took a page out of his book and returned to an earlier question that he'd answered with a question. "Why *did* you come to Las Vegas, Josh?"

"Following a lead. You're positive you've never seen Miss Lawrence?"

Emily lost her patience. "What are you asking me, Josh? Do you always interrogate in the guise of courting?"

"Only when I think the girl I'm courting has something to hide."

Her heart started thundering so loud she could barely think, but she managed to squeak, "Me? What could I have to hide?"

"That you're Emily Lawrence."

She started laughing, and she couldn't stop. He'd accused her right to her face of being someone else entirely. Just because she *was* Emily didn't make it any less audacious. And for some reason, that struck her as hysterically funny.

She laughed until she could barely breathe. And Josh got redder and quieter—and angrier.

"I don't think there's anything funny about that question, Emily."

"I'm sorry—but look at me! It's flattering that you think I'm that attractive woman in the picture you showed us, but hysterically funny."

"I think you look a lot like her."

She slipped the glasses back on and held out her hand. "Let me see that picture again."

He looked away. "I don't have it."

"Being such a conscientious lawman, Josh, I'd have thought you ate, drank, and slept with it twenty-four hours a day."

"It's lost."

"Well, that explains it. You obviously don't re-member what she looks like."

He glared at her. "I remember *exactly* what she looks like. It's my job to remember details."

"Fine, we'll forget about the picture, since you don't have it. But if I were a rich heiress, do you think I'd be working here? I love my job, but it isn't easy."

"Maybe you wanted a change. Maybe you were bored."

"Isn't New Mexico a bit of a stretch for a change? And serving rough cowboys a bit extreme to relieve boredom?"

"That's what Rose said."

Emily frowned. "You asked Rose about me?" Rose had never mentioned it to her.

"Of course."

"Rose would be less likely to tell the truth than I would."

"I figured that out."

"So that's why you asked me to dinner." For some reason that disappointed her, even though she'd known from the beginning why he'd asked. Still, she felt more like Emily Lane every day, and Emily Lane would love to be courted by a man like Josh MacKenzie.

Josh must have heard something in her voice, because he glanced at her quickly. A flush had started beneath his collar. He *should* be embarrassed to have taken advantage of a plain working girl.

"I'm sorry, Em. I wasn't being fair. I'll take you home."

She couldn't let this opportunity pass. Shoulders slumped, Emily stood and looked down at him. "That's not necessary. Women like me are used to finding their way home alone," she said, with just the right tone of sadness and self-deprecation. "Thank you for dinner, Mr. MacKenzie." She walked away.

"Emily!" he called, but she kept right on going.

Sarah Bernhardt, indeed, MacKenzie! Don't try and tell me I overplayed it this time.

He had to pay their bill, so she'd reached the

porch stairs of her residence by the time he caught up with her. When she stepped onto the first step he caught her elbow, then held on tight when she would have kept climbing. Slowly she turned, to discover herself face to face with him on an even level—only inches separating their mouths. Now, what had made her think about his mouth?

Maybe because he was so close his breath brushed her cheek?

The light of the moon made his beard appear darker, his lips fuller and more enticing than before.

"Emily, I'm sorry. Please forgive me."

"There's nothing to forgive, Josh. I understand: you were just doing your job. I should have known a handsome man like you wouldn't really want to take a plain woman like me to—"

His kiss cut off her words.

She'd been kissed many times before, but never—ever—like this. The men who'd kissed her would never have considered kissing a lady when they had a day-old stubble on their cheeks—and the contrast of his soft lips on hers and the scrape of his beard along her jaw created a throbbing sensation in her body.

His hold on her elbow gentled to a caress. Wrapping his arm around her waist, he drew her against him. His body was all angles and heat, while hers was curves and ice. They fitted together like two halves of an unknown whole—a whole she wanted to know very badly.

He moaned against her mouth—a rough, wild sound that added excitement to the kiss. Being the same height as him gave Emily a new sense of power: she felt the aggressor and deepened the kiss, moaning herself when his tongue met her own.

Then his hands were in her hair, yanking away the pins. The black strands tumbled to her shoulders. Before she could stop him, he tugged her glasses from her face, and her body went cold.

She wrenched her mouth from his. Had his kiss been a trick, too?

She lowered her lids to hood her eyes, then waved her hands about as if stone blind. "Josh, I-I can't see without them."

"It appears that you can't see with them, either."

His lips traced her jaw, gently soothing the scrape of his beard. "Close your eyes, Em. You don't need them to see me."

Closing her eyes, she sighed as his mouth ignited her body again. What could it hurt to let him kiss her a little more? He kissed like no other man ever had.

A door opened somewhere to the rear of them, and Mrs. McNamara, the housekeeper, called out in a pleasant voice, "Curfew in ten minutes, darlings. Everyone to their rooms!"

Josh froze and so did Emily. She had the presence of mind to keep her eyes hooded. Stepping forward, she fell against his chest, kicking him in the shin for good measure.

"Oops!" She hung limp in his arms and peered up at him. "May I have my glasses back?"

"Yeah." His voice was gruff, and she wished she could look at him without subterfuge to see if he was annoyed at being interrupted or annoyed that he'd been wrong about her again.

His hands fumbled near her face, and the glasses slid onto her nose.

"I have to get to my room. Thank you for the dinner and . . ." She broke off what she was about to say. The kiss might have been magnificent, but she'd be darned if she'd thank him for it. The blasted man had kissed her so he could weaken her defenses and take off her glasses to see if she was the lying, cheating thief he suspected her of being. After she'd spent an hour trying to convince him she wasn't! Talk about suspicious and underhanded . . . and . . . and . . . and sneaky!

"Em?" His voice was soft, his hand gentle when he grasped hers and kept her from running.

When she looked into his sapphire eyes, she found she couldn't run anyway. He had the puppy dog look again that just tore her heart to bits.

"What?" she asked in a trembling voice.

"I'm sorry."

"You said that already."

"I mean it. I'm sorry I thought you lied. And I'm sorry I took you to supper to question you."

"It doesn't matter."

"Yes, it does. Will you let me make it up to you?"

She tilted her head. "How?"

"I'd like to take you out again."

At her skeptical glance he added quickly, "This time just to be with you."

"You must think I'm crazy."

He grinned, and her heart flipped over. "I hope you're crazy enough to forgive me. Will you go out with me again?"

She opened her mouth to refuse and out came "Yes."

This man was trouble, no doubt about it.

Josh watched Emily run up the stairs, his mouth still burning from hers, his body hard and aching. What had gotten into him to kiss a suspect?

Was she still a suspect?

There was something odd about Emily Lane, but now he wasn't so sure she was actually Emily Lawrence. If she was, it was the best act he'd ever seen. And she was the most accomplished liar he'd met in years.

He had a hard time believing that. But why?

Was it because he wanted her to be who she professed to be? Did the attraction he felt for this woman make him want to believe she was in truth Emily Lane from Ohio—a hard-working woman who could take care of herself—rather than the spoiled girl from Long Island who would steal from her own father?

Emily Lawrence might be a beauty on the outside, but on the inside she was anything but; whereas Emily Lane had the sweet soul of an angel, even if she wasn't the most beautiful woman on earth.

He'd told the truth when he said he looked past the surface. In his business you had to. And when he looked past the surface of Emily, he found a woman he wanted to know a whole lot better.

So he'd stay in Las Vegas and get to know Emily better. If she was lying, she'd slip up sooner or later. And if she wasn't, he might come to understand why the sound of her voice made him shiver, the scent of her skin made him ache, and the touch of her mouth made him desperate for more.

The murmur of voices and the low laughter of Rose Dubois drifted through an open window. Josh smiled. What a woman Rose was. He'd like to see a face-to-face confrontation between her and his cousin Zach—that would really be a battle of the sexes.

Would he ever find the right woman, as his father

and uncles had? Would he ever stop feeling restless, inadequate, unsettled? His father said all those things were related. Once you found the woman who would be yours for the rest of your life, home became wherever she rested her head.

He headed for the tavern. He needed a drink, because sleep was now out of the question. These unanswered doubts were sure to haunt him long into the night.

Emily entered her room. Still shaken by the kiss, she went to the window and glanced up at the full moon that had risen over the New Mexico landscape. It seemed as if she could see every star in the heavens. And the moon shone as brightly as silver sunshine, making the distant landscape shimmer and shine like a magical world created just for her. She turned her head when the door burst open and Rose entered.

"How was it?" Rose asked eagerly. "Did you have fun? Did he kiss you good night?"

Emily glanced out again and saw Josh's silhouette still poised at the bottom of the porch stairs. "Fine. Yes and no. Yes."

Rose laughed. "And how was the kiss?"

Emily could still taste him on her tongue, feel him against her mouth. She licked her lips and sighed.

"That good, huh? I figured him for an exceptional kisser."

"Are you a kiss connoisseur, Rose?"

"Actually, yes, I am." Rose sat on her bed. "I see he took the pins out of your hair. Good man."

"And took my glasses off, too. He's very suspicious."

She glanced out again to make sure Mr. Suspicious MacKenzie wasn't listening outside. She doubted he'd lower himself to that level, but you could never be too careful. His shadow moved away from the stairs and headed across the street. She breathed easier knowing he was no longer hovering about, waiting for her to make a mistake.

"Being suspicious is his job. So what did you do?"

Emily sat down on her own bed and began to unlace her shoes. Sixteen hours in shoes was about six hours too many—and then some.

"I kept my eyes half closed and fumbled about."

"You're getting good at this, Emily," Rose said, laughing.

"But how long do I have to keep this up? When will he give up and go away?"

"Do you really want him to?"

"Yes! He's driving me crazy with all his questions."

"But what about his kiss?"

Emily shrugged and looked away. "That could drive me crazy, too."

"Ah, to be driven crazy by a kiss." Rose sighed. "I miss that."

The longing in Rose's voice made Emily look up at her friend. "Mr. Bridges was grumbling about how friendly you are."

"I can't imagine Fallen Britches grumbling," Rose said drolly. "And as for me being friendly, I guess I'd better stop that right away."

Emily laughed. "That'll be the day."

"You know me too well. And how well did Mr. Good-Looking MacKenzie get to know *you*?"

"Not as well as he'd like to."

"Ohh, that answer has all kinds of delicious possibilities. What are you trying to say?"

"That I fended off his questions. Emily Lane has become a girl from Ohio, working until she finds a man to marry." Emily grimaced. "That's exactly the life I ran from."

"Which makes it a good lie. The closer to the truth your story is, the easier it is to make it sound convincing. Do you think he believed it?"

Emily pursed her lips in thought. "I think so."

"Then maybe he'll leave and give you your wish."

"I doubt that. He asked me to go out with him again. What do you think that means?"

"That he likes your company."

"Well, I'm not going to, of course." Even though her traitorous voice had told him she would.

"Yes, you are. You have to. If you don't, he'll just wonder why. A man like that is not used to being denied, especially by a woman who looks like you're pretending to look. He'll wonder—and believe me, you don't want him wondering any more than he already is. You're better off keeping your eye on him—and your lips and hands, while you're at it." Rose winked. "If I were you, I'd enjoy the man while he lasts, honey."

Emily put her fingers to her lips and remembered the sensation of Josh's mouth on hers. Rose always gave such good advice.

In this case she planned to take it.

Chapter 7

Since Katie Cleary had disappeared into the sunset, as it were, the Harvey Girls in Las Vegas had been hopping to keep up with their duties. To Fallon Bridges's dismay the service was not as good as it should have been, being short not only the efficient Katie, but two other girls who had skipped New Mexico: one as soon as she discovered the work was hard and the hours long, and the other as soon as she discovered California lay at the other end of the Santa Fe Railroad.

"The youth of today just can't be trusted," Bridges mumbled as he ran about serving the fresh salmon fillets. "No one keeps their word. And to break a legally binding contract . . ." He *tsked* indignantly. "That is the height of irresponsibility—a true disgrace!"

"You can just leave Katie Cleary out of your grumbling," Rose announced. "She couldn't help what happened."

"She didn't return, either. Do you think that giant kept her tied night and day?"

"If she's lucky," Rose said.

The eight men at her table guffawed, and Bridges

turned bright red. Emily shook her head in amusement and continued to serve her first table of eight. Tonight she had an extra table as well, since they were taking turns making up the slack caused by the missing waitresses.

She hadn't seen Josh since the night before, when he'd left her with the memory of his kiss. She supposed he had other things to do besides hang around the Harvey House. Perhaps he had left on one of the trains that came through daily. The thought made her sad and then annoyed with herself for being so. Her problems would be solved if he went away and never came back.

She had just begun to start serving the next table when she noticed the man lingering in the doorway. He was handsome, with a neatly trimmed beard and mustache, and dressed like an easterner. She'd become used to men staring, but this one stared hard at all the girls and even at Bridges.

She made a trip to the kitchen, and when she returned, the stranger was looking under a table. Then he ran his finger along the windowsill and checked it for dust.

She looked around for Bridges, but now there was no sign of the manager. Well, she'd approach the man herself and suggest he sit down and eat. As she moved toward him, though, he disappeared into the kitchen.

"Oh, oh," Emily murmured, seconds before loud and furious Chinese erupted from that direction.

The intruder came running out of the kitchen, Yen Cheng in hot pursuit with a huge meat cleaver.

Bridges suddenly appeared, and upon seeing what was happening, he froze on the spot, looking like he'd swallowed his tongue. He crouched quickly behind a potted palm, which would have been funny if not for the severity of the situation.

Bridges had tried to talk to the cook about his temper before, but the language barrier prevented the manager from doing much more than yell louder in English. Yen Cheng would bow politely, then ignore him.

The little Chinese cook continued to chase the tall intruder about the tables, chattering furiously and waving the cleaver in the air. The tables cleared quickly, the guests grabbing their pie and heading for the door even before the train whistle blew.

As the last customer cleared the doorway, the stranger stopped and jabbed a finger at the cook. "That will be enough, thank you!" The crisp command brought a surprised Yen Cheng to an immediate halt. "This is precisely what I'm complaining about! Procedure is not being followed." A slight English accent contributed to the man's air of authority. "Where is Mr. Bridges?" he demanded.

Yen Cheng, Rose, Emily, and every girl in the room pointed to where the quaking Bridges peeked around from behind the plant. Caught in the act, he glared at Yen Cheng.

"I thought you didn't speak English? You understood that well enough."

"Yen Cheng understand English verlly good," the cook said, and shuffled back to his domain. At the door he turned. "Bigga boss man no matter to me. You keepa him outa Yen Cheng's kitchen." He shook the cleaver at the stranger. "You understand, boss man?"

The man nodded in solemn agreement, and Yen Cheng disappeared behind the swinging door.

The stranger turned to Bridges.

"Mr. Harvey, what a pleasure to see you again." Bridges's voice shook.

"Hmm," Fred Harvey said skeptically. "I understand there's a problem here in Las Vegas, Bridges."

Still trembling, Bridges hurried forward. "I can explain that, sir. I've had three girls run off in the past few weeks—ungrateful wretches. We are doing the best we can, but until my request for more waitresses is met, we must make do with the girls we have on hand." He sniffed in Rose's direction. "However inadequate they may be."

"May I remind you, Bridges, that my wife personally interviews each girl; they are neither wretches nor inadequate. I didn't notice any problem with the service I observed." He smiled at Rose and Emily, and they smiled back.

Emily knew they should get back to work and that they should let Bridges and Harvey talk privately. But she was too interested in hearing the legendary restaurateur speak and too curious to find out why he had come to New Mexico, if not to address the waitress problem.

"B-but, sir, then why—"

"One of the girls who has worked here since we first opened this station is getting married tomorrow. I have been asked to give her away at the wedding, since it is because of me, indirectly, that she comes to be getting married in the first place." The girls received the benefit of another smile. "I've given away quite a few brides since establishing these restaurants."

"Really, sir, I hadn't realized," Bridges said, still quaking. "The bride can only be Miss Cleary."

"That's correct. Seems like I'm keeping the West in food and wives." He winked at Rose and Emily.

"And when one of my girls asks me to give her away at her wedding, I have a hard time refusing."

Emily couldn't keep silent any longer. Stepping forward, she asked, "Is it true, Mr. Harvey, that there have been hundreds of babies christened with the name Fred or Harvey?"

"So I've been told, young lady. I've even heard it said there might be thousands. What is your name?"

"Emily. Emily Lane, sir."

"A pleasure to meet you, Emily. And where are you from?"

"Ohio."

"How lovely. Nearly as lovely as you. And what about you, miss?"

"Rose Dubois." Rose floated forward and held out her hand. "From New Orleans."

Harvey smiled and bowed over her fingers with the grace of a courtier. "Charmed, Miss Dubois. Miss Lane." He nodded at them, then moved to each of the other girls—who'd all stood staring, open-mouthed to find the legend among them—and repeated the courtesy.

"And now, Mr. Bridges, back to you. Have you heard what happened to the last manager of mine who tried to cut corners and save money?"

"Yes, sir. You fired him, sir."

"Then why am I finding a profit at this station months before there should be one? Are you cutting more slices to each pie? Giving the guests thin soup? Fresh fish only on Friday? Warm iced tea?"

"None of those things."

Emily blinked when Harvey almost shouted, "Then why, may I ask, are you making money?" When he raised his voice, it deepened, and with the addition of the English accent, it made her think of

God thundering from Mount Sinai. Bridges shook as if the burning bush had spoken to him directly. She almost felt sorry for the man. Almost.

"I-I-I don't know, sir. I follow procedure to the letter."

"He does that, all right, Mr. Harvey," Rose volunteered, and without the usual sneer. Emily was proud of her.

Bridges should have been thankful. Instead he hissed, "I can take care of this, Miss Dubois."

"Speak with respect to a lady, Bridges, or I'll teach you that lesson myself."

"Yes, sir. The only thing I can think of is that we use a lot of game here, sir. And because of Yen Cheng, who is a master in the kitchen, more vegetables in his creations. Has there been any complaint about the food itself?"

Harvey frowned. "No, I was merely informed that this station was making a profit, and that usually doesn't happen so soon. We expect to lose money until we establish ourselves firmly in an area."

"I understand, sir. I'm sure I can manage to lose money, if that's what you'd like."

"I'm sure I could, too," Rose murmured, and Emily smiled.

"And now, ladies," Harvey said, addressing the assembled waitresses, "I've been authorized to invite all of you to the nuptials this evening. After you close for the night, come to the hotel, and there will be a dance to celebrate the joining of another Harvey Girl with a man of the West."

The girls cheered and applauded. There were so few opportunities for merrymaking when you worked all day, every day, that tonight's respite would be a joy for everyone.

Would Josh make an appearance, and if he did, would they dance in the moonlight? Emily sighed at the prospect and set her sights on the coming evening.

Josh had purposely stayed away from the Harvey House all day. He was too confused over his feelings for Emily and his uncertainty over who she was. If she wasn't Emily Lawrence, he had no reason to stay in Las Vegas—and he didn't want to leave just yet. He had planned to avoid Emily, but after a day with nothing to do but sit at the window of his room and watch to make certain she wouldn't try to leave town, he decided he wanted to see her. Needed to, in fact.

But when he came downstairs, the music coming from the hotel dining room made him alter his course. The room had been cleared of tables, and people lined the walls, watching a dancing couple. In the center of the floor Katie Cleary, dressed in a white gown, waltzed in the arms of a tall, distinguished-looking older gentleman.

Perhaps her father? Certainly not her husband, though in the woman-scarce west, such a difference in age was not uncommon. As Josh watched, the man stopped dancing, bowed low, kissed the young girl's hand, and held out his other hand to the giant cowboy he'd seen the previous day. Then the older man left the couple to dance alone.

Their love was evident from the way they stared into each other's eyes. It was hard to look away from such beauty, and for several moments he just watched them and missed home even more.

"What happened to dinner?"

Josh turned at the gruff question. Another hotel guest stood, frowning, in the doorway.

"Sorry, sir," the desk clerk intervened. "The dining room's closed for a wedding. If you'd like, you can go to the kitchen, and the cook will fix you something."

The hungry patron gave a nod and spun on his heel. Josh sidled up to the desk clerk. "Who got married?"

"One of the Harvey Girls married Bull Burgoyne. Mr. Fred Harvey himself gave away the bride."

"Harvey is here?" Josh's gaze scanned the crowd.

"That's him there." The desk clerk pointed to the distinguished gentleman who had been waltzing when Josh arrived. "Nice man, although I wouldn't want to get on his bad side. Heard he nearly fired his manager over at the restaurant for not following procedure."

Couldn't happen to a more deserving fellow, Josh reflected, recalling the officious man he'd questioned about Emily. The man who said she'd been hired by . . .

With a nod of thanks to the desk clerk, Josh headed for Fred Harvey. If anyone knew about Emily Lane/Lawrence, it should be the great man himself.

Harvey greeted Josh with a smile that turned to a frown when Josh showed him his Pinkerton badge. "Is there a problem, Detective?"

"I hope not, Mr. Harvey. I've been hired to find a woman named Emily Lawrence."

"Is she some sort of desperado, like Cattle Kate or Belle Starr? I've heard that you Pinkertons have sworn to shut down those Dalton brothers; does she ride with them?"

"No, sir, nothing like that."

Harvey's face fell. Obviously he'd been reading dime novels. Unfortunately, they tended to glorify outlaws like Billy the Kid, who was nothing more than a crazy, murdering child—unless you read about him in a dime novel; then he became someone larger than life.

"What did she do?"

"She ran away from home. Her father wants her back."

"I see. And how can I help you?"

"I traced Miss Lawrence to Chicago, and then she disappeared. At that time, a train with several of your waitresses bound for the Las Vegas station was leaving. I was told you hire all the waitresses. Did you hire an Emily Lawrence?"

Harvey had begun shaking his head before Josh finished his question. "I'm sorry to say I no longer hire the girls. There just aren't enough hours in the day for me to keep my finger on everything, as I used to. I had to delegate that job. Did you ask at the restaurant?"

"Yes; there's no Emily Lawrence, only an Emily Lane."

"I met her this afternoon. Sweet girl, although a bit plain. Don't you have a picture of the woman you're looking for?"

"I did, but it's disappeared."

Harvey raised his eyebrow in such a way that Josh felt like an idiot. Some detective—he couldn't even keep a picture of his quarry long enough to find her. His father would never have been in this predicament, that was for certain.

"Describe this woman," Harvey ordered.

"Blond, beautiful, patrician features."

Harvey shrugged. "Haven't seen her."

"Me, either," Josh mumbled.

"Ah, but here are some of my lovely girls."

Harvey stared past Josh's shoulder, a smile of pure pleasure on his face. Turning, Josh found himself struck dumb. He hadn't seen the Harvey Girls in anything but their black and white uniforms. As attractive as they were in uniforms, it could not compare to how exquisite they now appeared wearing a kaleidoscope of colorful gowns.

Then he saw Emily, and the breath was sucked out of his body. Her hair was pinned in a bun on the top of her head and she still wore the thick glasses, but the body he'd only dreamed about in the heated nights alone in his room was now displayed to its best advantage in an emerald gown. The perfect cream of her skin was revealed by tantalizing cleavage at the low, rounded neckline.

His loins were on fire. He could hardly breathe, much less swallow or speak. He could only stare as his body responded to the sight of her.

Then she saw him and she faltered, her glance going from him to Fred Harvey. The uneasiness expressed in her face sent his suspicious nature to boiling once more. Why would she care if he spoke to Harvey? Unless she had something to hide.

Excusing himself, he hurried across the room. Her hand fluttered up to her chest, and her long, graceful fingers fanned out over the enticing swell of her bodice, drawing his attention to the luscious flesh rather than hiding it.

Just as he reached her, the band began another waltz, and without a by-your-leave he swept her onto the floor. She had no choice but to keep up with him or fall.

Still, she didn't miss a step. Either she had a natural talent for dancing, or she'd been schooled by a fine teacher. Emily Lane would not have had a dancing teacher—but Emily Lawrence . . .

He looked down at her but only encountered the top of her head. She stared straight ahead at what must have been a fascinating view of his Adam's apple, since she didn't seem to be able to take her eyes from it. Well, it was a fair exchange, because he couldn't take his eyes off the puff of lace tucked enticingly in the cleavage of her gown.

"Emily, I was just coming to find you."

"Really? What did you want, Josh?"

"I missed you, Em." He tried not to sound like a lovesick yokel.

"You just saw me last night, Josh."

"And I needed to see you tonight."

"Have you met Mr. Harvey?"

"Yes. Nice man."

"And what did the two of you find to talk about?"

"Just things. Nothing of importance."

Rose whirled past in the arms of a cowboy who chattered a mile a minute and vigorously stomped in time to the music. She didn't look happy and gave Josh a pathetic, help-me glance.

"I should go to her aid, but you dance so divinely, my darling Emily, that I hate to release you from my arms."

She smiled sweetly. "You embarrass me, sir. And you talk mighty prettily for a cowboy detective, you naughty boy." She lightly bopped him on his forehead with her fan.

"Why, Miz Emily, if I didn't know better, I'd swear you were flirting with me."

"Flirting? Me? Tsk, tsk," she murmured, shaking

her head adorably. "Now you truly are making me blush."

Clearly she was flirting with him, but it was so out of character for her that he could only wonder about the reason behind it.

"A blush which only heightens your beauty," he flirted back.

That earned him another rap from the damn fan. "Shame on you, Josh; you'll soon have my head whirling as fast as the music. So what kind of things?"

"Pardon?"

"What kind of things did you and Mr. Harvey discuss?" she asked, this time more firmly.

"Business and the like."

"Hmm. His business or yours?"

Josh decided he'd let her wonder. If she was hiding something, it would make her nervous. If not, then she shouldn't be concerned about the discussion. "Both."

She frowned; he smiled.

"Well, are you at least going to tell me where you picked up expressions like 'divinely'?" she asked.

"From the same person who taught me to dance."

Her brow creased, and she looked him in the eye again. Her eyes always appeared unfocused behind her glasses. At least, they were unfocused on him; his eyes were definitely focused—particularly on that piece of lace.

"I'm envious of the lucky woman. Who was she, pray tell?"

This time his hand was quicker than hers. He caught the fan before it could make contact.

"My mother. She once worked in a saloon."

"Your mother worked in a saloon?" Emily was so astounded, her mouth fell open.

"Does that shock you?"

"I guess so. It's not that I'm prudish, but you've just always spoken of your mother so reverently. I envisioned her as a paragon of virtue, and I've always been led to believe that women who worked in saloons were anything but virtuous."

"It's a long story, Em, and all part of how Dad and Mom met. And from that shocked look on your face, you'll be surprised to hear my aunt worked in a gambling saloon owned by my Uncle Cleve—and her father's a wealthy Spanish don."

"Serving drinks to men," she said disapprovingly.

"Isn't that what you do, in a manner of speaking?" She looked so horrified he burst out laughing just as Rose danced by.

"I'm glad you two are having so much fun, but give someone else a chance," she said.

He was confused until he realized Rose was now dancing in the arms of a different man. Had another song begun while he and Emily talked? He had no idea, which scared the hell out of him. Alertness was an essential element in his job. When had he lost his awareness of what was going on around him? When he started kissing and dancing with the suspect, no doubt. He'd been inexcusably careless—the kind of carelessness that, under different circumstances, could result in another bullet in his back. And the irony of the whole damn situation was that he could dance with a suspect and think of no one—nothing—but her.

He took a look at the sidelines and discovered a host of men waiting for their turn to dance with the lovely, ladylike Harvey Girls. But he had Emily in his arms and intended to keep her there—for as long as he could, anyway.

With a quick series of twirls, he maneuvered them away from the waiting throng. As he anticipated, she kept up admirably, and he again wondered where she had learned the skill of dancing. Smiling down at her, he discovered, she'd reverted to frowning.

"I guess you're right, Josh. In a manner of speaking I do serve drinks. Mr. Harvey serves a fine claret. But I don't consider myself a saloon girl."

Amused, he said, "I don't think my mother or aunt thought of themselves in that light, either. Interestingly enough, my aunt's situation was quite similar to the case I'm working on now. She was a wealthy heiress who was hiding from her father. Unlike Emily Lawrence, however, she didn't steal from him; she ran away to avoid an arranged marriage."

He watched Emily's face closely, but she only smiled. He had to admit she was good.

"And your uncle was her savior? Her Prince Charming?"

"In a manner of speaking." He smiled at the memory.

"You have a very interesting family, Josh."

"I do, at that."

The music ended with a flourish, and this time they had to stop dancing, since the band dispersed to take drinks from the bar. The crowd milled about, chatting, and when several cowboys headed in Emily's direction, Josh fended them off with a narrowed look. They shuffled off in search of a different girl.

"Would you like a glass of punch?"

Emily nodded, and he led her to a long table filled with pastries and punch. After filling a glass with the tepid, yellowish-looking liquid, he glanced longingly at the whiskey on the bar. If he left Emily unattended she'd be snatched up by another man, and he'd spend an hour trying to chase her down on the dance floor. While he remained in Las Vegas, she was his—whether she liked it or not. And he had a nagging belief that she definitely didn't like it. So, no whiskey.

"Why aren't you joining me?" she asked when he filled a cup.

"I'm not thirsty."

"Oh, what a shame. It's delicious, too." She took a sip, then held the punch cup up to his lips. "I insist you try some."

He couldn't have said what it tasted like, because the only thing he was conscious of was that her lips had just touched the glass. Something to think about besides that piece of lace.

Rather than stand gaping at her, he turned and picked up two plates holding slices of cake. He wolfed his down, but Emily ate hers slowly, savoring each bite. How in hell could it take so long to eat a skinny slice of cake? He tried not to stare at the piece of lace, but his gaze invariably was drawn back to it.

He almost yanked the plate out of her hand and thrust it aside when she finally finished.

Her hand moved to her bosom, and he watched, transfixed, as she withdrew the puff of lace. "I'm afraid you didn't eat all your cake, sir," she said lightly. Then she gently wiped the corner of his mouth. The handkerchief was warm from her body heat, and the scent of lavender drifted to his nostrils. He wanted to grab the piece of lace and bury his nose in it—or in the cleavage that had nested it. Before he could erect a defense, she raised up on her toes, leaned into him, and patted his brow with the distracting enticement.

"My goodness, Mr. MacKenzie, you're perspiring."

"Yes, it's hot in here." His throat went dry when she tucked the handkerchief back into its lavender-annointed sanctum. "Now that the sun's gone down, it should be quite pleasant outside. Shall we sit on the porch?"

She nodded. "I'd like that."

The outside of the hotel was as deserted as the inside was full. It seemed like everyone in Las Vegas had come to the party, and he couldn't blame them. Once the trains pulled out, there wasn't much to do in the town except go to bed to get ready for the next day. Tonight was a pleasant change, and people had taken the opportunity to enjoy the food, drinks, and music.

For a long moment they remained silent, drawing deep breaths of the cool night air, a contrast to the smoky, heated hotel. The street was a quiet relief from the pounding music, stomping feet, and myriad voices.

Emily took a seat on one of the benches that lined the hotel wall. "I'm glad so many turned out for the wedding. Katie and Francis looked so happy."

He sat down next her, their thighs touching, and she shifted away. *So she's playing cat and mouse.* She felt safe in a crowd but drew back when they were alone.

Josh laid his arm along the back of the bench behind her. "It was nice of Harvey to give the bride away."

"I understand he does that often."

"Yeah, so he said," Josh replied.

"What else did he say?"

She was like a dog with a bone on this subject. Well, he wasn't going to tell her he'd asked about Emily Lawrence again. She'd only shake her head and look at him like he was an idiot.

"We talked about desperadoes. There've been several train robberies lately, and it seems Mr. Harvey likes dime novels. He knows quite a lot about western desperadoes and their exploits."

"Really!" She looked as excited as a kid in a candy store and shifted on the bench so she could look at him. Her knee brushed his, but she didn't seem aware of it. He, on the other hand, was very much aware of the contact—too much for his own good.

"Who are these desperadoes?" she asked.

"Billy the Kid appears to be his favorite."

"Who's he?"

"Are you trying to tell me you never heard of William Bonney, alias Billy the Kid?"

She looked down her nose at him, a trait he found at once annoying and endearing. "I don't read dime novels."

"Too bad; some of them can be quite exciting. But I still can't believe you haven't heard of him. His exploits were written up in all the newspapers. Billy was quite a desperado."

She shifted closer, pressing her thigh to his. "Tell me about him." If this was more flirting to distract him, it wasn't going to do her any good. Of course, it wasn't exactly doing *him* any good, either.

He considered just kissing her, since that was what he wanted to do more than anything else, but the fascination on her face and the fact that she had moved closer and closer made Josh think a bedtime story was in order.

So he leaned back to tell her all he knew about the notorious desperado known as Billy the Kid.

Chapter 8

❝**W**illiam Bonney was born in New York, but he's a New Mexico boy all the way," Josh said.

Emily was fascinated by anything that had to do with the wild and woolly west. After living on staid old Long Island all her life, then discovering what life was really like out here, she loved this land with all her heart. She was a New Mexico girl, despite being born in New York—just like Billy.

"They say he killed his first man at eighteen, while working for the army."

"Oh, my! Why did he kill the man?"

Josh shrugged. "I really don't know, but that was usually the way with Billy."

Frowning, she said, "That doesn't sound like a hero to me. Or a legend."

"No. Anyway, he escaped and was hired by John Tunstall, an Englishman who had a ranch in Lincoln County."

"When was this?"

As Josh was thinking about the answer, Emily became aware that in her attempt to flirt with him she'd shifted so close to him on the bench that she was now pressed against his side. He didn't seem to notice or mind, and the warmth of him felt good in the chill of the approaching night. She stayed where she was.

"Billy died in '81."

"That long ago?"

Nodding, Josh continued, "Billy got a mite put out when Tunstall was killed. Took it on himself to avenge the man who'd taken him in."

"I can understand that—the code of the West."

He raised his brow. "I don't think Billy would have understood what that meant, let alone followed one. But he cut a nice swath through New Mexico during the Lincoln County War. Killed the sheriff in Lincoln, escaped from jail twice, put together a band of outlaws, and ran riot all over the place."

"How many men did he kill?"

"You are a bloodthirsty little thing, aren't you?"

"No, just curious."

She leaned back and discovered his arm lay along the bench. When her shoulder bumped his, his hand came around her shoulder and held her close. She stared out at the night, and as he held her, she couldn't think of a thing that felt as good as Josh's nearness.

"Well, the legend goes that he killed twenty-one men. One for every year of his short and violent life."

She gasped and turned toward him. Their faces were so close that if she had moved forward just a bit, she could have kissed him. His thoughts must have been the same as hers, because his hand tightened on her shoulder.

"Twenty-one?" Why did her voice sound so inviting, so husky, as if she'd just awakened from a long night's sleep to find this man at her side. Clearing her throat, she inched back from temptation. Josh loosened his hold but still kept his arm around her.

"It's hard to believe he was only twenty-one when he died."

"Violent people die violently. Billy was shot by a sheriff named Pat Garrett. But the Kid actually killed six men—not twenty-one like the legend goes. Like most legends, it's a lie."

"Even so, how did the total end up that high when he only killed six?"

Josh turned his head and looked out at the expanse of land that surrounded Las Vegas. "Because of that." He swept his hand at the shadows that shimmered in the night.

"I don't understand."

"Would you have ever believed the West was so big?"

Frowning, she contemplated the land along with him and shook her head. "No. I guess not. Coming from east of the Mississippi, I never guessed how vast the land is out here until I saw it for myself."

"That's what you easterners always say. You ought to see Texas. *That's* big. Everything in Texas is big."

She gave him a skeptical glance. "Everything?"

Grinning, he glanced at her. "Everything, li'l darlin'." His accent deepened, and she laughed out loud.

"I think you're trying to tell me something."

"Only that if everything is bigger out here, so are the legends. Billy the Kid killing six people isn't as exciting as Billy killing a man for every year of his life. The truth out here is usually what you make it."

For a long while, Emily thought about what he'd said. The idea appealed to her. She could become anyone, do anything in the West if she turned the lie into truth. She only had to get rid of Mac-Kenzie—and never see him again.

The thought made her heart ache.

Just then the band struck up a mournful, haunting tune that stirred her heart. Before she realized it, her eyes began to tear from a combination of the music and the thought of never seeing him again. She turned her head to look at him, just as he turned to look at her. They were so close their breath mingled.

"Em?" he whispered, as if asking her permission.

"Yes," she replied, in that husky, temptress voice that seemed to appear whenever he was near. Still he hesitated, his mouth hovering over hers. *Blasted man! Do it quickly before I lose my nerve.* She narrowed the tiny space between them and offered her lips.

The kiss was familiar, yet new. Would each kiss be like that? The same, yet excitingly different?

His lips were firm, full, and warm. She opened her mouth in a sigh, and he delved within, his tongue stroking hers. Hers stroked his in return. He outlined her lips, his hand cupping her neck in the warmth of his palm. Tilting her head, he kissed her more deeply, and she moaned against his mouth, her entire being coming alive in his arms. How could this man make her feel so much with only a kiss, when all the others had made her feel nothing?

He was dangerous, just like the land he'd spoken of. Josh MacKenzie was of the West, larger than life. He excited her; he thrilled her; he aroused her. He was a lawman, and he'd never stop until he had his man. And she was playing with fire by playing with him.

She pushed her hands against his chest to break

the kiss, holding him back when he would have dived in for more. His mouth was moist from hers, and those damnable sapphire eyes were on hers, searching, probing, waiting, as if he expected her to confess everything. But, she wasn't that far gone yet, and she prayed to God she never would be.

Although her hands trembled and her knees were weak, Emily forced herself to her feet. "I . . . I need to get inside. Rose will wonder where I've gotten to."

His lips twitched. "I'm sure Rose knows."

"Perhaps, but it's still rude of me to be out here when the celebration is inside."

"I'll take you."

"No!" His eyes widened at the force of her denial. She took a deep breath and ran trembling fingers down her skirt to smooth wrinkles that didn't exist. "I mean, that isn't necessary. I can find my way. Thank you for the dance, Detective."

He stood, crowding her, daring her to take a step back. She should have, she would have, but he grabbed her arms and drew her back against his body. "Is that all you've got to say, Em?"

"What more should there be?" she asked, confusion joining her nervousness.

"This." His mouth once again took possession of hers.

This kiss was different from the earlier one. The first one had been all gentleness and light. One of warmth, not hot passion—a kiss born of Emily. The second was rough and hard. Bold twists, turns, and dips—a kiss born of Josh.

She clung to him now, she couldn't help herself. If she didn't, she'd fall. The world narrowed to only them and the kiss, their mouths melded together, their bodies locked in an embrace for Lord knows how long.

The sound of applause broke them apart. Turning their heads, they discovered they were the center of the attention of Rose and several cowboys.

"Well, that was impressive, honey. And you, too, MacKenzie."

Emily blushed; Josh muttered an expletive.

Rose sashayed forward, her skirt swishing a tune of its own. The men followed faithfully behind her. She laughed and pulled Emily from Josh's embrace. "Time to go home now."

Josh put his hand on Emily's arm and pulled her back. "I'll take her home."

"No, you won't." Rose tugged on Emily's other arm. "You're not behaving like a gentleman, Mr. MacKenzie."

"I am, too." He yanked again, causing Emily to stumble against him.

"That's enough, you two," she declared, stomping on his foot accidentally. She pulled her arms away from both of them. "I can take myself home."

Josh looked lonely and bereft when she stepped away, but she could still feel his touch on her body, his kiss on her lips—and the blush on her cheeks. She needed time to think about this alone. So while Rose was occupied with her entourage, and since Josh was too much a gentleman to drag her back, she lifted up her skirts and ran all the way home.

Josh turned from the sight of Emily running away from him as if he'd sprouted Satan's horns, to find Rose shooing away all her escorts.

"Thank you gentlemen for the dance, but I need

to talk to Detective MacKenzie." They left, looking like lost lambs.

As soon as they disappeared, Rose turned to confront him.

"Honey, you're scaring that child to death."

"How do you figure that?" He sure as hell didn't like her butting in on something between him and Emily.

"You saw her face; what did you do? What did you say?"

"You know damn well what I did. You stood there and watched. So I kissed her—so what?"

"I don't think she's been really *kissed* before, if you know what I mean."

"I don't think I do."

"By a man who knows what he's doing. That's frightening the first time around."

"Why's that?" The conversation was becoming more amusing than irritating.

Rose smiled at him as if he were dense. "You lose a part of yourself every time you give to someone else. Now, if you love that person"—she sighed dramatically—"and they love you, it's a gift, and they give a part of themselves back to fill you up. But without love . . ." She shook her head. "It's downright terrifying when a part of your soul flies away."

He glanced down the street after Emily, but she was long gone. Turning back to Rose, he caught a dreamy look on her face that was in direct contrast to the worldly woman he'd come to know and like a whole lot.

"Rose, you're a dewy-eyed romantic, aren't you?"

Her face changed and the spice returned. "Me? How you do go on." Her hands fluttered to her bodice in a practiced motion.

Josh just smiled. He had her number. She might talk big about money and ranchers, but she was looking for love. He'd bet on that.

And because she was Rose, he sure hoped she'd find it.

Emily had all of half an hour alone before Rose hustled in. The time wasn't nearly enough to figure out MacKenzie or her response to him—but she doubted an eternity would do. Pretending to be asleep didn't fool Rose a bit; she lit the lamp and yanked the covers off Emily's head. "Honey, you need to quit playing with fire."

Not even bothering to protest, Emily sat up and arranged the pillows behind her head. "This, from the woman who agreed that I should allow Mac-Kenzie to court me."

"That was to keep an eye on him," Rose declared, pulling the pins from her hair. The curly red mass tumbled down. She shook out the tresses and grinned at Emily. "Not your mouth, lips, and hands, too, honey."

"I seem to recall a conversation about kissing while the kissing is good," she said, blushing.

"And from where I was standing, the kissing looked mighty good." They broke into giggles. Then Rose sobered and said in a serious tone, "Kissing is all right." She wagged her finger at Emily. "But nothing else."

"We weren't doing anything else!"

"Not yet, anyway."

"Rose!"

Rose came over to the bed and turned for Emily to undo the back buttons of her dress. "I saw what was going on. Another minute of that kiss and he'd have invited you up to his hotel room. And that would have been the end of you, Emily Lawrence."

"What are you talking about? MacKenzie wouldn't invite me to his hotel room." Tugging the last button free a bit roughly, she gave Rose a little push to indicate she was done. "And I wouldn't have gone if he had."

Rose snorted. "Yes, you would, if your mind was all muddled from his kiss. Don't tell me it wasn't."

She didn't bother to try, because Rose was right. Her mind was still muddled. "What am I going to do, Rose?" she asked sorrowfully.

Rose finished hanging up her gown and sat down on her bed. "I don't know. I talked to Mr. Harvey and found out MacKenzie was snooping around asking him questions."

"I know. He told me."

"He did?" Rose was clearly surprised. "Hmm, guess I'll have to give the devil his due."

"Well, he didn't tell me everything, but I figured it out. What did Mr. Harvey tell him?"

"Nothing. He only knew you as Emily Lane. So maybe the detective will run along now."

"Maybe." Emily sighed, and the sound was so lamentable in the silent night that Rose glanced at her, and they shared a commiserating smile.

"It's a shame he has to be a lawman," Rose said.

"Why's that?"

"I'd take him myself. He has a certain appeal."

The image of Rose "taking" MacKenzie put a fire in Emily's blood. But her friend was looking for a man, and she wasn't. "So why don't you, Rose?"

Lowering her chin, Rose raised a perfectly curved eyebrow at her. "I'm not one of those women."

"What kind of women do you mean?"

"Women who take any man available, even from their friends, just because they can. They tell themselves all's fair in love and war, and hog all the horseflesh."

"Oh, *those* women." Emily tried not to laugh. Rose really must have led an interesting life. "So you haven't found any prospects?"

Sighing dramatically, Rose fell back on her bed. "Not a one. Think MacKenzie has a rich, equally handsome brother?"

"Why don't you ask him?"

"I think I just might."

Silence descended between them, companionable and comforting. Feeling drowsy, Emily closed her eyes and listened to Rose rustle around until the lamp went out.

"What else did you two talk about?" Rose's voice came from far away and sounded as sleepy as Emily felt.

"Billy," she mumbled.

"Who's Billy?"

"Desperado. Outlaw. Lincoln County War."

"Billy the Kid? What kind of thing is that for a gentleman to talk to a girl about?"

"I like stories, and Billy's was a good one."

"Good and bloody, you mean. You'll probably have a nightmare."

"Uh-huh . . ." Emily drifted off while Rose was still talking.

"My name is William, ma'am."

The young man tipped his hat. His other hand held a rifle. He looked rumpled, as if he'd been riding for days on end with little sleep. As if he'd been chased for days, perhaps. The black horse behind him looked winded.

Glancing around in confusion, Emily found herself standing in the middle of nowhere—or New Mexico. How had she gotten here?

"And your name, ma'am?"

"Emily."

"Ah, Emily. I've heard of you."

"You have?"

"Yeah. Habitual liar. Thief of the highest order."

"I am not! You've been talking to MacKenzie or maybe my father."

"Not your father. Haven't been east of the Mississippi since I came across it the first time, and I don't plan to go. Leastwise not alive. Can't abide the East—too many people and not enough space. You know what I mean?"

Emily looked around the beautiful expanse surrounding them. "Yes," she said. "I do."

"Damn!" He stared at the horizon. "He's back."

Emily followed his gaze and saw the puff of dust indicating a rider. "Who's that?"

"MacKenzie. The man's a bloodhound."

"Don't I know it."

"Since you understand my predicament, you won't mind if we get on our way."

"Where?"

"Lincoln. I have a date with the sheriff."

Emily frowned. Lincoln. William. "You're Billy the Kid."

He grinned, and his sapphire eyes sparkled. Sapphire? Why on earth would Billy the Kid have sapphire eyes? But then again, why not? They were awfully pretty.

"In the flesh," he said.

"You're a desperate man."

"I am at that. And getting more and more desperate as we speak. Now we need to be hurrying along, because I doubt that there lawman will be too particular about who he shoots at this point."

"MacKenzie wouldn't shoot me."

"With him you just never know. Especially now."

Emily narrowed her gaze. "What have you done?"

"Nothing much." He shrugged. "Got in a little disagreement over cards in the last town."

"So you killed someone?"

"The man needed killing," he said with a shrug of his puny shoulders. "Let's go."

Short, puny—and young, she thought, hanging back. "Are you planning to ravish me?"

"Naw. I don't take to older women. Let's go."

"Older women! I'm not going anywhere with you."

"Yes, you are." He grabbed her arm and pulled her toward his horse. "MacKenzie might be more accommodating if he knows I have you. I think he's sweet on you."

She pulled her arm from his. "He is not."

"Is too," he said, grabbing her arm again.

"Is not!" They sounded like squabbling children, but what could she expect from someone called Billy *the Kid*? "Mr. Bonney, I am not riding off with you while MacKenzie chases us down like common criminals."

"But I am a common criminal."

"*I'm* not."

"Yes, you are."

"Am not!"

He sighed and rolled his eyes. "Are you always this much trouble?"

"I am not troublesome. You're the one with the bad reputation."

"I sure can't figure why MacKenzie likes you." He tugged on her again. "Let's go."

"No." She pulled away.

"Emily!"

Emily frowned. That sounded like Rose's voice rather than Billy's. But why would Rose be out in the middle of nowhere with Billy and her?

"Emily, wake up right now and quit arguing with me!" This time she was shaken vigorously.

Emily took a deep breath and drew in a lungful of smoke. She coughed violently and—woke up.

Rose stood over her. "Emily, wake up! There's a fire!"

Chapter 9

❀❀

"Wh . . . what did you say?" Emily felt dragged from the depths of an ocean of sleep.

"The restaurant's on fire, and I've been tugging on you and shouting, trying to wake you. "Here." Rose threw Emily her robe and some shoes. "You just kept mumbling 'Billy.' Who's Billy?"

"Never mind," Emily said. She quickly put on the robe and shoes. "We'd better get out of here."

"That's what I had in mind, honey," Rose said, staring out the window. "Looks like the fire started at the rear in the kitchen." When Emily started toward the door, Rose pointed at the glasses on the nightstand. "You'd better not leave those behind. I can't believe MacKenzie will sleep through all this."

Within moments they were both out the door and had joined the rest of the girls in the courtyard. Bridges was there, wringing his hands, in addition to Mrs. McNamara and Yen Cheng.

"Thank goodness! You two girls are the last out of the house," Mrs. McNamara said.

Bridges wrung his hands as Yen Cheng chattered away in Chinese.

"English, Chinaman. In English," Bridges shouted. "I know you can speak it."

"What good English now, boss man? Kitchen on fire in any language."

"Just what happened here?" Bridges asked.

"Yen Cheng sleeping. How he know? Poof, big fire. You no see?"

"I see it. I just don't believe it."

"Maybe we should try and put the fire out," Rose drawled, "rather than stand here worrying about how it began."

Bridges scowled at the black smoke billowing from the doorway, then back at Rose. "And how do you propose we do that?"

"With water."

"Spit on it? How do we get the water from the trough to the fire?"

"A bucket brigade," Emily said.

"What?" Bridges turned his sour frown on her.

"I saw one once in—" She stopped and glanced at Rose. "Uh, at home. You get a bunch of buckets and make a line."

"Great idea," Rose interrupted. "Let's go, girls, before the fire spreads to our rooms and we lose all our things. Man the wash buckets, maties."

Under the direction of Rose and Emily, the Harvey Girls soon formed a line from the horse trough to the fire and began passing buckets of water from hand to hand.

Just as they were under way, Emily saw Josh MacKenzie come barreling onto the scene. Obviously just awakened from sleep, he was annoyingly attractive: beard stubble, tousled hair, shirt awry—how could the man look so delectable when she no doubt looked a wreck?

His gaze immediately sought her out, and when their eyes met, his shoulders sagged in relief. A warm feeling flowed through Emily—he had been worried about her.

Without a word, he walked to the front of the line, and by the time the clang of a fire bell added to the shouting, the Harvey Girl bucket brigade was in full swing. Unfortunately, so was the fire.

A team of horses pulling a red fire engine raced down the street. The twelve volunteers of the Las Vegas Fire Department, wearing red helmets and white slickers, hurriedly ran a hose to a nearby cistern, then lined up on each side of the engine and began to hand-pump water onto the burning building.

"Good Lord, that engine has to be over thirty years old!" Rose grumbled.

By this time, the entire restaurant was engulfed in flames, and fiery sparks flashed in the dark smoke.

"Get back! Get back!" Josh shouted when the glass windows blew out from the heat, spewing glass shards over the street. "There's nothing more we can do here."

By this time, the townsfolk were out on the street, splashing water on the roofs and sides of nearby buildings, hoping to prevent the fire from reaching their homes and businesses.

The restaurant was destroyed, but Emily and the other Harvey Girls worked side by side with the townsfolk to prevent the fire from spreading to any other structures.

By the time dawn broke the eastern horizon, Emily and Rose, soaked, sooty, and unemployed, sat on the step of their boarding house and stared at the smoldering ashes of what once was the Harvey

House. Unless they could find some way to get the business up and running in another location, they would probably be leaving Las Vegas.

Emily's head hung, and she stared at the gray hem of her formerly white nightgown. A pair of muddy boots appeared between her shoes. She didn't have the energy to look up; she knew who those boots belonged to.

"You all right?" MacKenzie asked.

She nodded.

"Rose?"

"Fine and dandy," Rose replied.

MacKenzie squatted in front of Emily, and his face appeared on the same level as hers. He put his hands on her shoulders, and she looked up into his eyes. The tenderness there nearly undid her.

Reaching out, he brushed her straggling hair from her face, then rubbed his thumb over her cheek. Even as exhausted as she was, her body ignited at this touch, hotter than the flames they had just fought. She had to fight these flames, too. As Rose had said, she was going to get very badly burned if she wasn't careful.

"Your face is dirty," he murmured.

"So's yours."

He looked endearing with soot on his face, and the dirt made his eyes shine even brighter. Her heart made a funny sort of twist, and she sighed in defeat. How much harder must she fight what she felt for him?

"Are you going home now?"

He certainly had a way of saying the wrong thing at the right time. She jerked her face away from his touch. "No!"

"There's nowhere for you to work. Harvey will

send all of you home. Or back east until you can be reassigned."

"Where *is* Mr. Harvey?" Rose asked.

Emily frowned and looked around, her gaze moving over the crowd. Mr. Harvey was nowhere to be seen, which was odd, since a man like him would no doubt have been at the front of the bucket brigade. "Yes, where is he?"

"I heard he got on a train to California shortly after the wedding. He won't hear about the fire until later today. Then I'm sure he'll be back."

"Then we'd best find a way to be open for business before he gets here." Emily stood.

Rose did the same. "What do you have in mind, honey?"

"I'll come up with something. But you can be sure I'm not going home."

"Hadn't you better wash up and get some sleep?" Josh said.

Emily snorted. "Not now, MacKenzie. I'm busy."

"But . . ."

She walked off and left him sputtering at the foot of the porch stairs. Rose's laughter followed her as she headed down the boardwalk toward the deserted train station. Something tickled the back of her mind about the station, and suddenly she had to go see it.

"Where are we going?" Josh demanded from behind her.

"I didn't ask you to come."

"Well, I'm coming."

"Me, too," Rose chimed in. "But where?"

They crossed the railroad tracks, and Emily pointed past a building. "There."

"The roundhouse?" Josh asked.

Rose shrugged when he looked to her for understanding. "Honey, what has the roundhouse got to do with this?"

"The depot is where you get tickets, Emily. I'll see to it," Josh said.

"I—am—not—going—anywhere," she said through clenched teeth.

"Then why did you bring us here?" Josh asked. "Emily, I really think you should go back to your room and get some sleep. This whole experience has been very taxing for you."

She resisted the urge to scream in frustration. Rose looked about ready to burst from suppressed laughter. "Terrier," Emily murmured, and Rose caught the meaning at once. Her laughter trilled across the quiet train station.

At the sound, a man came out of the small ticket building nearby on the platform. "You folks want tickets?"

"No, we want those." Emily pointed to two abandoned boxcars sitting next to the roundhouse.

"What for?"

"The Harvey House will need a place to set up until the restaurant can be rebuilt."

The ticket man looked skeptical. "I don't know . . ."

"What are you using them for?"

"Nothing. There's something wrong with the wheels."

"Then why can't we use them temporarily? It's not like we're going to ruin them. You can always fix the wheels and hook the cars up when we're done."

The man continued to look confused and uncertain.

"Let me put it another way," she said. "Do you

want to have to tell each and every trainload of people that arrives that their meal tickets are no good because the Harvey House burned down? Once word gets east, they'll stop coming altogether. Or would you rather point to these cars and tell them that due to a fire, the restaurant has moved temporarily?"

He paled and waved his hand at the abandoned cars. "Be my guest, ladies." Then he disappeared back into his little house.

"What do you have in mind, honey?" Rose asked.

Emily bit her lip and stared at the cars, her mind churning with an idea. Though it wouldn't be as good as the Harvey House, it would be a heck of a lot better than going home. And she'd do anything to avoid that.

"We use one car as a kitchen, the other as a dining room."

"And what do you plan to use for tables and chairs? Food? Dishes? Need I go on?" Rose asked.

"We can get some men to start building tables right away. Bridges can send an emergency wire for dishes and supplies this morning. By the time we get the cars cleaned and painted, the new things will be here. If everyone pitches in and helps, with a little elbow grease, Rose Dubois, we can be serving dinner tonight."

"You think it'll work?"

Emily glanced at Josh, who was staring at her with a strange look. She tossed her head. "I guess we'll find out." Then she turned on her heel and headed back to the ashes of the Harvey House.

Josh stood on the platform and watched Emily march away without a backward glance. Laughing, Rose followed. He couldn't understand why she thought this was so funny, but he was coming to understand that to Rose, just about everything was an amusement. He wished he could see the funny side to a devastating fire, but somehow he just couldn't get his mind around that.

He couldn't get his mind around Emily taking over in the face of disaster, either. Calm head, cool voice, luscious body in white cotton.

When he'd arrived, her robe hung open and the breeze had blown her nightgown about her ankles and molded the material to her backside. He'd nearly swallowed his tongue before he forced himself to walk past her without touching her and stand at the front of her line. From there he fought the fire in front of him and ignored the one within him.

Then after fighting all night, she didn't collapse or whine or cling—though he'd almost wanted her to. No, she'd marched down the main street in her nightgown and found a place to set up shop.

He shook his head. If he didn't know better, he'd swear she was a MacKenzie woman. His mother would love her. The thought made him uneasy. What was he saying? How did he feel?

Emily was far different from any woman he'd ever courted. She didn't wait around for a man to help her; she helped herself. She didn't need him around; she didn't even *want* him around half the time. And while that could be annoying, it was also soothing. After a lifetime of admiring women who worked with their men and not against them, he held an image in his heart and mind of the kind of woman he would love forever. Lately, she'd begun to look a lot like Emily.

For the first time in a long time, he allowed himself to remember another woman he'd believed he might spend forever with. Diane Huntington's beautiful face had disguised a rotten core; her exquisite body had hidden a bleak heart. All her money and breeding could not make up for her spoiled and selfish ways.

He had been young and much more innocent when he had met Diane than he was now. He'd never known any woman but family—beautiful women whose faces reflected what lay in their hearts. It had never occurred to him that Diane was merely playing with him, attracted to his face and physique, but using him to catch a rich, blue-blood husband. He'd been a fool, but he'd learned his lesson. Women like Diane were not for the likes of Josh MacKenzie. Someday he was going home, and he wasn't leaving again. What had he been thinking when he'd asked Diane to return to Texas with him? That she'd happily "hop on a horse and ride west? Live on a ranch and bear his children in the Texas dust?" He flinched at the memory of her words.

Was the contrast with Diane's beauty what had attracted him to plain Emily Lane? Now, though, after getting to know her, he didn't think Emily was plain at all.

But at least she wasn't dazzling, like the Emily Lawrence he'd come to return home. His memory of the face in the missing picture was of an exquisite-featured girl with mischievous eyes. He'd been captured by those eyes the first time he'd seen them. But now when he thought of dancing eyes, he thought of them behind thick glasses.

The time had come to admit the truth. The Emily he'd pretended to court was nothing like the Emily he'd come after. Emily Lane was a self-sufficient, unselfish, quick-thinking woman. The kind of woman who adapted well to the West. Emily Lawrence was just the opposite, or so her father said. And since the two women were so different, he had no business remaining in Las Vegas. There was no time for his personal likes and dislikes. He had a job to do, and the time had come to get his mind back on that responsibility.

As soon as the boxcars were ready for business, he'd be on his way back to Chicago to see if he could find another trail to follow. If not, he'd send word to Long Island that Emily Lawrence was long gone. Then he'd come back here to Las Vegas—and find out if what he felt for Emily Lane was worth writing home about.

By the time Emily and Rose reached the remains of the Harvey House, the sun was up and everyone was sitting down, exhausted. Emily was exhausted, too, but she wasn't giving up yet. They didn't have time to sleep. There was work to do.

"I've found a place to set up the restaurant," she announced to her fellow workers. The girls groaned and put their hands over their faces.

Bridges, who was talking to a man who looked to be the sheriff, from the gunbelt at his hips and the star on his shirt, just scowled at her and went back to his conversation.

"Please, girls, listen to me. If we don't get up and running by the time Mr. Harvey comes back, he'll split us up and send us to different locations—if he even has room. If not, we're out of jobs."

Clapping her hands to get their attention, Rose declared, "Emily's right, ladies. Now, many of you are like me, and you know what other kinds of jobs there are for women alone."

That reminder was all that was needed. The women straightened up immediately, wiped their faces, and began to climb to their feet.

"That's right. Now march down to the store and get buckets and soap. We've got some cleaning to do."

Without a further word, the tired and dirty waitresses marched down the street.

"What other jobs were you talking about?" Emily asked, when the last girl had traipsed away.

"Honey, as smart as you are, sometimes you are so dumb." Emily raised a brow but didn't bother to argue. Rose was right. "In this world, a woman alone has very few choices. Find a man and get married."

"There must be others."

"Teach, if she has the education, can get a job, and can tolerate the children."

"What about shops and hotels?"

"Those jobs are for family. Sometimes they'll hire a woman on her own, but usually for a price."

"What price?"

Rose gave her a pathetic look. "What do you think the price would be, Emily?"

She realized how stupid she'd been. No wonder Rose thought she was dense. "There must be another option."

"Not until Fred Harvey came along. None of us plan to lose this job without a fight. We'll have that place ready by tonight, I'm certain."

"Miss Lane. Miss Dubois." Bridges said their names like he'd caught them rolling in a mud puddle with the pigs. "What have you done with my waitresses?"

"We haven't done anything but save your bacon, Bridges," Rose declared angrily.

Emily put a restraining hand on her friend's arm, and Rose stopped speaking. From the first time they met, Rose and Bridges had been like oil and water.

"Mr. Bridges, I spoke with the man at the train station, and there are two empty boxcars we can use temporarily until the restaurant can be rebuilt."

"Use for what?" Bridges asked.

"As a Harvey restaurant, Mr. Bridges."

His brow sunk to his eyes as he reflected on her words. "Hmm, I suspect that could work. It won't be up to quality, though."

"Better than what they'd get if they had to eat at the hotel," Emily observed, remembering the meal she'd had there with Josh. "Fresh fruit, fish, and produce will be coming in as usual on today's freight train. We could be operating by dinner time with some help from the town."

"True enough." Bridges gave a sharp nod and walked off mumbling, "I'll have to wire Lamy and Albuquerque for supplies." He began to tick items off on his fingers. "Tablecloths, dishes, glasses, silverware . . ."

Disgusted, Rose put her hands on her hips. "How do you like that?"

"What?"

"Fallen Britches didn't even thank you!"

"I don't care, as long as he agreed. I figured he'd turn tail and run as soon as the going got tough."

"I'm surprised he didn't. Must be because the fire's destroyed the potted palms to hide behind."

The sheriff with whom Bridges had been talking strode up to them. "Pardon me, ladies."

Rose hissed in displeasure. Emily laced her fingers through Rose's and squeezed her friend's hand, and Rose squeezed back. Someday she'd have to discover why Rose did not like the law. She figured that would be a story worth hearing.

"Yes, Sheriff . . ." Emily trailed off with an expectant raise of her eyeglasses.

The man brought a thumb to his hat. "Travis, ma'am. Ben Travis."

He was a nice-looking man, tall and broad. His warm brown eyes held a capable look, and his smile revealed healthy white teeth. He was young, too, probably MacKenzie's age. If he wasn't married already, he soon would be. One of the Harvey Girls would snatch Sheriff Travis up and never let him go. Too bad Rose had such an aversion to the law—and an affinity for money. Otherwise Emily would have shoved them together and run off.

Travis broke into Emily's matchmaking fantasy. "Mind if I ask you ladies a few questions?"

Rose's hand jerked. Emily pulled her closer, slipping an arm around her waist. "Certainly, if you don't mind me answering for both of us. My friend is a bit upset after all the excitement."

Emily gave Rose a nudge, and Rose put a hand to her forehead, sighed like a southern belle, and murmured, "Ah, me," in a forlorn voice.

The sheriff stared at Rose like she was an odd creature, and Emily's lips twitched in amusement. She liked him all the more for not being impressed by Rose's helpless act.

"Bridges told me, Miss Lane, that you and Miss Dubois room together."

"We do."

"And your room is in the building next to the Harvey House."

"Was," she corrected. "Or what's left of it."

He nodded. "What can you tell me about the fire?"

"Not much, Sheriff. We were sleeping."

"What woke you?"

"Rose. We threw on slippers and robes, then ran out. We managed to get a bucket brigade started until the fire department arrived."

"That was you?" He looked impressed, though she couldn't figure out why. From what she'd seen so far, the West was full of common sense.

"Yes, that was us. Is there some problem, Sheriff Travis?"

"No, no problem. Looks to be a case of the stove left smoldering with an unknown, ignitable item too close. Happens all the time, and with wood buildings . . ." He shrugged. "I could have lost a lot more of my town, but thanks to your quick thinking, ma'am, nothing more was destroyed."

Travis smiled again, and with a start Emily realized he was smiling at *her*. Beaming, actually, as if she was just the cutest little gal in town. He stepped closer. "Perhaps you'll allow me to call upon you some time, Miss Lane."

Emily tried out her customer smile on the sheriff. He appeared to like it, because his bright, white smile went up a notch. She stopped smiling, nonplussed. How could this man show interest in her with Rose nearby? The comparison must be mind-numbing.

"For the next several weeks," Emily said, "I'll be quite busy setting up the new Harvey House at the station."

His smile dimmed. "I see. Maybe when things are more settled, then?"

Although the man appeared nice enough, the thought of him coming to court her did nothing for Emily. Not like the way the mere sight and sound of MacKenzie sent her heart to thundering and her mind imagining. Still, a woman in her situation dared not make an enemy of the sheriff. Better a friend.

"Yes," she answered. "That would be fine."

Sheriff Travis stepped back. "Ladies." Tipping his hat, he spun on his heel and walked away, whistling.

Rose collapsed at her side. "I thought he'd never leave."

"He wasn't after you." An unpleasant thought occurred to her. "Was he?"

"Certainly not!" But Rose didn't meet her eyes.

"And he wasn't after me, either. He just wanted to ask questions about the fire."

"Silly questions." Rose stood up straight and brushed at her skirt. Not that it did any good; tiny burn holes from flying cinders had made an intricate pattern, and the soot would never wash out. "And you're wrong, he is after you now."

Emily rolled her eyes. "What's the matter with the man anyway? You were standing right next to me. Is he blind?"

"Honey, didn't you hear the song he was whistling?" Rose asked dryly.

"What was that? It sounded kind of mournful."

"It's a song the cowboys sing to their cattle at night to keep them calm—something about never making a pretty woman your wife if you want to be happy for all of your life. Goes on to say that a plain woman will do just as well to marry."

"Well, that's flattering."

Emily couldn't really be critical of the sheriff, though. Travis showed character in not being concerned about appearance—just like MacKenzie.

Then something struck her as odd about Rose's story.

"Wait a minute. Why do they *sing* to the cows?"

"Cattle, honey. It keeps them peaceful, I've been told. A stampede, especially with longhorns, is not a pretty sight. People die. Cattle, too. And for some reason, cowboy songs are always sad."

So Sheriff Travis was probably a cowboy. With a shrug, Emily dismissed him from her mind. "We'd better get over to the station and get to work."

"Yeah, or Fallen Britches will make a mess of it somehow."

As they walked off together, Emily posed the question she'd been curious about for a long while. "Rose, why don't you like lawmen?"

"I just don't."

"But you like MacKenzie."

"He's not a real lawman. He's been hired for a particular job, not to uphold the law."

"Are you running away from something?"

Rose sighed, and it was the saddest sound Emily had ever heard come from her friend. "Aren't we all running from something, honey?"

Chapter 10

⟨~∽◯∽~⟩

The Harvey Girls, along with most of the town, worked all that day converting the boxcars into a kitchen and dining room. The merchants knew that if Harvey meals were suspended in Las Vegas until a new building was built, they would lose untold business. They might even lose the rail stop altogether if the trains adjusted their schedules and went straight through without stopping for a lengthy period. So they happily pitched in to get the job done.

By dinner time, the Harvey Girls, looking trim and proper, stood at their tables and listened to the whistle sound as the first train of customers pulled into the station.

Emily smoothed her apron nervously. This was all her idea, and if it was a disaster, she had no doubt Bridges's long, bony finger would point right to her when he was asked what had happened. She also had no doubt that if it was a success, that same finger would point right back at himself. She didn't care, as long as she could keep working here.

MacKenzie had helped, too, and to say he'd been a distraction was a gross understatement. How was one supposed to work when the man took off his jacket and lifted huge blocks of wood with those hard, capable hands, then carried them about, muscles bulging against the confines of his shirt? Several times, she'd been irritated to catch the other women gawking instead of working. But she told herself it wasn't jealousy—it was merely distraction.

"Here they come," Rose said, rushing up with crossed fingers. "We'll soon find out, honey."

Guests filed in, looking around with great curiosity at the dining room within the boxcar.

Even if she had to say so herself, Emily thought they'd done a remarkable job in such a short amount of time. While some of the men had tackled the job of making tables and chairs, others had painted the walls of the two cars.

Chickens, eggs, and a side of beef had come from a nearby rancher who had heard of their plight. Potatoes and onions came from a farmer.

The women of the town sent tablecloths, napkins, and vases of fresh-cut flowers for the tables. Others had baked bread and rolls, pies and cakes.

Bridges's wire to the Harvey restaurant in Lamy was successful, and within a few hours of the time he sent it, a freight train arrived and proceeded to unload dishes, glasses, silverware, pots and pans, and cooking utensils, along with an assortment of condiments and spices.

Whatever was needed for Yen Cheng to have a workable kitchen had been toted over from the hotel, and he managed not to threaten those who carried the equipment into his new domain. Of course, once in operation, Yen Cheng had ordered everyone "out, out, out" of his new kitchen, just like before.

At dinner time, dressed in a spotless new apron and chef's hat—his long queue dangling from under it—he began ladling out steaming bowls of cock-a-leekie soup.

While the dining boxcar did not have the elegance of the permanent Harvey House, it was clean and cozy, with a vase of fresh flowers on each of the brightly covered tables lining the walls.

The girls bustled about doing their job. Bridges served the beef, and the guests ate everything in sight just as if there was nothing out of the ordinary.

At the sight of Fred Harvey entering the car, everyone froze. They'd expected him to show up, but to see him standing there in the doorway with his penetrating gaze staring at everything they'd worked so hard to accomplish in such a short time made Emily catch her breath. Rose came over to her side, and they glanced at Bridges.

He'd turned as white as a sheet and nearly dropped the platter with the remains of the beef. Emily groaned as he bobbled the piece of china, expecting the brand-new platter to shatter at the man's feet, but he managed to hold onto it.

"Please go on with your duties, young ladies," Harvey announced graciously to the waitresses. "You're all doing a wonderful job under the worst of circumstances. You've added luster to the Harvey reputation, and I'm proud of all of you."

The dining customers added their applause and approval to the owner's praise.

The girls exchanged smiles with one another. Besides the satisfaction they felt for a well-done job, no doubt there would be generous tips from the pleased diners.

Harvey moved about the room, checking windows, picking up soiled plates, and murmuring greetings to customers.

Emily had to remind herself to breathe in and out before she fainted away from loss of air. If Harvey had said the place was a disaster, a disaster it would have been—for he'd send them off to who knows where.

At the end of the meal, the train whistle blew, and the guests filed out. The waitresses began to clean up, and Emily watched Mr. Harvey apprehensively. What would he say? What would he do?

He strode over to Bridges and began to talk low and fast. Dare she sidle over and listen in? Rose had already done so.

Before Emily could do the same, Rose cleared her throat, slapped her hands on her hips, and declared, "That's not so, Bridges." She pointed at Emily. "*She* thought this up. She told you what to do. And she directed everyone in doing it."

Bridges sputtered his indignation, but Harvey was already walking toward Emily. Rose grinned and spread her hands wide as if to say, "Too late now."

"Miss Lane, is this true? Do I have you to thank for this brilliant accomplishment?"

"Well, I don't know about brilliant. I just wanted to keep working. And in the East I know that some of the trains have dining cars, so it seemed the practical thing to do. "

"Yes—practical, brilliant, inspired. I must say I am impressed, Miss Lane. I might very well do the same as you've done here in new towns on the line and begin the operation in a boxcar while the standing structure is being built. It would give us an extra month of service that we ordinarily wouldn't have."

"That's a wonderful idea, sir."

"And I have you to thank."

"No need for thanks. I just wanted to keep working."

He beamed at her. "That's exactly what an employer likes to hear. If you ever need anything, Miss Lane, *anything*, you've only to ask me."

Frowning, he turned back to Bridges. "And now, you and I have a few things to discuss in your office."

"I . . . ah . . . no longer have an office, sir."

"Then outside, Bridges."

With a harried look, Bridges nodded and scurried off, talking a mile a minute. "You'll be so pleased, Mr. Harvey. The fire is going to make us lose all the money I saved. We'll be right back in the loss column again."

As soon as the two of them exited the car, Rose broke into laughter. "That little weasel! He's finally getting a strong dose of the medicine he hands out. I can't believe he tried to take the credit for your idea."

"I didn't care. You shouldn't have said anything, Rose. I don't want him fired."

"I suppose not, but when I heard him pontificating about his brilliance, after first waiting to hear that Harvey was impressed, of course, I couldn't stop myself. He's such a little prig."

"But he's our prig."

"True."

They burst out laughing, relief overcoming anxiety. Then they pitched in next to the other girls, who had joined their laughter.

The Las Vegas Harvey House was back in business.

*　　*　　*

Josh heard her laughter before he even stepped inside the boxcar. She sounded happy, and he smiled wistfully. Nodding at Harvey and Bridges, who stood on the platform with their heads together, Josh went inside.

He'd come to say good-bye.

Standing in the doorway, he just watched her a while as she worked. There was so much energy in that woman's body. She flitted here, there—everywhere—doing her work, helping the others. The woman he'd thought she was would never have been able to serve with a smile, as this Emily did.

After working side by side with her throughout last night and most of today, he had to admit he'd made a mistake. And if the devil's advocate in him still said she she was Emily Lawrence, he certainly couldn't prove it. It was time to pull up stakes and move out. But oh, how he wanted to stay.

Emily caught sight of him, and her smile brightened the approachig shadows. Smiling, she held up one finger. "Just another minute to finish up here."

Rose threw a knowing glance his way and winked.

"Hello, Josh," one of the girls called out in passing.

"Good evening, Detective," another said sweetly, batting her lashes at him.

"Nice to see you, Josh," another cooed.

Several of the other girls greeted him in passing, but he merely gave them an absent reply. He couldn't take his eyes off Emily.

At last she patted her tables with a satisfied air and came toward him. He straightened up, only to feel his hands hanging heavy at his sides. Shuffling nervously, he fought the urge to pull off his hat and hold it in his hands. What kind of power did this woman have on him: voodoo or magic?

Halting in front of him, she glanced down at her feet in the shy gesture he found so endearing. A ray of last light from the window hit her hair, causing a shaft of yellow to run down the center in an odd manner that tickled something in his mind. Then she looked up into his eyes and smiled. "Hello, Josh."

He forgot about yellow rays of light.

She smelled like lemon drops and lavender. How could she smell that good after working all day? Her eyes behind the glasses looked soft and sweet. He wanted to take those damn glasses off and close her eyes with soft kisses.

Glancing behind her, he saw that all the girls were lined up, watching them. He took a discreet step backward.

"So how did it go?"

She clapped her hands with joy. "Wonderfully well! And Mr. Harvey commended me. He said he might try this idea when he begins building other houses."

"That's great, Em. This was an inspired idea. You have a quick mimd."

"Thank you."

An awkward silence developed between them. He shuffled nervously, became aware of it, and made himself stop. He'd come here for a reason. "Ah, would you like to take a stroll with me? It's a beautiful night."

"Stroll?" she repeated, as if he'd suggested they prance through cow dung.

Josh made up his mind to just say it and get it over with. Drawing a deep breath, he was about to speak when he glanced up and saw a grinning Rose watching them.

"Listen, can we go outside? I'm tired of being the prime exhibit on display at the Harvey House."

"Excuse me?" She wrinkled her nose and her brow. He wanted to smooth the lines on her face with his thumb and kiss away that frown on her mouth.

Clearing his throat, he nodded behind her. She turned her head, and all the girls waved. "I see what you mean." Sliding her arm into his, she whispered, "Let's go."

When they strolled outside, Bridges and Harvey had disappeared—no doubt to take a look at the damaged site. He doubted if the place had stopped smoldering yet. And it would have been a worse disaster if there'd been customers or if the flames had spread.

They walked down the main street of Las Vegas, returning nods and greetings. After the fire, everyone had become quite friendly. Just like a hometown, almost.

"And so, MacKenzie, where are we strolling to?"

"When you stroll there is no to. You just stroll."

"Really? I didn't know that."

"You must not do a lot of strolling."

"You're my first."

He slid a quick glance her way, but she walked on, oblivious to the double meaning of her words, which only made his body respond to them more. "Em, I—"

"Look!"

They'd reached the end of the boardwalk, and out on the darkening plain stood an antelope. The last remnants of the setting sun painted the sky in hues of pink, orange, and purple. The antelope stood in shadow, head raised proudly, as if posing just for them.

"The sunsets are so different here than back east. Sometimes it seems as if you could step right off the end of the world and straight into heaven."

He turned his gaze on her. Night slid across her face, highlighting the high cheekbones and delicate chin. He'd gotten to know her so well, he no longer could see Emily Lawrence in this woman, only Emily Lane. Reaching out, he touched her, a single slide of his finger across her cheek. She gasped. From surprise or arousal, he didn't know—and he didn't care. It was too late. He was lost in her.

She glanced at him warily, her eyes wide and lost behind those damnable glasses, and his mouth came down on hers.

She moaned, and so did he. He touched her only with his lips and tongue and teeth, taking her mouth and making it his. She tasted like strawberries. He wanted more. He wanted to taste strawberries until he could no longer bear even hearing the word.

Her hands clutched at his shoulders, as if to keep herself from falling, and he slid his arms around her, crushing her to him. This was all he needed to know. This was everything.

He made quick work of the hairpins, and her hair tumbled to her shoulders, cascading over his hands as he positioned her head so he could delve more deeply within her mouth. Their tongues met, stroked, retreated. He never wanted this night or this kiss to end.

She wrenched her mouth from his, and he wrapped a length of her hair around his fingers so she could not run away. His mouth moved along her jaw, tasting her, learning the scent and the softness of her.

Her head fell back. "Josh, this is getting out of hand," she murmured.

"Uh-huh." But her breathing heightened when he put his lips to the pulsing hollow near her ear.

She wove her fingers into the hair at his nape, pulling him closer, even as she tried to push him away with her words. "We need to stop, Josh," she warned breathlessly.

"Yes, stop." But his mouth had found the soft perfect skin where her neck met her shoulder, and he suckled. Her entire body jerked in response, and her fingers curled in a tighter grasp.

"Josh."

The sound of his name in a husky voice that hinted of panic breached the haze that had clouded his mind. Raising his head, he stared down into her dazed face.

Her lips were swollen from the kiss, but she looked ready for a whole lot more. And so was he. But did he want to tumble her against some wall in an alley?

No, that wasn't what he wanted. Stepping back, he held her steady when she swayed and gave her time to compose herself.

While he'd been ravishing her mouth, the sun had disappeared, and cold shadows of night spread across the land, as if God had turned a switch to change day to night.

"I apologize, Em. Whenever I'm with you, my good sense goes the way of the wind."

"What does that mean? You think it's stupid to kiss me?"

Her mood had changed as quickly as the light.

Misunderstanding his meaning, she looked annoyed, her arms crossed and her foot tapping beneath the hem of her black gown.

Tap, tap, tap, tap.

"Uh, no. Not stupid."

"What, then? You've never been at a loss for words before, Detective."

She was calling him Detective the way his mother called him Joshua MacKenzie.

"I . . . ah . . . uh—"

Tap, tap, tap, tap.

He had no idea what to say. The truth? That whenever he saw her, he wanted to touch her. Whenever he touched her, he wanted to kiss her. Whenever he kissed her, he wanted to touch her again—all over. Feel her flesh beneath his, feel her body jerk out of control with spasms of passion. And he wanted to drive into her until she groaned with ecstasy—until he answered with his own.

If he said that, she'd bloody his nose. The way she would if he told her he was leaving tomorrow, after kissing her like he just had.

Yeah, she'd most likely slap his face, shove him away, then turn on her heel and never speak to him again.

Perhaps he should wait one more day before leaving. What could it hurt?

For once he was going to do what he wanted to do. He was going to spend just a little more time with Emily. To lose himself in her one last time. And then he was going to leave.

"Would you like to go on a picnic tomorrow afternoon?"

She gaped at him as if he'd just asked her to dance naked on top of the piano in the saloon. That image took hold of his mind and stuck there. No more black widow's weeds for a gown; no more virginal white apron. She'd wear red satin that would slide along her body when she danced with a whisper that called his name.

"Josh?" Emily snapped her fingers in front of his face. "Where did you go?"

"Little side trip. Sorry."

"You're sorry about an awful lot tonight, up to and including kissing me."

"I'm not sorry I kissed you, Em. That was the best part of my whole day—hell, make that the whole week. I'm sorry I pawed you like a madman."

She tilted her head and contemplated him. "You didn't seem like a madman to me."

"When it comes to you, I can't seem to think straight. Or behave rationally. I was ready to ravish you on the boardwalk."

Her eyes widened. "You were?"

What a dumb thing to admit—but it was too late to deny it now. "So will you go on a picnic with me tomorrow afternoon?"

"So you can finish ravishing me?"

She baffled him. There was no longer any trace of anger on her face, and she sounded more amused—even pleased—than shocked.

She stepped back and contemplated him for a long time, and he feared she'd say no. Then she nodded slowly. "Yes, Detective, I think I will."

Chapter 11

 ❧⟋◌⟍❧

The next morning passed far too slowly. For the first time since becoming a Harvey Girl, Emily couldn't wait for work to end; so of course, it seemed like it never would. Although they were expected to work all day, every day, there were a few hours in the heat of the afternoon when the girls could kick up their feet and relax between lunch and dinner. She had asked Rose to cover for her during lunch, and with a smirk and a wiggle of an eyebrow, Rose had agreed.

The day was interminable—hot outside, stuffy inside, demanding guests, and they ran short of ice. By the time the lunch hour arrived, Emily wanted to scream. She had the beginning of a headache and wanted nothing less than to go on a picnic and spar with Josh MacKenzie.

Then he walked into the boxcar, and she nearly changed her mind. He looked fresh and clean, his hair still wet from a bath and curling about his crisp collar. He'd gotten gussied up for the picnic, and next to him she felt like a dirty, smelly, limp dishrag. Pushing back the damp hair from her brow, she scowled at him.

149

Josh winked at her and walked through the dining car to knock on the kitchen door. Yen Cheng appeared, chattered something, handed Josh a basket, then slammed the door in his face. Josh approached Emily and held out his arm. "Shall we, madam?"

"Oh, Josh," she sighed, "I feel so hot and messy."

"Wait until you see the place I found for our picnic. I guarantee you'll be glad you came." She gave him a skeptical look. "There's water. Lots of it."

"Around here?"

"Close enough." He inched his arm closer. "Water, Em. You could cool off with a bath. I promise I won't peek."

"You think I'm going to go somewhere with you and take a bath? You are mad."

He just grinned and kept holding out his arm. Rose suddenly appeared and shoved a package into her hands. Frowning, Emily looked at the bundle, then at Rose.

"Towel, soap, fresh clothes," her friend said.

Emily eyed her with a narrow look. "You two are up to something."

"Me?" Rose fluttered her hand up to her bodice.

She'd seen that gesture made by Rose enough times to know it meant anything but innocence. Scowling, she looked at Josh.

"Me?" he said, and spread his hands wide.

"Oh, just go, Emily," Rose said, pushing her forward. "You know that you want to. Get out of here before Bridges shows up and forbids it. Then you'll be sorry, and I'll have to listen to you whine about it all day. Besides, if you don't go, I will."

Since her uniform was sticking to her back and her hair felt glued to her head—which pounded with an ache that hovered between annoying and excruciating—Emily gave up and took Josh's arm.

Outside, a covered buggy awaited them. Josh had gone to great lengths for this picnic, and for some reason that made her nervous. Did he plan to spirit her away? Straight back to Long Island, for instance?

She stumbled at the thought, and his arm steadied her. "Are you all right?"

She nodded, unable to speak. She must never, ever forget that what was between her and MacKenzie was only a game they both were playing. She was lying; he was pretending to believe. When he ceased to pretend, or she ceased to lie, the game would be all over.

He helped her into the buggy, secured the picnic lunch, and climbed in. His grin was infectious. He couldn't possibly be plotting nefarious things with a smile like that. And he couldn't take her all the way back to Long Island in a buggy. Of course, he could take the buggy to another town and then drag her onto a train.

She hadn't realized she'd groaned aloud until he asked, "What's the matter, Em?"

"Nothing. A touch of a headache." That much was true.

His smile dimmed a bit, and she waited for him to say he'd take her home, as any gentleman would. She was tempted to suggest he do just that, torn between the fear of how this man could make her feel, of what he could do to her—physically and emotionally—and a desperate interest in that water he was offering as a bribe.

"The fresh air will help your headache, Em. Just sit back and relax." He flicked the reins, and the horse trotted off. "We'll be there soon, and the water will soothe all your aches."

"I doubt that," she muttered.

Leaning back, Emily closed her eyes and tried to put everything out of her aching head. That was nearly impossible, what with the oppressive heat, the jarring buggy, the snorting horse, and MacKenzie's hip pressed against hers in the close confines of the buggy. Every time the horse hit a rut in the road— and there were a lot of them—his leg rubbed along hers and she rolled against him. Within minutes her pulse pounded along with the ache in her head.

At least he wasn't the chatty sort. Today she might have confessed everything just to get him to be quiet. Instead, he watched the scenery, drove the horse, and let her be.

Amazingly, she must have dozed off, because she awoke when the buggy stopped and Josh spoke. "Here we are." He hopped down.

The fresh air did seem to have helped to make her head feel better. Cautiously, she cracked open one eyelid. Glaring sunlight hit the eye like a punch and nearly blinded her. The headache was not gone; it had only been lurking behind her closed lids waiting for her to do something stupid—like open her eyes. She moaned and snapped them shut.

"Come on, Em. You'll feel better once you get in the water. I'm sure of that."

"I'll feel better once I'm dead, too. I'm sure of that."

He laughed. "At least get out of the wagon. There's a breeze out here."

"Impossible. There isn't a breeze in all of New Mexico." She raised an eyelid again, and this time the pain wasn't so bad.

"I've found a magic place. Just for you and me."

The awe in his voice was enough to make her open her eyes and blink rapidly to clear them. His responding smile was so winning that she didn't have the heart to keep whining and hiding. After all, he'd driven all the way out here; the least she could do was see what had him so excited.

She took his hand and let him help her out of the buggy. "Mmm," she murmured when a soft breeze caressed her heated skin.

"Uh-huh." He held her to him in a quick hug that nevertheless made her body hum. Stepping away, he maintained his hold of her hand. "Come and see what I found for us, Em."

Up ahead there was an outcropping of rock and some trees—green trees—which meant . . . "Water," Emily whispered reverently.

Josh glanced over his shoulder and winked. "Didn't I promise you water?"

"I didn't believe you."

His face fell. "What do you mean you didn't believe me? I don't lie."

"Ever?"

"Hardly ever."

She laughed lightly. "Then how foolish of me to have ever doubted you." In truth, he certainly was being more honest with her than she was with him. That only made her feel worse.

She strode past him around the rocks and through the trees, where an entirely different world awaited her.

A pool of water, clear, cool, and inviting, lay beyond the rocks. Trees and bushes fed by the pool made an oasis in the midst of the arid land. Even in her most impossible dreams, she never would have believed such a place existed out here.

If she stood very still and listened, she could hear the slap of the water as the breeze lapped at it and smell its moistness on the dry air.

Stepping forward, she knelt down and put her hand into the water, wetting her shoes and the hem of her skirt. The temptation to jump in fully clothed was nearly impossible to resist.

"If I hadn't touched it, I'd think it was a mirage," she said, when Josh moved up behind her. "It seems too good to be true."

"There must be an underground feed for the water to surface here. Mother Nature is amazing sometimes, isn't she? I'm sure every animal for miles around comes to this pool. At dawn and dusk it's probably like a train depot here. But right now . . ."

Right now it was deserted. Just the two of them. She should be nervous, even frightened, but she wasn't. She was going to take a bath, and she knew if Josh said he wouldn't watch, he wouldn't. And right now she was too hot and sweaty to much care whether he did or not.

"Bath first or food?" he asked.

"Bath definitely."

"Your wish, madam, is my command. I'll get the basket and your things."

He moved off and she remained. She fought the urge to strip off her hot, soiled uniform without even waiting for him to return. But she still had some control left—some, but not too much. By the time he returned with her bundle of clothes and soap, she'd removed her shoes and stockings.

"I'll wait on the other side of the rock."

Emily looked at the rock, then at the pond. They

were a bit close and easily accessible. Was she being too trusting? Well, even if he said he planned to stand right at the edge of the pool and stare at her while she bathed, she was still going into that water. She couldn't wait one more minute.

Turning to him, she offered him her back. "Will you undo my buttons before you go?"

Bracing herself for the shock of his touch, she still started sharply when his hands gripped her shoulders. Briskly, he released the buttons on the dress. From the short time it took, it wouldn't have surprised her if a few buttons had come loose in the process. Confused, she turned her head, only to find his hands now clenched at his sides and his mouth drawn into a tight line. She'd never seen the man so tense.

"Josh?" she asked.

His sapphire eyes flicked to hers, and he spun on his heel, disappearing through the greenery and rocks. She didn't understand what she'd done, but she'd upset him somehow.

Well, he could take a bath after she was done. Maybe that would improve his mood. She certainly meant for it to improve hers.

Shrugging out of the dress and shift, she stood in nothing but her combination and stepped into the water.

"Ahh," she murmured in a sigh. Her headache was eased just by the coolness lapping at her ankles.

Still she hesitated, struggling with her virginal modesty. Dare she take off all her clothing? Only in the privacy behind locked doors did she ever remove all her clothing.

But this was the wild west; and if she was going

to stay here and thrive, she needed to be as bold as the land—and the people who trod it.

Without any further qualms, she removed her unmentionables and stood without a stitch of clothing and let the breeze caress her naked body. A feeling of freedom such as she'd never known came over her. Instead of diving into the pool, she stood and looked at the land. She loved this place with her heart and soul.

Raising her arms to the sky, she threw back her head and let the sun bathe her face. This time the heat felt like a balm, soothing the pain in her head and the ache in her heart.

She should have been born here, not on stuffy, boring Long Island. Here in the West, men were men—and the women were nearly as rugged in order to survive. Out here a woman could be what she wanted to be, could have a life of her choosing. She didn't have to marry because it was the proper thing to do, and if she did choose to marry, rich man or poor, the choice was hers to make.

MacKenzie's face flashed through her mind. That image, combined with the cool breeze on her body, raised gooseflesh on her arms. Her skin heated again, but not from the sun. A shuffle from behind the rock made her heart thunder in her breast.

Without a backward glance, she lowered her arms and dove into the water.

Chapter 12

He hadn't meant to watch. Really. Truly.

When Emily had innocently asked him to undo her buttons, he'd done so quickly, as if touching her back meant nothing to him. But even as he did the task, his body knew different.

So he'd spun around and run like a coward before she could see that the merest touch made him hard and wanting her. He'd slouched down behind the blasted rock and waited for her to go into the water, but he didn't hear a splash. Telling himself he had to see that she was all right, he peeked.

And was captured by the sight of her.

She stood at the edge of the pool, her back to him as she stared at the horizon. She looked like a water goddess, hair streaming to her bare backside, not a stitch of clothes on her.

As she lifted her arms toward the sun, the muscles in her shoulders bunched in an enticing hide and seek. Her hair swung back and forth, a dark pendulum brushing her buttocks.

As much as he wanted to, as much as he should, he just couldn't make himself look away from the pure beauty of Emily in the sun.

Shifting to relieve some of the pressure in his pants, his boot scraped the rock. She stiffened, her arms dropped, and she dived into the water like a wild thing retreating to safety.

He sat back and closed his eyes, but he could still see her. And he wanted her more than he'd ever wanted anything in his life.

Splashing sounds came from the pool, and he swallowed the lump in his throat. He'd need to cool off himself after this.

"Josh?" Her voice carried on the breeze.

"I'm here."

"How did you find this place?"

"Riding around."

"You just ride around?"

He heard the water splash and figured she must be kicking her feet as she floated. The thought brought an image of upthrust breasts and streaming black hair. He wiped his brow on his shirtsleeve.

"What do you think I do all day while you're working? Look for the Dalton Gang?"

"The what?"

How could Harvey employees not have heard of them yet, especially since the gang had taken to robbing trains? The Pinkertons certainly had.

"There's a new gang riding out here, the Dalton Gang. I'm surprised you people haven't been alerted."

"Really?" She sounded intrigued, so he settled in to tell the tale as he knew it. At least if he spoke of work, he would not think of those upthrust breasts and that streaming black hair—for a few moments anyway.

"They're three brothers: Bob, Grattan, and Emmett. Bob's the leader. Until now they've operated primarily in Kansas, robbing banks. Lately they've been operating in this area, holding up trains."

"How dangerous are they?" Splash, splash. Breasts and streaming hair.

He swallowed as the thought of long legs entered the picture. "Uh . . . they . . . ah, they used to ride with the Younger Brothers and Jesse and Frank James."

"My goodness—all these outlaw brothers! Do you have a brother, Josh?"

"No, just a sister, Kitty—ah, Kathleen."

"Mmm," she murmured. Splash, splash. Breasts, streaming black hair, and long legs. She was supposed to be taking a bath, so why in hell didn't she get to it, instead of floating images in a man's head? If it went on much longer, he'd be losing it like a green schoolboy the first time a whore touched his privates.

He'd better keep talking about the Daltons to try and stay focused on what he must do instead of . . . "Ah, Bob Dalton is the leader."

"Yes, you told me. How do you know this gang's robbing the trains?"

"They've been arrested before, and after they've robbed enough people and places, we're able to identify them."

"They sound very frightening."

"They've sure been a scourge in Missouri, Kansas, and now this territory. They have to be stopped."

"Do you think they'll be caught soon?"

"Probably. There are railroad detectives after them, as well as Pinkertons. If it weren't for the case I'm on, I'd probably be out looking for them right now, too."

"Hmm. The Dalton Brothers. Interesting." She sounded half asleep. "I'll be done in a minute, Josh."

Then for a long time he heard nothing but the lap of the water.

Emily sat on the porch of her little house, enjoying the view as she watched the sun set. She had a home of her own, money—and a secret that would surely curl the toes of her nosy friends on Long Island. Life just didn't get any better than this.

The water in the brook running through her front yard shimmered red from the glow of the setting sun. The sound of its babbling was loud in the still of the eve. She could almost feel the cool liquid surrounding her body. As the sun slipped beyond the horizon, she stood and went inside.

Her gaze took in the cabin, all her pretty western artifacts hanging on the walls or set on shelves. When she'd left Long Island, she'd never expected anything like this.

The house shifted and creaked under the bedtime caress of the night wind. Moving to her dark bedroom, she began to undress, sliding her gown off her shoulders. It pooled at her feet.

The sudden cocking of a gun caused her to gasp and spin toward the window.

A man sat in the rocking chair, watching her. The rising moon glinted off the pistol in his hand—the pistol that was pointed at her.

"What do you want?"

"You know."

A chill came over her that had little to do with the night breeze playing along her skin. She did know what he wanted. She wasn't that innocent.

"You plan to ravish me, then?"

"If I've a mind to." He made a motion with the gun. "Keep goin'," he ordered, his gaze upon her breasts, barely concealed beneath the lacy bodice of the combination she wore. Her hands trembled as she raised them to untie the garment.

His sapphire eyes held a heat of their own—a heat that she could feel like the stroke of his fingers—while his gaze roamed over her nearly naked form.

When the lacing was undone, the gaping opening revealed the shadow of her bosom in the pale moonlight.

"You heard me," he grunted.

Her hands gripped the thin straps of the garment, then she hesitated. At the slight motion of the gun, she slipped them off her shoulders, and the garment dropped to her ankles. She kicked aside the clothing at her feet and faced him defiantly.

Raising his gaze to her face, he said curtly, "Now the hair. Take it down." His voice held the twang of a Texan, a cadence she'd come to enjoy: soft, smooth, and so at odds with his menacing figure in the chair.

One by one, she pulled the pins out of her hair, and the tresses tumbled like a waterfall, cascading about her shoulders.

"Shake it out," he ordered.

She complied, and the soft strands shifted along her bare shoulders with a slide that made her shiver.

Uncocking the gun, he placed it on the night table. "Come here."

"Like hell I will. If you want me, you can damn well come to me."

He chuckled—strangely enough a warm sound coming from such a blackguard. He stood up and approached her, his spurs clicking in a staccato rhythm against the wooden floor in total disharmony with the pounding beat of her heart.

When he stood close enough to touch, he dragged one finger across the swell of one breast, dipped into the valley and then back out across the other breast, all the time holding her prisoner with those sapphire eyes.

The rasp of her breathing filled the room, and he smiled. "You ready to do anything I ask?"

Smiling slyly, she raised her arms and wrapped them around his neck, crushing her bare breasts against him. "I was born ready."

He kissed her as only he could. The man could kiss like the very devil, which at times she thought he was. He'd no doubt kissed a hundred women, but when he kissed her, he could make her believe she was the only one. He had that gift—damn him.

His big hand held her head, tangling his fingers in her hair. He positioned her mouth so he could delve more deeply. She was pressed to his length, her naked form flush against his hard body and the rough texture of his Levi's.

As always, the contrast between them excited her. He pulled away, and lowered himself to his knees. Taking a nipple gently between his teeth, he rolled his tongue around the hard nub until she began to whimper.

Raising his eyes, he asked, "Don't you like it?"

"What do you think?" she gasped.

Smiling, he cupped her other breast in his palm, rasped the nipple with a callused thumb until she thought she'd go mad, then brought it to his mouth and began to suckle.

Her knees trembled so hard, she could barely stand. "No," she pleaded, and slumped her torso against his shoulder. "I can't stand it, Bob."

"Baby, I've just started."

When he parted her legs and pressed his mouth to her, hot, blinding darkness clouded her vision and sweet, sweet sensation washed through her in a floodtide.

She felt like she was floating. Or was he carrying her? She forced herself back to awareness just as he laid her on the bed.

Raising her arms to him, she pleaded, "Hurry."

"I'm trying, but I can't get this damn buckle open."

She sat up to help him. "I've told you a dozen times to wear suspenders," she reproved him, struggling with the unrelenting buckle.

"If you tried looking past my privates for a change, you'd see I *am* wearing suspenders. This is the buckle of my gunbelt."

For the next five minutes they struggled unsuccessfully to release the belt. Finally, he turned away in disgust.

"Time's running out. I'm gonna have to get going."

"What! You just got here," she wailed.

"MacKenzie's hot on my trail. I swear that man is part bloodhound. He'll never give up until he catches me."

"Then you'll hang." To her embarrassment, her voice broke on the last word. She swallowed and refused to let the tears that burned her eyes fall free. When you loved an outlaw, tears were taboo.

He cupped her cheek and tilted her head to look deeper into her eyes. "Most likely." Then he turned away.

He was frightening her with the despair in his

words and the uncommon tenderness of his gestures. Bob Dalton had never been a man for either one.

She jumped out of bed and began pulling on her clothes. "Take me with you, Bob," she blurted. The words sounded like begging, and she wished them back as soon as she'd said them.

He frowned, looking at her in shock. "What are you talking about?"

"I've heard of other women going along; why can't I?"

"There ain't no other women in my gang. You trying to get me and my brothers killed?"

"I won't be a problem. I can ride as well as any of you."

"I still ain't taking you."

"Why not?" she challenged, pulling on a boot.

"You're a lady."

"*Was* a lady. I'm hardly one anymore."

"If they catch you, they'll kill you just like me."

"They wouldn't hang a woman."

"Tell that to Cattle Kate."

He had a point. She took a deep breath and plunged forward. "I don't care. If you die, I die with you. Just don't leave me here alone."

"You'll be okay. You've got plenty of money."

She shot him a dirty look. "Who says so?"

"What about all that money you stole from your pa?"

"If I've told you once, Bob Dalton, I've told you a dozen times: I didn't steal any of my father's money."

"Maybe so, but I ain't got time to argue, and you're not goin' with me."

He grabbed her and kissed her once more—hard and long—and she tasted good-bye. A final good-bye. Then she watched him ride off into the night.

Her tears fell, but she could not stop them.

Emily awoke and felt the tear tracks upon her face. She had dozed off on a protruding flat rock, her head resting on her folded arms, and her hips and legs floating in the water.

She couldn't remember ever awakening from a dream before and feeling as if she'd cried a river. She hoped she never would again. Obviously she'd dreamed of Bob Dalton because of Josh's story. But why had she dreamed of good-bye?

She stood up and waded to the bank, dried off, and quickly dressed in the clean clothing Rose had provided. She had just put on her glasses and was about to tell Josh she was ready when he came around the rock.

"I thought you were going to stay back there," she said pointedly.

"I was, but you were quiet so long I got worried." He looked at her face. "You okay?"

"Of course. That was wonderful, Josh. Thank you. If you'd like to bathe now, I'll set out the picnic."

Moving to go back to the buggy, she was startled when he grabbed her elbow and turned her about. "If you're okay, then what's this?"

Startled, she grabbed for his hand when he reached for the rim of her glasses. Shushing her, his callused thumb drew a line from the corner of her eye down her cheek. Confused now, she could only stare at him. After doing the same to her other cheek, he stepped in close and put his hand on her waist, almost as if he meant to dance with her. She tilted her head back to to see his face in the wide shadow of his hat. He looked both concerned and angry.

"What made you cry?"

His voice was just above a whisper and slid along her sensitive skin like honey over warmed bread. Captured by the blue of his eyes, she remembered her dream. What if he were leaving her and never coming back? What if this was their last day together—if this was the last kiss she would ever have from him?

Choking back a sob, she threw herself into his arms.

Josh caught Emily against his chest and met her frantic, feverish lips with his own. Though his body kicked into a higher level of heat, his mind clicked away at this mystery. What was the matter with her?

She'd been crying in the pool, and was now kissing him like tomorrow would never come again. For the first time he could remember, he was being kissed, not doing the kissing. It was too damn confusing to try to figure out and felt too damn good to stop her. Especially when her hands were clutching his shirt to bring him nearer as she used her lips and her tongue and her teeth to kiss him—like no woman had ever kissed him before. He sure as hell liked it.

Then he tasted the salt of her tears on his lips, and he pulled back. Fresh tear tracks traced her cheeks. She wasn't the kind of woman who cried easily. He'd seen her work from dawn until dark, day after day after day, and even at the height of exhaustion, she never complained. She'd come to New Mexico all alone, and though she and Rose had become the best of friends, she must have had to endure incredible loneliness and uncertainty on the way. Still, she toughed it out without a tear.

And the night of the fire she'd been truly magnificent. Not a tear dropped that night, either. She'd been in control of herself and everyone else—and he'd been proud to say he knew her. She had grit and an indomitable spirit. He had to know what had broken her down.

"What's the matter, Em? Tell me, and I'll make it right if I can."

She just shook her head and pulled him back into her embrace. "Make me forget, Josh."

He drew her gently into his arms. "Forget what, Em?"

"Everything in the world except you and me."

Damn convention! She wanted this as much as he did; why should he fight it? But he had to. She didn't know what she was asking for, but he did. And he knew that tomorrow he'd be climbing on a train and leaving her behind.

He headed for the buggy, and she followed. He knew he owed her an explanation. Wasn't that why he brought her here? He stopped abruptly and turned. Head bowed, she bumped into him and lost her balance.

Reaching out, he steadied her to keep her from falling. "Em—I" She looked up at him, wounded, vulnerable, her eyes brimming with tears.

Her hair was still damp, her skin still moist from the water. She felt cool, smelled sweet, and tasted even better. And for this moment, she was his if he was cad enough to take advantage of it.

He cut off his words, pulled her into his arms, and kissed her.

Then he spread his coat on the small patch of grass near the water, laying her upon it.

Stretched out before him like a banquet, she looked like the water goddess he'd seen at the pond, except for the clothes. He wished they'd disappear.

He yearned to see her body again freed from the clothes that concealed it, the way he yearned to see her eyes freed from the glasses that masked them.

Smiling, she held out her hand, and he grasped it, lowering himself along her. Their bodies fitted like a key to a lock.

Maybe just some kissing and petting was all she anticipated. Maybe that would be enough for her. But he knew damn well it wouldn't be for him. He had to keep control, to not venture past the point of no return. He could do it if he had to. Hell, all he had to do was take it slow and easy—not turn it into some uncontrollable, explosive moment of passion. A little kissing, a little petting.

She closed her eyes when he removed her glasses, and she lay back and parted her lips. He lowered his mouth to hers—and the world receded.

As if sensing his intent, she followed suit. How long they kissed, caressed, and tasted he couldn't say. She soothed him with contented sighs, he calmed her with tender strokes.

She opened beneath him like a flower at dawn, and he tasted her lips, her neck, her collarbone. Each foray drew him further into her, until passion sought a greater intimacy.

Freeing the buttons of her bodice, he parted the dress and freed her breasts, then dipped his head and tasted one of the taut peaks he had only imagined a short time ago. She responded with a sigh of delight and an urgent plea to go on.

Lord, how he wanted her. He was hard and aching, and he knew all he'd have to do was drop his trousers.

Crushing his mouth to hers, he soothed her with nonsense words spoken between quick, moist kisses, then traced a trail with his tongue to her breasts and once more took a rosy peak into his mouth.

Her hands clutched his shoulders, and he hesitated, uncertain if she meant to push him away or draw him near. When she tugged him and moaned his name, he knew he couldn't leave her unfulfilled, so he continued driving her mindless and torturing himself.

Sliding his hand beneath her gown, he discovered she was naked beneath the dress. He palmed that nakedness, and she gasped and arched into his touch. He probed deeper, increasing the rhythm of his action until she writhed and moaned mindlessly.

He could feel the sweat on his brow, his own body hard, ignited, and aching for fulfillment. He knew he must end this now or take her right there on the grass in the middle of nowhere. And while his body shrieked to go on, his mind calmly reminded him that if he did, he'd regret it for life, as she would come to do.

With a moan of despair he rolled to the side, throwing his arm over his eyes to shield them from the sun. He lay there, waiting for his breathing to slow and his body to stop shouting at him. After a few moments things receded to a dull roar, and he sat up.

"Josh?" Emily's voice wavered, and he turned his head, afraid she was crying again.

She lay tousled on his coat, her dress open and her breasts bared to the sun. Her mouth was red and swollen from his kisses, and her hair mussed into tangles.

The sight of her like that set his body to screaming again. Leaning over, he pulled her dress together gently, smoothed the hair from her face, and began to button her bodice.

She sat up and put her hands over his, stilling them, until he was forced to look at her. She had replaced her glasses, and the eyes he so longed to look deeply into were once again denied him.

"Did I do something wrong, Josh?" she asked, in a voice filled with sadness. He wanted to kick himself.

"Of course not."

"Then what happened? Why didn't you—"

"Em, this isn't the place for something like this."

She looked around, her gaze flitting over the pond, the birds, the bushes. Her sigh of contentment made her breasts rise and fall. He didn't miss it.

"It looks exactly like the place for a man and woman to make love."

"And you'd know a lot about that, would you?"

"Of course not! But I know about me."

He shook off her hand and continued buttoning her dress. "Believe me, you'd be sorry afterward."

"I doubt that."

He doubted she'd be sorry right afterward, too. But once she thought about it . . . "Besides, if my mother ever found out that I'd taken a woman's virginity on the ground in the middle of New Mexico, she'd most likely . . ." Josh winced. "I hate to even think of what she'd do. Or my dad, for that matter."

"You're a little old to be accountable to your parents, aren't you?"

He looked at her in surprise. "You missed the point. I was raised to respect females and treat every one of them like a lady."

"Even when that female isn't acting like one?"

"Em, you're a lady."

She turned her palms upward in her lap and contemplated the thick ridges that had toughened them since she'd come to New Mexico. "Not so much anymore."

"Yes, you are. Being a lady is not something that changes because your hands are rough or because you feel passion. It's in here." He tapped a finger along her breastbone, and she caught her breath. "And here." He put his finger to her temple.

"So I can never make it go away?"

"Why would you want to?"

"Being a lady isn't too much fun sometimes."

"No?"

She sighed deeply. "No, it isn't."

"Being a gentleman can have its drawbacks too, at times."

"Huh! Name one time," she scoffed.

"Right now, Em. Right now."

Chapter 13

⟨⟨⟨◦⟩⟩⟩

They had their picnic on the grass where they'd nearly had a whole lot more. Emily imagined she could still scent the remnants of their passion on the breeze. She'd never felt this way before and didn't know what to do. Ask Rose? She doubted that even Rose, who knew everything, could help, because she couldn't believe Rose had ever felt the things that she was feeling for Josh. If her friend ever had, she wouldn't be planning to marry a man for his money.

Conversation between them lagged, although long looks and heated glances abounded. Yen Cheng had outdone himself for their picnic, concocting a delectable version of Chinese fried chicken. There was also fresh fruit, thanks to the Atchison, Topeka, and Santa Fe Railroad, which continued to bring fruit, fish, and vegetables from all over the United States to Harvey restaurants along the route. And if the iced tea was no longer very iced, it didn't matter. They weren't eating much anyway.

Emily's appetite seemed to have died from the heat of the day—or could it have been the unfulfilled passion that sizzled in her stomach? Josh didn't seem to be too enthused, either.

Every time their eyes met, their gazes skittered away. Every time she looked at him, she remembered his mouth at her breast, his hands on her hips. She wanted to know what happened next, and she wanted Josh MacKenzie to teach her. But he had refused because she was a lady.

Or maybe because he didn't feel the same way— or couldn't. If he had felt the same mind-numbing need for completion that she'd felt, he wouldn't have been able to calmly button her dress or deny her his body. Men just weren't like that, or so she'd heard. Perhaps MacKenzie was more than a man.

"We'd best get back."

His words startled a bird from a nearby bush and Emily from her reverie. She nodded and began to gather the remains of their picnic, which was pretty much the entire thing. Yen Cheng would have a fit. She began breaking up pieces of the biscuits and strewing them on the ground.

"What are you doing?" Josh asked.

"Making sure Yen Cheng doesn't take his meat cleaver to you when we return with a full picnic basket."

"Why would he do that?"

"Because we hadn't eaten enough. It would be an insult, and he'd probably feel he'd lost face."

"Where would he lose it?"

Emily smiled. "It's an expression that means he'd be embarrassed. He's considered to be a cook of the highest order, and no one should be able to resist his meals."

"I see." He stepped closer and reached into the

basket, helping her with her task. "You know, Em, I brought you out here for a reason."

She shot a quick glance at the grassy knoll, and her cheeks heated. But if he'd brought her here for that, then why had he stopped?

Returning her gaze to his, she found him silently watching her. "Not for that," he said. "I'm not that kind of man."

Too bad, she thought, then blushed a darker shade of crimson. "If not that, then what?"

"To say good-bye."

Her hand froze in the act of tossing another bit of biscuit. The morsel fell unheeded from her fingers, and her eyes stung so badly she wanted to remove her glasses and rub them. This was her dream come to life. How strange. Had she instinctively known that today was their last? And why did her heart ache? Why did her eyes burn and her lips tremble? She'd been waiting for him to leave since the first time she saw him. If he'd decided to leave, that meant he believed she was Emily Lane. If he went away and didn't come back, she was safe in her new life.

So why did that suddenly seem like a bad thing?

"Emily?" Josh took the basket from her hand and set it aside, then placed his hands on her shoulders. Patiently, he waited for her to look at him.

She wanted him to stay more than she'd wanted anything in a long time. But if he stayed, sooner or later he'd discover the truth. She couldn't continue to wear these glasses, dye her hair black, and lie with every breath—although the lie was starting to feel like the truth, she'd lived it so long.

And if she told him the truth, after all they'd

shared, would he still take her home? Could she risk that?

Tucking a finger under her chin, he tilted her face until she was forced to look at him.

"You knew I couldn't stay here forever."

She shrugged, and his palm slid to her shoulder blades, a comforting touch she would miss. "I guess I didn't want to think about it."

"I don't want to, either. If I had thought about something other than you over the past few days, I'd have known I needed to move on. I have a job to do, and I can't just give that up."

"Why not?"

"It's a matter of honor, of commitment. I'd have little regard for myself—nor would others—if I didn't honor my responsibilities."

There it was again: the statement that his job was everything, just like her father's had been. She'd lived that life before and she didn't plan to do so again—especially in the role that her mother played. So as much as she wanted Josh to remain in Las Vegas and teach her all the things his body had hinted at, she'd let him go and do his blasted job.

She stepped back out of his reach, and his hands dropped to his sides. "I understand." Then she turned toward the buggy.

Grabbing the basket, he hustled to catch up to her. "Do you? You seem angry, Em."

"I'm not. I should have known this couldn't last forever."

As he helped her into the buggy, his hands lingered on her hips and hers on his shoulders. He climbed in beside her and sat close, hip to hip. How was she going to let him go when every casual touch set her heart to racing?

"Where will you go?" she asked.

He flicked the reins, and the horse moved out, carrying them back to the town.

"Back to Long Island, then home to Texas for a visit."

She nodded, thinking again how sweet he sounded whenever he spoke of home. She'd like to see his home someday, meet his family. Meet anybody who had the ability to influence him the way she'd failed so miserably to do.

But Josh was leaving and she was staying, and that was as it should be. They'd had a few laughs, shared a few kisses, and now the interlude was over. What had she expected? That the man would marry her and take her to live in Texas? Not hardly. She'd been living in a fantasy—quite a few of them, in fact.

MacKenzie was the enemy. He always had been and probably always would be. She had to remember that.

The rest of the ride was silent, broken only by the clip-clop of the horse, bird calls, and their own steady breathing.

By the time they got back, she only had ten minutes to get to work. Josh swung her down and took her hand.

"I guess this is good-bye, Josh."

He hesitated. "We've got one last night."

She arched a brow. What was he thinking? And was she willing to agree? Since she never expected to see him again, why prolong the agony of saying good-bye? A clean break was the easiest. But she knew she'd forever regret not sharing these few remaining hours together.

"Yes," she said, before he could even ask.

His brow creased in a confused frown. "Yes?"

She nodded eagerly and kissed him, then she ran inside to get ready to serve supper.

Yes, she'd said, although he had no idea what she was agreeing to. The woman was a mystery and had been from the beginning. He returned the buggy to the livery, then walked to his hotel. Deep in thought, he packed his bag and set it by the door.

He hadn't been able to read how she'd felt about his leaving. She'd seemed upset, but she hadn't said a thing—or even hinted—about wanting him to stay. She hadn't asked him to come back, let alone said that she'd wait for him. Why was he surprised? She didn't need him; she could take care of herself. Perhaps she didn't even want him. He'd been wrong about a woman before.

He slumped down on the bed. He'd so believed that Diane loved him as much as he loved her. She'd wanted his body, his touch, his kiss. But she hadn't needed his name or his love. After that experience, he'd felt like nothing more than a stud horse. It had taken him a long time to even contemplate caring for someone again. It had taken him until now.

His father always said, if you want something badly enough, you have to fight for it. Did he want Emily that badly?

Yes. So when he went back to see her tonight, he would ask her straight out how she felt. And if she cared for him at all, when his job was done, he'd come back here and convince her to marry him.

That decided, he felt a whole lot better. Perhaps when he went to see her this evening, he'd bring her a gift. He'd noticed her admiring some purple wild-flowers growing just outside of town. He had a bit of time and could go pick some for her. Then he'd leave them in her room.

Emily dashed into the dining car just as the other girls began to set the tables. She joined them in their task, and Rose hurried over.

"Any problems? Emily asked.

"Not one. Bridges had a headache and stayed in his room all afternoon."

"I appreciate you covering for me."

"Well, was it worth it?" Rose asked.

"What do you mean?"

"Did you have a good time?"

Emily thought back over the whole afternoon. The bath, the dream, the embrace. "Oh, yes," she said, with indrawn breath. "I had a very good time."

Grinning, Rose reached over and plucked a piece of grass from her hair. "I can see that."

Emily's eyes widened in embarrassment, and she reached up to brush at her serviceable hairstyle. "Do you see any more?"

"Relax, honey, there was just the one. And I won't tell. So how was he?"

"He's leaving," she blurted.

"Really? That's wonderful. Your troubles are over."

Placing silverware on her table gave her the excuse not to answer. Unfortunately, Rose was not easily discouraged.

"Isn't that what you've been hoping for?"

"I suppose so," she said desolately.

Rose put her hand on Emily's arm, stopping her from her work. "Honey, you knew he couldn't stay."

She nodded. "Yes, I knew."

"You don't sound so sure."

She looked into Rose's concerned eyes and sighed. "I'm not."

"I was afraid this would happen," Rose said, distressed. "You're just not cut out for casual flirtation, honey. I suppose that's not a bad thing. You're the kind of woman who'll only give herself to the man she loves."

"Rose, I didn't give him anything!"

"But you wanted to."

She couldn't lie to Rose or herself anymore. Grabbing a handful of forks, she kept on working. "Yes, I wanted to."

Rose snatched up some spoons and followed along at her side. "So what happened?"

"He didn't want me."

"What?" A spoon landed on the table with a clatter. "You've got to be kidding."

Emily repositioned the spoon where it belonged, glanced at Rose, and raised her eyebrow. "I am not kidding. I literally threw myself at the man, and he didn't want me."

"Hmm, that's interesting. Sounds to me like he's in love with you, too."

Emily dropped a fork on the floor. "I don't think so, Rose." She bent to pick it up and tossed the fork into the dirty dish pan.

"Hmm," Rose reflected. "What kind of man won't take a woman when she wants him to?"

"I'm not the one to ask. You're the expert on men."

"Well, it's either a man who isn't a man—and MacKenzie doesn't strike me as one of those—or a man who's contemplating marriage. I think he's going to ask you to marry him."

Emily dropped an entire handful of forks.

All the Harvey Girls turned to stare at her. Blushing, she bent down to pick them up. Rose knelt to help.

"Are you crazy?" Emily hissed. "I couldn't marry him even if I wanted to."

"Why not?"

"Have you forgotten that I'm living a lie?"

"So tell him the truth," Rose said offhandedly.

"And he'll drag me home to Daddy."

"Do you really think so?"

Emily thought about Josh's face when he'd spoken of his job and his honor. "No doubt about it."

"Then let him go, honey. If he can't live without you, he'll come back. And if he comes back, then he's yours forever."

Emily stood and threw all the dirty silverware into the dishpan. The clatter sounded like a final clap of approval to an important decision. Rose's advice was sound. She decided to take it.

Josh sneaked into Rose and Emily's room, feeling like a thief. But he wasn't there to investigate; he was there to surprise her. He'd felt silly walking around Las Vegas with a handful of purple wildflowers. But simple gestures often said what couldn't be expressed with words.

The room smelled of Emily—lavender—and Rose, an exotic scent that made him think of cinnamon and oriental spice. Their clothes were neatly hung on pegs, and their hairbrushes and the like were aligned neatly on a dresser with a mirror hung above it.

He went to the dresser and placed the flowers at the center of the top. Emily would most likely come here to fix her hair before meeting him, and then she'd find them. Or if not then, later, when she came to unbind her hair before bed. His body hardened at that image, and he sighed in exasperation. There were times he got on his own nerves.

His gaze wandered over the paraphernalia on the dresser: hairpins, perfume, powder, some kind of black water in a glass jar, and brackish yellow water in another. The flowers he'd just put down, a washcloth, and a photograph.

He'd already started to turn away when the implication of the last item hit him right between the eyes. He staggered and turned back to the dresser. Glancing in the mirror, he saw that his face had turned white and drawn. His hand shook as he reached for the picture.

He knew even before he picked it up what he would see. He'd carried the thing with him all the way from Long Island. Josh stared into the beautiful face of Emily Lawrence, and with a sinking sensation in his stomach, he knew he'd been deceived.

Not only had she lied about who she was, but she'd stolen, too. She'd kissed him, held him, and made him believe the lie. Then she'd stolen his heart, and now he could feel her stomping all over it.

Why did he have a weakness for spoiled, selfish little rich girls? It would be his undoing if he let it.

He did not plan to let it.

Glancing in the mirror again, he saw that his face still looked pale, but now with anger, not shock. His hand clenched the photograph, then he spun on his heel and left the room.

Miss Emily Lane/Lawrence was in for a big surprise. The next time she saw Josh MacKenzie, she'd discover that no one made a fool of him—at least not more than once in a lifetime.

As she served the pie to her guests, Emily kept glancing at the door, waiting for Josh to come into the boxcar. His usual pattern was to arrive at this time and wait for her to finish. By the time the passengers had left and the train whistle had faded into the distance, she'd begun to worry. By the time she'd finished with her chores and was ready to leave, she'd become very worried.

Had he left town after all—and without saying good-bye? If so, she doubted he'd be back. The thought made her eyes burn and her throat turn dry.

"Stop that," she chided herself. If he'd left without saying good-bye, then good riddance. Better to know what kind of man he was now than later, like her mother.

She walked past his hotel and hesitated. Perhaps he'd fallen asleep. She wouldn't blame him. She was exhausted herself after spending the afternoon in the sun and fresh air. She'd just trip up to his room, knock on the door, and wake him. No sense in getting angry when she didn't know the truth of the matter.

But she'd never gone to a man's hotel room before. What a scandal this would cause back home! No one looked at her twice, though, as she came into the hotel. The clerk told her Josh's room number without so much as a blink, and within seconds she found herself standing in front of his door.

And there she stood. She'd told him yes this afternoon, meaning to spend tonight in his arms. His room would be where it happened, if it did happen.

And she'd be sorry the rest of her life if she didn't find out what it was like.

Before she could talk herself out of the course she'd set, she raised her hand and rapped on the door.

Josh yanked it open. She gasped at the sight of him—pale, tight-lipped, and wild-eyed.

"Josh, what's the matter?" she cried, alarmed.

In answer, he grabbed her by the wrist and pulled her into the room.

Chapter 14

⚬⚬⚬⚬⚬

Josh couldn't believe Emily had actually shown up on his doorstep. But then, why wouldn't she? She didn't know he was on to her game.

She stumbled into the room and then into him. His hands steadied her before she could fall, and his treacherous fingers clung. The scent of lavender teased his nostrils, and his body responded predictably. A sigh of exasperation hissed through his teeth as he set Emily on her feet, then shut the door.

"Josh, what's the—"

He grabbed her wrists and tied them together with a length of rope. He couldn't bring himself to put the handcuffs he'd normally have used for a criminal on her small, feminine wrists. She stared in confusion at the rope, then with dawning understanding. Slowly, she raised her gaze to his.

He held up her photograph in his palm for her to see. "Miss Lawrence, I presume." Reaching out, he yanked the glasses from her eyes—Emily Lawrence's eyes. "Perhaps that will make it easier for you to recognize yourself."

His stomach churned at finally being able to look into the incredible green eyes that had haunted him for months. The eyes he had only been able to view in a photograph. They were everything he had expected—they were devastating. He balled his hands into fists. *Damn you, Em. Damn you*, he cursed silently.

"I can explain—"

"Don't bother. You're a liar and from the looks of this"—he indicated the portrait—"the thief your father said you were."

"I am not a liar. My father is. I didn't steal anything. I'm of age: the money was mine to take." She stamped her foot. "So you can't force me to go home."

"We'll see about that."

Desperation showed on her face, her eyes those of the trapped. "But . . . but . . . what about all that was between us, Josh?"

"Yes, what about that? How far would you have gone in your efforts to deceive me? I was a real fool to stop before taking what I wanted."

"You wouldn't have taken anything I wasn't willing to give," she said quietly.

The sincerity in her voice gnawed at his conscience. He hadn't been any more honest with her than she'd been with him. He lashed out in guilty anger. "Stop the act, Miss Lawrence. You and I both know the reason why we got involved: I was suspicious, and you were trying to throw me off the scent."

"You didn't seem too suspicious to me. Especially when you were making love to me."

"All in the line of duty, ma'am," he said mockingly.

The green eyes momentarily flinched in pain, then

she said scornfully, "And duty and honor before all else, Detective MacKenzie."

"You've got that right, lady."

You ought to be real proud of yourself, Mac-Kenzie, he thought bitterly. She'd hit the nail right on the head—even about making love to her. Once he'd allowed himself to believe in her lie, he'd let his suspicions go, because in his heart he'd wanted so badly for her to be Emily Lane.

Annoyance flashed through him, and he dropped the glasses to the floor and ground them beneath his boot. The crunch of glass filled the tense silence in the room for a moment, then she broke it.

"Thank you." He frowned, and she shrugged. "I hated those things."

So they *were* just a disguise. He'd suspected as much at first, but then figured she needed them, green eyes or not. The glasses had to have been a problem for her—all that stumbling around and bumping into things, and the greater quandary of making sure she wore them every minute of the day. He shook his head.

"Anything for the lie, is that it, lady? Keep up the deception on poor, dumb MacKenzie." He straightened his shoulders. He'd had enough of this to last him a lifetime. "First thing in the morning we'll get your things, then I'm marching you down to that depot, and we're climbing on the first eastbound train out of here. You can spend tonight reflecting on your sins."

"You mean you expect me to stay in this room with you tonight?" she asked, shocked.

"Isn't that what you had in mind when you came pussyfooting up to my door tonight, Miss Lawrence?"

Her eyes flashed angrily. "And you intend to lead me through town trussed up like a Thanksgiving turkey tomorrow?"

"Who's going to care?"

"I will. And I think Mr. Harvey will, too. It doesn't do his operation any good to have one of his waitresses led through town in bondage."

"I don't work for Mr. Harvey, and from now on, neither do you."

Her eyes narrowed into slits. "You're a real bastard, MacKenzie. You have no idea why I left, yet you're willing to drag me back for a few dollars. What if my father beat me? Locked me in a closet? Starved me? Did any of those possibilities occur to you?"

"Not a one. I met your father. He may be overbearing, but if I'm any judge of character, he's not a woman-beater."

Her nose went up in the air, and she glared at him, making him feel once again like even more of an idiot than he'd been already.

"And we both know how well you judge character, MacKenzie," she said sarcastically. "Particularly if the way you judged mine is any example. Whether you believe it or not, Josh, I had good reasons for running away from my father."

"I don't want to hear them. I was hired to take you back, and I aim to complete that job. What happened before you left, and what happens after you get home are none of my business."

"No? I would have thought that what we've shared—especially this afternoon—would have made me your business for longer than a few hours."

The memory of that afternoon, her body glistening

in the sun, water sparkling in her hair, only made his heart crack along an old wound.

"I suggest you stop thinking along those lines, Miss Lawrence. The only thing you are to me anymore is business. So remember that."

"I don't understand why you're so angry, Josh."

He yanked out his badge and waved it before her nose. "Detective MacKenzie to you."

"Fine, Detective MacKenzie," she spat. "But why can't you understand that I did what I had to do?"

"Because I have no love for liars and thieves. That's why."

"How many times do I have to say I'm not a thief?"

"You can try a few hundred more, and I still won't believe you."

"But why?"

Her voice sounded confused, sad, and a bit lost—just like he felt. And she was to blame for their miseries. Unable to contain his hurt for what she'd done, he grasped her shoulders and held her still as he stared into her naked eyes.

"Because you let me touch you, Em, and all along it was a lie."

Just as he threatened, he kept her there all night. She was furious. Not only would Rose think she and MacKenzie were making love, but she would be fired for breaking curfew. Emily laughed humorlessly to herself. She was going to be fired anyway, because she was being carted out of town by a blind, bull-headed Pinkerton detective who wouldn't listen to reason.

She hadn't slept, and neither had Josh, although they'd pretended to—he in the chair and she on the bed. But how could she sleep with her hands bound and her world near an end? So she spent the night trying to plot a way to escape.

As dawn tinted the horizon, he was up and moving about. As she watched him finish packing, her mind spun with exhaustion and the sudden turn of events. She didn't seem to be able to get her thoughts around the fact that she was captured by a Pinkerton agent and on her way back home. She'd let her guard down, though she'd known all along that MacKenzie was a bloodhound.

Why had she thought he would change for her? When would she ever learn the lesson her mother had spent a lifetime learning: with men you were never first, but always came after something that held a greater priority with them.

As she bit her lower lip, she tried to figure a way out of this mess. He wasn't going to listen to reason, so she would just have to do something unreasonable.

She stood and moved around the room. After a suspicious glance, MacKenzie ignored her. Her gaze lit upon the badge lying on the bed where he had tossed it last night. As long as he had it, his identity would be assured; but if he didn't . . .

She needed to create a diversion. Her gaze slid to the key in the door. She suddenly had a daring plan—so daring it just might work.

He paid little attention to her anymore, mistakenly believing that she was cowed and ready to go home. But he should have known her better by now: she was never cowed—and she was *not* going home.

When he stepped away from the bed, she leaned over and grabbed the badge, shoving it into the pocket of her apron. Then, very casually, she sidled over to the door and took the key, holding it out of sight within her fingers. Now all she had to do was wait for them to leave. MacKenzie, being a gentleman, would no doubt let her walk through the door first—a mistake which she intended to use to her advantage.

A moment of uneasiness came over her at what she was about to do. But out here in the wild west, it was survival of the fittest. Kill or be killed, trap or be trapped. If she didn't try, she'd be headed home for sure. If MacKenzie considered her a liar and a thief, he hadn't seen anything yet.

"Let's go, Miss Lawrence."

Hoisting his bag across his shoulder, he pointed at the door. He no longer called her Em in that way that made her melt; she doubted he ever would again. Just like she would never call him Josh with passion in her heart. What had been growing between them was dead, and he had killed it. She had best not forget that.

She tensed in preparation. As she anticipated, he opened the door and like a gentleman automatically stepped aside for her to precede him into the hallway.

Emily stepped through the doorway, and as he moved behind her to follow, she stepped backward, turned, and hit him square in the chest with her shoulder. The unexpected move combined with the unbalancing weight of the bag on his shoulder sent him stumbling backward into the room.

She didn't wait to see where or if he fell. Grabbing the knob, she pulled the door shut and slammed the key into the lock. A twist of her bound wrists, and she was down the hall and down the stairs. Seconds later, with a quick backward glance to see if

Josh was in pursuit, she rushed into the lobby—and collided with none other than Sheriff Ben Travis.

"Whoa, there, little lady." He steadied her. "It's Miss Lane from the Harvey House, isn't it?" Before she could answer, he saw the rope around her wrists. "What's going on here?"

Aaargh! Were all the fates conspiring against her? Only she could escape a Pinkerton detective and run right into the sheriff. *Think! Think!*

"He . . . he . . . he . . ." She couldn't catch her breath.

Travis scowled. "Who? What did he do?"

"He tried to . . . to . . . to ravish me." Travis's eyes widened with interest—this was going to be easier than she thought. "He enticed me to his room on false pretenses, then . . . then . . ." She broke off in a sob and held her bound hands out for his inspection. "He tied me up and was going to have his way with me, but I managed to escape."

His eyes narrowed grimly. "Where is he now?"

Emily held up the key. "I locked him in his room."

Travis took the key. "What's the room number?"

"Number Seven, second door on the right." She cast her eyes downward and slumped her shoulders in tragic despair.

He patted her shoulder. "Good girl. You did fine, ma'am. Who is this man?"

"MacKenzie. Josh MacKenzie."

Travis pulled a knife from his boot and sliced the rope about her wrists. Then he slid the weapon back into place with a determined look in his eyes. "We'll just see about MacKenzie, now, won't we? We don't take kindly to this sort of thing in Las Vegas."

Emily let her smile burst free. "I didn't think you would."

"I'll take care of everything now." He led her by the arm over to a lobby chair. "You're safe now. Just sit yourself down and wait here, ma'am."

She nodded. Travis drew his Colt and climbed the stairway. She hesitated a moment, not wanting MacKenzie hurt. But she trusted Travis not to shoot on sight. He seemed a reasonable man—and MacKenzie could take care of himself.

So as soon as the sheriff was out of sight, Emily ran.

Josh slammed his shoulder against the door, but the wood didn't so much as creak. His shoulder, however, screamed. He rattled the knob. He shouted. But no one came.

No doubt the other patrons were used to noise at all hours and just ignored it. That's what happened when you stayed in public hotels.

Damn the woman! He couldn't believe she'd locked him in his room and taken off. Well, she wouldn't be able to get away that easily. He'd be out of here soon enough, and then he'd drag her home—by her blasted fake black hair, if he had to.

Footsteps sounded in the hall. "Hey," Josh shouted, and banged on the door. "Let me out of here. I'm locked in."

"MacKenzie?" A man's voice inquired from the other side of the door.

Must be the desk clerk, Josh thought. "That's me."

A key rattled and the door flew open. He wasn't waiting for explanations and was halfway through the door when he saw the pistol in the hand of a stranger who definitely bore no resemblance to the desk clerk.

"Stop right there, mister."

Josh already had. He glanced from the barrel of the Colt to the holster slung low on the man's hip, the way Uncle Flint wore his. It was enough for Josh to know he was up against a gunfighter—and definitely on the wrong end of the Colt.

Glancing back up, he saw the badge barely visible under the man's vest. He relaxed. "I'm glad you're here, Sheriff. There's a fugitive on the loose."

"Not anymore."

The sheriff's hand and the pistol in it didn't waver. Josh met the man's gaze, and the gray eyes meeting his were like cold steel. Cold with anger. But why? He had never even met the man before.

"Name's Travis. I heard you tied up a young lady and held her captive up here. I don't take kindly to that in my town."

"What? You mean Emily Lawrence?"

"Lane," the man replied.

"Lane is an alias. I'm a detective from the Pinkerton Agency, hired to bring Miss Lawrence back to Long Island."

The man did not look impressed. How had Emily bamboozled him so quickly? Recalling the sound of her sweet voice, her soft skin, gentle smile, and those damn green eyes, his question was superfluous. "Travis," he said, stepping closer. The cock of the pistol froze him on the spot.

"Get your hands up," Travis growled.

"Now hold on, Sheriff, you don't understand." But he raised his hands just the same. "Can't you just listen to me?"

"Take off that Colt, and then we'll see." Travis raised a cautionary finger. "One hand."

He knew better than to argue with an irate lawman—especially one with a finger on the trigger of a Colt pointed right at his stomach. Making certain not to make any fast moves, he lowered his right hand and unbuckled his gunbelt, then tossed it aside.

"Over here," Travis ordered.

Josh shoved the gunbelt over to the sheriff with his foot. Travis bent down and picked it up and, keeping one eye on Josh, emptied the cartridges out of the chamber. He then uncocked his Colt and slipped it back into the holster on his hip. Apparently he felt that without a weapon Josh presented no threat to him.

"Let's go." The man flicked the barrel of Josh's gun toward the hallway.

"You said you'd listen."

"I didn't say where. I'll feel better about listenin' when you're behind bars."

"Sheriff, I'm a Pinkerton detective here on a case. I don't belong in jail. Hell, man, I'm on your side of the law."

"You got any proof of what you're saying?"

"Let me get my badge."

The sheriff bobbed his head in agreement. "Slow and easy, fella."

Josh reached into his back pocket. Empty. He patted the breast pocket of his shirt. Nothing. He knew it wasn't in the bag he'd just finished packing. His glance swept the empty room The bed . . . The dresser . . . Then he knew exactly where his badge could be found.

"Why, that clever little thief," he muttered. "She took my badge."

A snort came from the sheriff. "And tied herself up, I suppose."

"I admit I did that. She was my prisoner, and I didn't want her to get away. I intended to take her back to New York on the first train out of here this morning."

"So you're saying she stole your badge and the door key, then locked you in here, all with her hands tied together and you right in the room."

"I know it sounds ridiculous, but she's a desperate woman."

"Yeah, but don't try telling that tale to the judge. He ain't gonna buy it any more than I do. Let's go."

Josh could see he was getting nowhere. She'd already worked her charms on the man somewhere along the line. But he couldn't blame the sheriff; the story did sound phony. By the time they wired for proof of his identity, though, she'd be long gone.

Resigned to the inevitable, he marched off to jail.

He winced as the door clanged shut behind him and the key turned in the lock. "You'll call my agency and verify that I am who I say I am?" he said to Travis.

The sheriff shrugged. "Sure, can't hurt. But it'll take a day at least."

Josh sighed and sat down on the cot. By tomorrow, where would she be?

As if in answer, the long, low whistle of a train carried to him on the wings of dawn.

Chapter 15

⌒◯◯⌒

Emily cast a dismal glance around the town of Sand Rock. Nothing stirred on the street except dust—not even a stray dog or cat. She had a critical decision to make. Thanks to Josh Mac-Kenzie, her career as a Harvey Girl was over. Bridges was sure to discharge her for leaving Las Vegas without any warning. Besides, even if Bridges would reconsider, she couldn't go back there. No, she had to get out of New Mexico fast—but to where? In which direction? The smartest thing would be to head east, where there'd be less chance of attracting attention in one of the larger cities.

The trouble with that idea was that she loved the West. Surely she could easily be swallowed up in its vastness. After all, she was an educated, well-rounded individual. As much as she loved being a Harvey Girl, there had to be dozens of other possibilities for a woman. Maybe she could find a position as a clerk or schoolteacher in a small town—one so remote there'd be no train running through it.

The important thing was to get out of Sand Rock fast before Bloodhound MacKenzie was set loose to sniff her trail. Without knowing how long the sheriff would keep him jailed, she'd left Las Vegas so hastily that she only had time to explain to Rose what had happened as she hurriedly tossed a few things into a valise. Then she'd caught the only means of transportation out: a southbound stagecoach. Five minutes after he was out of jail, MacKenzie would have checked that out.

Oh, how she'd come to loathe him. To think she had believed she loved him! She'd even envisioned marrying him when, all the time, the sneaky cad had been spying on her. And worst of all, she'd wantonly thrown herself at him—willing to give up her virginity to him because she believed he cared for her. Then the rotten miscreant insulted her more by turning down what she offered. Rose had been right again—she was too naive to play games with these western men.

Well, she'd just see about that! If that detective wanted to play games, she'd give him something to think about. And for the next few minutes, Emily thought intently about what she could do to throw MacKenzie off the scent. Finally, she came up with a scheme: the one thing he'd never expect her to do was to go back to Las Vegas. But she'd have to get back there without being seen. That would mean no train, no stagecoach, no horse or buggy. That would make it too easy. She'd have to walk the twenty miles. Why not? And to confuse him more, she wouldn't check out of the hotel, and she'd leave her valise behind, as well. That way he might even suspect she'd fallen to foul play.

Let's see if you figure this one out, MacKenzie!

Hurrying to the general store, she awoke the dozing proprietor and bought a canteen for water, then she went to the diner and ate dinner. She wrapped the dinner rolls in a napkin and popped them into her purse.

Wishing to avoid being seen leaving town, she waited until dusk, then slipped out the rear door of the hotel to start her trek. Fortunately the road to Las Vegas ran parallel to the railroad tracks, so it wasn't difficult for Emily to stay on course. However, it wasn't long before the purple shadows lengthened and nightfall masked the trail in darkness, relieved only by silvery rays of moonlight and the glow of tranquil stars in the night sky.

She kept a steady pace, stopping for a few minutes every couple of hours to rest but not long enough for her muscles to stiffen up. She tried to concentrate on future strategy, but thoughts of Josh MacKenzie always interfered. She'd finally met a man with some intriguing qualities and she'd had to flee from him—just as she'd fled from lesser men. It appeared she was destined to a life of spinsterhood.

As she paused to tend to a blister that had formed on her heel, a northbound train chugged by. She watched it disappear and suddenly felt a sense of loneliness and despair. Maybe her strategy wasn't too wise. What was she doing on this lonely road in the middle of the night?

Desperate situations call for desperate measures, she reminded herself. Shrugging off her self-doubts, she resumed her trek.

The distant wail of a coyote reminded her of possible dangers that might lurk in the remote darkness stretching beyond her vision, but she trudged along unafraid, comforted by the evening lullaby of chirping crickets and the occasional trill of a pheasant calling to its mate.

The sky glowed with streaks of red and gray by the time Emily limped into the outskirts of Las Vegas, exhausted, blistered, but pleased with herself. A southbound train was just pulling out, and she ducked into the shadows to avoid being seen.

Emily reached the rooming house, and before climbing through the open window into Rose's room, she paused to look around. The street was deserted. She'd done it!

Rose woke up with a start when Emily sat down on the bed.

"Shh," she cautioned, with a finger to her lips.

"Emily, what are you doing back here? I thought you were heading south."

"I did, but I'm trying to throw MacKenzie off my trail. I suppose the sheriff's released him by now."

Rose nodded. "He questioned all the girls last night and claimed to be heading to Sand Rock this morning."

Just as she suspected, it hadn't taken MacKenzie long to find out where she'd gone. Gloating, she thought, *This time, Josh MacKenzie, you're not going to be so lucky.*

"I figured he would; that's why I came back here. Rose, I need your help. I have to dye my hair blond."

"Your hair *is* blond. Just let it grow out."

"I don't have time for that. MacKenzie thinks my hair is dark now, so that's what he'll be looking for. Then I'll have to pack some more of my clothes, because I left my valise back in Sand Rock."

"Why did you do that?"

"I wasn't about to carry a heavy valise while I walked back."

"You walked back here!"

"Yes, and I have the blisters to show for it."

Rose scrunched up her face in distaste when Emily pulled off her shoe and stocking to examine her heel. "Oh, Emily, that looks terrible. We better put a poultice on it."

"Let's get my hair dyed first before Mrs. McNamara and the other girls wake up. I don't want them to know I'm here."

"You can trust them, honey."

"I know that. But Mrs. McNamara is so honest, I doubt she could tell a lie convincingly if MacKenzie comes back and starts asking questions. Then I want you to go to the livery and rent a horse."

"What for?"

"I can't take a train out of here. That would spoil the whole scheme."

"What happens when I don't return the horse?"

"Tell the liveryman the horse ran off. I'm going to head west. When I get close to the next town, I'll set it loose, and it'll stray back here. Then I'll take a train from there. I figure MacKenzie will think I continued south from Sand Rock."

"My hat's off to you, honey. I can see you've thought this all out."

"What else did I have to do on that long walk here?"

They set to the task at once, and as soon as they finished restoring Emily's hair to its natural shade, Rose went to the livery to rent a horse while Emily treated her blistered heel. By the time Rose returned, the house had begun to stir.

"As soon as you all leave, I'll pack up some clothes and get out of here," Emily said, sitting on the bed and watching Rose change into her uniform.

"Where are you going, Emily?" Rose asked worriedly.

"I don't know. West, for sure. I'll find a little town and get a job. I'll write you as soon as I'm settled."

"Do you have enough money?"

"Yes. Money's no problem."

"Time to leave, ladies," Mrs. McNamara called out from below.

Brushing away her tears, Rose hugged her. "Oh, honey, what if we never see each other again?"

"Of course we will," Emily said, choking back her own tears. "Thanks for all your help, Rose. You're the best friend I've ever had."

"You take care, honey. And be sure and write me, or I'll set that detective on your trail myself." She ran from the room, dabbing at her eyes.

Tears slid down Emily's cheeks as she looked out the window at the girls talking and laughing on their way to the temporary Harvey House. For a moment Rose paused and looked back, then she turned around and followed the other girls.

Emily wiped away her tears. She'd miss them all—even that officious Fallon Bridges. Being a Harvey Girl had been the most enjoyable time of her life, and now it had ended.

Damn you, Josh MacKenzie.

Even though the train didn't make routine stops at Sand Rock, Josh convinced the driver to slow down enough for him to jump off.

He'd cursed himself ten times over for letting Emily Lawrence get the best of him. Now the lying little actress had a twenty-four-hour start on him, thanks to Sheriff Ben Travis. Even when it was obvious she was nowhere to be found in Las Vegas, the bullheaded sheriff hadn't believed she'd skipped town.

What a convincing little liar! She'd even made him believe she loved him enough to give herself to him. He wondered how many other men had been idiot enough to fall for that routine. Or the shy blushes. One minute maidenly and demure; the next standing buck-naked on a rock, pretending she didn't know he was watching. She knew damn well he'd watch; she'd stalled long enough to make sure he'd become curious. And boy, he'd sure as hell jumped at the bait she tossed out to him.

What bothered him the most was that if she'd faked all that, was she faking, too, when he made love to her? The sighs, the gasps, the writhing and moaning. Was that real or part of the price of the ticket? Recalling how aggressively she'd started them making love . . . her kisses . . . molding herself to him. Dammit! The truth became so obvious he wanted to punch his fist through the wall. She'd faked it!

Josh hopped off the train, and the porter tossed him his valise. The streets of Sand Rock were deserted except for the milk wagon making its morning deliveries. He headed for the diner, but it hadn't opened yet, so he decided to try the hotel.

There was no one at the front desk, and leaning over the counter, he could see a man sleeping in a room that wasn't much larger than a cubbyhole. He turned the register around to read it and saw that a F. Bridges had registered the previous day. He snorted. As in Fallon Bridges! Josh pounded on the bell several times until the clerk woke up.

Yawning and scratching his belly, the clerk came out to the desk. " 'Morning. Room's a dollar a day in advance, meals not included."

"I'm not interested in a room." Josh shoved Emily's picture across the counter. "Have you seen this woman?"

"You a lawman?" the clerk asked, picking up the picture.

Josh nodded, but his gaze never wavered from the man's face. He'd know if the clerk lied.

"What's she done 'cept look beautiful?"

"I'm asking the questions, friend. Have you seen her or not?"

"No, I ain't seen no blonde that looked like her." He put the picture down.

"She has dark hair now."

The man lowered his eyes. "I ain't seen her."

The bastard was lying to him—no doubt about it. "Well, if you do, I'd advise you to be careful. She likes to chop up fellas. Saw her last victim myself. Not a pretty sight." He shook his head sadly. "That is . . . what was left of him. I felt kind of responsible for it, too. I'd just talked to the guy about her, same as we are right now. And I no sooner left, than wham-wham-wham"—he slammed his fist on the counter—"she let him have it with an axe. Sure wasn't a pretty sight. Poor fellow—just doing his job, same as you."

The man looked like his eyes were going to pop out of his head. Josh picked up the miniature and started to put it back in his pocket.

"Let me see that picture again, mister." The fellow's hands were shaking when Josh handed it to him. "Could be she's the same gal who checked into Room Eight yesterday, 'ceptin' that gal's got dark hair."

Opening the register book, the clerk ran his finger

down the page. A senseless gesture, since only one person had registered yesterday.

"Here it is. Name's F. Bridges."

"Is she in her room now?"

"Reckon so. She came back to her room after dinner yesterday. Ain't seen her since, and she ain't checked out, neither."

"Give me a key to the room."

Now wide awake, the clerk shoved a ring of keys at him. "Number Eight."

Josh took the stairs two at a time and unlocked the door to Emily's room. It was empty, but a valise was on the bed. He went down the hallway to check the bathroom, but she wasn't there. Returning to the room, he riffled through the valise and recognized several pieces of clothing he'd seen her wearing— and surprise, surprise, his Pinkerton badge. So she'd been there, all right, but it was for damn sure she was gone now. The question was *where*?

After sliding his badge into his pocket, he closed up the valise and carried it downstairs. "She was here, but there's no sign of her now." He tossed the key ring on the desk.

"What if she's hidin' until you leave?" the clerk said, glancing around nervously.

"She's gone. I'm keeping her valise as evidence."

"Go ahead, mister. I don't want any part of it."

"Do you mind if I leave my bag and hers here while I check around town?"

"Yeah, I'll keep an eye on 'em."

As Josh started out the door, the man yelled. "Hey, mister, you sure she ain't lurkin' around here?"

"I'd stake my life on it."

"I don't care no hoot or holler about your life, mister. I'm worried about my own."

Josh hated to think of the poor yokel looking over his shoulder the rest of his life. "Hey, pal, come to think of it, she's not the axe murderer. It's some gal who looks like her. This one only whacked the guy but didn't kill him."

He left quickly and headed for the livery.

His luck wasn't any better there. The liveryman had never seen her.

"Anyone leave here on a horse or in a buggy last night or this morning?"

"Nope. Just telling my wife at breakfast that business has slowed down to a walk."

"What about the stage line?"

"Mondays and Fridays a southbound stage arrives and leaves at six in the morning; northbound is on Tuesdays and Saturdays at ten in the morning."

"Any at night?"

"Nope. You can set your calendar and clock by their coming and going. Trains, too, except they don't stop. Most of the weeks after ten in the morning, there ain't nothing in or out of Sand Rock 'cept the locals."

"Well, if she shows up and tries to rent a horse or buggy, will you let me know?" He didn't think for a moment she would. But where in hell was she? She hadn't ridden out last night or this morning; there'd been no stage in or out since she arrived yesterday; and the train hadn't stopped for her to board when he arrived this morning. Logically, she had to still be in town, but his sixth sense told him Miss Emily Lawrence was long gone from Sand Rock.

He was waiting outside the diner door when it

opened. Josh ordered steak and eggs, and when the proprietress brought his food, he pulled out Emily's picture and showed it to her. "She has dark hair now. Do you remember seeing her?"

"You're darn tootin' I remember her. She paid for her meal right enough but ran off with one of my best napkins."

What in hell was she up to? he wondered as he ate breakfast.

Upon leaving the diner, he headed for the general store. He'd found that most people ended up needing one thing or another from a store.

Squinting, the shopkeeper studied Emily's picture.

"Naw, I ain't seen her. I'd sure remember a handsome woman like that."

"Are you certain? She has dark hair now."

"Makes no never-no-mind. A good-lookin' gal is a good-lookin' gal, whether her hair's yeller or black. Had one stranger in yesterday, but she weren't that gal in that there picture."

"Did she buy anything?"

"Yep," he said.

Josh waited until it became evident the next question had to be his. "What was it, sir?"

The old man frowned. "Can't rightly remember."

"Was it something to eat? To wear?"

"Can't rightly recollect what it wuz."

"How about soap or shampoo?"

"Come to think of it, seems like it had somethin' to do with water. Slips my mind what it wuz, though. 'Sides, what difference does it make? Weren't the same gal anyway."

Josh saw he was getting nowhere, so he gave up. "Well, thanks just the same, sir." He turned to leave.

"Hey, wait up there, young fella. I remember now. The gal bought a canteen."

"A canteen?"

"Told you it had somethin' to do with water."

"Thank you," Josh said, and left the store.

Obviously the woman was Emily. He headed back to the hotel. The valise, a damn napkin, and a canteen? These were all pieces of the same puzzle; they had a common connection. And leaving his badge, knowing he'd find it. Was she toying with him?

Suddenly a light went on in his head. He had it: she'd *walked* away! That's why she'd left the valise behind, bought a canteen for water, and probably wrapped some food in the napkin. The question now was—which direction?

Altering his course, he hurried to the stagecoach office and checked the mileage between Sand Rock and the nearest town. He figured she wouldn't head south, because she'd expect him to follow her. That meant east or west. But one town was forty miles away and the other almost fifty. Actually, the only town within a reasonable walking distance was Las Vegas, the very place she'd run away from. But would she have doubled back?

Josh grinned. He'd bet that's exactly what she did.

"You little minx," he murmured. After buying a ticket on the northbound stage departing at ten o'clock, Josh hurried to the hotel to get the bags.

She was clever, but not quite clever enough.

Chapter 16

FULL MEASURE? 207

Winslow, Arizona

Emily felt very pleased with herself. Since fleeing from Sand Rock two days before, everything had gone exactly as she'd planned. Thanks to Rose she had her natural hair color back, and she'd ridden out of Las Vegas without anyone observing her. And this cup of coffee she was drinking tasted almost as good as the kind the Harvey restaurants served. She'd avoided those, because she was sure that's where MacKenzie would expect her to go.

Life is what you make it, she philosophized. A person had to take the initiative in their own life, or others would. She should have left home years ago rather than bow to her father's domination. He could send all the Josh MacKenzies in the world after her, and it wouldn't matter, because she was in charge of her own life now. The secret was to always think clearly and not let herself be intimidated by anyone—not even handsome Pinkerton agents. *Especially* handsome agents like Josh MacKenzie. If she could outsmart him, she could outsmart anyone.

I wonder what Bloodhound MacKenzie is doing

right now. She giggled at the thought of him somewhere down in Texas, showing her picture to people, while she sat in this diner enjoying a tasty cup of coffee. Arizona was as far west as she'd go. Now she'd take the next stagecoach out until she found a small town that she liked and, just as important, where she could find employment.

Putting down a nickel for the coffee, she got up to leave, only to stop abruptly and stare in astonishment at the man who stood in the doorway.

"We meet again, Miss Lawrence," Josh said, tipping his hat. His face stretched in a smug smile as he lowered his suitcase to the floor.

Her first instinct was to try and run past him, but he blocked the door. Looking around desperately, she saw that the only other person in the diner was a young man seated at a corner table. He appeared to be in his early twenties and about the same size as MacKenzie, so he probably would be able to hold his own against him. He even appeared to be interested in what was going on, because his gaze was on Josh.

Hoping he'd be an ally, she rushed over to him. "Please, will you help me? That man who just entered intends to harm me. I've tried to escape from him, but he keeps following me."

"It would be my pleasure, ma'am," the young man said. He stood up, and she saw that she hadn't been mistaken about his size. He might even have had an inch or two on MacKenzie.

"Mister, this here young lady would like to leave. I'd appreciate it if you stepped aside."

The grin left Josh's face, and his eyes turned cold. "And I'd appreciate it, sonny, if you'd mind your own business. This is between me and the lady."

"Not anymore. The lady asked for my help, green-horn. And out here in the West, we don't take kindly to seeing a lady mistreated. Now step clear and let her pass, or I might have to mussy up that fancy dude suit you're wearing."

Josh snorted. "Forgive me if I'm not scared, sonny."

"Gotta warn you that I don't like to be called sonny."

"I bet you don't like to be called stupid either, but I'm sure a lot of people do it anyway."

"You know, dude, you've got a real knack for riling up a man."

"A man? I usually don't make a habit of hitting children, but your ass is going to be wearing my bootprint if you don't haul it out of here right now, *sonny*."

"That does it," the young man said, sliding his hand to the holster on his hip. "Until now I was gonna let you off easy, but I hope you know how to use that iron you're packing, 'cause this fight's moving to the street."

Emily's mouth gaped open. "Packing iron? What do you mean?"

"Don't you worry your pretty little head, ma'am. I'm gonna put a hole in this guy big enough to stampede a herd through."

"A hole? Good heavens, you mean you intend to shoot him?"

"That's right, ma'am. When I finish with him, he won't be bothering you anymore."

"Can't you just restrain him until I can get out of here?"

"I'm gonna restrain him alright," he said with a

nasty laugh. "Nothing like a shot in the gut to restrain a man."

Until then she'd been fascinated by the whole exchange, but now the situation had taken a dangerous turn. They were actually talking about shooting each other. One of them could be killed! *Dear God, what have I done?*

"No, you mustn't do that," she cried frantically. "I only meant for you to punch him, or something like that. I don't want anyone shot."

"Ma'am, it's my pleasure. Out here, we don't tolerate anyone messing with our womenfolk."

"But I'm not one of your womenfolk," she screeched. "I mean I'm not from here; I'm from the East."

He tipped his hat. "That's all right, li'l lady. I ain't gonna hold that against you."

Seeing the diner owner leaning against the doorway of the kitchen, his arms folded across his chest, she turned to him for help. "Aren't you going to do something?"

"Yep. Mind my own business. And that's runnin' this restaurant."

"Why don't you cool off, sonny," Josh suggested. "I don't want to hurt you."

"I asked you if you know what to do with that iron you're packing, dude."

"Of course, but it doesn't have to come to that."

"Like hell it don't. You come out here in your fancy clothes, scaring our women and bad-mouthing us. Your luck's just run out. Let's go."

"No," she cried, grabbing the young man's arm. "You must stop. I lied. He's not trying to harm me."

"No sense in you trying to save him, 'cause it's too late, ma'am. He's said things that no man worth his weight in salt can let him get away with."

Emily rushed over to Josh. "Please, Josh, don't do this," she pleaded tearfully. "One of you could get killed."

"You should have thought of that, Miss Lawrence, before you told that lie."

Tears streaked her cheeks as she chased after them when they went outside. "I'm sorry. Please, I'm begging you. I'll leave with you, Josh, if you'll stop this insanity before it goes any further."

"You heard the fellow, Miss Lawrence. It's too late to stop now."

Sobbing, she sank to her knees as Josh drew the Colt from the holster.

"We'll count off ten steps, then turn and fire," the man said, sliding his pistol out of the holster.

"Just like ancient duelists, huh?" Josh said calmly.

"Yeah, that's right, dude. Ancient duelists."

As if in a nightmare, Emily watched, horrified, as the two men counted their ten paces then turned and pointed their pistols. Sucking in her breath, she closed her eyes and waited for the sound of the shots.

"Bang, you're dead," they shouted simultaneously.

She opened her eyes and stared as they began laughing. Then, covering the ground between them, they shook hands and slapped each other on the shoulder.

"God, Zach, how long has it been since we've played Ancient Duelists?"

"Reckon about ten years, cousin."

Emily struggled to her feet. She felt numb, as if she still languished in the throes of the bizarre nightmare. It wasn't real—couldn't be real. Dazed, she looked at Josh. "You know each other?"

"That's right, Miss Lawrence. This is my cousin Andrew Zachary MacKenzie, affectionately known as Zach."

"Your cousin!" Reality set in, and a hot wave of anger swept through her, incinerating the numbness that had held her transfixed. "You two men are unconscionable. Do you have any idea what you've just put me through?"

"Really, Miss Lawrence, aren't you being a bit hypocritical? You didn't hesitate to have me incarcerated and even possibly beaten as a result of your lies. You can dish it out, but you sure as hell can't take it."

"Mind telling me what's going on between you two?" Zach asked. "You're still with the Pinkertons, aren't you?"

"Yeah. Seems Miss Lawrence has run off with a big bundle of her daddy's money. I was hired to find her and take her back."

"Mr. MacKenzie . . . Zach," she said, turning to him, "I have been trying to convince your stubborn, bullheaded cousin that I did not steal any of my father's money. I took only the money my mother willed me. My father lied when he said otherwise."

"Reckon lying must run in your family," Zach said, grinning.

She rolled her eyes in exasperation. "And stupidity must run in yours!"

Zach had the audacity to grin and wink at Josh. "Whew! The little lady's got a temper, hasn't she? That kind of sass would have gotten her a spoonful of cod-liver oil from Maude."

"Maude? The keeper of the sanitarium in which the two of you were raised, no doubt."

"Miss Lawrence," Josh said, "as long as you want to spout off at the mouth, why don't you repeat the part where you're crying and begging us to stop. Especially where you promise to leave town with me if we do. I liked that part the best."

Emily glared at him. "Oh, if I only had a gun, I'd shoot you myself, you—you—*bounty hunter*!" She shoved him, and he stumbled backward, tripped over the horse trough, and toppled into the water, his long legs dangling over the side.

Hands on hips, Emily smirked down at him. "I believe, MacKenzie, it's the other end of the horse that goes in the water."

Zach MacKenzie clutched his sides, laughing, but Josh looked ready to kill. He stood up, dripping water.

Emily sensed danger. Stretching out a hand defensively, she started to back away. "It was an accident."

He continued to advance on her, and the gleam in his eyes was dangerous. She turned and bolted into the diner and tried to close the door, but his boot prevented it. He shoved it open, and she raced to the protection of a table. He continued to stalk her around it until the proprietor came out of the kitchen, shaking a wooden spoon at them.

"You two are messin' up the floor. Either sit down and behave yerselves or git out of here."

"We're getting out," Josh said. He made a sudden lurch across the table and succeeded in grabbing her arm. "Zach, grab the bags, and we'll go to the hotel. I've got to get out of these wet pants."

"Boy, lady, you sure are a greenhorn," the proprietor said, shaking his head.

Emily had enough of a problem with these

MacKenzies without tolerating this stranger's ridicule, too. "I beg your pardon, sir?" she said frostily.

"Lady, there ain't a soul out here who'd of fallen for that act. Folks would never of taken that fella for an eastern dude with that Texas twang of his. Greenhorn!" He snorted, then shuffled back into the kitchen.

Josh's hand on her arm felt like a vise as he led her out of the diner and strode down the road to the hotel. Stumbling and running to keep up with his long stride, she had all she could do to stay on her feet. If she fell, he'd probably drag her the rest of the way.

As Josh registered, the hotel clerk eyed the trio warily. Emily hoped the two disheveled men and the obviously reluctant female would be enough to make the hotel clerk suspicious.

"Just one room for the three of you?"

"That's right," Josh said.

"This is a respectable hotel, mister. We don't allow any hanky-panky. Whatever you three have in mind, it'd be more acceptable at the Alhambra at the other end of town."

"I like this hotel," Josh said belligerently. He dug into his pocket and pulled out his badge. "Now, how about that key."

"Of course, Detective MacKenzie," the clerk said readily, reading the register. He cleared his throat. "How long do you expect to remain?"

Josh smiled. "As long as it takes."

Emily wanted to scream upon seeing the obvious pleasure Josh was deriving from the clerk's misconception.

"That will be one dollar. There's no extra charge for the . . . ah . . . other occupants in the room."

"That's generous of you, Mr. Morris," Josh replied, casting a quick glance at the name plate on the desk.

"Room Twelve, upstairs, end of the hallway. More privacy there," Morris said with a weak smile, shoving a key at him.

As they climbed the stairway, Josh put a firm grasp on Emily's arm.

"I don't need your help," she declared, trying to shake off his hand without success.

"I'm not offering help, Miss Lawrence; just making sure you won't try to push me down the stairs."

"Sounds like you've got a tiger by the tail, cousin," Zach said.

"Yeah, with a snake's head."

The room was tiny, with only a bed, a nightstand, and—to her relief—a chair. She sat down in it immediately. It wasn't that she didn't trust the two MacKenzies; the desk clerk's innuendo had unnerved her. If she was going to get away from them, she had to get control of the situation. Surely she had the intelligence to outsmart these two Texas half-wits. She just had to relax—to think clearly.

Closing her eyes, she breathed slowly and deeply, shutting out the murmur of their voices. When she felt her body and nerves relax, she opened her eyes.

And bolted to her feet. "What are you doing?"

Naked except for his underwear and the Stetson on his head, Josh MacKenzie dropped his wet pants and turned his head to look at her. "Getting out of these wet clothes."

"In front of me!"

"You had your eyes closed."

"Well, they aren't closed now."

"Then I'd close them fast, lady, 'cause these drawers are coming off next," he said, reaching for the waistband of his underwear.

"You're a crude, unbearable vulgarian, Mr. MacKenzie."

"No, ma'am, he's a Texan," Zach said, choking back his laughter.

"Oh, you're as bad as he is!" she sputtered angrily. Pivoting, she folded her arms across her chest and began to tap her foot angrily on the floor. "Don't you MacKenzies have any respect for a lady?"

"We surely do, ma'am," Zach said. "That's why I'll be obliging enough to tell you when you can turn around."

"You're just as dimwitted as your cousin!"

Fuming, Emily reminded herself to remain calm. Losing her temper would not get her the freedom she coveted. If she was to escape from these two immoral degenerates, she had to formulate a plan. Divide and conquer wouldn't work; it was obvious the two men were very close. The younger one appeared to have some misguided blind loyalty to his cousin.

"You can turn around now, ma'am," Zach said.

Sitting back down, she resumed her train of thought. It sure couldn't be hero worship, she thought, with a scathing glance at Josh MacKenzie.

He'd replaced his three-piece suit with a shirt and Levi's. The change of clothing brought a dramatic change in his appearance. He looked more natural dressed in the casual clothing: rugged and—as much as she hated to admit it—sexier and handsomer.

"What're you doing up here in Arizona, Zach?" Josh asked, pulling on his boots.

Emily couldn't care less what motivated Zach MacKenzie to leave Texas, so she attempted to work on her own problem until she heard Zach's reply.

"I'm looking for Cole."

"You want to be a coal miner?"

"He's not referring to ore, Miss Lawrence," Josh said. At that moment, she could have used a pile of heated coals to ward off the iciness of his look.

"Cole is our cousin, ma'am; our Uncle Cleve and Aunt Adee's eldest child. Left home six months ago, and the family hasn't seen or heard hide nor hair of him since."

"Did you ever think that might be intentional on his part? You MacKenzies have a penchant for dragging people back to their homes whether they want to go or not."

"He just turned seventeen, Miss Lawrence," Josh said, with no attempt to conceal his anger. Then in a worried tone, he said to Zach, "I wish I'd known about it sooner."

"Uncle Cleve tried to contact you, but the Pinkerton Agency said you were on assignment, so I offered to try and find Cole."

"Any leads at all?"

"Yeah, ran into Webb Paige in El Paso. He saw Cole here in Winslow. Said our cousin was riding with a pretty wild bunch. That's why I came here. Found out the gang rode south."

"Dammit!" Josh cursed. "I wish I could go with you, but I've got to take little Miss Rich Girl back to her daddy."

"Yeah, I wouldn't mind the company. That kid always did have a wild streak in him. Remember the Sunday morning he bet old Billy Parsons that he could hit the church bell in the steeple? Did it, too," Zach said fondly. "Emptied his whole damn Colt into it without missing a shot. Really shook up the town."

"Yeah, and almost got poor Aunt Adee kicked out of the Ladies' Church Auxiliary because of it," Josh replied in a droll tone.

"And what about the time . . ."

Emily stopped listening. She had her own problems to solve, without concerning herself with the antics of a precocious juvenile. But by the time they left to get something to eat, she still hadn't thought up a good escape plan.

"You three back again?" the diner's proprietor grumbled, as he slapped menus down in front of them. "I don't want no trouble. The special today is corned beef and cabbage."

Josh nodded. "That's fine."

"Hope it's as good as Ma's," Zach said as soon as the man departed.

"Yeah, Aunt Garnet's a good cook."

"So's your ma, Josh. I remember when we were kids how we'd all stand outside the door, waiting, whenever Aunt Honey baked those big sugar cookies."

"And then she'd give us each a couple with a big glass of cold milk." Josh smiled fondly. "Can't remember the last time I ate one of Ma's sugar cookies."

"Well, she's still baking them, and they're just as good. And the younger kids are still waiting outside her door. 'Bout time you thought of coming home and sampling one for yourself."

Throughout the meal Emily listened as the two men reminisced about home and their families. They were both so homesick that it touched her heart. She thought of what a good life it must have been, growing up surrounded by a loving family: parents, brothers and sisters, aunts, uncles, cousins. She'd been the only child and had met her father's brother just one time. He'd been as stuffy as her own father.

She'd been so absorbed in listening to them that before she realized it, dinner was over, and she hadn't given a further thought to her own plight.

A loud burst of laughter sounded from a nearby table, where a half-dozen cowboys were having dinner. With Josh's attention fixed on Zach, somehow the six cowboys might give her an opportunity to escape. But how? She had to think of something quickly, because Zach had said he was leaving town as soon as he finished dinner.

She needed an incident. Hmm. What kind of incident could she start? Glancing at the other table, she saw that one of the cowboys was staring at her. Emily smiled at him, and he grinned and tipped his hat. As a Harvey Girl, she'd seen enough of such grins to know what kind of thoughts lay behind them. She returned the gesture with a seductive stare—at least she hoped it was seductive. It must have worked, because he grinned again and winked. This time she tried a demure smile and turned away. It didn't take long for the cowboy to approach the table.

"Excuse me."

Josh and Zach stopped talking and looked up at him. Emily didn't turn around.

"Beg pardon, partner, but I wuz hopin' you wouldn't mind if I spoke to the little lady."

Josh shifted his glance to Emily, and she gave him the most wide-eyed, innocent look she could conjure up. He didn't buy it for a moment.

"What are you up to now, Miss Lawrence?"

"Whatever are you talking about, Mr. MacKenzie? Do you have any idea, Cousin Zach?"

Zach grinned but didn't say a word.

"Sorry, cowboy, the lady's not interested," Josh said.

"Reckon that ain't my impression. Let's let the little lady speak for herself."

"You heard me. Now shove off, cowboy," Josh ordered, exasperated.

"What if I ain't hankerin' to?"

Josh drew in a deep breath and exhaled it slowly. "I don't want a fight, friend, so why don't you just mosey back to your table, and we'll all finish our meals peacefully and quietly."

The cowboy looked like he was going to back down. She had to do something fast.

"Oh, my, this has been so distressing. I think I'm going to faint." She started to get up, but Josh clamped a hand on her shoulder and forced her back to her seat. "Sit down, Miss Lawrence. You're no more about to faint than I am."

"That's no way to treat a lady," the cowboy said. He yanked Josh's hand off her shoulder, pulling him to his feet.

Zach groaned and stood up. "Dammit, stranger, why'd you have to go and do that?"

The fight erupted immediately, with the other five cowboys and Zach joining the fracas. The two MacKenzies stood back to back, fighting off their attackers.

Dodging bodies, Emily backed slowly to the door, sidestepping splintered chairs, smashed dishes, and splattered food on the floor. Suddenly a hand clamped around her arm.

"No you don't, lady," the diner owner said. "You ain't goin' nowhere."

He fired a shot in the air. All stopped what they were doing and looked at him.

"That's enough. You fellas have busted up my place good, and none of you are gettin' out of here till I get a sawbuck for all this damage."

"It ain't our fault," one of the cowboys said. "They started it."

"I don't give a hoot or a holler who started it. Start reachin' for yer pokes, 'cause yer ain't leavin' till ya do."

"Shucks, Charlie, you know we don't get our wages till the first of the month," one of the men said.

"Then you'll all sit it out in jail till then."

"I'll pay for the damage," Emily said, feeling guilty. Had she gotten away, she knew MacKenzie's integrity would have led him to pay for any loss to the proprietor; but since her scheme had failed, the least she could do now was pay for the damage. Digging into her purse, she gave him the ten dollars.

"All right, you cowpokes get movin'," Charlie said, pocketing the money. "And don't come back till you know how to mind yer manners."

The cowboys retrieved their hats and went out single file, tipping their hats to her and casting disgruntled looks at Josh and Zach.

When they picked up their Stetsons to leave, Charlie declared, "You three ain't goin' nowhere 'lessen it's the jailhouse till you clean up this mess."

Josh and Zach began picking up chairs and tables, but Emily wasn't about to obey so easily. "I said I'd pay for the damage. I didn't say anything about cleaning up the mess."

"I knowed you wuz trouble, lady, the minute I laid eyes on you," Charlie said. "Should of locked you up then."

"Really! Just who do you think you are, the sheriff?"

"You got that right, lady," he said. Reaching into his pocket, he pulled out a badge. "Sheriff Charlie Bowes. Either you get to scrapin' that food up, or yer gonna find yerself behind bars."

She knelt down and began to wipe up the floor.

"And don't try cuttin' yerself on them broken plates, 'cause it ain't gonna git you out of finishin' the job."

At the sound of Josh and Zach's laughter, she gritted her teeth.

When the room was cleaned to Charlie's satisfaction, he told them to get out and this time to stay out.

"Well, I best get moving if I'm gonna catch up with Cole," Zach said, once they were outside. He slapped Josh on the shoulder. "Thanks for the fight. Haven't had a good one since you left Texas, cousin."

"Zach, how do you know if your cousin Cole is even still traveling with this gang?" Emily asked.

"Can't say I do, but it's the only lead I have to go on."

Emily threw a disgusted look at Josh. "It's a shame your cousin can't help you since he's such a bloodhound—but he's too occupied rounding up hardened criminals like me."

"And you could make the job faster and easier, Miss Lawrence, if you'd cooperate," Josh said.

"What if I promise to remain here until you come back?" she said.

"Yeah, when mules fly like Pegasus," Josh said, brushing it off lightly.

They walked down to the livery with Zach, and as soon as he was saddled up, the two men shook hands.

"When you catch up with Cole, kick his butt back to Texas, cousin."

"That's what I intend to do."

"Wish I *were* going with you. Stay in touch, Zach. If I can get Miss Lawrence back to New York before the week's up, I might even be able to join you, if you haven't caught up with him by then"

"I'd like that."

Zach turned to her and tipped his hat. "It's been a real pleasure, ma'am."

"Good luck, Zach," she said. Strangely enough, she meant it. She sensed the concern both men had for their missing young cousin.

"And you take it easy on Cousin Josh, li'l lady," Zach whispered, grinning.

"Now, *that* I can't promise." Then for some inexplicable reason, which she found bewildering, Emily reached up and kissed him on the cheek. "Go with God, Zach," she murmured.

As they stood on the street watching Zach ride away, Emily stole a glance at Josh. His gaze followed his departing cousin—and she'd never seen such a longing look in anyone's eyes.

Chapter 17

~~~◯◯~~~

"**W**here are we going now, MacKenzie?" she asked, when Josh took her arm and began to walk.

"Back to the hotel. We have a train to catch at six o'clock in the morning. I don't intend to miss it."

"I hope you aren't expecting me to share a room with you again?"

"That's exactly what I expect. I'm not letting you out of my sight, Miss Lawrence."

"This is outrageous," she said when they entered the hotel. "Surely even you must be more of a gentleman than to compromise a lady's reputation by forcing her to spend the night with you."

"The lady's reputation has been compromised already. It's called theft."

"Oh, what's the use of trying to reason with you!" She turned away in disgust.

He led her up the stairs under the disapproving look of the desk clerk. When he closed the door and locked it, he held up the key. "Please note: me, key, pocket. Just in case you're planning to try that trick again." He slipped the key into the front pocket of his Levi's.

Removing her hat, she tucked it into her valise. "I hope you don't think I'm going to share this bed with you, MacKenzie. Just where do you intend to sleep?"

His amused grin was infuriating. "I hoped you'd offer the other half of the bed."

"Well, you can just—" She cut herself off. Maybe she was taking the wrong tack with him. From the time he showed up in Winslow, she'd been unpleasant and quarrelsome. Maybe she could gain his support by being sweeter—or even try to play on his sympathy. There had to be a tender spot somewhere in that hard wall of flesh and muscle. She'd caught a glimpse of it when he and Zach had been talking about home.

Sitting down on the edge of the bed, she began to think about returning to her home. It was enough to enable her to force out a few tears. Lowering her head, she began dabbing at her eyes.

"What are you crying about?" he asked.

"I'm not crying," she sobbed pathetically, and wiped a tear off her cheek.

Josh knelt down before her. "Look, Em . . . ah . . . Miss Lawrence, I wasn't serious. I intend to sleep in the chair."

"That's not why I'm crying. You had a happy home, so you wouldn't understand. But I can't bear to go back to mine; my father is cruel and tyrannical."

"Does he hit you?" His concern carried to his eyes.

"Hit me? He beats me."

"How old are you, Miss Lawrence?"

"Twenty-three," she sobbed.

"Then legally he can't force you to stay. Give him back his money and leave."

Her mock tears were forgotten in a rise of anger. "How many times must I tell you: *I did not take his money!* The money I took is mine. My mother willed it to me."

"So you say," he said, rising to his feet. "That was a sweet act, Miss Lawrence, almost as good as the one back in Las Vegas. Unfortunately, it didn't work any better than that one. I admit, though, you almost convinced me until you got to the beating part. Frankly, if I were your father, I'd be glad to be rid of you."

"Oh, you're the most infuriating man I've ever met. Between you and my father, I can't believe one woman can be subjected to two insane men in a lifetime." She flung herself face down on the bed.

Emily awoke and sat up, glancing around in confusion for several seconds before it all came back. How could she have fallen asleep?

The room was in darkness except for the glow of moonlight through the open window. She was able to make out Josh MacKenzie's sleeping figure in the chair.

Hoping the bed wouldn't squeak, she rose carefully, then crossed stealthily to the door. To her dismay it was locked, and she remembered he had put the key in his pocket.

She had to get out of there, but how? Tiptoeing to the window, she stuck her head out to survey the situation. The street was deserted, but she was on the second floor. There was a balcony but no stairway.

First things first, she decided. Grabbing her valise, she swung her legs over the sill.

Once outside, she leaned over the railing of the balcony, looking for a way to escape. Her only hope to get down to the street was an oak tree that stood at one end of the building.

Emily dropped her valise down to the street. Then, drawing a deep breath, she leaped across the gap and grabbed one of the branches. For a few seconds she dangled by her arms until she was able to swing her legs onto a limb. Then she worked her way down from limb to limb until she could drop to the ground.

Grinning smugly, she brushed off her hands, picked up her valise, and headed for the livery. The only thing she could do was ride as fast and as far as she could before MacKenzie woke up.

The liveryman did not appreciate being wakened at such a late hour. "Lady, where are you going this time of night?"

"I like the desert at night," she said.

"Is that why you're carrying that bag? I ain't renting you no horse. Looks to me like you're taking off."

"The bag holds my art supplies. I'm a painter, and I'm going out to paint the desert in the moonlight."

"And I'm Buffalo Bill."

"Then I'll buy a horse, Mister Bill. What have you got for sale?"

He led her over to a mare in one of the stalls. Emily shook her head in disbelief. "It looks older than Methuselah. Can it even gallop?"

"Buttercup's a good ole gal. She's still got lots of run in her. You want her or not?"

"How much?"

"Seventy-five dollars, and I'll throw in the saddle and bridle."

"Seventy-five dollars! That's criminal! I can see that not all the crooks in this town are in jail."

"Durn smart talk for a gal sneaking out of town in the middle of the night. What did you do, grab some old guy's poke and run off with his money?"

"Of course not."

"Make up your mind, lady, or I'm going back to bed."

"All right." While the livery man saddled the mare, Emily retrieved her hat and shawl from the valise and the money to pay for the horse.

Minutes later, she mounted the mare and rode north.

Having no idea how long it would be before MacKenzie woke up and discovered her gone, Emily goaded the horse to a gallop. Unfortunately, a ten-minute run was all the horse could do, so Emily stopped to rest it. She continued on, this time more slowly, stopping frequently to rest the tired animal.

"You're doing fine, Buttercup," she said, patting the winded mare. "I'm sorry, girl, I know you're tired, but we gals have got to look out for each other. It's a man's world, Buttercup, and they do nothing but take advantage of our good nature. But I'm sure you've discovered that already."

By the time the sun came up, there was no sign of a town or even a house. She had no idea where she was, but she kept heading north. After another hour's ride, the mare began to fight the rein.

"What is it, Buttercup?" she asked, dismounting. Was the horse too exhausted to continue?

The mare trotted over to a thicket of mesquite.

Emily chased after it, and to her relief, discovered a watering hole in the copse.

"Well, you smart little girl," she said, delighted. "You must have smelled the water." After quenching her thirst, she sat down, leaned back against a tree trunk, closed her eyes, and relaxed.

"It sure is peaceful out here, isn't it, Buttercup? I just don't understand it. There's water, the scenery is beautiful; but this is the most deserted country I've ever been in. Surely *someone* must live around here."

"Yeah, should be a town about five miles north."

Opening her eyes, Emily looked up at Josh MacKenzie smiling down at her. She might have known he'd catch up with her. "Too bad there has to be a snake to spoil it, Buttercup."

"There was one in Eden, too, Miss Lawrence," he said. Walking over to the water hole, he loosened the cinch on the mare. "Don't you have enough sense to rest a horse properly after a long ride?" He slapped himself on the forehead. "No, of course not. How stupid of me. You had a groom to do it for you." He pulled off Buttercup's saddle and tossed it aside. "Hate to see an animal mistreated."

"So it's only women you abuse, is that it, MacKenzie?"

Anger glittered in his glare. "You try a man's patience, lady. And waste a lot of his time." He removed the saddle from his own mount, and the horse trotted over to the water. When both horses had drunk their fill, he tied their reins to a clump of mesquite. Plopping down beside her, he asked, "So what did this latest fool move of yours accomplish, Miss Lawrence?"

"I decided to take a ride, that's all. It's very lovely

out here. If you remember, I told you how much I enjoy the beauty of the West."

"Yeah, I remember you saying that, but I figured that was as much a lie as the one you just told me."

She turned her head and looked at him. His eyes were closed, and he was stretched out on his back with his hands tucked under his head. Even relaxed, he emanated strength and vitality. She suddenly felt uncomfortably conscious of his virile magnetism. A flush of heat spiraled through her, sending a tingling sensation to her breasts and the core of her femininity. She bolted to her feet and hurried to the water hole.

Kneeling by the edge of the water, she drew a handkerchief out of her pocket and wetted it, then ran its coolness over her forehead and face.

As soon as she got up, Josh raised his lids enough to check what she was doing. His hooded gaze watched as she sponged off her face, then lifted up her hair and sensuously ran the wet cloth along the back of her neck. His loins knotted in response.

Lord, she was beautiful! Seeing her for the first time with that glorious mane of blond hair and those incredible green eyes not concealed behind that pair of ridiculous glasses had knocked the wind out of him like a punch to the gut. He'd had all he could do to stay on his feet. Then last night, watching her as she slept had been an exercise in restraint. He'd been fighting this growing desire for her from the time they'd gone on that picnic in Las Vegas. He had to remain objective and not let his personal feelings interfere. But how in hell could he do that when every time he looked at her, he wanted her? The sooner he got this whole damn thing over with, the better. Closing his eyes, he tried to put the vision of her out of his mind . . . standing naked on the bank of that pool.

He smelled the provocative fragrance of her before she even touched him. Then the silk of her hair feathered his cheek.

"I know why you keep pursuing me, Josh. What you really want from me." Her voice was a sultry seduction at his ear, and before he could say anything, her mouth covered his. Her lips were soft and moist, and he parted his to accommodate them. She found a fit—a perfect fit. Then her tongue took over: flicking, sweeping, coupling with his—plundering his mouth until hot blood pounded at his temples and loins. Her hand felt as soft as velvet when she slid it under his shirt to push that out of the way. Then she lowered her head and began to work his chest with sensual sweeps of her tongue as her hands fumbled at the buttons of his jeans. Every inch of his body was inflamed with an erotic heat. He wanted to touch her, but his hands felt too heavy to raise, his body too leaden to move; so he lay like a shackled prisoner and bore the exquisite torture—praying that it would never end.

"Stop," she cried out.

"No, don't stop. Don't stop," he pleaded.

"Come back. Come back, Buttercup." Her voice had begun to fade.

Buttercup! He opened his eyes and bolted to a sitting position. His shirt was wet with perspiration. He saw Emily chasing after the two horses, which were galloping away. Jumping to his feet, he angrily threw his hat to the ground. "Dammit! Dammit! Dammit!" he cursed. How could he have fallen asleep at a time like this? Then he clutched a hand to his privates; they were so heavy and full he thought they'd drop off.

Emily gave up the chase and came back to the water hole. As soon as she reached it, MacKenzie growled, "How in hell did those horses get loose?"

"How would I know?"

He grabbed her by the shoulders, and she winced from the pressure of his fingers. "You untied them, didn't you? Lady, you don't have an ounce of brains in that head of yours."

"Take your hands off me. How dare you manhandle me!"

Releasing his grip, he spun on his heel and walked over to pick up his hat. After slapping it several times against his thigh to shake off the dust, he plopped it on his head and turned back to her.

"You were trying to run away again, weren't you," he said calmly.

She doubted he was as composed as he sounded. "What did you expect me to do, sit and twiddle my thumbs until you woke up?"

"So you untied both of the horses. That was real smart, Miss Lawrence."

"I only untied yours and chased it away. Somehow Buttercup got loose and followed it. It's all your fault for not tying the reins properly."

"Miss Lawrence, I was raised on a Texas ranch; I know how to tether a horse."

"Very well, I untied Buttercup, and when I went to saddle her, she bolted away and followed your horse."

Wordlessly, he picked up his saddle with his valise tied to it, hefted it to his shoulder, and started down the road.

"Why are you taking the saddle?"

"Miss Lawrence, a cowboy never leaves his saddle behind. It's his most necessary possession after his horse."

"But you're no longer a cowboy, Mr. MacKenzie. You're a lowdown, conscienceless bounty hunter. In all probability we should be able to catch a stagecoach or a train in the next town; so why tote a heavy saddle with you?"

"I'm hoping the horses haven't strayed too far." He continued on his way.

She might have known he was too stubborn to take advice. He only applied logic to tracking down innocent victims like herself.

"Mr. MacKenzie," she called out, "what about my saddle and valise?"

He stopped and turned around, disgusted. "Lady, if you want that saddle and valise, you can damn well carry them yourself."

"But you said the next town was five miles away. If we don't encounter the horses, I can't carry that heavy saddle for five miles."

"You should have thought of that before you untied them." He spun on his heel and strode away.

She folded her shawl neatly and put it into the valise, then picked up the saddle. Her knees buckled as she hefted it to her shoulder, knocking her hat askew. She managed to straighten her hat, adjusted the load slightly, and started after him. What the heck, it couldn't be any more difficult than carrying a child on her shoulder. Except she'd never carried a child on her shoulder. She'd never even carried a baby in her arms before.

It soon became apparent there was no way she could keep up with MacKenzie's long stride. Apparently he noticed it, too, because he slowed his step to avoid getting too far ahead of her.

To make matters worse, the blister on her heel broke, and walking became very painful. After what seemed like ten miles to her, she called out to the tall figure ahead of her, "Mr. MacKenzie, we must have gone five miles by now. Are you sure we're headed in the right direction?"

"Do you see any other road? Besides, we haven't covered much more than a mile."

"Well, if that's the case, I'm not a pack mule." Halting, she dropped the saddle, untied her valise, and left the saddle where it lay. Whoever came upon it was welcome to it.

Favoring her heel, Emily was hobbling after him when they reached a battered sign that pointed westward up a hill. It read: TARNATION 1 MILE.

"What's wrong?" she asked, when Josh stood frowning.

"Seems strange. I figure we still have a couple more miles to go."

She snapped her fingers. "Tarnation, if that don't beat all! So you figured wrong, Mr. Detective. Guess the time's come to turn in your tin badge and call off searching for desperadoes. Give my regards to Daddy." She headed up the trail.

"Very funny, Miss Lawrence. May I ask why you're limping?" he asked, following her.

She had no intention of giving him the satisfaction of knowing that she'd developed a blister on her twenty-mile hike from Sand Rock. "I guess I picked up a pebble."

"Wouldn't it be smarter to remove it before continuing?"

Once again she snapped her fingers and exclaimed, "Tarnation, why didn't I think of that!" She continued limping up the hill. By now, her heel hurt so much she wanted to cry.

"Look at this road," he complained. "It's barely used."

"What's so strange about that? How many people, coming or going, have we passed since leaving Winslow?"

"None."

Arching a brow, she said, "Exactly, MacKenzie."

"At least there were ruts and evidence that the other road *was* used, whereas this is nothing more than a foot trail. I bet the sign has been turned."

"Tarnation! Now who in Tarnation would ever do a thing like that?"

He gave her a disgusted glance. "That wasn't that amusing the first time, Miss Lawrence."

In a short time they caught a glimpse of rooftops, and when they crested the hill, they came to a sign reading TARNATION.

Emily smiled smugly, then looked around. Her mouth gaped open in surprise.

"Well, tarnation, Miss Emily," he said beside her. " 'Pears Tarnation is a ghost town."

Chapter 18

"Oh, my!" Emily sighed and walked down the dusty, unpaved road of the abandoned town. She looked hopelessly around at the dozen or more buildings now a shambles. Several of the roofs were partially collapsed, and creaking doors hung off their hinges.

With the chain on one end already broken, a sign reading HOTEL dangled precariously from the remaining chain. She ducked to avoid the blur of fluttering wings that flew past her when they entered the building and heard the paws of tiny critters scurrying across the wooden floor. A thick coating of dust and sand covered the floor, registration desk, and the rickety stairway leading to the floor above.

Emily coughed and covered her nose and mouth when a breeze stirred the ragged, threadbare curtains at the broken window, launching a cloud of dust through the air.

She put her foot on the stairway, then drew back with a gasp when several lurking field mice scurried from under the stair.

"I wouldn't trust that stairway," Josh warned.

The mice had already diminished any curiosity

she might have had about the upstairs, and she moved away. "How long do you think this place has been deserted?"

"My guess is at least twenty-five years."

"I wonder why everyone left?"

He shrugged. "Who knows. Maybe Indians scared them off."

A chill rippled her spine. "Or killed them all."

He shook his head. "Naw. The place is stripped. It's been abandoned."

They went back outside and peeked into several more doorways. Emily smiled as dozens of the tiny mice scampered away.

"At least with all these little varmints around, you know there are no snakes," he said.

"They're kind of cute, aren't they?"

Josh looked surprised. "You've always been attracted to rodents, Miss Lawrence?"

"Only since I met you, MacKenzie."

She moved on, and her growling stomach reminded her she hadn't eaten since last night's dinner. "I don't suppose the citizenry left behind any tins of food?"

"I doubt it." He headed for the general store, and she continued her inspection, drawn to a cavelike structure at the end of the street. Poking her head in at the door, she saw that it was, indeed, a cave. Curious, she entered. In the faint light, she could see that it wasn't too deep. What purpose had it served?

"Miss Lawrence, where are you?" Josh shouted.

"In here," she called out.

Josh appeared in the entrance. "Get out of here. These old mines aren't safe."

"I don't think this is a mine. There are no tunnels in it, and it's not very deep. I can even see the rear wall from where I'm standing. Maybe the town used it for cold storage. Look, it even has a floor," she said, stomping her foot to prove her point.

"No-o-o-o," he shouted, and grabbed for her arm as the sound of splintering wood reverberated through the chamber. She screamed as the floor collapsed beneath them and they dropped into a deep hole. She landed sprawled on top of Josh, his arms around her.

"Are you hurt?" he asked when he got his breath back and the dust settled around them.

"I . . . I don't think so. Your body broke my fall," she managed to murmur, looking into his eyes. That close, she was mesmerized by the beauty of their sapphire color, since she'd previously had only viewed them this close through thick glasses. "What about you?"

"I'll know when I sit up."

Unthinkingly, she settled deeper against the long, muscled length of him. It felt good, secure. Funny, how she'd always felt threatened by his size but now drew comfort from this same power and strength.

"Maybe if I could sit up," he suggested.

"Oh, of course!" Startled into action, she crawled off him, and he sat up cautiously.

"Nothing feels broken." He stood up and flexed his shoulders, then glanced around. "Well, now we know why the town's deserted: the well went dry."

"You mean this was the well?"

"Looks like that to me." He leaned over and picked up his hat, which had fallen off during the fall.

She realized her own hat was askew and was almost covering her eyes. Sitting down against the opposite wall, she started to adjust it.

"Why don't you just take off that silly-looking hat?"

"I could ask the same of you, sir," she replied resentfully. This was her favorite hat; she'd left the others behind in Las Vegas.

"You just don't understand western culture, lady. A cowboy's hat is as essential to him as his horse."

"To help tell them apart, no doubt."

"Well, there are a lot of different styles, and everyone has their own preference." He began to pick up pieces of the wood that had dropped in the fall.

"I was referring to which was you and which was the horse, Mr. MacKenzie."

He snapped a piece of the wood with his fingers and angrily tossed the pieces against the wall. "We can forget about trying to use any of this wood to get out of here." He glanced up at the rim of the well. "Looks to be at least twelve feet to the top. This is another fine mess you've gotten us into."

"I'm sorry, it wasn't intentional. You don't have to be so nasty."

"I told you it wasn't safe, but little Miss Rich Girl doesn't have to take anyone's advice. Do me a favor and call out for help to one of your servants. I'd like to get the hell out of this hole."

"It's not necessary for you to get profane, either," she declared.

He looked mad enough to strangle her, so she thought it would be wiser not to say any more. When he continued to glare at her, she nervously adjusted her hat again and brushed the dust off her gown. Stealing a peek at him, she saw that his dark glare was still fixed on her.

Suddenly he bolted to his feet and yanked off one of his boots. "Take off your clothes."

"What did you say?" she asked, shocked.

"You heard me. Take your clothes off."

"I will not!" Good Lord, the man had gone mad; anger had pushed him over the edge, and he now intended to ravage her. She quickly pulled off one of her shoes and grasped it like a weapon. "I warn you, MacKenzie, if you come any closer, the heel of this shoe will end up in your eye."

"Don't get your hopes up, lady. I need your clothes to make a rope, so start moving. I'd like to get out of here while there's still some light."

She was too embarrassed to even apologize. Hesitantly, she removed her bodice, then untied her skirt and let it drop to her ankles. He had already stripped down to his drawers.

"Don't forget your stockings. Every little piece helps."

"I don't care what you say, I'm keeping on my unmentionables—and I hope, sir, you do not intend to remove your drawers."

To her relief, he sat down and began to tie the garments together, so she kicked her bodice and skirt over to him.

"Come on," he said impatiently, "you can move faster than that. Pretend you're in a hurry sneaking out of a window."

She turned away and raised the hem of her shift, then rolled down her stockings and pulled them off. "There you are," she said, tossing them over to him.

"The petticoat, too, Miss Lawrence."

When he had all the articles tied together, he tested the knots several times until he was confident they would hold. Then he draped the rope of clothing several times around her neck.

"All right, I'll lift you on my shoulders and, hopefully, you can reach the top. Then anchor one end of the rope to something solid and lower the other end down to me so I can climb up."

"What should I anchor it to?"

"Get my saddle. I left it in front of the hotel. Bring it back and tie the rope to the saddle horn, then sit on the saddle. That should be enough weight." He lowered himself to his knees. "Now stand behind me and give me your hands." She did as he ordered, and he took a firm grasp on each of her hands. "Okay, now climb on my shoulders."

Her legs trembled as she put a foot on each of his shoulders and he hoisted her off the floor. "I'm going to fall," she cried. For several seconds she wobbled precariously, trying to keep her balance.

"You aren't going to fall. I've got a firm hold on your hands," he said calmly. "Just relax, Emily, and when your legs feel steady, let me know, and I'll stand up."

When she felt her knees would not buckle, she said, "All right, I'm ready."

Slowly he stood up. "How close are you to the top?"

"I can just see over the rim of it."

"You'll have to climb over it. I'm going to have to let go of your hands, so you can climb up on the top of my head."

"Your head! Are you crazy? I can't balance myself on the top of your head. And if you let go of my hands, I'm going to fall backward."

"You don't have to balance yourself, you just have to push off from my head with your foot. And you won't fall. I'll be bracing your back with my hands. Now, let go of my hand and raise your leg enough to put your foot on my head, then shove off."

"I can't. You've got that darn Stetson on."

"Dammit! Kick it off with your free foot."

After several backward swipes with her foot, she succeeded in dislodging the hat, and it fell to the ground.

"Okay, you're doing great, honey. Now put your foot on my head."

Her legs returned to trembling as she placed her foot firmly on the top of his head. "Take your hands off my buttocks, MacKenzie."

"It's the only place I can put them to keep you braced," he said. "Will you just climb over the top?"

"I'm doing my best," she said. Her foot slipped off his head when she tried to shove herself higher.

"No, no. You're squashing my nose. Get your foot off my face," he shouted.

"I can't help it; my foot slipped."

He planted both hands firmly on her rear end and shoved her up. It was enough to get her head and shoulders over the rim, and she managed to wiggle over the edge on her stomach.

"I'm over!" For several seconds she lay still to catch her breath, then she stood up and unwound the rope from around her neck before peering down at him.

"Get the saddle," he shouted.

Josh plopped his Stetson on his head and sat down and put his boots back on. Then after several tries, he succeeded in tossing up her shoes. He could do nothing else but wait. Five minutes later she still hadn't returned, and he began to get suspicious. Had she taken off again? Surely she wouldn't run off and leave him here to die of thirst and starvation.

After five more minutes there still was no sign of her, and he began to call her every foul name he could think of. He looked around helplessly. The wood was useless. Digging into his pocket, he pulled out his jackknife and started to gouge holes for his feet and fingers with the idea of working his way to the top. He doubted it would succeed once he was off the ground, but he was desperate enough to try.

Just then her head popped over the rim, with that ridiculous hat still perched on top of her hair. "I'm back."

"Where the hell have you been?"

"Guess who showed up? Buttercup. I had to chase her down."

God had delivered him! he thought gratefully. "Okay, put my saddle on her and tie the rope to the saddle horn, then drop it down to me."

"I've already done that, MacKenzie. Look out below," she shouted and dropped the rope over the edge.

He grabbed the dangling end, braced his feet against the wall, and let Buttercup do the rest. Within minutes he reached the top, then grabbed and hugged Emily.

"We did it!" Without thinking, he lowered his head and kissed her.

It was a mistake. The pleasure was instant and explosive. He'd meant it to be a quick, spontaneous peck on her lips, but he'd been hungry too long for the taste of those lips. He devoured their softness, their sweetness, and she responded with her own hunger, which surprised as much as it pleased him. He knew he should stop, but he was helpless to break it off and deepened the pressure. Consciousness ebbed, passion replaced joy, and desire churned through him in a raging flood.

Emily pulled away and for a long moment stared up at him, her green eyes luminous and suffused with confusion.

He felt awkward, like a schoolboy after his first kiss—except his body was no boy's, and the ache in his loins wouldn't let him forget it. Releasing her, he went over and hugged the horse instead.

"Buttercup, girl, if we were on the Triple M, you'd spend the rest of your days in clover." After several pats to the mare, he turned back to Emily.

She had begun untying the rope to retrieve her clothing, and he couldn't help grinning. What a sight she made: barefoot in white cotton underwear and that silly bonnet perched prim and proper on her head. Yeah, what a sight—his grin slowly dissolved, replaced by a heated gaze.

"Thanks, Em." For her help or the kiss? He was unsure himself. He hadn't felt this uncertain about anything since he was six years old.

"I bet you thought I wasn't coming back," she said.

Despite her smile, there was no humor in her eyes; they were fixed on him intently.

"It crossed my mind," he admitted.

"It crossed mine, too, MacKenzie," she said succinctly, then pulled her petticoat over her head, turned her back to him, and continued dressing.

Emily sat down to put on her stockings and shoes. Her blistered heel was stinging, and she hated to think of putting on a shoe again. She was about to pull on a stocking when Josh asked, "What happened to your heel? It looks red."

"My heel . . . Ah, I must have scraped it climbing up the well."

"Let's see it."

She jerked her foot back under her skirt. "I already checked it. It'll be fine."

"Em, let me take a look at it," he said patiently.

Reluctantly, she extended her foot, and he cupped it in his hand. He had the nicest hands. She'd noticed them from the time they met. His fingers were long, his nails clipped short. Whenever he touched her, his hands felt warm and . . .

Her thoughts were becoming confusing about him. She resented him for what he'd done and was still doing to her, but at the same time, there was an element of integrity about him that she couldn't deny. And his kiss had shocked her—as much as it had him. She might have been naive, but she knew enough to recognize his physical response to her. How, after the way they'd deceived each other in the past, could they both still feel such excitement at the simple joining of their lips? And that kiss had been exciting. Her blood warmed at the thought of just how much. She raised a hand to her mouth—her lips still tingled from it. Like it or not, despite all the denials they made and the insults they threw at each other, deep within them was an undeniable attraction that neither could ignore—and every moment they spent together, they were becoming more and more involved. If only she could convince him that she was telling the truth.

He gently cupped her foot in his hand. His touch felt as healing as medicine. Frowning, he studied the blister.

"This is ugly-looking. How long have you had this blister?"

"I told you; I scraped my heel on the wall when I was climbing."

"This is no scrape, Miss Lawrence."

Miss Lawrence. So they were back to business as usual. She had liked it when he called her Em. It had sounded affectionate—even intimate. Her imagination really was running wild. It was time to put an end to such nonsense.

"All right, it's a blister."

"And there never was a pebble in your shoe."

"No," she lashed out. "There was no pebble; it was a damn blister!"

"That broke open again today. Bet you got it on that little walk you took from Sand Rock."

"What walk? I don't know what you're talking about," she sniffed.

"You made one big mistake, honey—the canteen."

"Well, you didn't expect me to walk twenty miles without water, did you?"

The darn seer figured out everything. There was nothing she could keep secret from him; he could almost read her mind. She'd better not let her fantasies wander down any more foolish paths.

"As long as you have this supernatural wisdom, MacKenzie, why don't you practice some divination and conjure up some water to drink? I'm thirsty."

He continued to examine the blister. "You should have told me about this sooner."

"And just what would you have done about it—kiss it and make it well?"

"I would have at least put something on it to protect it." He got up, went to his valise, and came back with a tiny round tin of unguent and began to lightly rub some of the balm over her heel. "Try to understand that things are a little more primitive out here than in the big city, Miss Lawrence. You've got to take proper precautions to protect yourself."

Yes, from you—and that tender touch of yours, she thought, closing her eyes. Within seconds the stinging pain had subsided.

"I think it'd be wise to keep your stocking and shoe off for a while. Let the air at it." She nodded. "Sit still while I pack us up." He gathered up her stockings and shoes, shoved them into her valise, then tied it on top of his.

Picking her up, he swung her into the saddle, then grabbed the reins. Leading Buttercup by the bridle, he guided the mare back down the narrow path that had led them to Tarnation.

Chapter 19

When they reached the main road, Josh continued to walk ahead, leading the horse by the reins. Apparently he was not going to take any chance of her riding away. But she doubted poor Buttercup could outrun him if she tried to escape.

After several more hours of the silent journey, there still was no sign of a town, and they hadn't encountered one living soul.

Josh was clearly disgruntled when they stopped to rest, and when he removed Buttercup's saddle, she could tell he was angry by the way he tossed it to the ground. She couldn't blame him. In a few hours it would be dusk, and they'd been without water since early that morning and hadn't eaten since the previous night.

"I'm so hungry," she said. "I keep thinking of all that cabbage and potatoes I left on my plate yesterday. How I wish I'd finished my meal. We should have returned to Winslow. We'd almost be there by now."

He spun on his heel and glared angrily at her. "No, Miss Lawrence, we never should have *left* Winslow to begin with. If you hadn't run off, we'd probably be in Las Vegas by now. But thanks to you, we're wandering around without food or water in this damn Arizona desert with a broken-down nag that can no longer be ridden." His voice had risen with every word, and he ended up shouting at the top of his voice.

"My goodness, how quickly they forget! Right, Buttercup? A few hours ago he was promising you a life in clover." The mare pricked up her ears and looked sorrowfully at her.

"You have no call to take your bad humor out on Buttercup, Mr. MacKenzie. If it weren't for her, you might still be at the bottom of that well."

"And if it weren't for you, Miss Lawrence, I'd never have been at the bottom of the damn well in the first place!"

His statement was too logical for her to think of a plausible response, so she remained silent. But that wasn't enough to shut him up.

"I wish I could figure out what I ever did to deserve getting mixed up with some harebrained heiress."

"Perhaps it's due to the profession you've chosen. I believe the term is poetic justice. If you think these explosive outbursts of insults, shouting, and looking fierce are going to intimidate me, Mr. MacKenzie, you're mistaken. I've endured the fury of a man far more vocally abusive than you—my dear father."

"So now he's *vocally* abusive. Gave up on that physical abuse story, did you?"

It was useless to argue with him, as it always had been with her father. She turned her back to him, folded her arms across her chest, and proceeded to ignore him.

Josh sat down and leaned back against the wall of

the granite butte. This whole damn thing was ridiculous. He should have known better than to take the assignment. He'd take his chances with a hardened criminal anytime. Thieves and murderers were predictable, their actions consistent. But how could anyone anticipate what Emily Lawrence would do next? She was the most frustrating woman he'd ever encountered—on either side of the law. He couldn't tell anymore when she was lying or telling the truth. And most of the time he was torn between wanting to strangle her and take her in his arms and let her cry out her misery. And *all* of the time, he wanted to take her to bed and stay there for about a week, screwing his brains out until he never wanted to see or hear of her again. And that's what scared the hell out of him. His mind was no longer on his job. They wouldn't be in this damn mess now if only he'd kept his mind on what he was doing. He was madder at himself than he was at her.

Sure, she was responsible for their being here, but he had made a couple of big mistakes today. As soon as he caught up with her, he should have turned around and gone straight back to Winslow. His second and biggest mistake was kissing her. No matter what his intention, not only had it kindled a fire that he couldn't put out, but it distracted him enough to forget that there was no blanket under that saddle. Now the poor mare was too sore for him to put the saddle back on her. If he'd had his head on straight, he'd have thought of using something from one of their valises as a saddle blanket.

He got to his feet slowly. Another dumb mistake. Sitting down to rest had caused him to stiffen up. He'd taken one hell of a fall and borne the worst of it to protect her. Now his whole body ached. If he didn't know better, he'd figure he fell on his head. It was time he started thinking straight.

"Time to get moving, Miss Lawrence. We've only got a couple more hours of daylight, and we still haven't found water."

"That must be why this area is so sparsely populated," she said, as casually as if they were taking a Sunday stroll. Next she'd be whipping a camera out of her bag and starting to take pictures.

"Yeah, the land's dry. Can't grow anything or run cattle. You're gonna have to walk from here on. Buttercup's back is sore."

"That's fine, I don't mind walking. Fortunately the Long Island Horticulture Society prepared me for long walks. I venture to say in my two-year reign as president, I must have tramped hundreds of miles through Long Island flora."

"Barefoot?"

Her light giggle was as refreshing as a cool breeze. "Well, no. I usually reserved that for the beach. But this is quite sandy, isn't it?" She picked up her bag and started out at a game pace.

For a long moment his gaze followed her briskly marching barefoot down the road. She did have a lot of grit, and he couldn't help admiring her for it. There weren't too many women who would walk twenty miles alone down a strange, deserted road in the dark, not knowing who or what she'd encounter, as she'd done back in New Mexico. Even now, she must be as sore as he was—especially that heel of hers—yet she didn't utter a complaint. He hoisted the saddle to his shoulders.

"Yeah, Buttercup," he said, taking the horse's reins, "she's got a lot of spunk all right—but if she had any brains she'd be dangerous."

He and the mare ambled after her.

About a mile down the road, they came upon a copse of elm surrounding a water hole. After drinking her fill, Emily stood up, wiped the water off her face with the bottom of her skirt, and then adjusted her hat.

"That was delicious. Now if only I had a bite of something to eat, I'd be content."

"Would a piece of beef jerky do?"

"What is beef jerky?"

"It's a thin strip of beef that's been preserved and spiced. A cowboy always carries some in his saddlebags. I've got a couple of strips in my valise."

"You mean all this time you've had food?" She could barely get the words past her clenched teeth.

He grinned. "I thought it'd be advisable to save it until you were really hungry."

"You thought! You thought! Oh, you're the most despicable, the most sneaky man I've ever met."

When she raised her hands, he guessed her intent. "Oh, no, not again!" He grabbed her just as she shoved him backward, and they both tumbled into the water.

For a few seconds they sputtered and thrashed about in an effort to untangle themselves. Then they both broke into laughter, and their actions turned playful as they began to splash and shove each other in the cool water. Buttercup continued to slurp away, oblivious to their frolicking.

They were still laughing when they waded out of the water.

Josh sat down and took off his boots, and after shaking the water out of them, he stripped off his stockings. "You'd better get out of your wet clothes, Em."

Surprisingly enough, she didn't give him an argument. He untied the bags, and as he gave Emily hers, he broke into a grin.

"What?" she asked.

"I think you overwatered that posy on your bonnet."

"Oh, my hat!" She clutched her head and removed the hat, then looked sadly at the prized possession. The artificial flower was so saturated, it hung limply over the brim, water dripping from the end of it. The straw brim was sodden and collapsed in spots. "It's ruined." She glanced up sorrowfully at him. "You hated it, didn't you?"

"Extremely," he replied solemnly.

He thought she was going to cry; instead, she burst into laughter. "What can I expect from a Texas cowboy?"

Picking up her valise, she headed for the concealment of a tree.

Josh quickly changed his clothing and was gathering firewood when she rejoined him, wearing a white bodice and gray skirt.

"The sun's starting to set," he told her, "so I'm gathering enough wood to get us through the night. We might as well stay here; at least there's water."

Once again she surprised him by sitting down without giving him an argument and began drying her hair, using a piece of clothing from her bag. By the time he returned with another armload of wood, she had spread out their wet clothing on the ground and over shrubbery. As he knelt down to build a fire, he stole a glance at her. She'd begun to brush her hair. Mesmerized, he watched her with open admiration. The sunlight glistening on the long strands created the illusion of a golden mist.

"It's awesome, isn't it?" she said.

"It certainly is."

It took him a long moment to realize they weren't speaking about the same thing. The plateau they were on overlooked the adjacent desert, and she was gazing at the colorful hues of the desert's sand and canyons.

"When the Spanish saw it for the first time, they called it *El Desierto Pintado*—the Painted Desert."

"That's very apropos. It's as if God took a brush and painted sections of it."

"Actually, I was referring to your hair before. It's the color of corn silk. Reminds me of the first time I saw my mother's hair."

She lowered the brush and smiled at him. "You've got a long memory, Josh. I've never been around many children, but I didn't think a child's memory carried back to infancy."

"I was six years old when I first saw her." At her questioning glance he continued, "I don't remember my real mother. I was only two when she and my grandmother were killed in a raid on the ranch. My dad and uncles were off fighting the war."

"Oh, how horrible. How did you survive the raid?"

"One of the outlaws helped our ranch hand, Juan Morales, to smuggle me away. Juan took me to Mexico, and I lived there until my father found me two years later. He became a lawman in California and married Honey Behr when I was six."

"Honey Behr!"

"My mother. She hated her name." He smiled with a private memory. "I adored her from the first time I saw her."

"That's refreshing to hear. So often children resent

another woman trying to take the place of their mother."

"I was too young to remember my birth mother. What about you? You mention your father often, but you never speak of your mother."

"She died three years ago. I loved her dearly and can't forget how miserably my father treated her." She was gripped by a momentary shudder, and her eyes clouded with resentment. "I shall never let a man destroy my life the way my father did hers. The man I marry will have to put me ahead of anything else in his life—especially his work."

Bitterness had crept into her voice, and for the first time he realized the trouble between her and her father went a lot deeper than the theft of money. But he didn't want to know what it was. His job was to take her back.

He shifted his gaze to her hair again. She'd resumed brushing, and it now lay across her shoulders like a golden mantle.

"Don't ever do it again, Em."

"Do what?" she asked.

"Discolor your hair."

Her green eyes filled with curiosity as she stared wordlessly at him. He lowered his head and resumed building the fire.

They ate the jerky, and although it didn't fill them up, the strips of beef helped to take the edge off their hunger.

As soon as the sun set, the area around them became cast into blackness, which the moon did little to brighten. Emily stretched out contentedly, lulled to serenity by the crackle and pop of the fire. Of course, knowing that Josh MacKenzie was lying nearby didn't hurt, either.

She tucked her hands under her head and gazed up at the stars. Whatever troubles lay ahead or behind were of no consequence. There was only the pleasure of the moment. A sigh of contentment slipped past her lips. "This is all so peaceful."

"You really do love the West, don't you?"

"What isn't there to love about it?" she murmured drowsily. "The remarkable colors, the astounding rock formations, the magnificent mountains. At moments like this, it seems almost pristine—untouched, untrodden, and untainted by humans."

"You wouldn't say that if you'd been around here five years ago."

"Why is that?"

"Let me put it this way: it wasn't God painting the sand red, it was more like Geronimo—with the blood of the settlers he slaughtered."

"Who was Geronimo?"

"You must have read about him in the newspapers. He was an Apache war chief. For a year he and his followers spread a bloody carnage in this territory."

"I gather he was finally killed."

"Captured, not killed. But not before a lot of people died."

"Well, that's just what I mean about this land. It's so vast. It swallows up these events as if they never happened and returns to tranquility. Silent and . . . mysterious." Her voice trailed off as she slipped into slumber.

Sensing someone's stare, Emily opened her eyes slowly and saw him, standing at her feet looking down at her, his copper face knotted in a fierce frown. He looked fearsome but glorious with the firelight glowing on his skin and the painted stripes on his forehead and cheeks. Straight, black hair hung to his shoulders, held back by a red band on his forehead. An eagle feather dangled from the band by his ear. Her gaze followed the beautifully proportioned muscular length of his body, clothed only in a breechcloth and knee-high moccasins. She stared in unabashed awe until a glint of light flashed on the tomahawk hanging by a strap from his right wrist. It galvanized her to action, and she bolted to her feet.

"Who are you?" Considering the circumstances, she was amazed at how calm her voice sounded.

"I am called Goyathlay by my people. You paleface call me Geronimo." His voice sounded husky, with a pleasant Texas twang.

She frowned, bemused. "You know, you look vaguely familiar. Have we met before?"

"If we had, you not be alive to ask such foolish question."

"I suppose it's your intent to crush me in your embrace and ravage me."

He snorted. "You must been drinking too much mescal juice, lady. Goyathlay is a mighty Apache war chief. He not spill his seed into worthless paleface woman who even steals wampum from her own."

She stamped her foot in anger. "I did not steal any money from my father."

"That's what you say, Golden Hair Woman Who Lies Through Teeth."

"Who told you that? Did my father send you? No, I bet that belly-crawling Josh MacKenzie is still spreading that lie about me. Furthermore, Mr. Geronimo, or Goyathlay, you are no one to be criticizing other people's actions, considering how you ride around the territory raiding and murdering."

He put his hands over his ears. "Silence, Golden Hair Woman Who Lies Through Teeth. Geronimo not come here to listen to carping tongue of paleface woman. Worse than twenty squaws. No wonder no man want you."

"I suppose my father told you that, too. It's an out and out lie," she declared. "I could have had any man I chose on Long Island."

"Humph," he grunted, folding his arms across his chest. "Among Apache, warrior choose his woman; woman no choose warrior."

At the sound of a growl, he jerked his head around and yanked a knife out of the top of his moccasin. "Hush. Geronimo hear growl. Could be wolf or bear."

"No, that's only my stomach. I'm hungry."

He looked at her fiercely. Her heart quickened as he took a threatening step nearer; but she stood firmly, bravely, and uncowed. Now his face was so close, she could see the color of his eyes. Funny, she thought an Indian's eyes would be brown or black: his were blue like sapphires. He reached out and touched her hair. "I no see such beauty before," he said, awestruck. "Like silk on corn."

"You really think so?" she said, pleased. "You're the second one who's said that tonight."

"I will give it much honor."

"Really, Mr. Geronimo!" She preened with pleasure. "That's so sweet of you. How will you do that?"

"Put on top of coup stick."

"Coup stick? But that's what you hang scalps from, isn't it?"

"Yes. Give yours much honor. Put scalp of

Golden Hair Woman Who Lies Through Teeth on very top."

She smiled confidently. "Oh, Geronimo, you're just teasing. You know you can't kill me."

"You in for one big surprise. Geronimo is great warrior. Take much coup in battle."

"But you see, this isn't a battle. This is a dream. My dream—not yours. And now is the part where you tell me you can't bear to kill me because . . . ah . . ."—she thought for a moment and then smiled triumphantly—"because you know you're in love with me."

"Now Geronimo know for sure you drink too much mescal juice. Enough talk. Time come for us to part company—and for you to part with scalp." He snorted with laughter. "Geronimo make good joke. He one funny fellow. No understand why people no like me." He raised his tomahawk to strike.

"Wait," she cried out. "You're just going to kill me? Aren't you going to kiss me and ravage me first?"

Shaking his head, he looked at her incredulously. "You one frustrated female! You need good man like Geronimo, but he no have time. Great scout MacKenzie on trail, so Geronimo do you big favor now and put you out of your misery, 'cause MacKenzie no want you, either."

"You don't know that!" she flared angrily.

"Boy, lady, you one dumb paleface. Should have stayed in the East where you belong."

She folded her arms across her chest and faced him defiantly. "I have just as much right to be here as you do."

"Famous last words," he said, raising his tomahawk to strike.

Emily managed to grab his arm. "If you do this, sir, you are no gentleman."

He slapped himself on the forehead, then, shaking his head in disgust, muttered, "Geronimo have much wisdom. No understand how he end up in your dream."

He grasped a fistful of her hair, and she looked up into his beautiful sapphire eyes full of menace. "No, stop! You know you want me, Geronimo. Don't kill me. Please don't kill me!"

"Em, wake up. Wake up."

She opened her eyes and looked into the same sapphire eyes, now darkened with anxiety. Josh was leaning over, his hand shaking her by the shoulder.

Struggling free, she shoved him away. "No, don't. Let me go."

"Em, it's me, Josh. You were having a nightmare and crying out to someone not to kill you."

She felt foolish—but still shaken from the dream. "Stay out of my dreams, MacKenzie," she lashed out irrationally, then rolled over and went back to sleep.

Chapter 20

⌒◯◯⌒

J osh woke her at daybreak.

"Let's get going before it gets too hot," he said.

Emily went to the water hole and rinsed her face, brushed her teeth, then drank her fill of water. Returning to her valise, she found enough hairpins to pin her hair up off her neck. Despite the state of her hat, she put it on; she'd need the protection against the intense sun.

Josh came over and hunkered down in front of her. "Let me see that heel of yours." His hand felt warm and comforting as he held her foot in his palm, his touch gentle as he smoothed a thick coating of unguent over the blistered area. She offered no protest when he ripped off a patch of her petticoat and folded it into a bandage. "This should protect the skin enough so that you can put on your stockings and shoes."

"Thank you," she said shyly. She didn't understand why she suddenly felt uncomfortable around him, unable to even look him in the eye.

She watched him as he went over and checked Buttercup's back. He gave the horse the same tender care he'd given her. Despite his gruffness at times, he had a gentleness about him that she found endearing. Not that she'd ever tell him so, though. She lowered her eyes when he came back to her.

"Don't suppose you have something that I can fold flat to put on Buttercup's back."

"I have a shawl."

"That would do fine."

She dug the shawl out of her bag and handed it to him. "You through with this?" he asked, pointing to her valise. She nodded, and he picked it up.

After tying a valise to each end of a piece of rope, he strung it over Buttercup's back and secured them.

"Won't that irritate Buttercup's sores?"

"I secured it where there are none. And your shawl will keep the rope from rubbing."

"What about your saddle?"

"I'm leaving it behind. I'm sure we'll reach a town today. Let's go."

It wasn't long before the heat became uncomfortable. What breeze there was blew hot air and granules of sand. Wherever possible they hugged the walls of the rock formations for any possible shade. Emily was tempted to remove her skirt and bodice and continue in just her shift. After all, he'd already seen her breasts, touched the most private part of her body. Her hot flush at the memory of it increased her discomfort. So why should seeing her in just her underclothes make any difference? Her shift was practically as good as a gown.

As she reached for the top button on her bodice, he shouted, "Hallelujah!"

Disgusted, she declared, "Really, MacKenzie, can't you be a little more adult about this?" Then she blushed when she saw he wasn't even looking at her; he was gazing at something in the distance.

"What is it—a town?"

"No, but see those tall spires up ahead?"

"Those trees?"

"Better than that. They're saguaros."

"And what's a saguaro?"

"A cactus. That means something to eat and drink."

That was all Emily needed to quicken her step. When they reached the clump of cacti, she gazed at them with amazement. Some had to be forty or fifty feet high, with long, creamy-white blossoms.

Josh took his knife and went to work on one of the small ones until he managed to dig through the spine-laden trunk. Then he hacked off a piece of the inside.

"Here, suck on this."

She took it and sat down. Gingerly, she put her lips to it. To her surprise it was moist, and she took a deeper draw of the watery liquid.

He cut out another chunk and squeezed the liquid into his Stetson. He carried it over to Buttercup, who lapped it up. "Ready for the next course?" he asked.

"What do you think?" she replied, grinning.

He pulled off several egg-shaped pieces of fruit from the cactus, cut them up into pieces, and offered them to her. She hesitated, glancing at them skeptically.

"Go ahead. They're not poisonous," he assured her, popping a piece of the crimson-colored pulp into his mouth.

Hunger won over caution, and she proceeded to eat the fruit as if it were a succulent orange or luscious strawberry.

"I don't understand how these cacti can thrive

without water," she said later, relaxing in the shadow of one of the huge saguaros.

"They're deeply rooted," he said, "so they suck it from the ground or an occasional rain. As you can see, they don't have leaves drawing out the moisture, so the thick trunks store the water like a water tank."

"Amazing. Everything about this country is fascinating. I always thought of a desert as something barren and devoid of life, but that's not really true, is it?"

He chuckled. "Well, there's deserts, and then there's deserts. I think saguaros are mostly found in the West and Mexico."

"Well, you won't find any on Long Island, that's for sure."

He gathered several more pieces of fruit and wrapped them up in his neckerchief, then tied it to Buttercup. "Time to move out."

"Yes, sir," Emily said, jumping to her feet and saluting.

He failed to hold back a grin. "Better save some of that energy, Trooper Lawrence. You might need it later if we don't find a town."

They started out again. He'd called her Trooper, she thought, smiling with pleasure. That had to be a compliment.

Shortly past high noon, they halted to rest and eat a couple of pieces of the fruit. Finally, nearing twilight, a town loomed up before them. A bullet-riddled sign identified it as Purgatory, but the dusty streets and sun-scorched buildings had the golden splendor of the lost city of Atlantis to Emily's weary eyes.

Please, Lord, don't let it be another ghost town. Her spirits soared when she saw several people on the street and horses tied to hitching posts.

Purgatory wasn't much larger than Tarnation, and their appearance drew curious stares from the few people on the street. Observing Josh, she could tell he didn't like the looks of several rough-looking men leaning against the front of the building as they passed the saloon. The seedy bunch looked like trouble to her, too, and he probably was thinking she'd make an attempt to escape.

"I'm not going to try to run away, if that's what's on your mind, MacKenzie."

"That's smart of you, because I think it's gonna take a lot of luck for both of us to get out of here with what we came with."

She thought of the money in her valise. Considering that it was the reason they'd ended up here, it would be ironic to lose it now.

He stopped in front of a run-down barn with the word LIVERY painted above the door. A young boy, sitting on the ground with his back against the wall, jumped to his feet and ran up to them.

"Put up your horse, mister?" he asked.

"Yeah, give her some feed and water," Josh said, untying their bags. "Where's the hotel in this town, son?"

"No call for one, mister. Ain't too many people visit Purgatory. If you and the missus are lookin' to spend the night, try the saloon. Ben Kerry's got a room he rents out."

"What's the best place to eat?"

"Saloon. It's the only place. Told you, mister, ain't too many people visit Purgatory."

"What about a stage? Is there one that comes through?"

"Used to be, but they stopped runnin' it a year

ago. Not enough call to make it worth the wear and tear. Ain't too—"

"—many people visit Purgatory," Josh said, nodding. "So how far is the closest town where a person could get a stage or train heading east?"

"Thata be Lordsburg. 'Bout twenty miles north."

"Thanks, son," Josh said. He flipped the boy a coin. "Take good care of Buttercup."

The lad's eyes practically bulged out of his head. "Wow! A whole dollar! Thanks, mister. I'll sure take good care of your horse."

Josh picked up their bags, and they walked back to the saloon, once again under the silent scrutiny of the men lounging against the building.

"Emily, listen to me and listen good," Josh said softly. "I don't like the looks of this bunch, so I don't want to leave you alone out here on the street. You'll have to come in with me. I'll get us a room, and we'll order something to eat. Don't say anything, and for heaven's sake, don't pull any of your crazy schemes to try and get away. Do you understand?"

"Yes," she said. "I have to agree the men do look unsavory. Do you think they're outlaws?"

"To say the least. Just let me do all the talking," he warned, as they entered the saloon.

Four men seated at a corner table stopped their card game to stare at them when they entered.

Josh put down the bags and pulled out a chair at one of the tables for Emily to sit down. "Don't move," he ordered, then walked over to the bar. Not more than a minute passed until he came back, handed her a glass of sarsaparilla, then returned to the bar.

As she sipped the tasty drink, Emily glanced

around the saloon, purposely avoiding making any eye contact with the four men at the table. A grayish haze of cigar and cigarette smoke collided with the dust motes floating in the air of the stuffy room. The pungent odor of stale beer and cigarette butts pricked her nostrils.

To her relief, Josh returned to the table and picked up their bags. "Our room's the first door on the right," he said as they climbed the stairway, each step creaking underfoot.

Emily flashed a smile at him. "I couldn't sneak away without being heard, even if I wanted to."

As Josh unlocked the door of their room, a burly, bearded man opened the door of the room opposite theirs. He paused in the doorway, looked Emily up and down, then his mouth curled into a salacious leer. She looked past him and saw a naked woman on the bed. Blushing, Emily turned her head away, and the big man gave a derisive snort, closed the door, and lumbered down the stairway.

It all happened so quickly that Josh didn't pay any attention. He opened the door to their room and started to step aside for her to enter. Emily shoved him in ahead of her and followed him, closing the door quickly behind her.

"What have you gotten us into?" she demanded.

He shoved his Stetson to the top of his forehead. "I beg your pardon?"

"Just what kind of place is this? I just saw a man come out of the room across the hall, and there was a naked woman on the bed."

"So?" he asked, confused. "It's not exactly an unusual situation."

"Is this a brothel, MacKenzie?"

"Your guess is as good as mine. I know this is

the only saloon in town, this is the only place where we can rent a room, and this is the only place where we can get a meal. It's not beyond my imagination to believe this is also the only place where . . . other services are offered."

"Well, do you think a bathroom might be one of those services?"

"End of the hall."

"Then I shall freshen up." She poked her head out of the door to make sure the hallway was empty, then hurried down to the door at the end of it. Turning her head to look back, she discovered that Josh had followed her. "What are you doing?"

"Accompanying you."

"No, you aren't. There are some places where I demand privacy."

"I merely intend to fill this ewer and check out the room in case there's an open window you might be tempted to climb out."

"Rest assured, MacKenzie, I have no intentions of attempting to escape from you. This town is creepy. It would be like jumping out of the frying pan into the fire."

"Gee, I'm flattered at the compliment," he said, checking the room. "No window. Too bad, Miss Lawrence. No hot water, either," he said, filling the ewer.

"What a surprise."

"Lock the door," he warned on his way out.

She gave him a disgusted look. "You can be sure of it."

As much as she would have liked to bathe, she questioned the cleanliness of the tub. The towel was just as suspect, so she removed her bodice and reached gingerly for the faucet, not knowing what would come out of that. Much to her surprise the cold water ran clear and cool, so she wet her handkerchief and proceeded to cleanse her body.

The quick sponge bath refreshed her, and when she returned to the room, she saw that Josh had shaved and freshened up as well. He now looked his usual clean-shaven and handsome self.

"How about something to eat?"

"If that's a dinner invitation, Detective, I accept," she said.

There were now several additional people in the saloon, some eating at tables, others standing at the bar. She was the only female, and with all eyes on her, Emily felt like a chicken surrounded by a wolf pack.

She saw no sign of the huge man she'd seen upstairs, and the table where the four men had been playing cards was now empty.

The bartender came over and swiped a wet cloth that looked like it hadn't been washed in months across the table.

"What'll it be, folks?"

"Steak and potatoes," Josh said.

"And the lady?"

"I'll have the same," Emily said. "With a fresh garden salad."

"A what?" he asked.

"A salad—fresh greens."

"Lady, we've got steak, potatoes, eggs, smoked ham, or beans and salt pork. We ain't got no fresh greens."

"Very well, steak and potatoes will do. And a glass of iced tea, please."

The bartender snickered. "Sorry, lady, the ice man didn't deliver today." That brought a round of laughter from several of the men nearby. "Lady, if we had ice, we'd sure as hell not waste it on iced tea." The choir offered another chorus of laughter.

Emily was becoming exasperated by his continuing mockery of her. "Which, no doubt, is why this place is called Purgatory," she declared.

"Bring her a glass of sarsaparilla," Josh interrupted, ending the exchange. "And I'll have a beer."

The man walked off, shaking his head, grumbling, "Iced tea!"

The steak was as tough as shoe leather, but after two days with nothing to eat except the cactus fruit, Emily ate voraciously. She chewed every bite of it and the fried potatoes that accompanied it.

"Do you suppose they have a general store in this town?" she asked, after finishing the meal.

"They'd have to; what do you need?"

"A jar of cold cream."

"Cold cream!"

"Yes. The sun dries all the moisture out of the skin besides causing freckles."

"You know, I'm beginning to believe that the sun made you a little touched in the head. If this damn town doesn't have ice, what makes you think a store would have cold cream?"

"Really, MacKenzie," she scoffed, "the cream's not *cold*. It's just called that because it moistens the skin."

"I know what it is," he declared. "I was merely pointing out the ridiculousness of thinking a store in this godforsaken town would stock such an item."

"Well, why don't we find out?" she asked smugly.

"I think we've attracted enough attention as it is. We're going to go straight back to our room, barricade the door, and hope we can get out of this town

in the morning with the clothes still on our backs."
He shoved back his chair and stood up. "Let's go."

Once back in their room, Josh said, "I have to
make arrangements for us to get out of here in the
morning. Can I trust you to remain in this room
while I'm gone?"

"Why can't I come with you?"

"Because I'm trying to avoid attracting any more
attention than we have already—and you attract a
lot of attention. It's dark now, and a man alone
won't be that conspicuous. I shouldn't be gone any
longer than ten or fifteen minutes. Don't open the
door to anyone but me. Do you understand?"

"Very well."

Josh slipped out the door and waited until he
heard the key click in the lock, then he took the rear
stairway and went out the back door. He remained
in the shadows as much as possible on his way to
the livery.

He found the young boy in Buttercup's stall. The
lad obviously had groomed and curried the mare and
was feeding her a sugar cube when Josh joined them.

"How's she doing, son?"

"Real good, mister," the boy said. "She's a good
ole gal." Buttercup nuzzled the boy's hand, and he
grinned widely. "And she likes me, too."

"Looks to me like you've grown just as fond of
her."

This time the boy's grin was shy. "Yeah, we took
to each other real quick."

"Do you have a horse of your own?"

"Kinda. We got a team for the wagon, but Ma
don't let me ride 'em, lessen one of 'em break a leg
or somethin'."

"Is there just you and your ma?"

"Yep," he said, giggling as Buttercup nuzzled him again.

"What happened to your pa?"

"Ain't never knowed my pa. Ma told me he dealt cards at the saloon when she worked there. Rode off afore I wuz born." It wasn't hard for Josh to put the pieces together as the boy continued, "When Ma got too old to work the saloon anymore, Mr. Kerry gave her the money to open this livery."

"How old are you? Say, what's your name, son?"

"Tim Jefferson. I'm twelve years old."

If the boy was telling the truth, he was rather small for his age. "Can you handle a wagon and team, Tim?"

"Heck, mister, I've been driving that wagon since I wuz nine."

Recalling his own youth on the ranch, Josh remembered he'd learned to handle a team just as young. "Do you think you could drive us to Lordsburg in the morning?"

"Sure can, mister. Ma's plannin' on sendin' me there fer supplies tomorrow, anyway."

"How about sunrise? We want to get an early start in case there's a morning train. Pick us up at the rear of the saloon."

"Sure will, mister."

"And, Tim, how would you like to keep Buttercup as your own?"

He shook his head. "Like to, but we can't afford to buy no horse."

"You don't have to buy her. I'll give her to you if you show up on time and don't pass the word around when we're leaving."

"You mean it?" he exclaimed.

"I sure do."

"Heck, mister, you bet I'll be there on time. And I sure won't say a word to anyone 'ceptin' my ma. I don't keep no secrets from her, mister."

Josh smiled and tapped him on the head. "That's good, son. Sounds like we've got a deal." He extended his hand. "It's customary for men to shake hands to bind a deal."

Tim grinned, puffing up with pride, and put his hand in Josh's. "It's a deal, mister."

On his way back to the saloon, seeing a light in the general store, Josh hesitated, then went inside.

"What'll it be, stranger?" the storekeeper asked. "Getting ready to close up, so make it quick."

The man was short and skinny and losing the battle with a head of thinning gray hair. Josh disliked him on sight. In his line of business, he'd learned to separate the wheat from the chaff in a glance.

"Couple of cigars." Although he rarely smoked, he figured cigars would cause less suspicion. He glanced around, hoping to spy what he was looking for. Seeing some toilet articles, he meandered over to the shelf and picked up a small white jar. The label read *Lady Godiva's Skin Moistener* and had a woman on horseback, her long flowing hair covering her obviously intended nakedness.

Well, I'll be damned!

"Anything else?" the storekeeper asked.

Josh handed him the jar. "Just this."

The storekeeper winked and grinned, exposing a missing front tooth. "Bet that's for Sally, huh?"

"If that's the name of the gal at the saloon."

"Yeah, she's the only one who uses it. Order it just for her. That be twenty cents for the cigars and a dollar for the cream." He grinned lewdly. "Can't figure out why she wastes her money on this here face cream. Her face ain't what fellas go there to feel. Heh! Heh! Heh!" he cackled. "Reckon she's costin' ya three bucks tonight, 'stead of two."

Tossing down some coins, Josh grabbed his purchases and got out of there.

Chapter 21

Emily opened the drawstrings of her purse, extracted a lacy handkerchief, and patted her forehead. Then, tossing the purse on the bed, she returned to the window and tried for the dozenth time to open it. The darn thing wouldn't budge. Disgusted, she returned to pacing the floor. She should have gone to the bathroom before Josh left, but he had said he'd be back in a few minutes, and it now seemed like hours. Regardless of her promise to him, she couldn't delay any longer.

Unlocking the door, she peeked out into the hallway. Seeing it was empty, she locked the door and slipped the key into her pocket as she scurried down the hallway.

When she was ready to return to the room, she opened the bathroom door to see if the coast was clear or if Josh was waiting outside the door of their room. But there still was no sign of him. As she hurried back, she heard the thud of heavy footsteps on the stairway. The lumbering rhythm sounded like that of the huge man she'd seen earlier. He was the last person she wanted to encounter in the hallway, and she dug into her pocket for the key. In her nervousness it slipped through her fingers and dropped to the floor.

The steps drew nearer, and she knew that any second he'd reach the top. Snatching the key up from the floor, she turned it in the lock just as he came around the corner.

The bearded behemoth drew up in surprise. "Well, look who we've got here," he said in a guttural voice that sounded like it roared from the pit of his huge girth. "How come ya been hidin', Blondie? I've been thinkin' of ya."

The key stuck in the lock, and she struggled to get it out. "I've got nothing to say to you."

"It weren't talkin' I had in mind."

Finally, the key came out, but he grabbed her arm before she could open the door.

"Ain't ya gonna invite me in, cutie? I bet this'll be two dollars well spent."

Her temper flared at the insinuation, and anger replaced caution. "How dare you!" She slapped him in the face. With a derisive snort, he pulled her against his bulk. He was too big to budge, so she followed Rose's schooling and did the next best thing—she slammed her knee between his legs.

Grunting, he dropped his hands from her shoulders and doubled over, clutching himself; his gasp of pain changing to what sounded like the growl of a bear.

Dashing into the room and slamming the door shut, Emily managed to get the key into the lock and turn it before he recovered. Leaning back against the door, she stood panting, trying to slow her pounding heart. At least she was safe behind the locked door.

Unfortunately, she'd no sooner begun to relax than his huge paws began hammering on the door.

"Your face ain't gonna look so pretty, bitch, when I get through with you," he shouted. The string of curses and threats continued, and the door vibrated from the force of his blows.

When the door began to crack, she knew it was sure to give way at any moment, and she'd be trapped in the room with no escape. Panic-stricken, she looked around for a weapon, and in desperation grabbed her purse from the bed just as the lock gave way and the door burst open.

His huge bulk filled the doorway. Like a young David facing a towering Goliath with only a sling-shot for a weapon, Emily whirled the purse above her head by the drawstrings to gather momentum. Then, with all her strength she swung it at him just as Josh appeared in the doorway. The bully ducked, and the purse struck Josh in the face, sending him reeling backward. Emily screamed and backed away as the man advanced on her.

Suddenly the bartender and several men arrived.

"Time to go to sleep, Orville," the bartender warned, and struck him on the head with a cudgel. The giant toppled over with a thud that shook the floor and rattled the glasses on the floor below.

"Orville gets a little crazy when he's had too much to drink," the bartender said. "Best to just keep out of his sight." Then her rescuers dragged the unconscious man out of the room.

Emily ran over to Josh, who was holding the side of his face. "Sit down so I can see what it looks like."

"What did you hit me with?"

"My purse."

"What have you got in there? Rocks?" he asked, lowering himself to the edge of the bed.

"I have a poke full of gold eagles at the bottom," she said, examining his face. "Your cheek's just a little red and swollen, but I'm afraid you're going to have a black eye."

"That's fine. That's just fine," he grumbled, and walked over to inspect the door. "The damn lock's broken, so now we won't be able to secure the door. I leave you alone for a few minutes, and look what happens."

"It's not my fault Orville broke in."

"I wouldn't bet on it. I've been around you enough to know you instigate trouble."

"Then why don't you leave? You're certainly not here at my invitation. Besides, I was only trying to defend my honor. He had no right to imply I was a prostitute."

"When did he do that?"

"In the hallway." She regretted the words the moment she said them. "Ah, that is, he was in the hallway and . . . ah—"

"So were you." He threw his hands up in the air in a gesture of hopelessness. "Can't you just once show some common sense?"

"I did. I *locked* the door when I went to the bathroom. And if I hadn't, I could have made it back into this room without being seen."

"I gave you explicit orders not to budge from this room."

"You also said you'd be back in a few minutes."

"And I would have been if I hadn't stopped for this!" He pulled a small jar out of his coat pocket and slammed it down on the dresser top.

Picking it up, she saw that it was a jar of cold cream.

"Thank you," she said, feeling contrite. He looked

ready to explode, so she thought she'd better not say anymore. She went over and gazed desolately out of the window. There was so much she wanted to say: how much the huge, drunken man had frightened her, how sorry she was he'd been injured. She wanted to hear him say he was glad she hadn't been harmed.

But mostly, she wanted him to hold her, to feel the comfort of his arms around her, soothing her body that still trembled from the incident.

He must have sensed her despair, because his voice sounded apologetic when he said, "At least we'll be out of here in the morning, Em. By this time tomorrow, we should be on a train heading east."

"Is that supposed to make me feel better?" she snapped. "I don't know which option is worse."

In a quick change of subject, he said, "I've got to get something for my eye before it swells shut. I'll try downstairs. I'll just be at the bottom of the stairs, so don't you budge from this spot."

"All of this wouldn't have happened if you'd taken me with you before."

"Maybe this wouldn't, but it's for darn sure *something* else would have."

So much for contrition, she thought, as she lit the oil lamp.

Josh returned within minutes, a hank of rope in one hand and a piece of raw steak on a plate in the other. After tying one end of the rope to the doorknob, he strung the other end to the bedpost, then shoved the dresser in front of the door. "Let's hope that does it."

She picked up the plate he'd set aside. "You'd

better do something about that eye. Lie down, and I'll give you a hand."

He bunched up a pillow and stretched out on the bed. She sat down beside him and put the steak on his eye.

The small lamp cast a pleasant glow, and she found herself relaxing. Josh, too, had relaxed, his face no longer etched with an angry frown.

"Does your eye hurt?"

"A little," he said. "How's your heel?"

"Fine. It stopped hurting."

"That's good."

She became more aware of the intimacy of the moment: he laying relaxed on the bed, she so near that his thigh was an exciting warmth against her hip.

"What did you do to that guy that made him so angry?"

"I slapped him in the face, and when that didn't help, I tried Rose's recommendation: I used my knee."

His chuckle brought a smile to her face and a warmth to her heart. "No wonder he wanted to kill you. You're lethal, Miss Lawrence."

This time there was no accusation in his voice, only a teasing huskiness that rippled up her spine.

"Does your eye feel any better?"

"Much," he murmured drowsily. Within seconds, the even rise and fall of his chest indicated he'd fallen asleep.

She returned the steak to the plate, then stared down at his sleeping face. This man was her nemesis, the biggest threat to the freedom she sought; yet she couldn't dislike him. On the contrary, her feelings were becoming dangerously the opposite:

she was falling in love with him. If she gave in to this growing attraction, she'd stop trying to escape from him—and as long as he put his mission ahead of her wishes, she couldn't let her resolve weaken.

She stood up and went over to the lamp, and after a final backward look at Josh, she snuffed out the flame, casting the room into darkness.

With not even a chair to sit upon, she had no option but to return to the bed. Fluffing up the pillow, she sat down with her back against the headboard to think about her confusing feelings for him. Her last conscious thought before drifting into slumber was that these feelings were coming from her heart, not her head, because there wasn't the remotest bit of common sense to them.

She woke to the feel of the slide of Josh's lips along her cheek. Opening her eyes, she looked up into the tenderness of his incredible sapphire eyes.

"You're so beautiful, Em." He lowered his head and covered her lips in a tentative kiss. When she parted her lips, he increased the pressure, sending sweet passion racing through her. "I've wanted to do this from the moment I saw you again in Winslow," he said in a husky murmur at her ear.

"This is a mistake, Josh. You must stop. One night of pleasure won't change what we face tomorrow."

He cut off her protests with a kiss that was more urgent, more demanding. Her emotions were in turmoil. She knew she should stop him, but the sensations his kiss created were too exquisite to forsake. Anything that felt so wonderful could never be a mistake.

"I want you, Em. I ache from the need of it. I've

thought of nothing but this moment for weeks: what I would do, what I would say."

"Then do it, Josh. Say it. Because I've thought of nothing else, too."

Her heart began pounding in her breast when he released the buttons of her bodice and pushed it off her shoulders. A tremor raced down her spine when his lips slid along the column of her neck, while his fingers made short work of the tiny buttons of her shift. Parting it, he freed her breasts. She felt the air on their nakedness and gloried in seeing his eyes fill with a mixture of awe and lust as he gazed at them.

"Lord, Em, everything about you is beautiful."

His words made her feel beautiful. She lay in sensual wantonness, reveling in the promise of what was to follow.

Lowering his head, he took one of the hardened peaks into his mouth.

"Oh, yes. Yes," she moaned, pressing his head to her breast as the flames of sweet passion ignited with exquisite sensation beyond any pleasure she'd ever fantasized. "Make love to me, Josh."

"I intend to make love to you—that's what you've been dreaming I'd do, isn't it?"

Yes. I want you to." When he reached for the band of her skirt to rip it off her, she cried, "No, stop that. You'll ruin my skirt."

"But you fire my blood, Em. I lust for you. I can't wait."

She shoved his hands away. "No, stop. Let me do it."

"Em, you've got to wake up."

She opened her eyes. Josh was shaking her shoulder. "I'm sorry, Em. I know you're tired, but we have to leave now."

"Yes, of course." She stood up, embarrassed and shaken by the dream. "I'll be ready in a minute."

Picking up the ewer, she poured some water into the basin, then hastily cleansed her face and brushed her teeth. After adjusting her disheveled hair and clothing, she pinned on her hat and closed her valise.

"Ready?"

He'd waited in silence, and as she turned around, she saw his black eye.

"How is your eye this morning?"

"Looks worse than it feels." He shoved the dresser away from the door and untied the rope, then picked up the valises, and they left the room. "This way," he said, when she turned to go down the stairway. "The back stairs."

"Sneaking out without paying, MacKenzie?" she said lightly.

"I paid the bill last night when I got the steak for my eye."

"Oh, darn!" she said. "You're no fun."

"Haven't you had enough fun, Miss Lawrence?"

"Got up on the wrong side of the bed this morning, did you?"

"No, just had a restless night. I didn't get much sleep."

True to his word, Tim was waiting at the rear of the building and greeted them with a wide smile.

" 'Morning, folks. Looks to be like a fine day." His eyes widened in surprise. "Wow! What happened to your eye, Mr. MacKenzie?"

"Wrong place at the wrong time, Tim," Josh said, tossing the luggage into the bed of the wagon.

"You look like one of them pirates in picture

books," Tim said, as Josh helped Emily up onto the seat. The touch of his hand on her arm was an exciting reminder of how real the dream had been to her.

"Move 'em out, Tim," he said, climbing up beside her.

As the town fell behind them, Emily turned her head and looked back. For a few moments, in the fantasy of her dream, Purgatory had been Heaven.

Seated between Josh and the young boy, she tried to listen to their conversation, but her thoughts continually returned to her troubling awareness of Josh MacKenzie. She was beginning to understand why the previous images in her dreams had always resembled him and last night had finally become him. In the beginning his pursuit of her had been a threatening thorn in her side, but now it was clear that the thorn had pierced her heart.

For the sake of her well-being, she had to get away from him and put romantic fantasies out of her mind—and heart—once and for all.

Josh still felt hornier than hell. Horny and irritable. Last night, when he woke up and found Emily sleeping next to him, he had to draw on every ounce of control to keep his hands off her. Any further attempt at sleep had become an exercise in futility. And now, seated beside her, the faint fragrance of her perfume was playing havoc with his senses, and the simplest contact of her arm or thigh sent jolts of arousal through him—an unwelcome sensation that distracted him from his purpose: getting this blond-haired temptress back to Long Island.

The narrow wagon seat had not been intended for three people to sit comfortably. Her nearness was too disturbing ... too intoxicating ... and sure as hell, too arousing. He had to get away.

"I'm tired. Think I'll climb in the back and get some sleep."

With his valise as a pillow, Josh stretched out on the wagon bed. But closing his eyes didn't help to shut out her image.

"What's that in the distance, Tim?" Emily asked a short time later. "It looks like a church steeple."

"It is, ma'am. We're nearing Lordsburg."

An actual church! She couldn't believe it. It seemed as if she'd been wandering through a god-forsaken wilderness forever, though it had only been a few days.

As the wagon rumbled down an actual paved street, Emily glanced around. There were several stone buildings; a couple of them were even three and four stories high. They passed a bank, a pharmacy, the city jail, and a hotel—which could mean a hot bath!

"Where's the railroad station, Tim?" Josh asked, climbing up front and settling down next to her.

"Just a little ways up ahead, Mr. MacKenzie."

Turning a corner, they saw it—railroad tracks stretching as far as the eye could see.

As soon as Tim drew up in front of the depot, Josh jumped off, then swung Emily down. She glanced around with interest. Strange, how much all railroad depots looked alike.

"Thanks, Tim," Josh said, after retrieving their luggage.

"Hope you folks have a good trip," Tim said. "Where you headed, Mr. MacKenzie?"

"East to New York."

"New York! Wow! Hope some day I'll get to see New York. Heard a lot about it."

"I hope you will, too, Tim," Emily said, thinking of the desolate town of Purgatory. "And take good care of Buttercup."

"Sure will, ma'am. Much obliged to you for givin' her to me."

"Good-bye, son," Josh said, slipping a gold eagle into the boy's palm as they shook hands. "Thanks again for your help."

With a heavy heart, Emily watched silently as the wagon creaked down the road. From the sadness on his face, Emily knew that Josh's thoughts were the same as hers: what future lay ahead for a young boy raised in Purgatory?

"Let's see when the next train's due," Josh said, picking up their bags.

She sat down on a wooden bench while Josh went up to the ticket agent's cage. He came back, smiling, two tickets in hand.

"What a coincidence: there's a southbound Lone Star train due in an hour. We can make a connection with the Santa Fe in Winslow."

"Oh, my, yes, what a big coincidence," she replied, disgruntled.

"My father's cousins own the Lone Star."

"Small world, isn't it?"

"Gotta admit, Miss Lawrence, it's becoming one."

"I hoped I could bathe before leaving."

"If you hurry, you can get in a bath; but if you're planning on dawdling, hoping we'll miss the train, it's not going to happen. I'll yank you out of there, ready or not."

She nodded in agreement. "I can be in and out in thirty minutes."

They walked down the block to a bathhouse. "No tricks, Em. I'll be right outside the door, waiting," he warned, handing Emily her valise.

At the moment, the thought of a bath was far more appealing than any attempt to escape. She hurried inside.

The bathhouse was divided into two rooms in a division of the sexes. A man at the desk gave her a towel and bar of soap when she paid her dollar. He informed her the towel and soap were to be returned when she left.

The women's room was empty and much to her relief appeared to be clean and tidy. A partition created two shower stalls. She would have preferred the comfort of sinking into a hot bath but quickly shed her clothes and turned on the shower.

It was heaven. Refreshing. Stimulating. She sang out like an opera diva as she soaped herself thoroughly and revelled in the feel of the suds and water cleansing her body. She would have loved to linger under it longer, but she didn't doubt for a moment that Josh would do exactly what he'd threatened if she wasn't ready on time. Soaping her hair, she rubbed it vigorously to make sure she rid it of every particle of dirt and sand, and had just finished dressing in fresh clothing when Josh rapped on the door.

"Time's up, Emily."

"I'm coming." After one final stroke to her hair, she shoved the brush into her valise. She could always pin up her hair later, when it dried.

Grabbing her valise, she hurried to the door, only to rush back and gather up the towel and bar of soap.

Clean-shaven and wearing a change of clothing, Josh stood waiting. At her look of surprise, he grinned.

"I was in the shower stall next door. Do you always sing in the shower?"

"No, I usually limit my operatic inclinations to the bathtub," she said, laughing.

The distant wail of a train whistle brought the conversation to a quick close. "Let's get going," Josh said.

Five minutes later, Emily leaned back into the velvet plushness of a seat in the lounge car as the train puffed out of Lordsburg. Freshly showered, ensconced in a comfortable chair, and sipping an iced tea—with ice—she closed her eyes and reflected on the past few days. As much as she loved the beauty and vastness of the West, she had to concede that much could be said in defense of civilization.

Chapter 22

Emily screamed as the bedroom door splintered. She jerked up, clutching the sheet to her neck. The tall figure kicked aside the broken wood and strode into the room, a long black cloak swirling at his ankles.

"Who . . . who are you?"

He moved nearer. In the dim light she saw that wisps of dark hair had slipped from under a red bandanna tied at the back of his neck. A gold loop hung from his ear, and an eyepatch covered his left eye. Heavy dark whiskers masked his jaw.

"What do you want?" she asked, grasping the sheet more firmly.

"Why, what else, my lady, but you?"

Pulling off his cloak with the flair and grace of a matador, he flung it aside. An open white satin shirt exposed a tapering trail of dark hair that vanished under the waistband of skin-tight black trousers. Her gaze paused momentarily on the intriguing bulge at the junction of his legs before continuing down muscular thighs to where his long legs disappeared into knee-high boots.

"Do you mean you intend to ravage me?" she asked, in a quaking voice.

"Ah, but it will be a rapturous ravage, my lovely."

"You sound just like my friend, Rose," she declared, recovering her composure. "That clearly is an oxymoron. Ravage indicates violent destruction; rapture, on the other hand, is an emotion of divine ecstasy. Therefore, one could never experience an ecstatic—"

"All right, all right; I get the picture!" he growled. Then his voice softened to a mesmerizing huskiness again. "Ah, my lady, once I whisk you away to my ship, you will never know such bliss. We will sail the seas, plundering ports during the day, but the nights . . . ah, the nights, my lovely, will be filled with mindless passion."

"Plunder? You're a pirate!"

"Of course. What else could I be dressed in these clothes and a gold loop hanging from my ear?"

"I thought you were Josh. He's the only one who invades my dreams. Plunder, indeed! I would never steal anything."

"Rumor has it that you stole money from your own father, my lovely Emily."

"First, Mr. Pirate, I am not your lovely Emily; and secondly, I'm tired of hearing that bold-faced lie my father invented repeated to me. I have never taken one thing that didn't belong to me."

The brow over his visible sapphire eye arched in skepticism. "Nothing? What about the booty you plundered from the very admirable lawman MacKenzie?"

"Booty? I've never plundered any—" Her eyes widened in recollection. "You mean his badge?

Surely you aren't considering that stupid badge booty!"

He cocked his brow again. "A rose by any other name, my lady."

"Well, I don't wish to go with you, so get out of here, or I shall start screaming."

Grinning wickedly, he sat down on the edge of the bed, gently pressed her back, and lowered his head until their breath mingled. "Then you force me to convince you."

He covered her mouth with a masterful, drugging kiss that melted any hope of resistance. She trembled with excitement as he trailed spine-tingling kisses down her neck. Raising his head, he reached out and slowly slid the gown off her shoulders.

"No outcry, my lady?" he asked, gently tracing a finger around the taut peaks of her breasts.

"You're an unconscionable blackguard." Her breath began coming in gasps when his moist mouth closed around a hardened peak, sending erotic shivers through her.

Lifting his head enough to meet her gaze, he said, "You want me to believe that you do not enjoy this?"

"What does it matter whether I do or not? I still won't change my mind and go with you." He lowered his head again. This time his tongue toyed with the peaks, and the tantalizing sensation was exquisite. "Oh, please, you must stop!"

Cupping his hands around a breast, he took it in his mouth and suckled like a nursing babe. Moaning, she closed her eyes, writhing beneath the rapturous assault to her senses. "Indeed, you are a merciless pirate, so ravage me if you must, for I no longer have the strength to fight you."

His eye gleamed with mockery. "Strength or will, my lady?"

"Call it what you wish. You'll have your way regardless."

He sat up. "Unfortunately, so will the clock. Time is fleeting. We must hurry or we'll miss the tide. And like it or not, you are coming with me, Emily."

He grabbed the pillowcase, put it over her head, and swept her up in his arms. She swatted and thrashed to try and free herself, but the more she struggled, the more enveloped she became. "Let me alone! I don't wish to go with you. Do you hear me? I'm not going with you!"

"Yes, I heard you. The whole train heard you. Will you please be quiet?"

Emily opened her eyes. Her tangled hair was wrapped around her face and mouth. Brushing it aside, she saw Josh peering at her with a disgruntled look made more fierce by the discoloration around his left eye.

"Good Lord, Emily, everyone's looking at you. Why do you insist upon making these ridiculous scenes in public? They don't work."

"I wasn't trying to escape. I was dreaming."

"You're dreaming, all right, if you think you're going to get away." He stood up and got her valise. "We'll reach Winslow in a few minutes. I suggest you do something with your hair; even that dumb bonnet you wear would be an improvement."

"It's not a bonnet, it's a hat," she said, snatching the valise from him. "And it's not any dumber than the one you wear." Gritting her teeth, Emily pulled out her hairpins and brush. Hastily pinning up her hair, she adjusted the drooping flower and put on the straw hat. Then she sat back, folded her hands primly in her lap, and waited to disembark.

When she stepped off the train, she looked around at Winslow. Nothing appeared changed. It didn't seem possible that only a few days ago she had climbed off a similar train and seen the town for the first time. And now it was hard to believe that some of the bizarre events of the these past days had even occurred.

After a short conversation with the ticket seller, Josh paid for their tickets, and a porter took their bags. *He looks pleased with himself,* she thought as Josh walked over to her.

"We're all set. Train arrives in ninety minutes."

"Do you ever feed your prisoners, Detective MacKenzie?"

"I was about to suggest it. This time we'll go to the Harvey restaurant." He took her arm. "I don't think Sheriff Charlie Bowes would take kindly to our showing up at his diner again."

"It's unbelievable what a contrast a Harvey restaurant is to other western restaurants," Emily remarked a short time later. She looked around with admiration at the luxury of the spotlessly clean establishment and popped the last bite of a light and fluffy egg soufflé into her mouth.

During the course of their meal the train had arrived, and the restaurant was now full of passengers eating breakfast. An attractive waitress with a pleasant smile, garbed in her meticulous Harvey Girl uniform, immediately came over and removed the plate. "Would you like another cup of tea, ma'am?"

"No, thank you. Everything was delicious," Emily replied wistfully. Her heart felt heavy as she recalled that just last week at this time she, too, was a Harvey Girl.

"If you're finished, I'm sure we can board," Josh said.

She sighed deeply. "I don't suppose I could convince you to change your mind about this."

"Don't waste your time trying. If I don't do it, someone else will track you down and take you back. If what you say is true, you shouldn't have a problem proving the money you took was yours. And since you're of age to do what you wish, once you prove your innocence, your father can't force you to remain."

She threw down her napkin. "You still don't get it, do you, MacKenzie? My father is a powerful and influential man. He doesn't even have to bribe people to get what he wants. You're naive if you think any bank president would risk losing the account of Hiram Lawrence just to prove my innocence."

"Even so, I can't believe your own father would have you incarcerated."

"I didn't say he would. In his own despotic way, I'm sure he loves me, but that doesn't mean he'd give me my freedom. He needs me there under his thumb to marry one of those effeminate minions who grovel around him swelling his ego, and to produce an heir to follow in the footsteps of his illustrious grandfather, Hiram Bertram Lawrence."

"Pretty tough shoes to fill," Josh said.

"The only reason I got away from him was because he didn't expect me to run away. But once I'm back, he'll have me watched every moment."

"That's your story; I've been told a different one— and if it goes beyond theft, it's none of my business. I'm being paid to find you and take you back."

"Duty and honor before all else, is that it, Detective MacKenzie?" she said bitterly. "Forgive me, I didn't know such noble qualities existed in mercenary bounty hunters."

He stood up, his face hardened with restraint. "Time to leave, Miss Lawrence."

For a long moment she sat staring up into his impassive sapphire eyes, then she got to her feet, and they left the restaurant.

Outside, the shouts of porters and brakemen could be heard above the hiss of steam as the train idled, waiting for the passengers to reboard.

Josh sent a wire to his home office, and after a short conversation with the porter, the man picked up their luggage and they boarded the train. He led them to a private Pullman sleeping compartment.

"We'll be departin' soon, suh," he said, putting down their luggage. "If you or your missus need anything, just ask for Jeb."

"Thank you, Jeb." Josh tipped him, then closed and locked the door.

"A private compartment," Emily remarked. "If I'd known you were wealthy sooner, MacKenzie, I'd have called it to Rose's attention. She's looking for a rich husband."

"I'm on an expense account, and it should please you to know that your father is paying for this. Considering the public scenes you make in your attempts to escape, I thought this would be an easier and less embarrassing solution for the rest of the trip."

"Surely you don't expect me to remain cooped up in this small compartment with you for the next few days?"

"That's exactly what I expect. This can be as pleasant or unpleasant as you choose to make it, because like it or not, Miss Lawrence, that's exactly what you'll be doing."

Oh, how he infuriated her. Every time she lowered her guard enough to trust him, he showed his true colors—the lowdown, bounty-hunting, snake in the grass!

She flounced into the room and sat down, and began drumming her fingers on the table. It would take some serious thinking to get herself out of this situation, but she wouldn't go down without a fight. *Where there's a will, there's a way,* she reminded herself; and the one thing she had was a strong will.

Josh removed his jacket and hung it on a peg. Then he loosened his tie, rolled the sleeves of his shirt up to his elbows, and pulled a folded newspaper out of his coat pocket. He sat down and buried his face behind the newspaper.

Emily sat deep in thought until he lowered the paper.

"Is it your intent to drive me crazy with that finger-drumming?"

"Oh, does it bother you? Sorry, MacKenzie." She intensified the drumming.

It produced a grin from him. "If you wear down those lovely fingers too much, Miss Lawrence, they'll be worthless for picking your father's pocket." His face disappeared again behind the paper.

She sat for several minutes looking across the table at the upraised newspaper, then she stood up and removed her hat. A glance in the mirror reminded her of the necessity for some hair grooming, so she dug into her valise and retrieved the last of her hairpins.

By the time she finished pinning her hair up properly, the train had pulled out of the station and Josh was still engrossed in the paper.

Returning to her seat, Emily leaned back and stared out the window at the passing countryside.

It was a long way to Long Island.

Josh could almost hear the wheels grinding away in that beautiful head of hers. He tried to concentrate on the newspaper but couldn't remember one word he'd read. His awareness of her was too distracting. The essence of her filled the small compartment with a tantalizing combination of the scent of lavender and seductive female. If he could bottle it, he'd die rich.

Lowering the paper enough to peek over the top, he saw she was fussing with her hair. For days he'd been fighting the overwhelming need to dig his hands into that gorgeous mass of sunshine and feel the golden silken strands curl around his fingers. Just the thought made his fingers itch, and the paper crunched when he curled his hands into fists.

Despite the serene look on her face, her body hummed with the steadfast determination to escape— a clarion warning that the battle between them still waged. She wouldn't go down without a fight. Not Emily Lawrence.

In a few days it would all be over. He was too cautious to be celebrating a victory yet; he had no intention of falling on his own sword. The end was too near to allow himself to be distracted by romantic thoughts of her.

There were a dozen things he wanted to say to her—to offer the reassurance that he was on her side, would stand by her and help her get through this mess with her father. He hoped she wasn't lying about the money, because if she was, he had no idea how to pay it back or even how much she still had left of it. She couldn't have squandered it all away, but she'd been working her little butt off for seventeen dollars and fifty cents a month—which seemed unlikely for someone sitting on a cache of stolen money.

What he did know for certain was that she was in his blood. He couldn't just dump her on her daddy's doorstep like a sack of grain and walk away.

But for now, he had no intention of lowering his guard. He dared not even hint of his intention. If she sensed his vulnerability, she'd use it against him in an effort to escape.

Oh, he definitely had future plans for the very lovely Miss Emily Lawrence. She was too much woman to let her slide through his fingers.

But until then . . . it was a long way to Long Island.

Chapter 23

❧ ⌒◯◯⌒

When Emily finally got over her snit enough to relax, she settled back on the seat and allowed herself the pleasure of enjoying the scenery. Red rock buttes and cliffs jutted majestically against an azure sky. In a blink of an eye, shifting shadows would deepen the rock formations to orange, and they resembled a huge, terra-cotta canvas, too brilliant and spectacular to be real.

The train stopped at Albuquerque for lunch, and when it was time to reboard, the conductor announced there would be a two-hour delay for an emergency repair on the engine.

Even though they had done enough walking in the past couple of days to last her a lifetime, Emily was relieved when Josh suggested they take a walk. Remaining cooped up in the small compartment with him was too disturbing. She'd been too aware of him sitting across from her, too aware of him filling the small space. No matter how much she reminded herself that the man was destroying her life, he excited her. And whatever lay ahead for her future, the memory of him would always be foremost in her mind.

As they strolled away from the depot, they both seemed to relax and become comfortable with each other again. By the time they reached the plaza the tension between them had completely dissipated, and they were laughing and enjoying the sights of the old city with its colorful adobe buildings, tepees, and the signs of western civilization—cowboys in boots and Stetsons.

Despite having just eaten, neither could resist stopping at a stand where an old woman was preparing tortillas. Each sampled one before continuing on to where an Indian woman sat cross-legged on the ground beside a blanket laid out with turquoise and silver jewelry. Josh bought Emily a brooch she admired, and as he pinned it on her, they stared deeply into each other's eyes.

"Is my father paying for this, too?" she asked softly.

"No," he said simply, his gaze still locked with hers.

This must be how lovers act, she thought. And for a few precious moments, she felt as if they were two young lovers instead of sworn adversaries.

The toll of the bell from the steeple of a century-old church reminded them of the hour.

"We best get back to the train," Josh said, "or it might pull out without us."

She glanced up at him and saw the same regret in his eyes that she was feeling: the holiday had ended, and the real world had closed in on them again. "And that would be terrible, wouldn't it, Detective MacKenzie?"

He didn't respond, and they reversed their course.

"What an interesting city," Emily declared on

their way back to the depot. "A fascinating blend of Spanish, Indian, and Anglo cultures."

"I think you'll find that's true of most of the towns in this region. Four flags have flown over this city since the Spanish founded it: Spain, Mexico, the United States, and even the Confederate flag for a brief time during the Civil War."

Shortly after their return to the depot, the train's whistle blasted a warning call to alert the passengers.

"All aboard," the conductor called, and within minutes the train chugged out of town.

As the train rolled along the plateau toward the Sandia Mountains to the east, Emily waved back at several cowboys herding cattle.

"Were you ever a cowboy, Josh?"

"Sure. Reckon it's true of most of the men in Texas. When the men went off to war, they turned their cattle loose, because the women couldn't take care of them and the land, too. For nearly five years the cattle roamed wild, until what was left of the men came back."

"And what happened when the men came back?"

"The cattle had bred and roamed wild in the brush. If there was no brand on them, the cows were free for the taking. So a lot of the men rounded up the cattle and became cowboys. In the years that followed, Texas cowboys drove over four million steers from the Rio Grande to the Canadian Rockies."

"I've read about those cattle drives," Emily said. "They sounded so heroic and dangerous—herding hundreds of long-horned steers over hundreds of miles, through swollen rivers, across arid land, Indian territory—"

"Not to mention the weather, which could range

from blazing heat to snow, lightning storms, and hail. And let's not forget the snakes and animals— wolves, cougars, bears—and the beasts of human variety: discharged soldiers of both armies, outlaws, and Jayhawkers."

"What are Jayhawkers?"

"Pro-Union gangs in Kansas who tried to charge the Texans, who'd fought for the Confederacy, for driving the herds across Kansas. If the Texans wouldn't pay, it usually ended up in a gun battle. They tried it on my dad and uncles once."

"And what happened?"

He looked at her, grinning. "If you knew my dad and uncles, you wouldn't have to ask."

She sighed, caught up in the heroics of it. "And despite all those dangers, the expanding country needed that beef, and thanks to those heroic Texans, the nation was fed. It's no wonder you Texans are so proud of your heritage."

"There's a lot more than just cattle drives to our heritage, Em. We fought alone for our independence." His eyes glowed with pride. "The Mexicans at the Alamo and San Jacinto; the Comanche and Apache just to stay alive. Nobody helped us. We formed the Texas Rangers to keep law and protect our borders. That's why we call ourselves the Lone Star state. Gotta admit, though, the advent of trains helped to settle things down a bit—not only in Texas, but the whole country. Once those herds were driven to Kansas, it was the railroads that carried the cattle to the Chicago stockyards; brought California grapes to the midwest, Wisconsin vegetables, Iowa corn, and Georgia peaches to the whole damn country." He grinned broadly. "And most important—thanks to the Atchison, Topeka, and Santa Fe Railroad— brought beautiful Harvey Girls to the West."

Emily's thoughts still hovered on the marvel of those inspiring cattle drives. "I admit that the coming of the railroad was significant, but I just think those Texas cattle drives were awesome."

"I went on one when I was younger."

Her eyes glowed with anticipation. "Really! You must tell me about it."

"Well, after Dad traced me to Mexico, he took me to California and became the sheriff of Stockton."

"What happened to your uncles?"

"They missed each other in the coming and going. They both were hunting down the gang that killed my mother and grandmother, particularly the leader, a guy named Charlie Walden. Dad was doing the same thing, because he heard the Walden Gang was active in California, but he was handicapped by having me to take care of; he couldn't live on the trail like Uncle Flint and Uncle Cleve. That's when he got the idea to send for a mail-order bride."

"Your father's second wife was a mail-order bride!" she exclaimed. "Oh, this is getting more interesting by the moment."

"Actually, she wasn't. Mom had taken the place of the woman Dad actually had sent for." He grinned. "That's another story in itself. Dad arrested her, hoping she'd stay and be a nursemaid to me. I was six years old then. Well, I reckon I don't have to tell you that they fell in love and married."

"It's tragic about your mother and grandmother, but the rest is so romantic," Emily said. "Now where does the part about the cattle drive come in?"

"After Charlie Walden shot my dad in the back."

"Shot in the back!" Emily's eyes almost bulged out of her head.

"Another story," he said, offhandedly. "My uncles heard about it and showed up, and we packed up and headed back to Texas. They took off again to track down Walden, while Mom and Dad got the ranch back in shape. Dad rounded up a herd, but Texas was dirt poor by then—it hadn't recovered from the war. Dad heard that the previous year one of the ranchers had driven a herd to Kansas and got big money, so he talked my uncles into trying it. I was seven years old that year, and I'll never forget it. For safety's sake, Dad wouldn't leave us behind— not that Mom would have stayed." He smiled that remarkable smile that always appeared whenever he mentioned her. It was clear to Emily how much he worshipped the woman who'd raised him.

"There was my Dad and Mom, Uncle Cleve, Maude Malone, Uncle Flint, Aunt Garnet—but she wasn't my aunt then. Uncle Flint had saved her from a Comanche massacre." His warm chuckle sent a ripple down Emily's spine. "Everyone knew Uncle Flint was in love with her, even though he kept denying it."

"But that's another story," she added, grinning.

His smile carried to his eyes. "Yeah, that's a whopper!"

"Well, go on—the cattle drive. Were there any others on the drive with you?"

The smile drained from his face. "Yeah, Joey and Jeb Boone, they were twin brothers."

"You said 'were,' " she remarked cautiously, sensing something ominous.

Once again his eyes filled with bitterness. "Yeah, Charlie Walden caught them alone on the drive and hung them for spite." He paused for several seconds, then continued, "Anyway, my family drove that herd to Kansas. Those remarkable women rode alongside their men, doing men's labor, fighting off attacks from Indians and Jayhawkers, and going to bed each night aching; but not a one of them would have had it any different. My folks and my uncles and aunts are the most incredible people I've ever met. They may not be the geniuses who make the world's wheels go round, but they're the best at what they do."

"You talk about them with such pride," Emily said. "It must be wonderful to be raised in a family that has so much love and respect for one another."

"Guess I never thought about it. It's always been there, something I've taken for granted."

"Well, I can tell you from experience that it's not true of all families, so don't *ever* take it for granted."

She was surprised to see a guilty downward shift of his eyes. "It can have it's drawbacks too, Em. I've always held such respect for my dad and uncles that I feel I can never live up to their level."

So Josh MacKenzie had an Achilles' heel after all. The knowledge should have given her satisfaction, but instead, she felt sad thinking about a young man feeling he was never quite good enough to follow in the footsteps of men he loved and respected. "With such role models, Josh, I would think you'd just want to try harder," she said softly.

"Or run off and join the Pinkerton Agency."

He turned his head and gazed out of the window. The conversation had ended.

What was left of the day soon passed into another breathtaking sunset.

"These sunsets and rises are so beautiful," Emily exclaimed, brushing out her hair as she prepared to go to bed. "If I lived out here, I'd be up every morning just to see the sun rise."

"Well, don't wake me if you decide to do so tomorrow morning," Josh groused.

"The trouble with you westerners is that you take everything for granted. You don't appreciate what you've got."

He looked at her with a disgusted expression. "Sometimes I can't believe the arrogance of you folks from the East. My Uncle Cleve tells a story about this lost easterner out west who rode up to an old-timer sitting on the porch of a rundown shack and asked, 'Could you tell me the way to Tombstone?' The old-timer raised his hand and pointed west. 'Can you tell me how many miles?' The old-timer said, 'Nope. Ain't never been there.' The man became impatient. 'Well, can you tell me how many miles it is to the nearest town?' The old-timer said, 'Nope, ain't never counted 'em.' Exasperated, the man declared, 'You don't seem to know much of anything, do you?' The old-timer thought for a moment, then spewed a stream of tobacco juice at a scorpion crawling past. 'I knowed I ain't the one that's lost.' "

He raised his brows, waiting for her reaction.

She frowned, "I don't understand the connection. What has that got to do with your statement regarding eastern arrogance?"

"Because, Miss Lawrence, we westerners don't need you visiting easterners to tell us how lucky we are. Why do you think we chose to live out here?"

"I apologize," she said. Kicking off her shoes, she crawled up onto her bunk and lay down. "I simply should have said that I envy you folks out here."

He came over and stood beside the tier of bunks. "Your left hand, please."

"Why?" she asked, but raised her hand.

He snapped a handcuff around her wrist, and heartache replaced her initial surprise.

It must have shown on her face, because he said, "I'm sorry, Em, but I can't take any chances of falling asleep and letting you escape, like you did at Winslow."

"How would I escape from a moving train?"

"You'd figure out a way somehow, I'm sure." He pulled the key out of his pocket. "If you give me your word you won't try to escape, I'll unlock it."

She was too devastated to challenge him further. In fact, despite his being right, she felt hurt that he continued to consider her nothing better than a thief and liar. If only she could make him understand that the only reason she lied to him was to avoid arrest.

"I can't do that, Josh." Her eyes welled with the tears she refused to release. "Try to understand—I have to do whatever I can to escape from you."

He looked at her sadly and slipped the key back into his pocket. "And you must understand, I'm honor bound to prevent you from succeeding."

She closed her eyes when he attached the other cuff to the side rail of the bunk. The click of the closing cuff was deafening. She fell asleep to the sound of rain pelting the window.

Emily awoke with the lingering sting of salty tears still in her eyes; she'd been crying in her sleep. Josh had not drawn the drapes when he went to bed, and she saw that the rain had stopped; moonlight now cast eerie shadows on the walls and ceiling as the train streaked through the night.

Leaning her head over the side of the bunk, she was able to discern Josh, stretched out on his back, asleep.

The key to her freedom was in his pocket—but how could she get it out without waking him? At this point she had nothing to lose. If he woke up, she'd be no worse off than she was now.

And if she succeeded, what then? How would she get off the train? They had to be nearing Las Vegas. If she managed somehow to get there, she knew she could count on help from Rose.

Somewhere, sometime, the train would have to slow down, and she could jump off. All she could do was hope it would happen before Josh woke up.

But first things first—she had to get the key.

Thankful for her height, she lowered herself from the bunk despite her arm still being cuffed to the side.

For a long moment, she gazed down at him. His face was shadowed with stubble, but he looked so peaceful and endearing, she wanted to reach out and caress his cheek.

I wish I could hate you, Josh, but I can't. It would be so easy if I did, but, there's no one I'd rather be with than you. The thought of leaving you is breaking my heart. If only I were Emily Lane—then we could have so much together. Instead . . .

She shook aside the thought, took a deep breath, and gingerly reached into his pocket.

She gasped when his hand clamped on her wrist like a vise.

"Is this what you want?" He held up the key.

She was too stunned to take it, so he unlocked the cuff on her wrist. Freed of the restraint, her arm dropped to her side, her gaze shackled to his.

She knew she should move away, but she remained bent over him, transfixed by the raw passion glimmering in his eyes. She'd missed that look in the past few days. At moments like this, it was hard to forget the intimacy they had once shared.

He released her wrist and reached up and wove his fingers into the thick hair at her nape, then slowly brought her head down to his until their breath mingled.

"Or is this really what you want?" Josh asked.

He pulled her down on him until she lay stretched out on top, her slim body molded to the hard muscle of his.

Oh, it felt divine. She wanted to relax and sink against his firm warmth and let him have his way with her—to finish what they had begun that beautiful day beside a pond near Las Vegas. Yet that could spell disaster for her; her womanly instinct told her she'd lose any hope of ever fleeing from him if she made love to him. She'd be his for the taking—and the taking was a trail leading straight back to Long Island.

Forcing a breath into her heaving lungs, she tried to reply. "No, I—"

His mouth snatched the words from her lips as he took possession of them. Whatever feeble protest had entered her mind was obliterated as she parted her lips beneath the electrifying pressure of his.

The kiss was deep and passionate with an intensity that aroused a need for more, deepening even as it drained the breath from her until she thought she'd swoon before he finally released her. She gasped for breath as he covered her cheeks and eyes with quick, moist kisses, each one an ember that fueled her passion. The glorious pressure of his lips reclaimed hers, his tongue ravishing her mouth until her senses were deafened by the blood pulsating in her head. His male scent, his touch, his taste all combined into a powerful force bombarding her already weakened resistance.

Closing her eyes, she threw back her head in a feeble effort to pull away, but the move only gave him freer access to her throat. He accepted the invitation willingly and opened the front of her bodice, then proceeded to run his tongue across the swell of her bosom. Impatient to free her breasts, he mumbled a curse when he encountered her combination. He tugged at the front of it, and tiny buttons popped in all directions.

It was so wrong, but it felt so divine. His recklessness, his impatience, his need, made her whole body tingle. She'd never felt this womanly before, and she gloried in her woman's body and his urgency to possess it.

She throbbed with rapturous sensation as he suckled and played with her breasts. Then he reclaimed her mouth, driving his tongue past her parted lips, the stroking heat like a bellows stoking the flames of her passion until the draw in her loins had her shifting beneath him. Instinctively she parted her legs, and the hardened pressure of his arousal filled the gap, intensifying a greater need. She wrapped her legs around him.

His mouth moved to her cheek, and he slid his tongue to the sensitive pulse at her ear. His warm breath ruffled the hair at her ear when he murmured hoarsely, "I want you, Em."

"Yes, yes. I want you, too, Josh. Now, please. Take me now."

Her fingers fluttered along his neck and inside his

shirt. She made as short work of his buttons as he'd made of hers, then her smaller, softer hands touched his chest. He buried his head in the valley of her breasts, inhaling her fragrance, brushing his cheeks along the softness of her skin where no one else had ever touched. Her fingers tangled in his hair, then she cradled his face and pulled him back to her mouth.

Shifting to his side, he slid her down so they were face to face. When he reached out to close the gap between them, her hand splayed against his bare chest. At the sound of his quickened breath, she glanced up in surprise. His face was taut and drawn, as if he were holding his breath and waiting. Had her touch caused this reaction? She slowly ran her hand down his chest, and he sucked in his breath. Could it be her touch had the same tantalizing effect on him that she felt under his?

Her own passion soared as she discovered this new power. She ran her other hand along the slope of his shoulder. The muscles jumped and contracted beneath her fingertips. Daringly, she pressed her lips to one of his nipples, and his whole body tensed.

Oh, this was amazing. For an interminable moment she tested, tasted, and stroked him, kissing until he groaned aloud. And each nip, each bite, every stroke of her tongue buily her own passion until it threatened to explode.

With a feral growl he rolled over, pulling up her gown as he flattened her to the bunk. Her breath came in ragged gasps as his mouth tortured her breasts, and his hand sought and found the sensitive, heated core of her. It tightened in an exquisite urgency that kept building and building, fed by his touch.

"Josh, please, I can't—"

He cut off her plea with a kiss, then shifted his mouth to her breasts again. Her head began whirling in a maze of sublime sensation when his finger teased the nucleus of her passion, the rhythm of his strokes increasing until she moaned with ecstasy as her body vibrated, inundated by love's tremors.

"Now you're ready for me, baby. You're so ready," he murmured at her ear. Shifting, he straddled her and began to open his jeans.

She'd been ready from the moment he pulled her down to him. The thought of something even greater to come was inconceivable.

The sudden, horrendous screech of metal against metal brought Emily back to earth abruptly, and then she and Josh were flung out of the berth.

They landed in a heap on the floor.

Chapter 24

❦❦❦

"What in hell!" Josh exclaimed. "Em, are you okay?"

"Yes."

The train came to a shuddering stop with another jolt that slammed them back against the floor of the berth.

"What is it? What's happening?" she asked.

She'd no sooner spoken, when the sound of gunshots rang out and several riders galloped past the window.

"Stay down," Josh cautioned urgently.

"What is it?"

"Looks like a train robbery."

She gasped. "Maybe it's that Dalton Gang you told me about."

He pulled on his boots as the gunshots continued. "Sounds like somebody up front is putting up a game fight." Emily's stomach leaped to her throat when Josh strapped on his Colt. "They might need some help."

She felt like the breath was being squeezed out of her. It no longer mattered that he was taking her back to Long Island against her will. The only clear thought she had was that he could get hurt—or killed. Grabbing his arm, she pleaded, "Don't go, Josh."

"You'll be okay, Em. Just stay down away from the window, and keep the door locked. And whatever you do, don't light the lamp. They'll probably figure the compartment's empty."

"I'm afraid, Josh."

He cupped her cheeks between his hands and smiled down at her. "You'll be okay, honey, if you do what I say." Then he kissed her.

She'd meant she was afraid for him, but couldn't find her voice to tell him. Then it was too late. He'd already squirmed over to the door.

"Lock this door," he said, and slipped out into the darkness.

Emily crawled over and locked the door. Her hands were shaking as she managed to rebutton her bodice and pull on her stockings and shoes. The sound of gunshots continued to ring out, and she could only imagine what was going on up front.

Her anxiety increased with every shot fired; each passing minute seemed interminable. It became hell waiting, not knowing what was happening. What if Josh was lying wounded and bleeding? Or worse, what if . . . She wouldn't consider it, wouldn't let that thought enter her mind.

The time had come to admit to herself that her feeling for him was more than just an attraction. Somehow, someway, by some crazy twist of fate, she'd fallen in love with him. It made no sense, but the truth was undeniable—and there was no way she could bear another minute in this room while he was possibly hurt out there.

Emily unlocked the door.

There wasn't a soul stirring in the car and, hunched down, she made her way to the platform and stepped off the train into the predawn dark. Her heart was pounding so loudly in her ears, it sounded like a drum roll announcing her arrival. Staying in the shadows, she started to work her way along the line.

Suddenly the firing stopped. Were all the defenders wounded—or dead? Panicked, she began to race along the side of the train, sobbing Josh's name. In her rush she tripped and fell, and was almost trampled as several men rode by.

"What the ... will you look what we got here, boys," one of the men said, reining up. The others halted.

Lying on her stomach in the dirt, Emily looked up into the coldest pair of steel-gray eyes she'd ever seen, in a face almost obliterated behind a heavy black beard.

"Whatta you know, boss," one of the men said.

Smirking, the leader said, "Yep, boys, could be this weren't no loss after all."

If this man was Bob Dalton, he sure didn't look anything like the one in her dream.

Josh had discovered that the returning fire had come from the conductor and a railroad detective who was on the train due to the recent robberies. He'd joined them, and the three men succeeded in holding off the robbers. As soon as the outlaws rode away, Josh helped the train crew assess the damage to the train, while the porter and conductor checked the passengers to make certain no one had been hurt in the attempted robbery.

A barricade of felled trees had been dragged

across the track, derailing the train. The engine was off the track, and it would take time for another engine to be dispatched. To Josh's amusement, the nearest town with an available engine was Las Vegas. If he hadn't known better, he'd have suspected Em had something to do with the robbery. He grinned to himself as he walked back to their car.

But the delay wouldn't bother him and Em in the least—they had some unfinished business. As a matter of fact, the delay could be very entertaining.

Josh encountered the porter as he entered the car. "Any passengers hurt, Jeb?"

"No, suh, Detective MacKenzie. They're all fine and accounted for 'ceptin' your missus. I knocked on that there door, but she ain't there."

Josh laughed. "No problem, Jeb. I told her to keep the door locked and not to make a sound."

"No, suh, she ain't there. Door's open and there ain't no sign of her."

No! He couldn't believe she'd be foolish enough to run off in the midst of a gunfight. But she'd warned him as much when he put the cuffs on her. He was a damn fool to have unlocked them. When he found her again, he'd keep the damn cuffs on her all the way to Long Island.

Suddenly his anger drained from him as he realized that if she'd tried to escape, she could very well be lying wounded someplace. Or worse, she could be . . . No, he wouldn't consider that.

"Em," he shouted, hoping she was nearby.

Jeb chased back to the caboose and returned with lanterns. The two of them began searching the area around the train. If she'd been wounded by a stray bullet, she'd probably be close by.

The rising sun was a big crack in the horizon by

the time they returned from the unsuccessful search, and Josh saw an area that showed the trampled hoof-prints of several horses. He examined the area more closely, drawing on all the knowledge Uncle Flint had ever taught him, and this time his eyes were drawn to a tiny object so obscure it could barely be seen in the dirt. Kneeling down, he picked up a hair-pin.

They had her! The thought was like a punch to his stomach, and he started gulping for air. But if they'd grabbed her, it meant she was still alive.

At the sound of approaching horses, he spun on his heel, whipping his Colt out of the holster. Two riders rode up to him.

"Hey, don't shoot, mister," one of them yelled.

"Keep your hands away from your sides. Who are you?"

"We ride for the Circle R. This here track runs through it. We were camped nearby and heard all the shootin'. What's goin' on?"

"Train was held up. I need a horse right away. The outlaws rode off with one of the female passengers."

"You sure she weren't one of 'em?" the other cowboy said.

"I'm damn sure." He pointed his gun at the cowpoke. "Get out of that saddle. I haven't time to argue."

"All right. Just leather that Colt before it goes off," the man grumbled, climbing down. "I'll warn you now, the boss don't take kindly to horse thieves."

"You'll get your horse back."

Josh swung into the saddle and headed in the direction of the prints. It had been damn foolish of the outlaws to try and rob a train so soon after the rain; a novice could follow the trail. His greatest concern was that he'd be too late by the time he caught up with them. If one of the bastards so much as touched Emily, he'd . . .

Lord help him, he loved her. Emily Lawrence was a liar, a thief, and a schemer. A spoiled rotten, little rich girl who didn't concern herself about the consequences of her actions. He'd let himself believe the attraction was just an itch in his loins which would go away once he scratched it. But she was like a damn tick that had sunk her teeth into him and wouldn't let go—she was in his blood now.

But she was Emily Lane, too. He'd seen the way she didn't shirk hard work, the way she'd pitched in the night of the fire. He'd seen her grit and spunk as she traipsed across a desert. He'd seen how the beauty of a sunset could bring tears to her eyes.

And there was the Emily who inundated his senses. The woman he'd held in his arms, whose softness he could still feel beneath him. He'd seen her green eyes glow with desire for him, had tasted her passion, smelled her scent, heard her moans of pleasure when he touched her.

All three were the Em he now loved. All three had burrowed so deep in his hide, there was no burning them out.

Not now—not ever.

After several miles, he reached a spot where the riders appeared to split, two going straight ahead and a single rider veering westward. Which way had Emily gone? Dismounting, he examined the ground carefully for several yards in each direction and finally found another hairpin in the dust.

"You're doing great, baby. Keep it up," he murmured. "I'll never complain about those damn hairpins again." Climbing back on the horse, he headed westward.

She'd known he'd follow, and she must be alert and okay since she'd had the presence of mind to leave a clue when necessary.

The countryside soon became rocky with shale bluffs and cliffs. At times he was forced to dismount to follow the trail, a displaced stone or a partial print the only signs he had to go on.

Reaching a level spot, he picked up additional prints. It appeared that the other two riders had rejoined their comrade, or else he'd been joined by others—a possibility he hoped was not true. His instinct told him it was the same three riders.

The terrain leveled into a narrow trail with rocky bluffs overhanging the trail on each side. Dismounting, Josh followed it slowly, pausing when it widened into a canyon.

"I don't like the looks of this, boy," he said, patting the horse. "If that's a box canyon, and they're in those rocks above, they can pick me off like a fish in a barrel." He shoved his Stetson to the top of his forehead. What would Uncle Flint do in a situation like this? The canyon would be quicker, but he figured his uncle would take the time and climb.

Josh tied the horse to a scrub, spun the chamber of his Colt to make sure it was fully loaded, then slipped it back in the holster.

When he'd scaled the rocks, keeping low, he glanced down and saw it was indeed a box canyon, but there appeared to be no sign of the outlaws. But there was always the other side.

After climbing back down, he scaled the other side and met with the same result—no one.

Where in hell were they? Their tracks led right to the mouth of that canyon, the only way in or out.

He went back down and untied his horse, then led it into the canyon, barren except for scattered clumps of scrub. A man on foot didn't make as easy a target as one on horseback.

His back was stiff with tension; nothing about this smelled right. Why in hell would the tracks lead into the damn thing and none appear to lead out? His gaze scoured the canyon walls. There was nothing to indicate a cave or anything to conceal at least three horses and four people.

As he passed a huge boulder, he caught a flash of sunlight on an object on the ground. He picked it up and recognized it at once: the turquoise and silver brooch he'd bought Emily in Albuquerque.

This had to be the spot. A closer inspection of the boulder revealed it was not part of the canyon wall, but a flat rock concealing an opening wide enough to lead a horse through.

After he had entered the cave, it took several seconds for Josh's eyes to adjust to the dark. And in the silence, the low murmur of voices carried to him through the darkness. He saw three horses tethered nearby and tied his own with them, then proceeded cautiously toward the voices.

The ceiling of the cave had dropped, and he had to lower his head slightly to continue. Rounding a curve of the rocky tunnel, he saw that it opened into a large circular cavern with a high ceiling.

The early Spaniards had buried caches of treasure in caves such as this when they came to New Mexico. This had to be one of them.

A lighted torch burned from a sconce on the wall, revealing four figures sitting in a circle in the center of the room: Emily and the three outlaws. Hugging the shadow of the walls, he inched closer and saw that Emily's hands weren't bound. These guys didn't know they were playing with fire in leaving her arms and legs loose, he thought with dark amusement.

He finally worked his way close enough to overhear the conversation.

"I can assure you, gentlemen, my father is very wealthy and will pay a large sum to ransom me." Emily sounded frightened; her voice lacked its usual spunkiness. She was in trouble, and she knew it.

One of the men scoffed. "Lady, you must think we're dumb. Just how would we get the money from him? Pick it up at the nearest bank?"

The others burst into laughter. "She's just trying to stall, boss. Let's flip to see who gets her first."

"We don't have to. I'm the boss, ain't I? You fellas work it out between ya till I'm done with her." He yanked Emily to her feet.

"Take your hands off me, you brute!" She began kicking him.

He picked her up and slung her over his shoulder like a sack of grain. "Won't do you no good to fight me, Blondie, I've got a blanket over yonder, and me and you are gonna have us a real good time."

That's what you think, you bastard. Pulling his Colt, Josh began to work his way toward them.

Behind the curtained blanket Emily appeared to be putting up a solid fight, for the man's tolerance turned to anger.

"You bit me! You're gonna pay for that, you little bitch, 'cause I've got teeth too—and it ain't gonna be your arm I'll be biting."

Josh heard her scream and the sound of ripping

cloth. He broke out in a sweat, trying to reach them unobserved before the bastard hurt her.

By the time he'd worked his way over to them, the outlaw had pinned her arms to the ground above her head with one of his hands and was trying to hold down her thrashing legs with his own as he ripped the bodice off her with his free hand.

"I'm gonna like this, Blondie. Ain't nothing like straddlin' a wild filly and breakin' her. And, sister, when I'm through with you, you're gonna wish you were dead—but you ain't gonna be that lucky, 'cause the other fellas are gonna take their turns with ya. And you better hope Brogan gets you last, 'cause he likes to do little tricks with burnin' cigarettes. If you're lucky enough, you won't have to suffer too long afore you kick off."

She looked up, horrified, just as Josh moved behind him. The shock of seeing him caused her to freeze, and her fear turned to relief.

"That's right, Blondie. Ain't no use to fighin', 'cause it ain't gonna—"

He collapsed on her as Josh hit him on the head with his pistol, then kicked him off her.

He pulled her into his arms, and she clung to him, whimpering and crying uncontrollably. The sound of her sobbing reverberated through the cave, and the men started laughing.

"Sounds like the boss is taming that gal down a mite," one of them said. "Hope he don't take all the fight out of her."

Josh would have liked to shoot the two of them right where they sat, but he didn't dare take the chance of Emily getting hurt. She was shocked enough as it was, and he'd have his hands full just trying to get her out of there before any bullets started flying.

"Honey," he warned in a whisper, "we've got to get out of here, so you're going to have to be quiet." As he spoke, he tried to close the remnants of her bodice. "Do you understand?"

She nodded, and her sobs trailed off to an occasional one or two. Crouching in the shadows, they moved toward the entrance of the cave, trying not to make a sound.

They'd just rounded the curve in the wall when something scampered across Emily's foot. She screamed reflexively.

"Hey, Yancy, what's goin' on?" one of the men shouted.

There was no time for caution. Josh tightened his grasp on her hand. "Let's get out of here fast." They started running and reached the horses but could hear the shouts of the outlaws coming closer.

Josh quickly hefted Emily onto his horse. "Get goin' and don't stop."

"What about you?" she cried out.

"I'll be right behind you." He smacked the horse's flank.

Grabbing the reins of the other horses, he drove them through the gap one by one as the sound of footsteps drew nearer. Swinging up into a saddle, he fired a couple shots, and the horses raced toward the mouth of the canyon.

With blazing pistols, the outlaws burst from the cave. Bullets whizzed past his head as he pushed his horse to a full gallop. He felt a slug hit his shoulder but kept going. Emily had already cleared the entrance to the canyon and was about fifteen yards ahead of him.

By the time the outlaws reached the entrance on foot, the two of them were well out of pistol range. Only then did they ease up on the reins.

As soon as they got back to the train, Emily dashed into their compartment to change her gaping bodice. The new engine had arrived from Las Vegas along with a crew that had almost completed repairing the track. A sheriff had ridden in with the repair crew and was getting ready to ride out with a posse of Circle R riders. Of all people, it was none other than Sheriff Ben Travis.

Josh quickly drew a rough map of where the outlaws could be found.

"I know that canyon," one of the cowpokes said. "Don't remember any cave, though."

"There's one there, all right," he said.

"That shirt you're wearing looks pretty bloody, MacKenzie," Travis said. "You best tend to it."

"It's nothing, Sheriff. Good luck in catching those guys. They sound pretty rotten to me. Robbing trains isn't their only crime."

"We'll get them. Now you better get that wound tended to."

Josh watched the posse ride off, then wearily climbed onto the train.

When he entered their compartment, he saw that Emily had changed her clothes and pinned up her hair. She looked none the worse for the frightening experience she'd gone through.

Turning her head, she smiled at him; then her eyes widened in alarm.

"Josh, your shirt! It's soaked with blood."

"Yeah," he said, just as the floor came up to meet him.

Chapter 25

"Josh! Dear God, no! No!" Emily cried out as she rushed over to kneel by his unconscious body.

The rise and fall of his chest indicated he was breathing, but he looked so pale that she feared it would just be a short time before he stopped.

Turning him on his side, she saw the bullet wound, seeping blood. He'd lost so much already and was losing more with every breath he took. She had to stop the flow somehow.

Glancing around desperately, she spied the discarded garments she'd tossed aside. She snatched up the skirt, folded it into a compress, and stuffed it against the wound.

Her mind was spinning in a dozen directions. What should she do next? Scissors. She needed scissors to get the bloody shirt off him. Where was her valise? She scrambled on her knees over to the corner where she'd put the bag. Her hands were trembling so badly, she could hardly open it. Rummaging through the bag, she found the small kit that contained her tiny manicure scissors. Returning to his side, she tried to jam her fingers through the small round holes of the scissors. When had her fingers gotten so large? She sobbed in frustration. Why couldn't she hold them steady? Every moment of delay was a moment out of his life.

"Get a hold on yourself, Emily. You're not doing him any good this way."

Closing her eyes, she took several deep breaths and clenched her shaking hands into fists to steady them. When she felt the trembling lessen, she picked up the scissors, this time with no trouble, and tried to cut the front of the shirt. But the scissors were too small to be effective.

"Damn! Damn! Damn!" she cried. "Think, damn you! Think!" Tossing them aside in disgust, she looked around for a sharper instrument. Her eyes came to rest on Josh's valise.

She rushed over to it and began pulling out clothes, tossing them helter-skelter until she found his shaving mug and razor. Grabbing the razor, she hurried back to Josh and succeeded in slitting the bottom of his shirt, then ripped it up the front.

His chest was streaked with blood, and she had the horrifying fear that he'd been shot more than once. She sought the ewer. Empty! The damn thing had spilled when the train crashed.

She used her torn bodice to wipe him off, and to her relief, there was only a single puckered hole at the back of his left shoulder. The blood on his chest had come from the soiled shirt. Then she realized the ramifications of there being no exit wound: the bullet was still in him.

She needed help. Yanking the light quilt off his bunk, she covered him and ran out the door smack into Jeb.

Clutching the startled porter by the shoulders, she

cried, "Help me! Josh is unconscious; he's been shot."

The porter hurried into the compartment and knelt at Josh's side. After a few seconds of examining Josh, Jeb stood up.

"You stay with him, ma'am, while ah get some help." He rushed out, leaving her alone.

Emily sat down and cradled his head in her lap. "We're getting help, my darling," she said, gently brushing back the hair on his forehead. "Open your eyes, Josh. I have to look into them again to know everything will be okay. Please, Josh, open your eyes."

She hadn't realized she was crying until her tears dropped on her hand and she felt the sting from the salty moisture. She wiped her hand on her skirt and saw that she must have nicked her hand with his razor, for she was bleeding. Or was it his blood?

"Our blood is blending together, Josh. Can you feel it, my love? Draw strength from it, from my body, as I've done so often from yours."

That's how they found her when Jeb and another man arrived on the scene: Josh's head in her lap, and her hand pressing the compress against the back of his shoulder.

After a quick examination, the man said, "Mrs. MacKenzie, I'm Conductor Bellows. Your husband's been shot, madam."

"I *know* he's been shot, Conductor Bellows, and did you notice the bullet's still in him? So while we're standing here discussing it, instead of doing something about it, *he's bleeding to death!*"

Bellows stepped back. "Shouting will not accomplish anything, Mrs. MacKenzie."

"And I'm not—" Apparently, Josh had not told

anyone she was his prisoner. Better to let them believe she was his wife, or the conductor might feel a responsibility to keep her confined—or even worse, make her leave Josh's side. She couldn't bear to leave him now.

"If you'll move away, Mrs. MacKenzie, the porter and I will lift him into a bunk."

As Emily glanced over to the bunks, the first thing that caught her eye was the handcuff dangling from the upper one. Had Bellows seen it yet? If not, he'd surely expect an explanation when he did.

"Wouldn't it be easier to remove the bullet right here and now?" she said.

"We have nothing more than that first aid kit," he said, nodding toward a white box in Jeb's hands. "In a few minutes we'll be under way, and we're not much more than forty miles from Las Vegas. They'll have a doctor there. It's better we leave it to him than try to do it ourselves without the proper instruments or supplies."

Emily got to her feet. "Very well, give me a moment to put his bunk in order."

"I'll do it, ma'am," Jeb said.

"No, you help Mr. Bellows, Jeb. I can take care of the bunk."

Putting herself between them and the bunk, she shoved the dangling cuff under the mattress of the top bunk, then bent down and smoothed out the sheets on the lower one. What happened to the key? Not encountering it in the bunk, she glanced around and saw it lying on the floor near the foot of the bunk. "It's ready." She stepped away, placing her foot on the key.

The two men struggled to put Josh's tall frame

into the bunk, and she prayed they wouldn't jar the upper bunk and dislodge the cuff.

"I'd keep a compress on that wound, madam, to stem that blood flow," Bellows said. "And we'll leave you the kit to bandage the wound. In the meantime, we'll wire ahead to make sure the doctor will be ready when we get there."

"Thank you, Conductor Bellows, and you, too, Jeb," she said, practically shoving them out the door. Since they couldn't be of any further help to Josh, she wanted them out of the small compartment.

"Do you need anything else, ma'am?" Jeb asked.

"If you could bring some warm water, Jeb, I'll be able to clean him up a bit."

"Yes, ma'am," he said, picking up the ewer. "We've got a pot of coffee boilin' in the caboose, Miz MacKenzie. You want me to bring you a hot cup?"

"No, Jeb, thanks just the same."

"Might help to perk you up some, ma'am."

She shook her head. "Just some water and a clean washcloth and towel, if you have them."

"Right away, ma'am," he said.

She closed the door behind him and turned back to the figure on the bunk. Placing a hand on Josh's forehead, she sighed. At least he wasn't running a fever, but why didn't he open his eyes?

Pressing an ear to his chest, she heard a steady heartbeat; a reassuring sign. To have to just let him lie there was frustrating, but Bellows was right to suggest they leave the bullet removal to a trained doctor.

Awaiting Jeb's return, she unlocked the handcuffs, then shoved the key and cuffs into her valise to get them out of sight.

Jeb was back shortly with a ewer of water and the linens she'd asked for. She removed the heavy gunbelt from around Josh's waist and sponged off his chest. Then, being careful not to jar him too much, she managed to turn him over onto his stomach and removed the rest of the bloody shirt and the compress.

The kit held bandages and tape, and after washing off his back and arms, she folded some bandage into a fresh compress and taped it to his back.

Emily had just finished the task when the train lurched to a start, and they were finally under way.

She removed his boots and covered him with the quilt from her bunk, and then there was no more she could do except pace back and forth in the small compartment. If only he were to regain consciousness, she'd feel a little better, but he showed no sign of stirring. As worrisome as that was, though, at least it helped to slow the blood seepage.

The ride to Las Vegas seemed like the longest hour of her life. Her frightening experience with the outlaws now seemed a long time ago, since her worry over Josh pushed everything else out of her thoughts.

What if he'd lost too much blood? What if the doctor couldn't remove the bullet? What if he never regained consciousness?

She wanted to scream aloud, because the *what if* that was eating her apart was, what if she'd remained on the train the way he told her to? He'd never have been wounded then.

She was to blame for this. He was lying there with the blood slowly seeping out of him, and she was to blame.

If the worst should happen, how could she live

with herself—how could she live without him?

Kneeling on the floor, she clasped his hand; then, laying her cheek on the bunk, she sobbed in heartache.

When the train chugged into Las Vegas, Emily recognized the doctor at once, for he had frequented the restaurant often. That explained Rose's presence beside him on the depot's platform.

It was comforting to see her, and when Emily stepped off, they hugged in silence as the doctor supervised the transfer of Josh's body to a stretcher. Rose tucked Emily's arm firmly through hers, and they followed.

The wait in his office was tense as the doctor performed the surgery behind a closed door. Rose managed to get a few words out of Emily but didn't press her to talk any more than she wanted to. Knowing her friend was there for her was comforting, and Emily wondered if Josh somehow knew she was there for him.

When the doctor appeared, she bolted to her feet, and Rose took her hand. Grim-faced, he said, "Well, I removed the bullet successfully, and even though he's still unconscious, his body signs are very encouraging."

"Oh, thank God!" she cried, hugging Rose and then turning back. "Thank you, Doctor."

"He's not out of the woods yet, Emily. The young man's lost a great amount of blood, so right now I can't promise anything. Do you have someplace where he can stay? I recommend rest and quiet."

"I'll get a room at the hotel," she said.

"Fine. I'll see to having him moved, and I'll come by later today to check on his condition. Right now, keeping him in bed is the best thing you can do for him. When he regains consciousness, I'm sure he'll try to get up. I don't advise it for a couple of days."

"I'll make certain he doesn't get up, Doctor."

He took her hand and squeezed it. "My dear, wipe that fear off your face. From what I can tell, he's a healthy young man. I'm sure in a couple of days he'll be sitting up wanting a thick, juicy steak." His eyes twinkled with mischief. "Or something else."

Emily blushed at the innuendo but was too relieved to take umbrage.

Rose started chuckling. "Why, Dr. Hughes, whatever are you suggesting?"

"Thank you, Doctor," Emily said quickly, before the two could carry the topic any further.

"And the doctor's orders are that you get some rest, too. You look as pale and drawn as he does, my dear. He'll need your strength when he regains consciousness, so take advantage of the opportunity and get some sleep now."

"I'll make sure she does, Doctor," Rose said, sounding as relieved as Emily now felt.

"Good. Now let's see to getting the hotel accommodations so we can get Mr. MacKenzie into a bed."

A short time later, Josh was securely ensconced in the same room he had occupied before, overlooking the charred ruins of the Harvey House.

Rose had returned to work for the evening meal. Their valises had been delivered to the hotel.

The doctor had arranged for Emily to have the connecting room, but she had no intention of leaving Josh's room—or of sleeping in a different bed. Her place was beside him. If the doctor expected her to rest, she'd for darn sure be lying next to Josh.

She kicked off her shoes and lay down beside him. Clasping his hand, she closed her eyes and felt the tension ease out of her. She hadn't realized how tired she was until then.

Suddenly her eyes popped open, and she sat up, certain she'd felt him squeeze her hand—and stared down into the most beautiful pair of sapphire eyes she'd ever seen.

"Em, what happened? Where are we?"

"We're in a hotel in Las Vegas. The doctor just removed a bullet from your shoulder and you've lost a lot of blood, so you're very weak."

"Yeah . . . feel . . . weak." He drifted off again. Lying on her side, she propped herself up on an elbow, cradled her head in her hand, and stared down at his face. Dark stubble covered his lower jaw, and she lovingly traced a finger across his bristled chin.

"Detective MacKenzie, I think I'll try shaving you tomorrow."

Leaning over, she whispered, "I love you, Josh." Then she pressed a light kiss on his lips, lay back, and closed her eyes.

Before falling asleep, she reached for his hand.

Emily awoke to a persistent rapping on the door. A quick glance at the clock revealed almost four hours had passed since she had lain down. She got up and opened the door to Dr. Hughes.

"I'm sorry about the late hour," he said as he hustled in. "My, this has been a busy day. I've delivered a baby since the last time I saw you."

"A baby—how wonderful." She lit the lamp.

"And how is our patient doing?"

"He regained consciousness for a few seconds,

Doctor. Asked what happened and where he was. Then he fell asleep."

"That's good news. Sleep's the best medicine for him at this time. I'll examine him and change the dressing on the wound."

He looked at her expectantly, and it dawned on her that he was waiting for her to leave the room. Excusing herself, she left, closing the connecting door behind her.

Since she'd been banished from Josh's room, she used the opportunity to go down the hall to the bathroom and freshen up. By the time the doctor tapped on the connecting door, she had changed into a nightgown, securely concealed behind a belted robe.

"How is he, Dr. Hughes?"

"I'm afraid he's running a fever, Emily." At her startled look, he added, "That's not unusual. His body's undergone a shock. I suspect by tomorrow the fever will have broken and he'll be able to remain alert for longer periods of time; but for now, I've put a bottle of tablets on the table. I want you to give him one every two hours. And get as much water down him as you can. We don't want him to become dehydrated."

"Are you sure he's going to be all right, Dr. Hughes?"

"I'm only a doctor, Emily, not a prophet. Medically speaking, it will be touch and go for the next twenty-four hours. But his body signs are good, the wound doesn't show any sign of infection, and as I said, fever's a common occurrence when the body's been traumatized." He closed up his black bag. "Just follow my instructions, my dear. It will be a long night for you, but once the medication takes effect, the fever should break by morning. If he gets restless during the night, sponge him down occasionally—and remember, get as much water down him as you can. I'll come by in the morning."

"What about food?"

"I don't think he'll need any for a while. The water will do. If he is alert enough to ask for some, I advise soup to begin with. Perhaps Rose can bring you some hot soup from the Harvey House."

Rose! She'd forgotten about her. Her shift would have ended hours ago. Had she come back earlier when Emily was asleep?

Emily had so much to tell her dear friend, so much to talk over. A lot had happened since the last time they'd had a good chat. She wanted to tell Rose how deeply she'd fallen in love with Josh MacKenzie.

But despite her feeling for him, she suspected he'd be more determined than ever to be rid of her once he was fully alert and realized that she'd nearly gotten him killed.

As soon as the doctor departed, she began to pace the floor, stopping at his bedside every few minutes to check his condition.

Remembering one of her mother's cures, she wet a washcloth and put the cool compress on his forehead. It had always felt good to her whenever she'd run a fever as a youngster.

Her vigil continued for several more hours: administering the medication, forcing water down his throat, changing the cloths on his brow. Sometimes he'd be docile, other times thrashing and murmuring in delirium.

Shortly past midnight, a light tap sounded on the door. "Emily."

Recognizing Rose's voice, she hurried over to unlock the door.

"I saw the light from my window, so I figured you were awake. How's Josh doing?"

"Not well. He's feverish right now. The doctor left some pills for him to take."

Rose grasped her by the shoulders and stared deeply into her eyes. "Honey, when was the last time you slept?"

"Earlier. I slept for four hours while Josh was burning up with fever."

"And now you feel guilty, is that it? You're exhausted. Go into the next room and get some more rest. I can take care of Josh."

"I can't sleep knowing he's—" She stopped and drew a deep breath. "Rose, I'm in love with him."

"Honey, you don't have to say it. It's written all over your face."

"And now . . . it's hopeless."

"You don't know that. So he's been shot, and he's running a fever. That doesn't mean he's going to die, Emily. If you weren't so exhausted, you wouldn't be talking so foolishly."

"You don't understand. If it weren't for me, he'd never have been shot."

"What do you mean? It's not your fault the train was held up."

"He wasn't shot during the holdup. He was shot because I didn't listen to him when he warned me to stay put. We had a private compartment, and when he left to help out in the attack, he told me to stay quiet and keep the door locked. But I left the train." She shuddered, recalling the incident. "The outlaws caught me; there were three of them. Josh tracked them and rescued me just when the leader had started—" She broke off and forced the image from her mind. "Josh got wounded when we escaped. And now he's . . . he's—"

"Oh, honey," Rose said, hugging her. "What does Dr. Hughes say?"

"He's still optimistic."

"Then you should be, too. Have you told Josh how you feel about him?"

"No, I'm sure he'd only laugh—or think I'm just trying to keep him from taking me back to New York."

"I doubt that, if I'm any judge of men. And believe me, honey, that's one topic I'm familiar with."

"Josh has said repeatedly what he thinks of women like me. And now, since I'm responsible for his getting wounded . . ." She threw her hands up helplessly. "What's the use?" Walking over to the bed, she took the wet cloth off his forehead and rewet it. "I should try to contact his family. The way he talked about them, they all seem very close."

"Emily, sit down, dear. Please," Rose said worriedly.

"He worships his parents." She looked at Rose. "Did you know his real mother was killed during the Civil War?"

"No, I didn't," Rose said.

"Oh, yes. So was his grandmother. Quite tragically, too. His father and uncles had gone to war. They fought for the Confederacy, you know."

"I suspected as much, since he's from Texas."

Emily knew Rose was indulging her, but she felt driven to keep talking. It was that or cry.

"A band of outlaws attacked the ranch and raped and killed them." She looked at Rose, unaware of the tears sliding down her cheeks. "The men were all gone to war, and the poor women had no one to protect them. I've heard stories of the war in the North, of course—I even had a cousin who was killed at Gettysburg—but I hadn't really ever thought of what it must have been like for those poor women living in the South: left alone to protect themselves, conquering armies tramping through, most of their male population killed or wounded— fathers, husbands, sons, lovers. An entire way of life dying before their very eyes."

"I know," Rose said sadly. "My momma was in New Orleans when Butler occupied the city. They still call him Beast there because he told his men they could accost any woman in the city as if she were common trash."

"He said that?" Emily asked, horrified.

Rose shrugged. "I don't know if those were his exact words. But if a woman was insulting to a Yankee soldier—and what would you expect them to be toward enemy soldiers occupying their city—then the soldier had the right to arrest her as a tramp."

The tears were openly running down Emily's cheeks, but she knew as well as Rose that they were tears she'd been trying not to shed all evening. The sad story had merely been the wheel that opened the floodgates.

Rose didn't try to stop her; tears were as essential to Emily's healing as the pills were to Josh's. And by the time Rose left, Emily felt better for having shed them.

Chapter 26

⌒⌒◯◯◯⌒⌒

After a night of anguish, watching Josh thrash in the throes of fever, Emily's spirit had begun to wane by the time the sun broke the horizon.

She had forced the pills down him at timely intervals, had cooled his brow with wet cloths, and had held him up to get water down his throat.

In desperation, she finally forsook modesty and stripped off his drawers to sponge his fevered body. She'd never seen a man nude before, and found herself distracted by the beautiful symmetry of muscle, bone, and bronzed flesh—even more so because it was Josh.

He had seen and touched so much of her body, and she realized she had seen little of his.

She sponged him gently with loving strokes: arms, powerful shoulders and chest, long, muscular legs. She even cleansed his most private parts, feeling a sense of possessiveness—a feeling that no one but she had a right to view them.

The bath seemed to soothe him, and he lay quiet. Tempted to carry through her previous intention of shaving his face, she opted against it when his restlessness resumed.

The doctor's arrival did nothing to buoy her spirits; he seemed unperturbed, checked the wound, and changed the dressing. He then told her to continue with the medication and sponge baths and departed with a fatherly pat on her shoulder.

Rose arrived shortly after with a basket of food. Emily accepted the hot tea it contained but declined the soup and hot rolls.

Rose sat down and folded her arms across her chest. "I'm not leaving until you eat it. You know how temperamental Yen Cheng is; I wouldn't dare return with the food uneaten."

"Rose, I can't. I'm just not hungry."

Sighing, Rose picked up the basket. "All right. If Yen Cheng doesn't take his cleaver to me, I'll come back with lunch. Maybe by then you'll be willing to eat something. You aren't going to help Josh by getting sick, you know."

"I know. I promise I'll eat some soup then."

By lunch time, Josh's condition appeared improved. When she gave him a sponge bath again, his temperature wasn't as high, and he lay still. By late afternoon, when Dr. Hughes examined him, Josh's fever was gone, and the doctor declared that any crisis had passed and that Josh was now out of danger.

That's all Emily needed to know. With Josh finally sleeping peacefully, she felt it safe to get some sleep herself. But first she wanted to bathe. Aching, exhausted, and bone-weary from worry, she would have loved a long, hot soak, but she didn't want to leave him alone too long, so she hurried through her bath, donned her nightgown and robe, then returned to her room, hoping to catch some sleep before he awoke.

Shedding her robe, she was about to lie down when she heard a sound in the next room. Had Josh awakened?

When she pushed the door open, Emily was startled to hear the unmistakable sound of a gun being cocked. She froze. She'd forgotten to light the lamp before leaving, and the room was dark.

If anyone had dared touch Josh, they'd have her to reckon with.

"Who's there?" she demanded.

"Em?"

At the sound of Josh's voice, hoarse from fever and disuse, she felt dizzying relief. She hurried into the room and lit a lamp.

He was sitting up in bed. He looked as tired as she felt, but seeing him awake lit joy in her heart. "Where did you get that gun?"

"From the valise in the corner."

"You got out of bed!" she exclaimed. "Why did you do that?"

"I woke up and didn't know what was going on, so I looked for my Colt."

"I'll tell you what's going on: you've been sick and feverish for two days."

"Two days!" he exclaimed. Uncocking the gun, he placed it on the nightstand near the bed. "You've been taking care of me all that time?"

"Of course. Why wouldn't I?"

He gave a snort of laughter. "You've been trying to escape me at every opportunity. Hell, Em, I've even handcuffed you. Now you say I've been unconscious for two days, and you had the perfect chance to take off." He crossed his arms over his bare chest and narrowed his eyes. "Why didn't you?"

Emily discovered that Josh wearing only a sheet while unconscious was a whole lot different from Josh in the same condition while lucid and sitting up in bed. The way he crossed his arms made the muscles of his chest and shoulders bunch in an enticing manner.

She'd been touching that chest for days, but she'd never felt about it then as she did now. She wanted to run her fingers over every ridge and valley, discover if his bronzed flesh stretched soft over the sleek muscles, and if the dark mat of hair that surrounded his nipples felt as crisp as it looked.

"Emily?"

She raised her gaze from his chest to his face and encountered an expression she couldn't read. But the look in his eyes made her shiver. It was as if he could see into her soul.

"Why didn't you leave?" he repeated.

She blinked, then flushed. She'd been so engrossed in his body that she'd completely forgotten his question. And try as she might, she just didn't seem to be able to keep her thoughts from straying back to his body, her body, their bodies—together— naked. She had been in this room alone with him far too long.

"I . . . ah . . . felt you needed me." Her face heated further at the double meaning to those words, before she realized just how true they were. But she'd never embarrass herself by admitting to him that she stayed because she loved him. She was too weary to withstand his mockery. "You saved my life, so I couldn't very well leave you when you were wounded and unconscious. How could you think that I would?"

"I don't know what to think anymore." He stared at her for a long moment, his gaze wandering down her body in such a way that she could almost feel the touch of his fingers on her skin. Confused, she looked down, but there was nothing untoward in her appearance. Why on earth was he staring at her as if he'd never seen her before?

"Come here." He patted the bed at his side.

Heat flashed over Emily again at the thought of joining him on the bed—her hip brushing his thigh, her hair brushing his chest; kissing him, touching him, whispering against his skin the words she'd been hiding in her heart even from herself. She had fallen deeply in love with this handsome and heroic man, who considered her to be nothing better than a liar and thief. How could she have been so foolish?

If she told him how much she loved him, he'd push her away. Just as her father always pushed away her mother—because like her father, Josh MacKenzie only loved his job.

She stiffened her spine in anger at the unjustice of his stubborn refusal to believe her.

"I've just spent the most exhausting, gut-wrenching, heartaching, sleepless two days that I've ever known, MacKenzie. From now on, if you want anything, you can damn well get it yourself, the way you got that gun—because now, if you don't mind, I'm going to my room and get some sleep. And if I'm lucky, maybe I, too, can find out what it's like to sleep for two days." She stalked toward the door, then turned back. "And by the way, we're even now. All debts are paid. So if it will put your mind at ease, Detective, I'll humor you and cuff myself to the bed."

Her tirade appeared to have rolled off him like

water. He leaned back against the pillows, and a lock of hair drifted over one eye. He flicked it back with a toss of his head that was all Josh. Her heart turned over. How would she ever forget this man?

"Humor me, huh?" He grinned. "I'm sick and wounded, remember?"

"Not half as sick as you were."

"And how sick was that?"

Suddenly all that had happened in the past few days came back with a force that made her dizzy, and she grabbed the foot of the bed to steady herself.

"Hey," he said, "I was just kidding. What's the matter?"

She was too exhausted for any more of this word game. "You scared me to death, Josh. I thought you were going to die."

"Die?" He snorted. "I've got a shoulder wound. MacKenzies don't die from shoulder wounds."

Maybe it was the combination of fear and exhaustion with the realization that she loved him and he could never love her back. Or maybe it was the way he dismissed as nothing something that had looked so deadly to her.

Whatever it was, her tenuous hold on her composure broke again, and she hollered, "I suppose MacKenzies don't bleed, either? Well, you were bleeding, Josh—a lot! You were unconscious for two days, raving and thrashing around in that bed with a fever. Maybe that's not unusual in Texas, but I'm from Long Island, where people don't get shot every damn day. I'm not used to it." Her voice broke, and she whispered again, "Not used to it."

The silence that followed her outburst was so deep she could hear the hiss of the flame in the lamp behind her. She turned to leave.

"I'm sorry, Em. I'm sure you were scared, and I didn't mean to make light of it. It's just—well—in my family, people get shot at all the time."

"Your mother must like that."

"Actually, no. She gets pretty hot about it. In fact, I seem to recall *her* shouting and crying a few times, too. But only when my dad was being shot at, because she—" He stopped abruptly, and she knew he'd figured out her secret. "Because she loves him so much."

Emily didn't want to look at him and see the pity in his eyes before he told her he didn't love her. So she kept looking at her feet, wondering where in blazes she'd put her shoes, because her toes had gone ice-cold.

"Had a fever, did I?" The nonchalance of his tone made her nod before she could stop herself. He grinned, all innocence. "I think I still do. Come feel my head."

He pushed his chin out, raising his forehead and closing his eyes. He looked harmless, childlike, adorable. Her lips tightened, and she repeated, "The fever's gone."

He opened one eye. "Really, I feel so hot."

She frowned, and her heart began to beat a staccato tap of fear. What if his fever had returned? With a sharp sigh of anxiety, she moved to the bed and reached for his forehead.

Cool and dry. Her relief was short-lived when his hand clamped onto her wrist and he yanked her forward. She sprawled over him. Several strategic buttons on her nightgown popped, and her breasts threatened to erupt from the gap. She gasped, which only made the material pull tighter; then she started to struggle.

"Ugh!" he groaned, sucking in a breath. "Hold still, Em."

"I will not! Let me up."

"No." His arms closed around her back. His fingertips brushed her buttocks, and she stiffened. Something pressed against her stomach, and when she shifted again, he moaned.

"Emily, quit wiggling."

Lifting her head, she looked into his eyes, and her hand bumped his shoulder. He hissed in pain. "Oh, I'm sorry, Josh. You've got to let me up."

"Stay and make it better, Em," he said as his eyes met hers. "Tell me you love me—because I love you. Then kiss me. Make all the pain go away."

She wouldn't. She couldn't. She shouldn't.

But Josh didn't let her run this time. Instead, he held her in his arms and stared into her eyes. "I love you, Em."

Then she was lost, because she loved him, too, and suddenly she understood why her mother had stayed all those years with her father, even though she was miserable and alone. She loved him, and when you loved a man, what went before and what comes after doesn't matter.

Chests pressed together, their hearts beating in the same rhythm, the gasps of their breath as one, their lips met—and the world became new again.

They had kissed before. She had touched him, and he had touched her. But never like this. Because now they loved, and love made everything magical.

Those lips she had dreamed of took hers, no longer gentle, but demanding. Demanding things of her she did not really understand. But she wanted him to teach her.

His tongue swept within her mouth—teasing, retreating, advancing, mating. He nipped her lips, her chin, her neck. His large, hard hands learned her body through the thin fabric, then found her skin beneath.

He was so clever with those fingers, loosening what was left of her gown, baring her to his touch, his gaze—a gaze that made her want everything he had to give. She had always wanted that.

When she rolled off his body and the sheet fell away, the sight of his arousal made her gasp. For just a moment, he seemed too big, too rough—too male.

Reaching out slowly, he gently cupped her breast in his hand. The sensation was exquisite, especially when he rubbed his thumb across her taut nipple. But when she looked into his face and saw the reverence, the gentleness, the love there, everything she felt increased tenfold.

Arching her back, she pressed herself into his palm. "Josh," she whispered, "please don't wake me this time."

He looked perplexed. "Wake you?"

"Do you know how many times I've dreamed of this moment? Wanted this moment? Tell me, show me, what to do."

His eyes darkened, and his other hand snaked around her waist, pulling her back against him. Then he reclaimed her lips.

The brush of his teeth along her lip matched the brush of his hands on her skin. She shivered, despite the heat of their bodies, and she ran her hands all over him, giving in to desire. Light from the lamp flickered across his chest, turning the dark whorls of hair gold. A sigh shuddered through him when she traced the defined muscles, her fingers splaying across his skin and tangling in the chest hair, familiarizing herself with his body in a way she'd only dreamed of before.

Caressing him, her hand encountered the bandage on his shoulder. He would have a scar from that bullet—a scar from defending her. While the thought upset her, it also made her want him even more.

He buried his face in her hair. Drawing a deep breath, he rubbed his cheek along the length. "You smell like sunshine," he whispered.

Her lips curved against his shadowed jaw, and she traced his ear with her tongue. "You taste like a man."

A shudder went through his body. Concerned that his fever had indeed returned, she pulled away and studied his face. Eyes closed, jaw clenched, he looked more vulnerable somehow than she'd ever seen him. After all, he'd been very ill. Had passion driven him beyond his body's limitations?

She loosed one hand from behind his neck and cupped the sharp plane of his cheek. He was warm, but not from an illness. Fever born of passion was a different story. She felt it, too.

She expected him to open his eyes at her touch. Instead he rubbed his cheek against her palm, as he'd rubbed his face in her hair. Her heart leapt in a sharp jig, and she swallowed hard.

"Josh, perhaps this isn't wise. You've been very ill. You shouldn't tax your strength."

Opening his eyes, he pushed her back upon the bed and loomed over her. "This is the best medicine I could have."

With a shiver of anticipation, she waited as he unbuttoned the rest of her gown and pushed aside the material. Then he slowly lowered his head, and his lips closed over the peak of one breast. Shifting restlessly against him, she gasped when the hair on his stomach rasped across her throbbing center.

"Did I hurt you?" he murmured against her skin, his breath cooling the dampness that surrounded her nipple.

She tangled her fingers in his hair and shook her head. "No. You'd never hurt me."

That was true. She'd known it from the moment she'd first seen him. He might be dangerous—rough and tough, and a man on a mission—but he would never hurt her. And no one else would, either, when Josh was around.

Raising his head, he stared down at her. Her breasts throbbed as his gaze caressed them, then continued along her body. What must she look like with her hair tumbled all about her shoulders, lying there in the faint glow of lamplight, her gown bunched every which way and her breast wet from his mouth? She did the only thing her instincts allowed—she reached out for him.

"Wait," he whispered. "Let me touch you, Em."

His hand skimmed her thigh. A finger traced the line of her hip, teasing, promising. Then his thumb rubbed her center, and she arched into the sensation, quivering at his touch.

Trailing his lips to her navel, he dipped his tongue and swirled it, then moved lower and kissed her where she'd never dreamed to be kissed—a stroke, a circle, and she shattered into more pieces than she'd ever dreamed there were. Behind her eyelids she saw more colors than she'd ever imagined, and in her heart she felt more love than a woman had a right to feel in one lifetime.

Reaching out, she brazenly cupped him in her palm, learning his most intimate secrets as he learned hers. She slid her finger up his length as he'd slid his thumb along hers. Cursing, he grabbed her hand, and she smiled at the realization he was not so in control after all.

Seeing her smile, he raised a brow; then with deliberate movements, he pushed her gown from her shoulders and threw it to the floor.

The flame of the lamp seemed dim compared to the heat that lit his eyes. She'd never known how exciting a mere look could be.

He traced her lips with his fingertip with such incredible gentleness that her eyes burned from unshed tears. Smiling, he pressed a gentle kiss where his finger had been.

"Touch me, Em," he whispered against her lips. She complied willingly, running her fingers and mouth all over him, tracing his contours with the slide of her palms along the plane of his chest, the ridge of his belly, and the rise of his nipples.

Time ceased to have meaning. The lamp burned low; their passion burned high, as each came nearly to the peak and then down, only to come nearer and nearer each time as they touched and kissed, murmured and gasped, and tasted.

Her body burned, and when he nudged her legs apart, his hardened shaft probing at the source of the fire within her, their gazes locked as, flesh against flesh, mouth against mouth, he made her his forever.

She had heard there would be pain the first time, but with the burning ache came a sense of urgency as the heat at her center built to a nearly unbearable longing. He moved slowly, drawing himself out until she begged him to come back, then filling her so completely she never wanted the sensation to end. At last, when the pressure seemed almost too much to bear, he pushed inside her one last time, and as he pulsed deep within her body, the tension broke into waves of sensation, and she cried out his name.

When her breathing returned to normal, she turned her face and kissed his cheek, the day's growth of beard scraping her lips and making her smile at the bittersweet sting.

Raising his head, he stared at her for a long moment. Then he bent forward and kissed her temple in a tender gesture that said so much about the man she had come to love.

"You've never said it," he said.

"Said what?"

"You know."

She frowned. Her mind was fuzzy. It seemed like she'd said everything there was to say with her body and her heart. She stared deeply into his eyes and saw a spark of fear there that confused her. What could Josh MacKenzie have to fear?

She kissed him, hoping to make the shadow go away, but when she looked again, it was still there. "What is it?" she asked.

"You . . . ah . . . well, I know you would never give me this gift if you didn't love me, but . . ." He sighed, struggling.

Suddenly she understood what he was afraid of, and she wanted to weep: he was afraid she didn't love him.

"Oh, Josh, I adore you."

He continued to avoid her eyes until she grabbed his head between her palms, put her nose to his, and said very slowly, "I love you, Josh MacKenzie."

Then he smiled and kissed her again—and the night was still very young.

Chapter 27

Emily awoke to the gentle touch of Josh's lips on hers.

"Ah . . ." She sighed deeply. "Oh, Billy, kiss me again."

"Still trying to fool me," he said. "That's not going to work." His mouth covered hers again, this time with a kiss that curled her toes.

Opening her eyes, she said, "Oh, it's only you." Her attempt to look disappointed failed miserably, because her treacherous mouth kept turning up at the corners.

"You've slept the day away," he said, leaning over her, his hands on the pillow framing her cheeks. "You planning on doing the same to the night?"

Slipping her arms around his neck, she murmured, "Well, I promise I won't *sleep* the night away, if you get back in here with me."

"Gad, you're a brazen wench! I'd consider doing just that if it wasn't time for you to get up and dress. We've got to get out of here." He walked away. "Time's come to make an honest woman of you."

His words stung like a slap to her face. She bolted out of bed, oblivious to her nudity. "You mean after

353

all we've been through—after last night—you still believe I'm a liar and a thief?"

"Em, I didn't—" The words stuck in his throat when he turned. He stared at her from head to toe in a slow, hungry, perusal. Swallowing, he said in a husky murmur, "God, you're beautiful, Em."

That would get him nowhere. The damage had been done. Snatching the quilt from the bed, she covered herself. "Beautiful but bad. Is that it? And much too unworthy for Mr. Upright-Noble-Job-Comes-First Detective MacKenzie. Well, be sure to add dumb to my other failings, because that's the one undeniable fault I'll admit to."

She strode toward the connecting door, and as she passed him, he reached out, caught an end of the quilt, and pulled it off her.

"You're better off without that on, honey. You need to cool off."

She'd never felt such betrayal before. "Oh, I hate you, Josh MacKenzie!" She clenched her teeth and fists. "I'd like to . . . to . . ."

"Go on, baby, you're getting me excited," he said, stalking her. "What would you like to do to me that you didn't try last night?"

"So help me, Josh, if you touch me, I'm going to scream at the top of my voice."

He bent down and picked up her nightgown from the floor. "I was only going to suggest you put this on, although it's not a very proper wedding gown. But it certainly will help speed things along as soon as the service is over."

"Wedding gown?" At the devilish grin on his face, everything became clear. "Do you mean . . . Are you—"

"Asking you to marry me. Like I said, Em, I have

to make an honest woman of you. Will you marry me? All the arrangements are made. Everyone's waiting."

"But I thought . . . I mean, you think I'm a liar and a thief."

"Are you?"

"Of course not. I've told you that a dozen times."

"And I believe you."

"Why now?" she asked suspiciously. "You didn't before."

"Because now I'm in love with you."

Still uncertain of his sincerity, she asked, "And what if I told you I *did* steal the money?"

"Then I'd have to say you're lying, because you're not a thief, Em. I think I always knew it, but I didn't want to admit it to myself or I wouldn't have had an excuse to keep you near me. Now, will you get some clothes on? We've got a roomful of people waiting for a wedding."

"Let them wait, MacKenzie," she said, advancing toward the bed. "I have this fantasy about a stranger—who strangely enough looks like you and even speaks with a Texas twang—who ravishes me until I agree to wed him."

"Hmm," he said. "Stranger, huh?"

"Never saw him before. He breaks into my room and chains me to the bed—most likely with hand-cuffs just like yours in my valise."

"He chains you to the bed, does he?"

She nodded.

"Ravishes you?"

"Uh-huh." She stretched out like a nubile tempt-ress. "Madly. Passionately."

"Until you agree to marry him?"

"Until I agree to marry him," she said, casting her eyes downward in maidenly modesty.

"Well," he said, unbuttoning his shirt. "Since all those wedding guests have waited this long, a little bit longer won't make much difference. Wouldn't you say . . . li'l stranger?"

Despite her not fulfilling the terms of her contract, in deep appreciation for her dedication at the time of the fire, Fred Harvey had ordered that no effort or expense be spared for Emily's wedding.

The wedding reception was held in the temporary dining room of the Harvey House, with all the girls, Mrs. McNamara, Fallon Bridges, Dr. Hughes, and Yen Cheng attending.

The high point of the evening was when Sheriff Ben Travis appeared and informed them that the three outlaws who had attempted to rob the train were now incarcerated in the Las Vegas jail, awaiting the arrival of the territory's marshall.

As soon as they left the reception, the sheriff asked if they'd stop in at the jail to identity the culprits.

Seeing the brutal men again, Emily shivered with revulsion.

"We'll see you soon, Blondie," the leader called. Then, smirking, he looked at Josh. "And you ain't seen the last of me either, Mr. Pinkerton Man."

"That's good to hear, you bastard, because you and I have some unfinished business. If you ever get to Texas, look me up. Name's MacKenzie. Josh MacKenzie."

They both signed affidavits swearing to the identity of the outlaws, then Emily couldn't wait to leave.

"They give me chills, Josh. They're so evil. Especially that Yancy." She shuddered. "And that sinister Brogan. They sure have cured my romantic notions about outlaws."

"Don't worry, Em. I'm sure we've seen the last of those three hombres."

Later, as she lay in Josh's arms, she knew her fantasy had come true—she'd married the man of her dreams.

"Where are we going to live, Josh?" she asked.

"What would you feel about living in Texas?"

"Texas!" She sat up, surprised. "I thought your job was in the East."

"The job isn't important to me anymore, Em. I'm a rancher; it's in my blood. But if you want to live in the East, that's all right. I want you to be happy."

If she were any more ecstatic, she'd burst with joy. She couldn't believe he'd put her happiness ahead of his own. Emily knew then that she couldn't love him any more than she did at that moment.

"I love the West, Josh. And I'm sure I'd love being a rancher's wife."

"It's not a glamorous life, honey, but it's a good one. And you'll never get lonely on the Triple M. We'll build us a house in the compound, and our kids will grow up with their cousins, the way I did."

"It sounds wonderful, Josh. Why did you ever leave there?"

"I had to prove something to myself, Em."

"And have you?" she asked, looking into his eyes.

"Yes. I was trying to become the best of three men, instead of just the best at what I am."

"You're the finest man I've ever known, Josh."

"That's all I need to know. I never want you to

stop believing that, because that's the goal I want to live up to: your belief in me, not my father's or uncles'." Hugging her tighter against him, he said, "So as soon as we finish in New York, we'll head to Texas."

She stiffened in his arms. "New York? You can send a wire to resign from the Pinkertons. Why do we have to go back there?"

"Em, we've got to settle this business with your father once and for all."

Her blood ran cold. "You don't know him, Josh. Somehow he'll find a way to break us apart."

"Honey, he can't hold you against your will. And you're my wife. There's not a thing he can do to prevent you from leaving."

She'd seen too many of her father's ways to believe that. He always got what he wanted. "Then why even go back? I'll wire him and tell him I'm married."

"No, Em, that's not enough. That's still running away. I want to look him in the eye when I tell him we're married. I have a few things to say to Mr. Hiram Lawrence—and one of them is to make it clear to him that he no longer poses a threat to my wife."

She settled back in his arms, but long after he slept she lay awake, fearful that somehow her father would find a way to end her happiness.

The next morning, she still harbored misgivings as they prepared to board the eastbound train.

Rose and the other Harvey Girls came out on the platform to say good-bye.

"We'll stop on our way back to Texas," she assured Rose. "And if I find you a rich husband in Texas, will you move there?"

"Honey, if the price is right, I'll move anywhere."

"All aboard," the conductor called.

Yen Cheng shuffled out and handed Josh a basket. "Yen Cheng fix you and Missy fine lunch."

"Oh, thank you, Yen Cheng. I'll miss you."

"Yen Cheng miss you, too, Missy."

"Come on, honey," Josh said, taking her hand. They boarded the train.

"Oh, isn't it romantic," Sally Stewart, a Harvey Girl from Iowa, exclaimed. "Emily's so lucky. Josh is so tall and handsome. And heroic. Look how he rescued her from the evil clutches of those outlaws." She sighed deeply.

Rose's mouth curled in a slight smile. "Yeah, honey, he sure is. But he ain't rich, or he wouldn't be working for that damn Pinkerton Agency. For me, handsome or not, the guy's gonna—"

"Have to be rich," the Harvey Girls chimed in collectively.

As the train puffed out of the station, Emily stood on the observation deck, waving a handkerchief at the cluster of white-aproned figures waving back at her.

When they were no longer visible, she turned away—her heart made heavier by the uncertainty of what lay ahead in New York.

The cabbie turned his carriage, and the team trotted up the long driveway toward the front of a stately mansion with a columned portico set in the splendor of century-old oaks and a manicured lawn.

The house might just as well have had bars on the windows, for to Emily it had been a prison that had held her confined for the twenty-three years of her life.

And since Josh had wired the time of their arrival, she knew the prison's warden would be waiting in the luxury of his paneled den, seated in his huge, cushioned, leather chair behind the mahogany desk that had been authenticated to have been made by the hand of Thomas Jefferson.

The carriage rolled to a halt, and a young groom quickly appeared to open the door. Josh got out and reached for Emily's hand. She took a deep breath and stepped out. A large Irish setter padded up to the carriage and sniffed her gown.

"Hi, Red," she said, patting the dog's head. It was the cook's dog; Emily had never been allowed one as a pet, since they shed hair.

The door opened, and James Wallace, the liveried butler, greeted her. "Welcome home, Miss Emily."

"Thank you, James."

He stepped aside for her to enter, and she paused for an instant, scanning the familiar walls of the marble-tiled atrium. Nothing had changed—why had she expected it would? It had remained the same for as long as she could remember. Pieces of carved ivory and jade still sat on a polished Duncan Phyfe table. The Waterford chandelier still sparkled in the sunlight. And the dark mahogany railing of the winding stairway still glistened with polish.

"Mr. Lawrence is awaiting you in the—"

"I know," she said.

"Your hat, sir," he said to Josh.

"James, this is my husband, Mr. MacKenzie."

If the news came as a surprise to the man, he concealed it behind an impassive facade. James had been trained well in the service of Hiram Lawrence.

"Congratulations, sir."

"Thank you," Josh replied, handing his Stetson to the butler, then following Emily.

She paused outside a pair of wide double doors. "Well, Mr. MacKenzie, if I recall an earlier conversation, you said there were no cannon to the right or left of you when you were once shot. Well, hold onto your saddle, my love, because you're about to ride boldly 'into the jaws of death, into the mouth of hell.' "

With a dramatic flourish, she pushed open the doors to her father's study.

Hiram Lawrence didn't even look up when they entered. The scratch of his pen was the only sound as they crossed the costly Oriental carpet that adorned the floor. Emily sat down in one of the twin gold brocade Queen Anne chairs in front of the desk; Josh followed suit in the other.

Finally her father replaced the pen in the well, and without raising his eyes, he said, "So my prodigal daughter has returned."

"Against her better judgment, Father."

Lawrence ripped the check he'd been writing out of a large, bound checkbook and shoved it across the desk toward Josh.

"My compliments, Mr. MacKenzie, on a job well done. Here's your check, and you're dismissed. Please close the door on your way out."

"I'll be glad to when I leave, sir, which will be after I say what I came to say."

"Mr. MacKenzie, I said you're dismissed. I have not the time—much less the inclination—to hear anything you have to say."

"Very well, then, I won't waste either my time or

yours trying to convince you otherwise." He stood up. "Let's go, Em."

That got his attention. "What in hell are you talking about? My daughter's not leaving with you."

"My wife is," Josh declared.

Lawrence bolted to his feet, his glare falling on Emily. "Is this true? Have you married some fortune-hunting detective just to spite me?"

"Hardly, Father. You flatter yourself. I married Josh because I'm in love with him."

Smirking, Lawrence said, "And he, no doubt, holds the same affection for you."

She lifted her chin defiantly. "Yes, he does."

"I believe he may be more in love with your wealth."

"Oh—you mean the inheritance Mother left me, which you accused me of stealing from you? That wealth, Father?"

"I just hope you didn't spend it all, because you'll need it to buy you out of this escapade. He's not getting one penny from me."

"Excuse me," Josh declared. "If the two of you don't mind, I'd like to speak for myself."

"I'm not interested in listening to what some gigolo has to say," Lawrence said.

"You're going to hear it anyway. I didn't marry Emily for her money. I married her because we're deeply in love." Lawrence snorted in contempt. "Frankly, sir, I don't care whether you believe me or not. We're here because I felt it only fair that you were informed of our marriage by us and not by a stranger. As for your money, sir, I don't want a damn cent of it. Seeing what it's brought you convinces me that it's worthless."

"What would you know of what it's brought me, MacKenzie?"

"I have a sister about Emily's age, and she sure as hell isn't running away from home to get away from an overbearing despot of a father. You're the biggest fool I've ever met, sir. What has your domination gotten you except this empty mausoleum?"

Hiram looked at Josh as if he were a mosquito he was about to flick off his coat sleeve.

"Do you know to whom you're speaking? I don't think you're aware of what the name of Lawrence means in these parts, MacKenzie. I can have you thrown behind bars before you can reach the end of the driveway if I choose."

"I'm aware of that, sir. However, the name of MacKenzie carries a lot of weight where I come from, too."

Lawrence snorted. "Maybe you should enlighten me as to why."

"It means loyalty and honor."

"Which won't buy you a five-cent cup of coffee here on Long Island."

"Perhaps not, sir, but a MacKenzie's word is worth far more than your bank account. I took an oath to love, honor, and protect your daughter, sir—and I take that oath seriously."

"Humph! Loyalty can be bought, MacKenzie."

"I'm aware of that, sir."

"I bet you are." A smirk appeared on his face. "I think we're beginning to understand each other perfectly."

"I think we are, too."

"So how much will your *loyalty* cost, Mac-Kenzie?"

"A great deal. Undoubtedly much more than you expected."

Lawrence looked at Emily. "You see, daughter, everyone has a price." Sitting back down, he opened his checkbook and reached for the pen. "So what's it going to be, MacKenzie?"

"Your daughter, Mr. Lawrence."

Frowning, Lawrence looked up. "I don't understand."

"Emily's the most precious thing you have, sir, and the only reason you could ever buy my loyalty. She loves you, to her credit—not owing to any effort on your part—and that's the only reason I've brought her back here."

"You brought her back to get the money coming to you."

"I'm not a bounty hunter," Josh said, winking at Emily. "Let me make one thing clear, Lawrence. Emily's my wife, and I won't tolerate any more interference from you in her life: no more false accusations, no more of your intimidation, and no more Pinkerton agents. Lord help you if you try."

"Are you threatening me, MacKenzie?"

"No, where I come from, we call it horse trading."

"And Emily's the horse." Lawrence appeared amused.

"Figuratively speaking. You get what you want—an heir—and in exchange, she gets peace of mind."

"And what do you get out of it, MacKenzie—long-range plans for a rich inheritance?"

"Long-range plans? You bet!" He met Emily's gaze and saw curiosity coupled with confusion in her eyes. "A lifetime together." He smiled lovingly.

Emily closed her eyes, and when she opened them, tears had washed away the uncertainty, and love glowed through the tears. He squeezed her hand.

"And do feel free to drop into the Triple M whenever you have an urge to see your grandson, sir," he added.

"The Triple M?"

"My family's ranch. That's where Emily and I will be living."

"And your grandson, Father," Emily interjected. "At least until he's old enough to make that decision for himself."

"You're serious about this, aren't you, Emily?" Lawrence said, for the first time showing a sign of bewilderment.

"I've never been more serious about anything before, Father."

Folding his hands behind him, Lawrence strode over to the fireplace and gazed in deep concentration at a framed portrait of Emily astride a pony.

After a long silence, Emily looked at Josh. He shrugged but said nothing. Lawrence finally picked up the picture and turned to them.

"I remember the day this picture was taken. It was your birthday—"

"My sixth birthday, Father. I'm surprised you even remember, because you didn't make an appearance until it was over."

"I bought you that pony, over your mother's objections."

"As you did everything."

He paused as if pondering her words, and finally replied, "I suppose I did."

"I used to pray during those tense moments between you and Mother that just once you'd agree to do something to please her." Her voice dropped to a whisper. "But you never did." Josh slipped his arm around her shoulders. "If only you had, things might have been so different between us now. I'm sorry, Father; I love you . . . but I don't like you. I can't forget what you did to my mother."

He smiled sadly. "Perhaps I was too occupied to pay your mother the attention she deserved—but do you think I haven't mourned her loss, missed her gentle voice and ways?"

"You never said so, you never showed a sign."

"There are many things in life one takes for granted and never appreciates until they're gone. It's too late for me to change my mistakes of the past."

"Not to your daughter, sir," Josh reminded him.

Lawrence looked at her. "I do love you, Emily. I may never have said it, but I thought you understood that. And I'm proud of you, my dear. Proud of your courage, and, believe it or not, your independence. If only your mother had had more of that independent spirit—" Emily arched a brow in disapproval. "And I had had a little less imperiousness," he said somewhat sheepishly, "how different our lives might have been." He looked contrite. "I also believed that I knew what was best for you, but I underestimated you. I never gave you credit for the intelligence you obviously possess—as evidenced by the choice you made of a husband. I'm impressed with this young man of yours, Emily. Is it too late for me to say I'm sorry?"

Josh glanced at Emily. This was the turning point. After over twenty years of resentment, could she now find it in her heart to forgive him? He hoped she would. He hoped the Em he loved with all his heart could find the charity in her own to recognize the plea of this lonely and penitent man. But he had not borne the heartache of a little girl growing into womanhood under a domineering father. His own father had been a taskmaster but a fair and loving man. He'd never had cause to doubt his father's love as Emily had throughout the years.

And bitterness ate at one's soul. Could she make a break from her father without having that bitterness destroy her?

Emily glanced up at him, her lips quivering, eyes beseeching him for guidance.

"Follow your heart, honey," he said tenderly.

She hesitated for a long moment. Then, arms outstretched, she ran to her father. "Oh, Father, I love you, too."

Josh was so proud of the extraordinary woman he'd married that he wanted to hug her, but at the moment, her father was busy doing it himself.

When Lawrence turned to him, moisture glinted in the older man's eyes.

"As for you, Mr. MacKenzie, I, too, am a man who stands by his word. You'll have no further trouble from me. Any man who can control this daughter of mine holds my highest esteem. I'm surrendering her to good hands."

He reached out, and the two men shook hands.

"I don't suppose I could convince you to consider a position with my organization."

"Thank you, sir, but I'm a rancher. I hope you'll accept the invitation to visit us on the Triple M."

"You can be certain of that, young man. It's time I let others run the business, so I can get around more. I especially want to see Texas—you Texans appear to be a rare breed. I've only met one other before, a young fellow named Carrington who was into railroads. He invested in my steel company.

You remind me a great deal of him: forthright, honorable, and with a self-assurance that comes from confidence, not arrogance."

"By chance, would that gentlemen be Michael Carrington?" Josh asked. "Of the Lone Star and Rocky Mountain Central Railroad?"

"Yes, by Jupiter! Do you know him?"

"Yes, sir. My father's cousin is married to him: Elizabeth MacKenzie Carrington."

"Well, that is a coincidence, son. It's a small world, isn't it."

"Maybe on Long Island, sir." Then he grinned. "But nothing's small in Texas." He tucked Emily's arm through his. "Time to go, Em."

"You can't stay for dinner?" Lawrence asked hopefully.

"I'm sorry, sir; we have a train to catch."

Emily kissed her father's cheek. "My lord and master has spoken, Father." She giggled and leaned into Josh. "All I've done is jump out of the frying pan into the fire."

"Is that so?" Josh teased. "Then how come I'm the one who's always getting burned? Black eyes, bullet holes." He shook Hiram's hand. "We'll look forward to seeing you again, sir."

"You can expect to see much more of me, son. Especially when that grandson you promised me comes along." He slapped Josh on the shoulder.

"Actually, I had in mind a little girl with blond hair and green eyes."

Lawrence thoughtfully nodded. "That wouldn't be too bad, either."

Darkness had descended by the time their train pulled out of New York. Josh lay stretched out on the bunk with his hands tucked under his head, watching Emily brush her hair. His fingers began itching to mess it up again.

She put down the brush and walked over to him, her slimness encased in a white satin nightgown that clung to her curves. More than just his fingers began itching.

Smiling, she stood and looked down at him. "I'm really happy about my father. It seems like the yoke I've worn around my neck my whole life has suddenly been removed."

"Yoke? Honey, you don't remind me of any oxen I've ever seen."

"That's right, if I recall, you were horse trading with my father."

He grinned. "Cute little filly that you are."

Sitting down on the edge of the bunk, she said, "Seriously, Josh, I'm so grateful to you. My father and I would never have made peace with each other if it weren't for you." She flashed the pleased little smile that always raised hell with his libido. "I suspect I'm married to the smartest man in the world, just dripping with all that honesty and integrity he's been taught by his father and mother and uncles and aunts and all those dozens of Texas cousins."

"You've got that right, Mrs. MacKenzie—except some come from Colorado, too."

She chewed her lip, and he realized she wasn't feeling as light-hearted as her tone would indicate. "What if your family doesn't like me, Josh?"

Pulling her down, he rested his forehead against hers. "They'll love you, Em," he said, with a tender smile.

They held each other, familiar yet always new and

exciting. That was the amazing thing about their love.

"I can't wait to meet them." She sighed. "Texas is so far away. It'll take forever to get there."

"Well, you're gonna have to take your girlfriend Rose's advice," he said, unable to keep his fingers out of her hair.

"About what?"

"About learning how to enjoy a train ride." He slid the straps of the gown off her shoulders. "Remember? She said it all depends on who's in the berth with you."

Epilogue

~~~⌒◡⌒~~~

Honey Behr MacKenzie stood in the doorway of the barn and watched with pride as her handsome son waltzed his lovely bride around the floor. The MacKenzie clan had gathered in force to celebrate Josh's wedding, and, as always, when they were all together, laughter and gaiety was the order of the day. Honey loved them all dearly: Flint and Cleve, their families; Luke's three cousins and their families.

Josh's wife was a delightful girl, and the love shining in Emily's eyes when she looked at her husband warmed Honey's heart. They were so in love.

Honey thrilled at the thought of it, remembering back to the days when she and Luke had fallen in love. Her eyes misted, recalling the sad little six-year-old boy with big sorrowful eyes.

Well, there was no sorrow in those eyes tonight; they were glowing with love and pride as he waltzed his wife around the floor.

Josh waved to her as he waltzed past. Emily turned her head and waved, too. Smiling, Honey waved back, then felt the unexpected tears that had begun to slide down her cheeks. Hastily she tried to wipe them away, when a strong pair of arms circled her waist and drew her back against a warm, muscular body.

She didn't have to turn; she knew the feel of those arms, that body, had gloried in the feel of them for the past twenty-two years. Sighing, she settled back comfortably against her husband.

"What are you thinking about, Jaybird?" Luke murmured at her ear.

"I was just thinking how much Josh and Emily love each other and how happy I am for them. They're so perfect for each other."

"Yep, I'd say Josh has a good eye for the right woman."

Honey closed her eyes as he trailed a string of kisses to her ear. Even after all these years, his touch still excited her.

"Like father, like son," she teased lightly.

"In more ways than one. Haven't you thought about the other similarity?"

"Of course; Josh is the spitting image of you."

"I'm not talking about that. Think about how they met, why they met."

She spun around in his arms, her eyes glowing with perception. "Of course! He arrested her and fell in love with her."

Luke grinned. "Sound like anybody we know?"

She turned around and settled back in his arms. Sighing, she murmured, "Us."

And that's how they remained, watching in companionable silence. When the bride and groom finished their wedding waltz, another tear slid down Honey's cheek and dropped on Luke's hand.

"Hey, are you crying, Jaybird?"

"I can't help it; I'm so happy." Smiling through her tears, she snuggled deeper against him, and murmured, "He's home, Luke. Our son's come home to stay."

Coming next month
Two terrific historical romances
By
Two unforgettable writers

Only from Avon Romance

The de Montefortes are back! . . .

Danelle Harmon's de Monteforte men are some of the most sinfully sexy heroes you've met in a long, long time. Now meet Lord Andrew de Monteforte, *THE DEFIANT ONE*, who meets his match in the sassy Lady Celsie Blake.

And don't miss Gayle Callen's latest . . .
MY LADY'S GUARDIAN. Beautiful and rich, Lady Margery is a prize for any man—but the king has decreed she must choose a husband quickly. So she asks Gareth Beaumont to pretend to be her suitor . . . never dreaming he wanted her in his arms—for real!

THR 0200

Dear Reader,

Next month is June, and romance—and weddings!—are in the air. So if you've enjoyed the Avon romance you've just finished, then you won't want to miss any of next month's delicious Avon love stories, guaranteed to fulfill all of your most romantic dreams.

Love and romance in the old west is the theme of Susan Kay Law's sensuous, spectacular Treasure *THE MOST WANTED BACHELOR*. The richest man in town knows he has to take a bride, but he'll be darned if he'll marry someone who's just after his money! Then a pert young gal catches his eye—could it be that the most eligible man in town is about to marry?

Every now and then you can't help but wonder what it would be like to marry a millionaire. In Elizabeth Bevarly's contemporary *HOW TO TRAP A TYCOON*, Dorsey MacGuinness has written a bestseller that's become a handbook for single gals across the nation. But sexy Adam Darien isn't about to succumb to some gold-digging female . . .

Historical fans will be thrilled—Danelle Harmon's de Monteforte men are back! This time, *THE DEFIANT ONE*, Lord Andrew de Monteforte, meets his match in sexy Lady Celsie Blake, and when they're caught in a compromising position wedding bells ring . . .

Lady Margery Welles has the uncommon privilege of choosing her own husband, but she's in no hurry to wed. So she selects dashing knight Gareth Beaumont to pose as her suitor in Gayle Callen's *MY LADY'S GUARDIAN*.

Yes, June is the month for weddings—and none are more romantic, more beautiful, more sensuous than the ones you'll find here at Avon Romance.

Enjoy!

Lucia Macro

Lucia Macro
Senior Editor

Avon Romantic Treasures

*Unforgettable, enthralling love stories,
sparkling with passion and adventure
from Romance's bestselling authors*